Nightwolves Siren's Song

Clarrissa Lee Moon

(Book Three of Memoirs of the Nightwolves Series)

World Castle Publishing

http://www.worldcastlelpublishing.com

Book Three of Memoirs of the Nightwolves Series
This is a work of fiction. Names, characters, places, and incidents are products of the author's imagination or are used fictitiously and are not to be construed as real. Any resemblance to actual events, locations, organizations, or person, living or dead, is entirely coincidental.

World Castle Publishing
Pensacola, FL

Copyright © 2011 by Clarrissa Lee Moon
ISBN: 9781937085124

First Edition Smashwords January 2011
Second Edition: World Castle Publishing July 1, 2011
http://www.worldcastlepublishing.com

Cover Artist: Fantasia Frog Designs
Editor: Lea Ellen Borg

Note from the Author

I realize that the names of the dark Gods in this book (and future books in this series) are completely fictitious, yet I used the correct names for the Gods and Goddesses of the Light. Orochi is actually a Japanese demon, not a dark God, so using his name won't matter. Those who are in the know, will know why it is so. For those that don't, read the books on Magick, then you'll understand why.

I used the spelling for Magick with a 'k' to differentiate magic (no k) being used by magicians and stage artists from those who actually practice real magick and run with WILL on the astral planes. Though there are some stage magicians in whom I wonder about if they have should the 'k' included. Some are just that good to be hiding in plain sight. However, like them, this book was made to entertain you and I hope you enjoy all of my new exciting worlds and travel with me often as more are created.

I'd like to thank my boys, Jerimiah, Cody and Cameron for letting me use the computer for hours on end. I want to thank Jerimiah, personally, for being the one who came up with most of the chapter title names. I want to personally thank Cody for keeping me fed when I would forget. And I want to thank Cameron, for reading all my stories and giving me feedback and ideas when I would write myself into a corner. Having the three of you as my sons has been a blessing and a pleasure. Also, thanks to Laurie and Kenny for getting me the research I needed for more authenticity in my stories. Finally, thanks to Liz and Lea Ellen, who busted butt in editing my books! Thanks to Penny Nichols for beta reading! Good work guys. Keep on astral running. Ride hard, Ride free!

I'd like to thank my favorite Rock band, Nickleback, and my favorite Heavy Metal rock band, Godsmack, for rocking me through my writing. Keep rocking! Also, a thanks to my favorite Rap bands, ICP, Twiztid and Eminem. The love scenes were inspired by a CD mix I made with my various favorite "Mood" music. Oh yeah, it worked. HA!

(The typos below are deliberate)

Just one More note: i have Three very special people i hope read the whole series. You know who you all are. if you do, hey, i am here, still

3

Alive, bring me in from The cold. Sushi and Margaritas until the End Of time On our own island in Nature's paradise.

In Loving memory of R.J. Kirkham, the 'hood took you too young. We miss you, bro.

Table Of Contents

Catrina's Prologue

Finding your soulmate is a great gift. No gift of the Gods, however, comes without a price and when you are a child of the Gods, the price can be even steeper. In order for my mates and I to find each other, we had to stay celibate. The Gods also tacked on a 'save the world' quest.

Thanks to a prophecy that is told in many of today's religions, by the end of 2012, four and a half billion people or more could die. Great plagues, famine and wars will take their toll. "The end of days", which is really not the end of mankind as most people think, but a change of life as we know it.

The reason for this is twofold; one scientific and one metaphysical. The scientific side is this: A major shift in the Earth's gravitational pull has been happening slowly for the past ten or so years. Surprisingly, not a lot of people know this, but it is a scientific fact. On December 21, 2012, we will see the full end of the "Shift" in the polarity of Earth. Even its' axis will be tilted more than it is now. Minor Shifts have happened to some degree, every 5,000 years or so. Some shorter and some longer time has spanned between shifts. With these shifts, depending on the severity, they can cause earthquakes, tsunamis, flooding, Earth temperature changes and many other weather deviations. Some believe that in 2012, we will see a shift on a magnitude that hasn't been seen in thousands of years. At one time, our Earth's surface was one solid piece of land. Then, after the first 'Great Shift', the tectonic plates moved so far, that many smaller continents were made. The Ice Age happened and the Neanderthals perished.

For the metaphysical side: Myths and legends record that during this time, all of the magickal races (dragons, vampires, werewolves and the like) were sent to other various dimensions through portals and astral doorways, which can only be opened or closed during a major polarity shift. Hence, the reason they are myths and legends in today's cultural histories. This was done to protect man from races that were stronger, faster, smarter and much more lethal in magickal uses than man who had no way of protecting themselves against it. Man too, eventually would have been wiped out as the Neanderthals were. The Gods and Goddesses decided to separate the pure magickal races and let ingenuity and science rule man for a time. Not all magick was lost to Earth, but the greater magicks and the beings that can wield it were removed. Science has ruled heavily, but with science, too, there is a price. Pollution, skepticism, and a disregard for nature and natural cycles; as well as the imbalance of feminine and male roles in most cultures and newer religions got the attention of The Gods, once again. Now, They want the door opened to hopefully bring balance back between the female and male aspects, as well as a healthy respect for the Earth and The Gods themselves. Therefore, a great change is coming and most are completely unaware. And with great change, always comes a great price.

The Gods and Goddesses of many of the older religious pantheons of Earth got together and decided to have children that would be mated to other pantheons, to combine and amplify power, like in the days of old on Earth. The merging of two powerful houses' of Lords in marriage would have influence over a more vast area. By putting us in human physical bodies that were birthed by human women, it gave Them a channel of power here on Earth for a more effective use to help bring down the death toll, ease those left through the new changes here on Earth and to protect them from the more aggressive magickal races that are coming back. I am one of those children: the first born daughter of the Triple Goddess and Her Consort, from an ancient Celtic pantheon. There are six of us - three daughters and three sons, all placed into separate physical mothers at conception. Only my youngest brother and I share the same physical father - a High Dark Adept, who also happens to be a Mafia Don. Lucky us. Searching for my soulmates, using astral magicks, opened a whole can of worms on my astral spiritual heritage; more than I was ready for, in many ways. It could be part of the reason why it took fifteen long years to find my mates on the physical plane.

The prequel to this story (which may be written sometime in the future) will tell the tale of how I had learned to use my powers and astral project out of my body. Using this method of astral projection for finding my soulmate, I met Antonio, one of my mates, briefly, for about three seconds. I tried again, sometime later and made it to Demitri's mansion, Antonio's eldest brother. Their middle brother, Andre, had felt me coming; curious, he followed me home using the same technique. I fell in love with all three of them and when made to decide which one, I said all or nothing. They chose all. We found out later that's the way it was supposed to be and made peace with it. I had also met my brothers and sisters (who had different physical parents then me) but we had the same spiritual Mother and Father. During this time, my evil physical father, a High Dark Adept, tried many times to keep us apart and even tried to kill me a few times. Then, another new enemy joined the fray.

The outcome was me being cursed and my powers brought down to minimum levels. Many of my psychic powers were blocked and without those powers, I could not find the physical location of my mates (though we now lived in the same town). We had gotten that far, before I was cursed. Even blocked, I would not stand down, and many magickal battles ensued, leading up to a battle with the dark God Orochi. We won, and that lifted my curse; but, lost because we died. The Goddess brought us back and "Blessed" us by modifying our physical bodies. I, then, finally got to meet my mates. They brought my brothers and sisters to their home and I got to meet them physically, as well. We were then wed by my youngest brother, Gerard. Unfortunately, fifteen years of darkness had left its' toll on me and I froze on my wedding night. This story is what happened after that. And I thought the hard part was over....*sh'yeah.*

These memoirs I have written, were not only written by me, but by the other Nightwolves. I think of them as the true heroes of this tale, months before The Great Shift happened. I can't really claim to be a hero, since I was born and made for this job. To me, a real hero is one who chooses the path of great danger, even though they may be the most ordinary of us all. It takes great courage to face the Great Shift with no extra tricks up ones sleeve. I had them write their own memories from their view point and I put them together within this story, here and there, as best I could. This story is for them, as it should be, for the truly great heroes of our time.

Chapter One

White moves first

Cassie and I were late for the meeting in the war room at the base in Truax Field with General Pierce and the Nightwolves. We had been paged right in the middle of healing some soldiers in the East Wing of the base hospital and couldn't stop what we were doing to answer our pagers. It was a hazard of the job of being mercenary, as well as magick users, who couldn't ignore the pain of a wounded soldier. Using our gifts for good has always been a priority in our training, but lately, times have made it seem we used our gifts mostly for defense, rather than for good deeds. We had been trying to rectify that by spending more time in the hospital at Naval Air Station, more commonly known as Truax Field, and volunteering time as nurse's aides at the local hospital in Corpus Christi, Texas.

Though, we had to hide what we were doing from the locals and even had to watch ourselves on the base, where they sort of knew what we were doing, but pretended ignorance for the sake of budget and personnel cuts. We couldn't be too obvious in our healings in either place, lest word got out witches were real and burning us females at the stake became all the rage again. I definitely wasn't into torture; which I'd found out recently and would happily pass up being ousted as a witch.

I really was one, but I was also more than just a witch and not one of the evil kind. However, after having just recently healed, both physically and psychically, from being tortured by an evil General who was also a High Dark Adept, who was trying the 'ole rule the world' ploy (which when you think about it, it's really a stupid plan). It's been tried so often

11

before by others, it's practically a cliché now. Movies, books and real life evil-doers have been trying the same 'ole, same 'ole, for so long. Can't the bad guys think of anything new to try, to ruin someone's good day? I mean, come on! Although, what I thought was worse than wicked bad guys, were people who, either out of ignorance or just plain stupidity, helped the bad guys by vilifying the good guys, like us. Yes, we may be different and yes, we may be magick users, but that didn't make us worthy of death. The Gods and Goddesses themselves put our spiritual bodies into human infants to be borne by human mothers so we could grow up and help save the world from those who would enslave it. Yet, because of what we were, half demi-God children and witches, we would still, to this day, be burned at the stake, if the sheeple could get away with it. Then, who would protect them and this world from the dark covens and dark Gods, hmm?

Stupid mortal humans, I grumbled to myself. Why we risked ourselves to save this dumb assed planet full of sheeple sometimes eluded me, until one of my mates would point out some smiling infant with wide, beautiful, innocent eyes that hadn't been shut closed by this world's society yet. Then the baby would burst into a joyful giggle when they saw me. Every time I saw one of those cute, chubby cheeked babies, my heart would melt and I would pray this child would grow up smarter and more tolerant than his or her parents. That would make all this crap worth it then.

My attitude had been mellowing so much lately though that I couldn't even get up the old angst of how much I really hated people in general. My mates were the culprits in taming my usual hot temper, turning me into a much more relaxed version of my usual self. Everyone, at one point or another, has done double turns at watching me smile for no apparent reason. Smiling wasn't what I usually did. Snarling, sneering or throwing wicked evil grins was more my style, but lately, I just couldn't tap into the anger needed for any of that. I had found my happy place and my mates were the center of that warm safe retreat. No one was used to it; even the General looked at me oddly from time to time these days. I couldn't even care enough for that as I looked around my environment and remembered how blue and clear the sky was this morning as we rode to the base for the big test to see if I had healed enough, on all levels inside, to use my powers without causing my brain any more damage. I smiled happily as my sister and I walked down the long corridor to the war room to meet up with the rest of the team for the big meeting.

My sister took a long sideways glance at me, but she wasn't smiling. "Sister..."

"Hmmm?"

"Are you sure you are all right?"

I looked at her, and asked, "Why wouldn't I be?"

Her expression grew pensive. "We have noticed how distracted you've been lately. Not that anyone could blame you."

"Distracted?"

"Well, yes. Distracted would be the best word to use. It's just that you haven't really gone after General Robertson like we had expected you to."

I stopped walking and turned to her. "Shamus said not to use my power to even tap into the watcher. Everyone has been on my case about not using my powers so I don't blow anymore blood vessels in my brain, and now I have been distracted?"

"That's not what I mean. It didn't come out right." She took a deep breath. "It's good that you followed orders so well this time, but, that's the problem. You don't usually follow anyone's rules and now you just seem to be flowing along without any direction. No goals. The Coven follows you, and without any direction, we don't know where we should be putting all of our energy."

"You guys ride my ass when I do things my way and then you ride my ass when I follow orders. I really wish you would make up your friggin' minds," I snorted and started down the hall again.

She moved to catch up to me. "I am sorry. You're right, but after what happened to you, we thought you would want to retaliate immediately. We thought we would have to literally tie you down to hold you back and here you are just going along with things...well, it's a little disturbing for those of us who've known you for so long. The General and the others too, know that there is something different about you. They just don't understand exactly what - and frankly, we don't either." She looked up at me, her brown eyes wide with concern. "We are worried you're losing your edge and what that might mean for you when we go up against the Dark Coven," she rushed her explanation so fast, I barely caught on to what she was saying and that wasn't her usual MO She had a precise way of talking and rushing her words together wasn't normal. This showed me how upset she was.

Half of me wanted to get pissed, but the other half understood what was upsetting the rest of The Coven. Nothing was more dangerous to a mercenary team than a leader who has lost their edge. My anger had given me my edge, I knew this subconsciously, but I also knew that I had never been so happy in my life and by the Goddess, I friggin' deserved to be happy after all the crap that I'd been through. It's not my fault my other siblings have had fifteen plus years of peace and quiet to enjoy their mates and have the blessings of children and the time spent with them, while I was trapped in my own personal hell the entire time. This was my time. This was my chance. I knew they didn't understand just how close I had come to losing my mind. It was a miracle I hadn't gone completely, fucking insane from being so close to my mates, but still not being able to touch them. To hold them. To get to know them as my siblings knew their own mates. They would never understand. How could they? They couldn't even fathom it. Sure, they'd seen me go through it - unable to help me undo the curse that had trapped me - but they could never understand the pain, mentally and emotionally, that I'd gone through; or how often I came to offing myself just to stop the nightmare.

I still couldn't really get angry at her, though.

"Listen, the Coven doesn't have anything to worry about. For one, what I went through with General Robertson wasn't anything worse than what I went through as a kid. Ok, maybe not quite that bloody, but still, nothing that I haven't been taught to handle a long time ago. So, me getting pissed and wanting revenge isn't going to happen." I looked over at her. "Oh, we will even the score. Never doubt that. But, we are going to do it smart, when they least suspect it." I smiled again with the ghost of my usual evilness. "Let them relax and let down their guard before we strike at them and make them regret fucking with us." I saw her shoulders loosen up and her own smile reappeared. "We can't let what they did slide, but we can pick our time when the odds are more in our favor."

"All right, Sister," her tone relieved. "That sounds like a valid move and a smart one. You know we are behind you all the way. Just let us know what we need to do to get things moving towards that goal."

Who would of thought the Coven would be hungry for immediate action and I would be the one who was willing to wait for the right moment to strike? Maybe I really had lost my edge. I didn't let it worry me, though. I knew things would be all right in the end. I didn't know how yet, but I knew it would be all right. Meanwhile, I was going to enjoy every minute of finally being with my mates and damn the consequences.

"Never fear, sister dear. I will." I winked at her and we continued down to the war room together.

We were just about to walk from the building that was used mostly for hospital staff and patients, to the base, as a young man walked by us and accidentally bumped up against me.

"Excuse me...miss?" he said and stopped dead in his tracks. "You're the one!" he exclaimed, incredulous.

"I think you have made a mistake," I said, nicely.

"No, it's you. You saved me. You're real." He couldn't seem to get over actually seeing me in the flesh.

Actually, he really shouldn't have recognized me at all. Most coma patients never remembered anything from their time in a coma such as Juan Rico had suffered from. A few weeks ago, I'd brought his spirit back from the astral planes after healing the rest of his body the doctors couldn't fix. He was an Air Force pilot and had had a really bad day and almost lost his life. Until I brought him back and for some reason he seemed to recollect it.

"You must have me mixed up with someone else. Is there a doctor we can get for you or something?"

"No, I know what I saw and what I heard. You said I had to come back and help save the world. That this world was in danger. Now you're here and that means it was all real. My mother was right."

Confused I asked him, "What do you mean?"

"My mother came here when I woke up from the coma and I told her about this real-seeming dream I'd had. She said it was no dream that I had been saved and brought back. She said if I ever saw you, I needed to do whatever God had in plan for me, because it would be important. That it was why I came back, when the doctors had told her to be prepared in making arrangements for my funeral. Then, I woke up, and I'm completely healed. I just got back from my checkup and they said it's a miracle that I don't have any long range problems. Most face months, if not years, of rehabilitation, but not me. My mother was right."

Oh, shit. Mexican families were more superstitious then in most cultures. They still remember the times of magick working and had earlier myths and legends then most races of people here. They were also more attuned with the Earth, as were American Indians. They were steadfast in their beliefs and were really hard to sidetrack when it came to esoteric situations. Especially dreams. They were really big on dreams. In a nutshell, it was going to be a pain in the ass getting this guy off of my trail.

15

I had read his file before taking on his case. He had scored highest in his class and was one hell of a pilot. The crash was not his fault and if it hadn't been for his flying skills, the crew aboard would also have been killed or badly injured. Because of his skill, only he'd suffered the worst injury on that flight. That, in and of itself, was a freakin' miracle.

"Come outside with us," I told him. I didn't ask, it was more of an order. Cassie had that look in her eyes again. Probably thought I was going to off him or something. Back in the old days, I would have, if the situation called for it, but today I had a better idea. I went with my gut instincts.

Outside, where there was less chance of having ears on the walls, I turned to him. "Fine. I did and yes this world is in for some shit. We might need you but not right this minute." Before he could ask any questions, I gave him answers he would have asked about, making it easier for me. "No, I don't know when or how, but do me a favor. Don't talk about it or your dreams, and if you don't have a problem working with a pagan High Priestess, I sure don't have a problem working with one of God's people. I like God and Jesus just fine but I really hate the church, so if you have a problem with that, keep walking and forget you ever saw me."

"You're a Bruja?"

A Bruja was a Mexican witch, and most of the time, they weren't nice guys. It was why most Southwestern houses had painted their doors blue. The myth was, a witch couldn't cross into a house with a blue door, or spell anyone in the house. They were right on that one. That didn't stop me from going into a house with a blue door, though. But my intentions had always been good.

"Witch, yes, Bruja, no. Like I said, I like God; I think Jesus is very cool, hate the church. My Goddess is Celtic. Is that going to be a problem?" I gave it to him short and sweet, because I was pressed for time. I was supposed to be at the meeting in the war room.

He thought about it and said, "No. No, I don't have a problem with it. Things felt too light, too good, for it to have been evil, but why do you hate the church?"

"I'm supposed to be in a meeting right now. In about five hours, go see a General Pierce in that building over there." I pointed to the building we were heading to. "General Pierce will give you some papers to sign and a list of books you'll have to read for yourself, if you want an answer to that question and make your own decisions. Like I said, I am very late."

16

He understood I was pressed for time. "All right, I understand. Maybe later, we can talk?"

"Sure, if I can get some down time. Take care." I started to turn away then turned back to him. "Oh, General Pierce may tell you many things that may blow your mind. Just remember to breathe and know it's all part of a grand scheme of things. Just don't ask me what. I'm still trying to figure it out myself."

We turned back to the building.

"All right, and hey, thanks!" he yelled after me.

I waved and kept walking.

"You're sure that was a good idea?" Cassie asked.

"You had another?"

"We could have just told him it was nothing more than it was a dream, a coincidence. You didn't have to verify any of it for him."

"Sister mine, pieces keep being thrown in my path. I am going to start collecting them and someday use them. We've got Marines, We've got Special Forces, now we've got Air Force, or a start, in that branch now. Robertson and Williams have got their players. We need to gather ours."

"I can see how that would be a good idea for a mundane operation, but the risk of exposure to us greatly increases with every person who knows what we really are."

"True, but when have I ever played it safe?" I grinned at her. "Sometimes, you got to say what the fuck, make a move, and see what happens."

She shook her head at me. "Just make sure what happens isn't pitchforks and stakes."

"Well, if we get bored, that could be fun, too."

She laughed at me.

Chapter Two

Double Space Pawn

General Pierce stated the obvious as we walked in. "You're late." But his tone wasn't clipped yet. He was getting used to working with magickal Mercs. He was waiting for a plausible excuse.

We usually did have one and this time was no different. "Sorry, General, everyone," nodding to the group. "Healing in the East Wing was needed today." I'd tell him about Lieutenant Juan Rico after the meeting, privately, in his office.

Cassie and I took our seats and waited for the General to either roast us or get on with the reason for the meeting of all of my family of mercenaries, O'Hara's Special Forces team, and Captain Holland with all four squad leaders of the Marine Alpha 53rd Recon.

My Kla' din mates were there, as well, looking more American by the day with Andre's shopping sprees. Andre was one of three mates I had Earth-side. My other two Earth-side mates were Andre's brothers, Demitri and Antonio. They were the heart and soul of Caberelli Corporations, second only to Bill Gates according to Forbes, but not nearly as mercenary in business, even though we were Mercs for the military. Ironic, really.

General Pierce had made a coalition of his Special Forces and my family of mercenaries to help save Earth from the effects of the Great Shift that was happening. We also fought with blade and magick against dark forces that threatened this world's freedom.

19

"Yes, well then, we have several items on the agenda today. Let's start with the most important one." He slid a file across the table to me where I sat with most of the Nightwolves. A few had to stand behind their respective mates when we ran out of room when these larger meetings were called. We would definitely be over crowded if the rest of the Alpha 53rd Recon were also posted to the meetings, but they usually had to wait until the meeting was over, for the squad leaders to return with news of whether they were needed in the field or not.

Wizard, who was part of O'Hara's Special Forces team, showed me a file with the information he and one of my mates had been investigating for the past two weeks. "We've managed to ascertain that besides a hurricane in Manitoba, Canada in '07, classed as an F-5, and one in Iowa in '08, neither is showing on up our radar with an open portal, still to this day."

Antonio inserted, "We think, for a portal to be open, a natural disaster of huge proportions has to occur. A F-5 or a lot of tornadoes like the nine that showed up in Tornado alley at the same time. An earthquake of no less than a 6.5. Anything less, and no portals are opening. On this supposition, we looked at the history of natural disasters and found another portal hiding in the Pacific Ocean, from the tsunami that hit in '04 near Indonesia. Wizard and I think that because of the large body of water, this portal has hidden itself, because of the pulse disruption with the tides messing with the signal."

"The only anomaly is Saudi Arabia. No major disaster happened there, but a portal was there allowing in those werewolves that attacked on that one mission, infecting Craven," Wizard finished the outline for the group.

"So, how did a portal show up there?" General Pierce asked.

O'Hara tapped another file that General Pierce hadn't shared with the group yet. "We think General Robertson has a witch who is able to predict major disasters before they happen. They go to the site before it strikes and gather the energy that it makes and then directs it to open a portal instead."

I was shocked. "So, they actually stopped a disaster from happening and used it to direct a portal opening? Talk about irony. But, why stop the disaster? Why not let it hit and then find the portal?"

Antonio said, "Well, if they have no quick way of detecting it like we do, the next best thing would be to use the energy from a major earthquake and make a portal right where you want it. That would give them first contact and total control of the portal from the start."

20

General Pierce slid another file over to our side of the table. "Case in point that supports your conclusion. After that F-5 hit Greenburg in '07, there was a rash of missing people reported, then suddenly it stopped in late '09. We are assuming that's when General Robertson found the portal and put the mesh over it. It would stop the vampires from their world from coming into ours without his permission."

"Great, so we owe another thank you to the jerk for stopping people from being kidnapped?" I groaned. Although, I didn't think stopping natural disasters was necessarily a good thing, either. The Earth has to move as she will, or there will be a high price to pay for it, later on.

"Who's to say there isn't more people being fed to the vampires? With Robertson's contacts, he could easily have kids and women taken a lot more discreetly from other places and shipped to Kansas. From there, he could then gain favors from the vampires for being the one supplier, like a drug lord would be," Demitri added.

I nodded my head, "Now that would be more his MO. He did tell me, while he was torturing me, he and some pastor had 'young delights' they tortured in his basement many times. They wouldn't be able to do that if they kept taking kids from that town and it not be noticed, sooner or later. The town's population isn't that large. They would have to traffic the victims in from other areas, so as not to draw notice to what they're doing."

"So, since we now know he controls the one portal, how many others does he control?" Cassie asked.

Antonio shrugged. "There is no telling how many, if he has a witch who can predict them before they happen. They can then have an untold number, since there wouldn't be a natural disaster to mark it. With the black mesh Cat was stuck in when they had captured her, we can't pick it up with the tracking system or with any of our other abilities."

"Do we know how many, or who, is in his dark coven?" Cassie asked.

"Nine were killed in Kansas. Funny, how the base there isn't making a big noise about it, which tells me most of the brass there, either know about Robertson, or is also involved in the Dark Coven directly. Further investigations brought about these names of people he meets with most frequently. There is brass from the Pentagon in this folder. It would behoove all here not to repeat these names outside of this room, even in private." General Pierce arched his eyebrows and gave everyone at the table a deep look. Everyone nodded their agreement, as he slid the file over for us to look at it (the O'Hara had tapped on earlier).

21

The list of names was scary. There were so many in the Pentagon, it amazed me we have been able to operate as we have, since I knew General Pierce answered to a few of the movers and shakers there. Luckily, none of their names were on the list.

One name caught my eye though. "Hey, this guy is a weather man. How much you wanna bet here is our dark witch weather predictor. Says here he works for my favorite news station, which I love to bash, for their pontificating bullshit."

Demitri looked over my shoulder and snorted, "Yes, I remember hearing you yell at the TV screen when they were preaching at every newscast like it came from God's own lips. You are so cute when you do that."

He winked at me. "Do you think they're going to hear you, or what, babe?" Andre chuckled, shaking his head at me.

I turned a nice shade of pink. "Well damn, they piss me off. What they do isn't journalism, its brainwashing crap for crying out loud. They are making a mockery of the Fourth Estate and that makes me mad."

Antonio leaned over, "But you yell at scary movies, too." With a high falsetto voice, he mimicked, "Dumb ass woman, don't you know you should never go outside when there's a scary noise? You deserve to die, ya dumb ass."

Everyone started laughing at me, which I could only grin at.

"Dumb ass always dies though, don't they? I mean, come on, a scratching noise? Oh look, let's go outside so the mad man with the pick-ax can whack me." I rolled my eyes at the movies coming out lately.

Demitri laughed, "But, it's just a movie, honey."

"Well, let's go make scary noises at the weather witch and see if we can get him to do something dumb?" I smiled. "Maybe he'll do the predictable thing and tell us all. Then we can whack him."

General Pierce grunted, "We can detain him, but I don't know about the whacking part, Cat."

"There is only one way to stop a dark witch, General, and that's whacking its head off." my eyes narrowed at him.

"I understand that, but he still falls under the guise and the laws of a civilian. Legally, the only thing we can detain him on is a suspect in terrorist activities. We can't prove he is using magick to create portals to hostile worlds."

I grinned evilly. "Exactly. So, he now falls under our laws, which after a serious interrogation, we can whack him."

General Pierce sighed, "Your laws aren't recognized by the U.S. You'd be putting me in a bind, Cat."

I understood his predicament. Premeditated murder just wasn't in his makeup. Neither was it in mine, but if the weather witch confessed to not only helping General Robertson, but participating in black rituals, then, by his own admission, he would have to be executed. That was something I could live with. So long as the confession wasn't done by torture. I didn't agree with torture for anyone. A person would confess to a crime even if he didn't do it, just to get the pain to stop. So torture, in my opinion, was useless as a tool.

General Pierce's hands were even more tied, being military than mine. He was used to upholding his oath as an Officer and defending the Constitution. Although, with the Patriot Act in place, it took away most of a person's Constitutional and Civil rights which is one of my other soap boxes. However, being what we were, we had our own Laws and Regulations that superseded, right or wrong, even America's Constitutional Laws. The problem being, first and foremost, the American justice system wouldn't and couldn't deal with a black witch. First, they wouldn't believe it, and secondly, they couldn't hold a true magick user, even if one could be proven to be breaking laws in the first place using magick. General Pierce was still bound in upholding the Laws he had sworn to protect. This could cause friction between his military mind-set and our way of dealing with black witches.

"How are you going to stop a black witch from casting spells against you and your men, General?" I asked.

"Couldn't we just use that potion your brother made for your cell at The Nightwolves Lair?"

"Sure, we can spray paint it over a silver mesh and coat one of your cells here." I leaned closer over the table. "It would work, but sooner or later, you will have to either charge him, which by your own laws, civil or military, you can't, so you'll have to let him go. What then, General?"

He closed his eyes and it looked like he was slowly counting to ten. I tended to make him do that often.

"If, by some chance, he goes missing before I can send a team over to pick him up, make sure I don't find him anywhere here. Are we clear?"

"I get it, General."

"Anywhere here. Are we clear?" His eyes were hard.

"Crystal."

I leaned back and contacted my youngest brother with telepathy. *'Brother, make a call to New York. Ask one of the Major Mafioso families to detain the weather witch for us. Make sure they know how to contain him and move him, unharmed, to the portal in Japan using one of Demitri's planes. Once he's through the portal, move him to Trinidad. We'll deal with him there.'*

'Consider it done.'

This was one of the few times being related by blood to a Mafia Don came in handy, when one had to walk on the other side of the law. Again, I thought how ironic it was, that The Mafia would play a role in helping to save the world. Not everything bad was evil and sometimes being bad was necessary to make something even better happen. This was one of those few times. I knew we would have conflict from time to time with the Military and American laws, but the real problem would be our physical father, if he decided to step into the game and oppose us. He was not only The Don for our family, but also the High Priest for The Families own Dark Coven. Every member was Family, by blood, or marriage. My father's Coven practiced a more Stregarian dark side of magick, where if a human sacrifice was needed, it was done. My brother and I formed our own Coven, since we sided with the Light, and that infuriated my father to no end, to the point that he had ordered a hit on me…twice. Our father thought I had turned my brother against the family- which I hadn't. I just told my brother I would love him, no matter what path he chose to follow. I loved my father, too, even though he still didn't believe it nor would he admit I was his daughter by blood. I was only half Sicilian and that wasn't good enough for the Family. And to make matters worse, I was female, so I was utterly useless to them in their eyes. With my brother choosing to be a part of our Coven instead, and turning his back on being groomed to take over as the future Don and High Dark Adept for the Family, my death was still greatly desired by my father. I felt like I was putting the General in the same category as my father, by having to circumvent around his ethics, though our goals were one and the same. Not so, with my father and his Dark Coven, but then again, I still didn't know that if a choice had to be made, what side my Family's Dark Coven would chose. As the prophecy drew nearer though, I knew without a doubt, that day would come. I would dread it, because even though they worshiped the dark most times, I would still loathe hurting any of my Mafia family. Most of them may be evil, but I still cared about their well being, regardless. Another thing for my siblings to worry about, I supposed.

O'Hara broke me out of my musings. "So, when do we detain the weather witch?"

He and his team would be the ones to bring the weather witch in for questioning, apparently.

"Let's save that for after this list of portals has been dealt with. We'll send someone to keep an eye on him until then. Gather more evidence and such." I understood he was giving me time to handle things our way. I would also have to clear it with my Kla' din mates later, for moving the weather witch through their lands to my portal. I made a mental note to ask them after the meeting was over.

"Now, what do we do about the voodoo people who may be sending these tornadoes in retaliation?" General Pierce asked me.

"I can send word out to talk to them about it. *If* they are even doing it, that is," I suggested.

The General nodded. "True, that F-5 didn't happen for over two years. Your theory doesn't quite track with that kind of time table."

"Ah, but it does, actually. Have you seen New Orleans lately? It still has damage and people from there are still scattered over five other states. The list of families still looking for their kids is over four hundred, to this day. When a people are scattered like that, it would take time to settle somewhere else and build up a power base, General," I informed him.

He looked confused. "What do you mean?"

"It's like this. No matter what flavor of magick you run, you have to build a power base before you can do major magick, in most cases. I am one of the few, who can raise power without a power base and only because I have my mates bonded to me. If I were alone, my magick levels wouldn't be as high for one, and then I may need a power base to build up, before I could throw any major spells around. Voodoo people are even more tied to their power bases, because of what they call an Oum' phor. It's a sacred place of worship that takes many sacrifices and spells done in one purified area, before they can muster enough power to throw a major spell. Even I, who have lived here in Corpus Christi for only a few months, have my power base built up to only a fourth of the power I would need if I were alone. My altar is my sacred space and the more spells I perform at my place of worship, the more power builds there for me. Now, someone who has been displaced because of Katrina, would need time to find a new home, and time to rebuild their power base. Only a few true Vaudouns have that kind of power."

"But, the TV evangelist made their snide comments and those nine tornadoes hit Kansas pretty damn quickly," O'Hara interjected. "How did the Haitian voodoo priests get powered so fast?"

25

"You're talking about Haitian voodou verses New Orleans voodoo, buddy. Haitians come from a long line of voodoo practitioners that goes back to Africa, and if you're talking Africa you're talking about the primordial of magick. People say Africa is the birth place for mankind. Well, if that's true, it is also the birth place of Magick; Primordial Magick, which was carried in its most pure form to Haiti. Haiti, after all this time, has deep pockets of this primordial magick and even after a disaster, you can bet their Vaudouns can pull some pretty powerful stuff off with no waiting. New Orleans voodoo is also mixed with French and Catholic influences. Well, Haitians also incorporated some of the Catholic Saints into their Voodou, but it is still more pure then New Orleans Voodoo, which is a slightly different flavor of Voodoo."

"So, can your laws do anything with these people? What they did caused the loss of innocent lives," the General asked.

"You honestly need to understand Vaudouns and their sense of justice. If they did what we think they did, then they are justified under their own laws in retaliation. You and I might not think so, but under their own flag, they would have the right. We cannot and will not roll up against them. It would be trying to push our form of magickal laws onto them, which is just as bad as the church trying to make everybody live by what they consider right, with birth control and marriage rights worldwide."

The General wanted clarification. "So, you won't act against them?"

I shook my head. "We don't have the right to. I can ask them to let us take care of this from our side, but we can't force them to. It's out of our jurisdiction, magickally speaking."

"You'll ask?" O'Hara looked surprised.

I nodded my head. "And I'll ask nicely, too. Vaudouns are a power to be respected. True, we might be able to take them in a magickal fight, but it would cost us dearly. Very dearly. I would rather take on a horde of Draugralls; it would be easier."

O'Hara shook his head. "They are that powerful?"

"Oh yes, the primordial of magick; never forget that. But also, as I said, mainly because, according to their own laws, they would have had the right to respond as they did. I know innocents got hurt and that sucks. If there is a price to be paid for that, they'll be paid by the Laos, but we can't interfere with their ways. We can ask them though, to think about the fact that innocents got hurt that had nothing to do with what the asswipe said, nor the woman from a Baptist Church who tried stealing their children. But, as I said, their sense of justice is quite

26

different from ours and we don't have the right to stop them. That move would be up to the Gods themselves, not us."

Wizard snorted, "Yet, you would cut off the head of this black witch?"

I frowned at him. "Yes, because his form of magick is the dark side of what we do. He then falls under our jurisdiction. The best we can do is to send protection for those in Kansas and others in tornado alley, which we have done. Though, they would never thank us for sending what protection we can, they would burn us for sure if they knew. But, still, we'll protect them by shielding. I don't know if it will help and we have to let nature do what nature does, but if any storms aren't started naturally, we can deflect those."

O'Hara asked, "Why not stop all storms and earthquakes, if you could do that?"

"Because, nature has to do what nature does. We've talked about this at some length and have come to the decision of not getting in Mother Nature's way, but to use our powers to ease the suffering from the effects of any disasters. Hurricanes being the exception, if they are affecting a land mass. Plus, think of the ramifications if we did stop all natural disasters, if we had all of the abilities needed to do so. The world needs to move and blow off its steam one way or another. If we were to stop an earthquake in one area, it would only release itself somewhere else and it could be twice as deadly. Hurricanes, I can slow down, but only if it is affecting a land mass; otherwise, I am not allowed to touch them by Law. The ocean has to breathe and the ocean is under the jurisdiction of Neptune, not the Triple Goddess. We have no say there and He told me hurricanes are a way for the ocean to breathe and grow in marine life at the bottom of the ocean. If we stopped all hurricanes, we would stop life from moving under the ocean. That would be a very bad thing, eventually."

Wizard was curious. "What happened with Katrina once it affected the land? That one didn't slow down at all."

"It did for a bit," I corrected. "It went down to a category three, but then, in the last three hours before it was to hit New Orleans full force, for some weird reason, it got a huge boost in energy and went back to a category five. After that, no matter what I did, it wouldn't slow down. I often wondered if someone wasn't helping it gain speed and shielding me from it. That storm felt wrong from the get-go. I remembered that and asked Dar, my trainer at the time, about it. She, too, thought it felt wrong; that it was goaded by something else, but we never could find out by who or what. It was before I found my mates so my power levels weren't at full strength at the time, but I did try." I felt sad that I couldn't have done more.

I loved New Orleans and its' people. I had a respect for their ways of life there and their various religions. New Orleans was such a unique American culture that blended in various creeds of people that made that city a wonder that can't be found anywhere else in America. I felt sad for its loss and knew it would never be the same again, but I also knew that New Orleans would someday make a comeback and some of their shine would live again. It was such a diverse place and had such strength, I knew it would find a way to grow again, being even stronger, diverse and more beautiful once again.

General Pierce asked, snapping me out of my thoughts, "So, Tornado Alley is now protected?"

I took a deep breath. "As best as we can make it. The natural ones will have to be let loose, but for anything unnatural, we should know about it and be able to stop it. Most tornadoes get going between three pm and seven pm. Scientists call it the 'magic five' hour; weird how they put metaphysical idioms to things they are trying to learn to explain in a scientific manner," I grinned at the General. "So, between those hours, we'll keep our own eyes on it our way."

"Good. Are you healed enough now to get back into action?" he asked.

"Yes, that's why we went healing in the hospital today, just to make sure. Shamus gave me a clean bill of health." I had been driving my astral familiar, Shamus, nuts with begging him to let me use my powers over the last few weeks.

I had been hurt badly when I closed a large vortex alone and the blow-back had messed me up, spiritually speaking, in a bad way. I had been held back from using any of my gifts because every time I did another aneurysm would show up physically in my brain. I had just recently healed enough, finally, to be able to use my talents once more.

General Pierce nodded, "Good. Then you and yours have a lot of work ahead of you. Four more blips made it on the radar recently."

A radar that one of my mates, Antonio, and one of O'Hara's Special Forces men, Wizard, came up with to alert us when a portal opened. I called it PETS (Portal Echo Tracking System), just to irk Antonio. He said I didn't get to name anything else ever again, except our future children. And maybe not even then.

28

"We need teams out on each of the portals that have opened and see if we can either make a peace treaty or close the portal against a hostile magickal race," the General said tiredly.

Lately, we've been running overtime, with racing all across the globe, every time a major natural disaster happened due to the Great Shift pulling the tectonic plates that raised enough energy to open a portal earlier than expected. We all groaned over the number of portals that had opened all at the same time. Two, were nearly in the same place in Baja, California. We had just gotten back from doing another one in Haiti. That one too, turned out to be hostile and had to be closed right away.

I suggested to General Pierce, "For this one in Baja, we would only need one team with two squads attached to save on time and Mercs." The General and I were all for cutting corners and costs in man power and money, so long as it didn't endanger the mission and the safety of our Nightwolves.

We weren't in it for the money ourselves, though we were Mercs. Working for General Pierce gave us a chance to uphold our mandate with a military backing. Our mandate consisted of saving as many lives as we could when a natural disaster struck, make treaties with the Greater Magickal Races that were coming through portals being opened early because of the energy from the natural disasters, and defend Earth from the more aggressive Magickal races that didn't want to live in peace with those on Earth. With the General's Special Forces team, his Marine Recons and my mercenary family, together we were the Nightwolves.

"That would be a good idea, because of the second bit of news I have to tell you all today, which is the reason for the large meeting." He took a deep breath and folded his hands together on the table in front of him. This was never a good sign.

"Certain people in the White House have gotten wind of the higher than normal activity and expenses being spent here on this base, which was supposed to have been realigned. Meaning downsized to the bare minimum operations. We basically have one of two choices facing us; either we close up shop and pray for the best..." An outburst erupted, even from a few of the squad leaders, who knew firsthand what we faced almost on a daily basis lately.

The General raised his voice and his hands in a calming gesture. "Or, we can allow a few more people to know of our situation here."

Everyone went quiet at that option. The more people who knew about us, what we do, could expose what we were and put us in a very bad situation. Burning at the stake would seem more humane than other things some government labs were doing to people like us, in secret, already.

"Who, and how much would they have to know?" I asked, since I led the Mercenary part of our Nightwolves operations.

"I have a General chum who is one of the Joint Chiefs of Staff. If we could get him on our side, he could help keep this from going to the Oval Office. Who, from what I've seen lately, wouldn't be too sympathetic to our cause and would lead the witch hunt if it was of a political advantage," he said gruffly. No General was comfortable speaking ill of the Commander in Chief in any public forum. Their careers didn't last long if they did. Luckily for this General, he could voice his true opinion and not worry, so long as it was our people he was speaking to.

I had to admit, however grudgingly, "Well, he is getting the country back on track, slowly but surely, economically speaking; can't fault him for that." Though, I still thought of him as 'He who has no balls'. I knew most of the people at this table thought the same way. Though, being natural born fighters, it was hard for any one of us to have respect for a person, especially one in power, who couldn't have enough cajones to fight for his own policies with any passion.

"And that's the problem," General Pierce responded. "They have an eagle eye on every dime being spent and since this base wasn't supposed to have that kind of budget, they're asking questions. With the politics focusing more on Church and God, instead of the science of what is going on, this could be a powder keg in our laps. Though, to be fair, we do use a lot of magick in our operations. Things we can't prove scientifically."

I snorted, "Most of those hypocrites are magick users themselves, of one flavor or another. That would be the pot calling the kettle black." I held up my hand before he could say anything. "I know, most of them are publicly saying they're church goers for the votes, so proving what they are would be futile and they would get away with it. They've got their asses covered too well," I rubbed my face. "Ok, so let's take a page from them and get our own asses covered. How can your Joint Chief of Staff shield us and what would we have to do?"

"Hal is one of the few White Knights in politics today. He actually does what he does for love of country and the betterment of the people. High ideals that don't usually flourish all the way to the Joint Chief of

Staff level, but he did it." General Pierce sounded very proud of his old military buddy.

His face got serious. "I am not saying he hasn't had to bend every now and again. Politics are politics, but on the high level matters, he has never caved in and has stuck to his guns. He is cleaner than most, in that respect. That, I can promise you."

"Ok, so what is he going to want? And what can he do for us?" I was curious about a man who can stay relatively clean to that high of a level in politics. That's a rare breed of man. I knew there were a few good guys in politics and I said a prayer for them every day. If they weren't there, then only the bad guys would be running the country and that would spell disaster for everyone on this planet. I was willing to work with one of those rare White Knights in politics. If he could be trusted, then he could be a huge asset for our operations.

The General looked relieved that I was being reasonable over this. "He'll want proof, for one. I was thinking of a trip to Kla' din and maybe to Trinidad. They would be relatively safe examples to show him. Providing the rulers of Kla' din have no objection? And you, of course." He looked over to my Kla' din mates, who as one, nodded their assent. He looked to me and I nodded my assent, as well. "Good, then. He would also want to bring along a few of his people. Between the people he works with and himself, they know where a lot of the bodies are buried and could use that knowledge to stop the ones we don't want starting investigations down here over the money issues."

I looked around our table, taking note of the expressions on my siblings and their mates faces. A few seemed uneasy about the extra exposure, but I could tell just from sizing them all up, they were also realistic. If we wanted to keep the military help we had, we needed to bend a bit for the General, who has to this day, bent over backwards for us.

I let the silence hang for a few more moments waiting to see if any of my people were going to voice a negative vote. No one did, trusting my judgment again in this type of situation.

"Fine, we'll play nice with the Brigadier General and his men. Cassie and her mates would be the best choice for smoozing and guiding them around to the other places." I had absolutely no ability to assimilate, often speaking my mind before thinking to whom I was speaking to. Cassie had a real gift for not only numerology, but being able to act as a diplomat. She had a knack of keeping the peace with people I would soon lose patience with. She was also way prettier then I was, in my opinion, not that I was jealous of it. But, it does help smooth the road with other people when on one hand you had Cassie, who was half Japanese, who had a precise way of speaking and an infinite level of patience. She was small, almost petite, and hid her dangerous side very well under a veneer of civilized, polite manners.

People took one look at me, however, and usually moved quickly out of my way. I was pretty enough, with long brownish hair and blue eyes, but more of your Xena warrior type with my black leather boots, leather jacket and sporting my latest Harley or Rock concert shirt; usually in black. I was your typical biker chick with tattoos and all. People with a more civilized background didn't smooze with people like me; they ran, if they had a half a brain. My Earth-side mates were the exception to the rule; they loved me no matter what I wore or how many tattoos I had and they came from the way upper class of the one percent club. Even my Kla' din mates loved me and they were rulers of their own world, but they didn't know better than to love a biker chick. Nope, for the most part, Cassie was definitely the better people person for this mission with the General's friend.

Relieved, General Pierce made notes in his file. "That sounds fine. I'll make the arrangements for him and his staff to come for a visit and see if we can't get his cooperation on our operations."

Chapter Three

En passant

The General looked up at me. "Speaking of operations, who are you assigning for the portals from your family's side?"

"I'll send Gerard, Cendra and Crimson to Baja, California. Antonio, Christoph and I, will deal with Rio de Janeiro…" I began making my own notes.

"Mother." Christoph had moved forward, closer to the table so I could see him.

At twenty years old, he was growing into a fine young man with his blond hair and bright blue eyes. Deadly at martial arts and with swords, my eldest son could hold his own with most everyone here.

"Yes, son?" I was concerned, because he had never interrupted a meeting before.

He stated simply, "I feel the call, Mother."

Silence thundered in my ears. Every single Merc in the room knew what he was saying and what it meant. My mouth dropped open and I blinked my eyes for a few seconds. "Are you sure, honey?" My baby boy couldn't be that old already. He was much too young for a calling. I hadn't gotten my own calling until I was twenty-nine. Antonio reached over and squeezed my shoulder to comfort me. I realized then that my breathing had accelerated.

Christoph leaned forward to peer into my eyes to show me he was serious. "I feel it in my soul. She calls to me, Mother."

"Do you have a name, a place to start?" I asked him, my voice low.

"Andrea? Somewhere Northeast of here, I believe." His gaze wandered off into a place only he could see.

An American mate or maybe a Canadian one, I thought to myself. Well, that would be nice. Nothing like trying to find your soul quest in another country you're unfamiliar with. I had heard of a few cases and they didn't end well.

I gathered myself together and said the only thing I could say. "Good hunting then, son. I hope your quest is met with joy," giving him a High Priestess' blessing.

"What's going on?" The General, who had until now just watched the proceedings, seemed confused with what we were allowing for Christoph.

"My son has been called. He must answer it. He won't be with us again until his quest is fulfilled," I explained to General Pierce and those of the military who were in the room with us.

"Called? A Quest?" General Pierce looked around at our group. "You never told us of this? What does it mean, exactly?"

I couldn't take my eyes off of my son. "It means the soul of his mate is calling him and since he is open for a mate, he must seek her out and complete their bond. He won't be available for any other mission until this quest is done, one way or another."

"But, we have a case overload here." General Pierce leaned forward in his seat. "Can't it wait until we have at least caught up? Surely this is more important than finding a mate for your son."

Every single Merc in the room stood up, showing support for Christoph and the call that was made to him. I stood as well. "General, this is exactly why we are Mercs. Some things have precedence over duty. Soul calls are top priority with us and if he has been called, he must answer. To deny a soul quest is to risk damage to his soul, to his destiny. It could harm the Coven as a whole. He has our blessing and support." I gentled my tone for the General. "It would be nice if he had yours, as well."

I knew Christoph also valued General Pierce's opinion, but he wouldn't allow that to stop his soul quest mission, even if it hurt him to do it.

"General Pierce," O'Hara had cut in, "I have read of these. They used to be rare, but apparently for this Coven, they are more frequent and we have to learn to live with them. If the call isn't answered, it could drive him insane. He could wind up 'soul lost'. Inside, he'll be split into two. There would be nothing that could be done for him. He has to finish this according to the texts I have read or things could go badly for him, for the Coven; and by extension to us, the Nightwolves."

I was impressed that O'Hara had studied that far into the texts and understood the implications of a soul quest.

"That serious, eh?" Pierce was beginning to comprehend how important a soul quest was to one of my kind. He stood as well, "Son, we'll miss you. I hope you find what you are looking for and make it back to us as soon as possible." General Pierce couldn't keep the order out of his tone, but Christoph only smiled at him for it.

"Yes, Sir. Thank you." He walked over to me and gave me a hug. "Thank you, Mother." Demitri slipped him a credit card and clapped his shoulder.

"Good luck, son." I kissed Christoph good-bye and gave him my silver dagger with its blessed silver sheath. He knew all he had to do was cut himself a bit on this blade and I would come running if he needed me. The silver blade and sheath were spelled for many things that could help him on a quest. Others were touching him as he moved slowly towards the door, being stopped every now and again for a hug and someone slipping him money or phone numbers for places he could use as shelter or call for help.

The General, seeing how we were giving him things for his journey, offered his own. "Does he need a car?"

"No General, he has a car, though it could impede, as well as help. Some of the old ways still apply even in this modern age where doing it by foot would be better in some cases. But, thank you for the offering." I smiled at him, grateful for his support; even though I could tell he still didn't quite understand just how significant this was. I could tell he thought the portals being closed should take precedence, but he was willing to let this go, knowing we would cover for Christophe's absence somehow.

"Oh, well then, call us if you need us for anything, Christoph." The General told him.

Christoph nodded to him. "Thank you, General." As he moved past the Dai' Khans of Kla' din, Ja' Kelo stopped him. "Here son, this is from our world. It is a speaking crystal. Rub this side of it three times, speak to it and we will hear you if you need us, even if we are in our own world, as long as the portal is open."

AH ha, now I knew how the rubbing the genie lamps myth had gotten started! The People of Kla' din were descended from the Mage-Wizards of the old Egyptian lore. Since the ancestors of Kla' din were too powerful for this world, the Gods and Goddesses had them moved to another world during the last Great Shift, as they had done with the other Great Magickal races all over the planet. It was why they still worshiped Amun-Ra even to this day and some of their traditions where rooted in Ancient Egyptian Lore. Being cut off from this world for so many millennia, they had developed differently than most of the Middle-East had on Earth. Their traditions were more 'woman caring' than in those of this world, but some of that could have stemmed from having to protect their womenfolk so fiercely from their dreaded enemy, the Draugrall; fierce vampires that seemed to have descended from the Lithuanian vampire clans.

Segregation didn't help the Draugralls become nicer vampires. It only made them more vicious and bloodthirsty. The Draugralls had found a way to open temporary astral doorways into Kla' din and steal their women for food and breeding. They took some men and a ruby-like stone too, but women were their main targets when raiding Kla' din. I had a full fighting wing of Dragons from Trinidad, my own world, guarding Kla' din now, while the Dai' Khan's were visiting Earth, trying to help us with our own problem of portals opening too early every time a natural disaster struck. The energy from an earthquake or the like would open a portal and some of these portals led to very aggressive Greater Magickal races. Vampires, werewolves, and others that had become myths and legends in Earth's cultural histories wanting to come back to Earth and rule as they did in the days of old. The polarity of Earth was shifting with North becoming South and vice versa. We called this the Great Shift. The shift would complete its process on December 21st, 2012. Meanwhile, the pull of the tectonic plates was causing havoc and disasters planet wide. It was our job to safeguard Earth from the more aggressive races, make treaties with those who wanted to live peacefully, as the rulers and people of Kla' din did, and save as many lives as possible during the disasters that were happening with greater frequency. It was bad timing to be starting a soul quest, but when a call came, one could not ignore it, even if Earth itself was falling into chaos.

My son looked surprised and pleased with the gift Ja' Kelo had given him and clapped him on the shoulder in thanks. Christoph made it to the door and was gone to start his own journey, as I had done sixteen years ago. I prayed to the Goddess, his quest goes much more smoothly than mine had. I still had nightmares from the long, lonely nights it took me to find my own mates and the battles I'd fought to keep my own sanity until I actually did find them physically. My soul quest had almost cost me my sanity as well as my life several times. I was still missing pieces of my soul because of the length of time it had taken to finally complete my calling. I hoped my own son wouldn't know that kind of hell.

"May The Goddess watch over him and guide him on his quest," I intoned, the blessing being repeated by several of our kin and a few of the military men as well, I was pleased to note.

The General sat back down in his seat. "Well, back to business then people."

We all took our seats again. Ja' Kelo leaned forward, whispering in my ear, "I can take Christophe's place if you'd like, Meshama." I thought about it and nodded in agreement. His power would be helpful in protecting or closing a hostile portal, if negotiations faltered with the beings inside it.

"Thank you, Ja' Kelo." I looked to General Pierce and O'Hara who would make up the military part of the team going to Baja to deal with the portals there. "General, Ja' Kelo has graciously offered his blade and power in Christophe's place, if either of you don't mind?"

General Pierce looked to O'Hara who nodded his agreement. O'Hara had fought side by side with the Dai' Khans of Kla' din before and felt comfortable working with them.

"That would be fine, then. It solves that problem for us. And to further help them here in our world," General Pierce slid three more folders to me, "these are faked personal histories, making your Dai' Khans citizens of America. Driver's license and birth records, as well as school records have been made up for them. Have them memorize the information in case they are ever questioned. Wizard and your mate, Antonio, have circumvented certain data bases," he gave a slightly disapproving glance at the two mentioned, but continued anyway, "so they'll pass muster even with the deepest of scans from any branch of law enforcement."

"Thank you, General, and you two as well. This will be helpful the next time Ja' Kelo is pulled over for speeding on his Harley," I raised an eyebrow at him. My brother, Grant, who was now a Corpus Christi detective, has had to fix several tickets for my Dai' Khan mates already.

"They now have Americanized names, so you should start getting used to calling them by those instead," General Pierce advised me.

I looked at the folders and scanned for their new names; Jack Allen for Ja' Callum, Jameson Elms for Ja' Monel and Jake Lords for Ja' Kelo. "Cute, real cute. I bet I can blame Andre for Jake Lords' last name."

"Is that not a good last name for me, Meshallima?" Ja' Kelo peered over my shoulder.

"It kind of does fit, since you are a Lord in Kla' din. It's a play on words, actually. I was just giving Andre shit for it. Don't worry, I like it. It does fit you." I smiled reassuringly at him and he grinned back. Andre was chuckling behind his hand, the creep. Giving Andre a mock glare, I handed the Dai' Khans each their folders. I started to repeat their new names over and over again in my mind, so I wouldn't make the mistake of calling them their Kla' din names anymore in public. They had gotten better at not calling me Meshallima, Dear Wife, or Meshama, Dear daughter of Goddess, in public and fell back to calling me Cat when we weren't alone or in a safe place to talk freely.

"The next thing on my list is finding out how far along you all are on those investigations with missing kids?"

Gerard, my youngest brother, sat forward to be seen by those at the table. "I have found two churches trying to pull what Cat calls a 'Maggie'."

O'Hara cocked his own eyebrow, "Come again?" He had earned his call sign, The Rock, not only for the 225 lbs of pure muscle in a 6'3 frame (needed in a leader for the best Special Forces team in America today) but also for this habit of cocking his eyebrow when asking a question or if he was pissed off at someone.

Gerard pulled a book from his briefcase and slid it across to O'Hara. "Up until 1994 supposedly," he said sarcastically, "there were instances of young girls being placed into convents for a variety of reasons. Pregnancy, not listening to parents and the whole host of reasons parents allow someone else to take a troubled teen off their hands. The church takes these young girls and uses them for slave labor. Back-breaking work doing laundry, landscaping and the like. The priests come in after hours and rape the girls; the nuns beat them with whips, sometimes to death, for tempting the priests or rape the girls themselves."

O'Hara had been leafing through the book Gerard had given him. "Fuck, this ain't right."

Gerard's ice blue eyes, not usual for someone with pure Italian blood, were hot with suppressed anger. "I know. Even though, after the investigations in 1994 were supposed to have stopped this practice, Cat was afraid that it was still going on." Gerard nodded to me, "She is right. The whole thing about the Maggie's is when the parents allow their daughters to be taken into the church, they change their names to take their identity away and make them feel bad about themselves by calling them Magdalene Marsha, Magdalene Rose and so on; ergo, the 'Maggie's'. Since Mary Magdalene was a prostitute and Jesus cleansed her soul of her wickedness, the church adopted the attitude of vilifying Magdalene instead feeling blessed that she was cleansed. They used her as an example to beat these young girls down. When they are killed, their bodies are thrown into a grave with others who have died from abuse. There was a church where they found over 150 bodies of dead girls that the nuns were supposed to take care of. It happened in a lot of countries as well. Ireland, America and Canada were the worst offenders in taking young girls and making them into vilified Maggie's." Gerard's voice had gone deadly cold, as he told the results of his and his mates investigations.

"Didn't the parents ever wonder what happened to their daughters?" General Pierce was incensed now himself.

"Of course some did," Gerard snapped, not at the General, but because he was so pissed, "but the church would always tell them some story that they were moved to another church, sometimes to another country. They would say that the child was fine and doing well, but unfortunately they couldn't see the young lady anymore due to the fact it might upset the teachings the church was doing for her."

General Pierce shook his head. "And this still goes on?"

"Yes, though not as flagrant as it was before. But, there is a church or two that are the heaviest in using the girls for prostitution, then beating them for it when they are returned to the church. Twenty more young girls are completely missing. I think they, too, found their way into a mass unmarked grave." The look in Gerard's face promised retribution-with interest.

"What happens to the pregnant teens?" Major Pearson, one of the Alpha 53rd's Recon squad leaders asked, shocked to his core.

One of Gerard's mates leaned forward, knowing her mate was on his last edge. "The babies are put up for adoption at a nice profit for the church, then the girl is raped by a priest, getting her pregnant again and the same thing is repeated."

"That's disgusting," Pearson spat. "Why wasn't the church held accountable for the bodies that were already found?"

"Church politics," Lucy, Gerard's mate, explained. "Same reason their priests who were brought up on molestation charges for raping altar boys never made it to trial or were stonewalled by the church. M-O-N-E-Y. That billion dollars of our tax money paid yearly, violating separation of church and state laws, is helping the churches lawyers keep their priests out of jail. Politics and church laws is what makes Congress go round these days."

I gave an evil chuckle. "Word on the streets, is that the new Pope, who helped keep all that stuff quiet and the priests out of jail, is what got him his Papacy. Well, boys and girls, it is now finally biting him on the ass. Seems some want the new Pope brought up on charges for crimes against humanity. Problem is, because the church is not part of the U.N., but does have an auditor there, in between the lines, 'a church spy', it will be hard to hold him accountable for his crimes or the church itself for that matter on an international level."

"As all of this is highly criminal and ought to be stopped, but how can we here at the base help?" General Pierce was stuck between a rock and a hard place. Since this crime wasn't causing harm to the planet itself for putting people in harm's way on a wide spread level, he really didn't have any authority to actually use resources of the military to do anything about it.

I, however, had other plans and resources. "First, the only thing we may need of you, General, is the use of your computer to hack into certain data bases. If we can drop enough evidence, on the QT., it might get the investigation going by departments where it is their responsibility, both by law and financially. We just need to nudge them in the right direction. However, if that doesn't get the ball rolling the right way, we may need a man or two for some rescue operations for those poor kids trapped in those churches."

"Not enough," my brother bit out, his lips pressed thin with fury. "I want them to bleed. I want to capture the offending priests and hang them by their own balls."

"And become what they were with the inquisition, brother?" I understood his anger and felt it myself, but I couldn't allow our Coven to go down a road already trodden by the church several times. "We would be no better than they are, if we become judge, jury and executioner; as much as my hands ache to rip a few of the balls off the priests myself and break every bone in the hands of the nuns, we can't be as they are. We don't have the authority, for one, and for two, this is not our mandate."

"So we let them live?" he hissed at me, too close to losing his temper to contain his fury, even from me.

"Not comfortably, no." I wasn't in the least of afraid of his temper. I knew he loved me deeply and wouldn't hurt me. "What are we, if not witches, brother dear or did you forget how to do a karma spell?" I grinned mischievously at him. His temper was slowly cooling as he got the idea. His own smile grinned just as wickedly as mine did, as it dawned on him.

"Hmm Cat, can you please share with the class. A Karma spell?" O'Hara was watching our exchange with great interest. The General and others too, were looking expectantly at us both.

"A Lords of Karma spell. I am practically famous within the pagan underground with it. My brother here is just as good as I am in bringing about a Karma spell. On the astral planes, O'Hara, which you should have read about by now, " glancing at him archly. He was falling behind in his studies again if he didn't know about the Lords of Karma yet. "There are The Lords of Karma. They are the ones who, either at the time of death or during a person's life, decide when their karma, good or bad, will hit them. It doesn't matter what faith, creed or religion they come from. The Lords of Karma hold power over all before their souls are brought to their particular God or Goddess for judgment. We, as witches and Daughter and Son of the Lord and Lady, seem to get special attention when we ask them to bring a person's karma back on them quicker than was planned, even by The Lords of Karma. Now, here's the trick. The person gets his bad karma, it comes on them times three and since they deserve their karma, it isn't our bad for throwing a negative spell. Remember, you get what you put out, sooner or later, so tossing about negative spells will build up negative karma or negative brownie points on the astral, but since we are just asking for justice now for these asswipes instead of later, it isn't considered our bad and we won't have to pay the penalty. The person getting the karma is karma deserved, not us making bad stuff happen that wouldn't have happened to them anyway. Quite a nice little loophole I found in the astral law books." I was grinning smugly, seeing the wheels turning in my brother's head.

This will keep him busy doing spells against those that deserved it instead of lopping off their private parts and violating the harm none law. It was one thing to defend country and home, quite another playing vigilante when you weren't appointed as one by the Gods and Goddesses. That thought just gave me another idea. "Oh brother, mine. You could also have your mates track down those appointed by the Gods and Goddesses for justice, as well. Bring them the evidence and let them roll heads instead, all nice and legal, witch-crafty speaking. None of our laws will be broken that way." His mates were now grinning, as well.

Good, I was able to stop them from doing something that could have some real negative consequences later. Although, if I didn't see a drastic change for protecting these kids soon, I may say screw the laws myself, pick up my own fucking sword and damn the consequences. There was only so much I could take and I empathized with my brother's first instincts on just killing the damned pedophiles and abusers and let the Gods sort them out. It was a guaranteed way to make sure of no repeat offenders.

I closed my eyes and counted to ten. I was the leader here for our Coven. I had to keep my head and control my emotions better than this. I felt a hand gently hug my shoulder and I opened to see Ja' Callum look at me with understanding in his eyes. It helped me calm down enough to continue the meeting with the General as he was speaking to me again and I missed the first part of his question. "So, it seems then, you have a handle on this situation and don't need very much from us." He sounded both happy and disgruntled he couldn't be more of a part in getting these kids safe.

"Sir, if I may?" Major Pearson asked.

The General granted him leave to speak. "Go ahead, Major."

"If you need men for muscle, please call me. I would be happy to volunteer for a rescue operation." He appeared incensed and needed to do something about it. I nodded my head at him. "You'll be the first I'll call then, if the General and your Captain allow it."

"Please apprise me of the exact details, if this move needs to be made. So long as you don't get my men's hand caught in the cookie jar, so to speak, I won't have a problem with it." The General seemed happy to have some hand in helping these kids even though it wasn't a military problem.

Captain Holland had his bulldog face on, as usual. "I have a difficulty using military men for a civilian operation. If they're caught, my men could be brought up on charges. It could reflect on the platoon as a whole. Sir, I disagree with letting her use my marines like this."

The thing was, he had a problem no matter what with me. He hated Mercenaries and female ones just rubbed him the wrong way. Taking him down in a match as easily as I did, when proving to him I could fight, didn't help. Not even when he found out I was part vampire and said I had cheated, so no wonder I won against him. His disagreement didn't surprise me, even though I offered yet another olive branch in including his opinion on such an operation, if they became necessary. I could have superseded him anytime I wanted too, depending on how I played my cards with the General.

"I trust her not to expose any of our men unnecessarily, Captain," the General assured him, "so I don't think you'll have to worry. Besides, it isn't written in stone yet that she or her family will have to put such an operation in motion. They may cause enough havoc that the situation will be worked out in due course."

"That's all they do, is cause havoc." I and a few others could hear Captain Holland say under his breath. General Pierce caught some of it too, from the expression his face, since Captain Holland wasn't but two seats from him. The general glared a warning look at him, as if to say, behave yourself or else. Captain Holland took the hint and with eyes forward, refused to even glance my way for the rest of the meeting.

"Now, about the one in Rio. Who will take that one?" General Pierce was getting back to business.

"Two of my mates, Ja' Kelo and Antonio, and I will, Sir. I am the best with flooding and can ease the flow down faster, therefore save more lives." I shook my head in disgust, "If they hadn't cut their damned forests, they wouldn't have had such a bad problem, but with the razing of the rain forest, they have now left their cities exposed to just this kind of thing. I wouldn't be surprised if this happens more often now, since they have devastated so much of the rain forest already."

General Pierce sighed heavily, "True, but there isn't anything we can do about the rain forest, but we do have to deal with the portal. O'Hara, have you thought about which teams are going with which Mercs?"

"Cat, which portal do you think will have the most trouble?" O'Hara had gotten into the habit of asking me if a portal is going to be potentially hostile. I had a high rate of calling it right, so far. I've only missed once or twice. "The Baja ones are going to be the worst, I think, which is why I'm sending my brother and his team to deal with it. He needs to hit something, so what better than a hostile?" My brother shot me a dirty look. "What, bro? You know you need to bust a few heads. It'll make you feel better, trust me."

A few people burst out laughing at my managing who needed to break heads and who needed to just quiet things down this time around. Usually, I took the hardest ones, being in a bad mood most of the time, but lately I'd been feeling pretty mellow. With six handsome mates, what woman wouldn't be smiling most of the time? I wiped the grin off of my face before someone caught me at it and got my game face back on. I was supposed to be cold, hard, and ruthless. Yeah, I can do it.

"Fine, which means Special Forces should back your brother this go around with Pearson's and Mitchell's squads for back up. You take Miller's squad with you to Rio. And, who is handling Sumatra, Indonesia?"

"I'll be sending Demitri, Craven and Gavin with that one." I wrote down in the file who was going where and with what squad so they can have a get together later and establish their games plans. Demitri had a corporation out in Indonesia, so he'll use his private jet to get everyone there and do both the mission and checking on his business at the same time. It would save General Pierce expenses in sending a military plane, plus Demitri could use it as a business expense tax write-off since he really was doing business there once the portal was either closed or a treaty was made with the inhabitants.

General Pierce knew of Demitri's businesses and agreed with the use of the private jet to ferry his marines out on the mission. Andre and Ja' Monel were planning on going around and adding shields that my Kla' din mates had shown Demitri, Andre and Antonio how to do. The shields were most interesting and never seen here on Earth before. It would definitely help keep hostile businesses from using their magick successfully against the Caberelli Corporations; not that they had too much trouble before, but it's always good to err on the side of caution. A lot of businesses used magick, either for their protection, or against their competitors. Most people didn't know about that aspect of Corporate America, though.

"That leaves just getting two planes ready on the base." The General was writing his own notes. "Demitri, if your plane needs any artillery, let me know and I'll set up the outfitting for it. I'll also have codes you can use for the base in Indonesia that will get you past the Commander there as a black OP. There won't be any questions when you land a private jet that way."

"Good enough. I'll have a list for that artillery later today, General," Demitri told him. I could see the gleam in his eye. A private jet fitted with weapons. He was probably having a male moment right now. Sheesh, I was grinning again. My mate being outfitted like 007; yeah, that's just what he needed. I held in my chuckle and hoped we'd have time before he flew out, just so I could reap the reward of the male moment for myself.

Game face, Cat. Come on, game face. Oh, I hoped that's all the General had for us right now. The question was, hop on the male moment now or wait until the plane was outfitted and the male moment would even be harder? Hmm, I don't think that answer would be in my Martha Stewart handbook, either.

Clarrissa Lee Moon

46

Chapter Four

Domination

Crimson stealthily made his way down an alley on his way to his hook-up with Vanessa. Slipping past the guards that had been assigned to him and Craven to has become almost too easy. Just say you'll be in the gym alone for a few hours and they never come to check on you. Go to bed early, slip out the window and you can be gone all night. Christoph was the only one who didn't get a guard and that was because he'd put his foot down over his age. Crimson was eighteen, but that excuse didn't work for him which he thought was totally unfair. He had always been a loner, never quite fitting into the family unit as well as his brothers did. Mom always tried to make a connection though once she saw how distant he had become from the family, even within the house itself. He would often ghost out, not letting anyone see him as he slipped outside to pace in the yard or just to avoid chores he knew his mother was going to ask him to do. He had been practicing not being seen for many years, even as a child. It wasn't that his home life was hard to handle; it was the fact that he didn't know how to relate to anyone in the house or out of it; until Vanessa had come into his life.

When he'd first met Vanessa, everything seemed to finally make sense. With her, there was no pressure to relate, or even talk. It was just them, with no one else to live up to or try to connect with. The connection was already there. Sweet, warm and soft spoken, she was everything he could want and she never put any pressure on him. She just let him be himself without any expectations. Her long black hair and deep warm whiskey colored eyes would always smile when he showed up at her door. Slim and small, she was perfect for him. They had met last summer when he'd first moved here with his family. At first, he was

47

incensed they'd had to move here from Tucson, Arizona. He was born and raised there and never did well moving around. He liked being in one place, so long as he could move around within his space. Highly territorial, he didn't like leaving the only home he'd ever known and was pissed at his mother for moving them so abruptly to a place he had never seen before. Then, Vanessa was there and his life was all right again. Stability had been reestablished and Vanessa was the only reliability he could depend on now.

His mother had changed. Their family had changed with them moving into the house of his mother's mates. Now, Christoph was gone and again he felt shaky inside. Once more his world had been redefined and he didn't like it. He needed Vanessa tonight to feel stable inside again. Going up to her door, he knocked and waited for her sweet smile to appear through the door screen. The outside light turned on, the front door opened and she was there.

"You're late tonight, Caro," she told him, with a teasing lilt to her voice.

"I had to wait for the guards to sleep. Everyone is on edge and I only have a few hours tonight." He opened the screen door himself, so he could look at her without anything in his way. She wore nothing but a sheer black teddy, as if she knew he would be there tonight, though, he never promised to show up.

She smiled at him. "Why only a few hours?"

"I have to leave at 5 am." He moved closer to her, feeling her warmth already seeping through his jacket, her hands wrapping around his neck.

"Where are you off to now, Caro?" she whispered in his ear, pressing kisses along his neck.

He shuddered. "Too far away, but I'll be back in two or three days. I'll sneak away again and come to see you as soon as I get back," he promised her.

"You sure there isn't another girl you're seeing? You go away so much lately and you won't tell me where." She pressed her fingers to his lips, "I know. Don't ask questions and I won't. I have been very good about that. But, don't you think after all this time, maybe you should take me to meet your mother or to that bar you talk about all the time?"

"Vanessa, you know I can't take you to the Nightwolves Lair. It's strictly for family members only." Crimson kissed her back, slowly edging her into the house towards the back rooms.

"The Nightwolves Lair? You told me the name weeks ago Caro," she smiled sweetly at him. "It still sounds interesting."

Crimson sighed into her neck, "Remember, only family can go in."

"How will I ever be family if you don't take me to your mother?" She danced with him, the same dance they made every time he came over. He didn't want to share this with anyone else though. If he took her, she would be a part of the rest of it, and he didn't want that; at least not yet. He just recently told Craven one night and only parts of what he did when he snuck out, making his little brother promise not to tell their mother. She would want to know everything from the time Vanessa was born to this very minute. His mother's over protectiveness had always driven him up a wall.

"Maybe, someday I'll take you to my house, but not now. Besides, I have to leave in a while. We can argue or we can dance." He left the choice up to her. She searched his face and slid the bedroom door shut, silently inviting him in.

False dawn was barely breaking to true dawn, as Crimson slipped into his room.

"Busted bro," a growl from the corner had him spinning around with his right hand ready with a blade.

When he realized it was his little brother, Craven, Crimson straightened out his stance. "You asshole."

"Out seeing the girl, again?" Craven moved towards his brother's bed and sat on the corner of it, spinning his Tonfa against his forearm, then kicking it out to hit an imaginary target. Crimson watched him spin the Tonfa, and then kick it out, over and over again.

He preferred sharp blades to Craven's preference of wooden weapons. "Yeah, anyone notice I was gone?"

Craven grunted, "I did. You move like a pregnant baboon."

"Oh, don't get started on that," Crimson groaned.

That was mom's favorite game to play. Mention a movie quote, and then the person had to remember which movie it came from. Mom could have a whole conversation with a person, using nothing but movie lines. It drove Crimson nuts, sometimes.

"Remo Williams. And no, no one else noticed you gone. Mom's been busy with her men, knowing she won't see a few of them for a week or more." Craven sounded jealous to Crimson's ears.

Crimson snorted. Good for mom. It was the one change he did like. After seeing her alone for so long, which just wasn't natural, it was good to see her smiling more often now. Craven just didn't like it that her attention wasn't all on her sons anymore and resented the time spent with her mates. Craven always started growling when the bandanna was hanging on her bedroom knob. A sign to keep out, or her kids may be scarred for life seeing shit she felt they didn't need to see. Too damned overprotective, thought Crimson.

"Good. Move. I gotta get my bag out." Crimson bent down to retrieve his black bag to load it up with things he'll need for his mission to Baja, Ca.

"You haven't packed, yet? I'm done and waiting to go." He would be. Craven lived for this shit; Crimson didn't. "You should have had this shit done last night, just in case."

Crimson put in his shirts and spare pants, as well as his own Gaileyah. "Fuck off."

He added a few extra blades and went to his drawer to get his guns and load them with silver bullets. Mom had warned him that Baja might be a bad one.

"How come you get Baja and I get Sumatra? Being a Were, I should have gotten the possibly more dangerous one," Craven was sounding jealous again.

He added extra socks, both black and whites, in case he needed to dress up for something. "Maybe, because you haven't gotten a hold of your Dire Wolf form yet? Just a shot in the dark."

"Nope, can't remember the movie." Craven was pacing back and forth, excited over the nearness of taking off for another mission.

"What the fuck are you talking about?" He was getting irritated at his little brother. Though they were the same height even when they were little, Craven had always been just as tall as he was and outweighed him by twenty pounds. Another thing that irritated him as he grew up.

"Just a shot in the dark," Craven said, as he checked his hair out in the mirror. He was such a fucking fashionista, thought Crimson. "It came from a movie, but I don't recall which one." Craven spiked his hair more with gel and combed it just so.

Crimson cursed, "Fuck, now she's got me doing it."

"Still pissed at Mom for moving us here?" Craven cocked a grin at him.

"No," he said sullenly, "but the game is stupid."

"Dude, you'd be pissed at her no matter what she did." Satisfied with his now perfected hairdo, Craven started fussing with his black shirt. "You love everything she hates and hate everything she loves. The

only things you two agree on are politics and history." Craven
shuddered, "I don't know how the fuck you two can go on for hours
about those two boring-assed subjects."

"Not as bad as you two going on about magick and paganism. That's
boring." Crimson shot back.

"Man, lighten up." Craven lightly hit him on the shoulder, ever
mindful of his new strength now. "So, how was it?"

Evading the questions, as always, "How was what?"

"Your girl. You haven't even told me what she looks like yet." He
had been pestering him for weeks about Vanessa, but he still didn't want
to go into it, even with his brother.

"Same ole." Crimson zipped up his bag and was ready to go after
running a comb through his own hair.

Craven decided to poke some more. "Time for a new girl then if
that's all you got to say about her after all this time."

"You wouldn't know shit about it." He was tired already and he
hadn't been home for more than fifteen minutes. "You haven't even had
a girl yet, yourself."

"Why does everyone automatically assume I'm going to be
straight?" He looked pissed. Craven had proclaimed to his family two
years before their mom found her American mates that he was bi-sexual.
Mom just shrugged her shoulders at him and said, whatever. Later,
Mom had taken him and Christoph out for a talking to, saying that if
they gave Craven shit over it, she would ground them until the end of
time. She warned the older boys that he was their brother, their flesh and
blood no matter what his sexual orientation was, and she wouldn't
tolerate any teasing of Craven over it from either of them. She looked so
serious about it, they both took it to heart and were careful never to even
joke about it.

At least he got Craven off the subject of his girl. "You just like the
attention it gets you." Right then, both of their pagers went off and it was
time to call in and get rolling to the base.

"Finally! Countdown to fun." Craven was always excited before
every mission.

"If you say so." He hated the missions because it took him away
from home and into places he'd never been to before. He really hated the
unstable feeling he got when that happened. He also didn't want to be
left home alone while his other two brothers were out getting the glory.
So he forced himself to go every time his name came up on the roster.
Now Christoph was out on a quest and that was one thing he hoped like

hell never happened to him. Mom said that mate quests only happened if both mates were ready. So by that logic, since he didn't want a mate at all, it should never happen to him and that would be just fine. Vanessa was better than a mate, anyway. She didn't make him feel tied down to a ball and chain and that's was just what he wanted. Freedom.

Craven grinned at him, happy to be rolling at last. "Cheer up, bro. It's Showtime."

Crimson, picking up his black bag, thought to himself, 'I hate that stupid game.'

Chapter Five

Fianchetto

To save time on debriefing the teams, General Pierce had waited until everyone had returned from their various missions. Once again, the whole Nightwolves force was sitting around the table inside the war room. Those that returned the fastest didn't go to the Nightwolves Lair, unable to settle and relax until they knew that all of the teams had made it home in one piece. Tonight would be different, as they were all reunited again and would celebrate their victories at the bar, each filling the others in with their own war stories.

The General waited until everyone was in place. I noted that, yet again, Crimson was the last to come in, and he'd set himself apart from the table, leaning up against the wall, trying to be invisible even in here. So, the mission hadn't helped him to relieve any of the suppressed anger he had. I would have to come up with another tactic with him somehow. Craven still looked morose that there hadn't been any fighting done in Indonesia. It was exactly what I'd hoped for. I didn't trust his control over his Dire wolf form yet and a violent mission wouldn't have been a good way to try him at this point.

General Pierce addressed the teams. "Four men injured in the field, who were taken care of while most were in flight. According to the reports, these men will need only a day or two of rest and they'll be fit for duty at that time. Other than that there were no losses for our teams. Good work, Nightwolves."

We took our due with a smile. It was a good run for everyone, for the most part anyway. General Pierce got to that part. "Extreme hostiles were reported in Baja, California. Apparently, they didn't even try to dialog at all. It seems a raiding party had made it to a small town two miles South of one of the portals and killed every man, woman and child there. They were on their way up the highway, on foot, to the next town, when O'Hara's team and your Mercs found them. Due to the violence done to the townspeople, they were dealt with extreme prejudice. Three men were injured, but not critically. Both portals led to the same world and both were closed; permanently, we hope. Local authorities have been handled and will not be asking too many more questions." The General looked up from the report O'Hara must have handed him late last night. "What made these hostiles so violent and what breed were they?"

O'Hara glanced over the table at me. "I was hoping Cat could tell us. There was nothing obvious at the first town we tracked them to, to tell us what might have made them go on a rampage like that. None of her family on the site could ID. their tribe or breed. Gerard didn't even know if they were vampires or something else. We took pictures and tossed their remains back through the portal before closing it as a warning, but knowing their origins, just from looking at them couldn't be determined." He slid a pile of pictures at me and I took a look at them.

The pictures showed what appeared to be a male with long white hair, very pale skin, but humanoid for the most part. No vampire teeth were showing, but their eye color was pure red, with black elongated pupils, like a cats eyes. I'd bet they either came from a dark world or were just nocturnal by nature. O'Hara had done a good job of taking a picture of each corpse. There had been ten bodies they had to take back and put thru the portal. Each body was wearing trousers and a black cloak, like capes. One had more style and a golden emblem on it. His weapons, too, were more stylish, set with jewels and etched with scroll work on the blade and hilt. This one must have been the leader for this hostile group. The symbols on his weapons weren't anything I recognized, but I sent a mental picture to Shamus, my astral familiar, asking him telepathically to go to the Akashic Records to see if he could find a match. If it can't be found in the Akashic Records, a library of mass proportions of every person on every world, their histories and past lives- then we be screwed. There was something about their features that reminded me of an old myth called the Fomroii. An underworld dark Fae, that had been defeated by the Tuatha De Danann. If they were the same race, we could be in serious trouble sooner or later. I didn't know of any portals that lead to Tuatha De Danann, yet. And they weren't exactly warm and fluffy, either. On the sly, I passed my suspicions to Shamus. I didn't want to worry anyone until I had confirmation.

I asked O'Hara, "Do you know if they had done their killing at night?"

He shrugged, "Quiet possibly, since most of the bodies in the town were found still in the homes or in their beds. I can't confirm one hundred percent, though. We found them during daylight hours, which is why we ruled out vampires. Plus, there weren't any bite wounds on any of the victims in the town."

"There are vampires that can run during daylight hours and there is more than one kind of nocturnal Magickal Race. I asked, because some won't kill during the day at all. If that were the case, it would shorten my list of suspects." I tossed the pictures back at him. "I don't recognize the breed, but we'll dig into it." I turned to Gerard. "You didn't have any gut feelings on what type they were?"

Gerard's eyes were still hard and cold. "No, the closest thing I was able to determine was dark Elf, except the skin color didn't fit." It wouldn't, if they were Fomroii.

"Did any of the Unseelie Sidhe tribes fit the portfolio?" If we had a portal to the Sidhe, even if Unseelie, they could be dealt with by negotiations. You just needed to know how to approach them the right way. Much less dangerous than dealing with the Fomroii.

"None that I had read about in the old texts," he admitted.

"Let us know if you find anything. This was one rough group." O'Hara took the pictures back and slid them into the folder.

"In Sumatra, we only had one injury; the other three were in Baja because of the fighting," the General continued with his summery, before asking us for further details. "Demitri's team reported a quiet portal. They walked in for few feet and waited, but nothing happened, good or bad, except one of the men twisted his ankle. Craven healed the injury on site and they backed out. Neither Demitri nor Craven could smell any tracks on Earth's side. The Bokaris were placed and a trip-wire signal was put in place. If there is any activity we'll know about it."

General Pierce looked up at Demitri. "Any other feelings on this mission, Demitri?"

"Nothing, other than one of the marines twisting his ankle badly. For some reason, that rubbed me the wrong way." Demitri was rubbing his chin thoughtfully.

I was silently agreeing with Demitri. Our marines were not clumsy, but sometimes things did happen. However, in this case, it did seem a bit off and I wasn't even there.

"We'll keep a weather eye on the place, then." General Pierce turned to me. "All was quiet on your portal the report says. Nothing but a water world?"

"Yes, it didn't help the torrential flooding already happening in the area. Then again, it could have been a Kismet kind of thing. Since the portal led to a water world, Rio had problems with water flooding. Things like that do tend to reflect on each other when you're talking metaphysics and magick." I slid a file to him. "With no trees to absorb the rain or the water flowing in, the damage was severe. Over three hundred deaths in the area. We closed off that world's portal permanently, but I can't guarantee there won't be another flooding for any of the surrounding cities through other natural means." The report I'd given to the General included both mundane and spiritual facts. "I had to do a lot of Veil transports for departed spirits, so at least there will be a minimum of haunting in the future. Only a few refused to go. I can't do anything about those spirits, free will being what it is; they have the right to refuse crossing over."

He glanced up at me from viewing the report I'd given him. "What if they change their minds in the future?"

I shrugged, "Then I'll reopen the tunnel through the Veil and guide them through to their particular heavenly plane."

"Will that mean another trip or trips to Rio?" the General's voice held a note of concern.

I bet it was the finances. "No, I don't even have to be in the country that has had a high death toll to open a tunnel through the Veil, though it does take quite a bit more energy from me."

He grunted, trying to hide his relief. "How will you know if a tunnel is needed again in Rio?"

"It's all part and parcel of being a High Priestess. I'll get an astral jingle, so-to-speak." I had used one of his favorite catch phrases.

General Pierce grinned at me. "That's good. That will save us time and money. Good work down there." He peered around the table. "Good work, everyone. I have Brigadier General Halbert Bruhest coming in for a first hand visit next week; until then, go enjoy yourselves, but stay out of trouble. That's all. Dismissed."

Chapter Six

Indian Defense

J looked in the walk-in closet at the choices of clothes and turned to Demitri asking, "Which outfit, hon?"

"I like the black leather mini skirt with the boots that go to your thighs," he said, as he ran his hand lightly over said thighs, making them shiver. I turned into him, smiling at his warm brown eyes that were turning hot with passion.

Andre was sitting on the foot of the bed watching us. "I like the black jean skirt with the slit on the sides with her mid calf black suede boots."

Who would have thought I, bad-assed biker chick that I was, would be discussing what to wear for the party at the Lair? Usually, I would throw on what I wanted and to hell what anyone else thought. I had never given a shit before. Yet, here I was, wanting to wear clothes to please my men. Problem was, with six mates it was damn near impossible to please them all at the same time.

"What Meshama has on looks beautiful to me." Ja' Monel glided into the room, already dressed for a night out at the Lair.

I gazed down at the towel I had on and gave a saucy grin to my men in the room. "You think this would be good on the dance floor?" I swiveled my hips to expose more flesh and got a strong reaction from all of them.

"We would have to kill any man ogling you sweetie, and that would be a bad thing. They are family now, after all," Andre growled. He stood up from the bed and prowled over to me grabbing the front of my towel and pulling me towards him.

He kissed me deeply as I heard Ja' Monel say to Demitri, "She is not issuing a mating challenge?" his voice was tinged with worry.

"A mating challenge?"

57

"Yes, a female can issue a mating challenge to see if there might be a stronger male to bond with. This only happens when the bond is not a white-blue bond, but a mix of other colors. I checked our colors and we have the right colored bond."

I felt his anxiety and pulled away from Andre. He allowed the move because he could feel Ja' Monel's feelings as well as I could. "No, Ja' Monel, I am not thinking of issuing challenge. It was a joke. Honest." I reached out to touch his face and pulled him down for a kiss. I felt his relief wash through my soul and then his feelings of desire overtook us both.

I heard Demitri whisper, "You shouldn't ever worry about her changing her feelings for us. Once her heart is given, it is for life. No, until the end of time," he corrected himself. I felt his surety, his conviction and joy swept through me. I had never felt so at ease, so understood and accepted before. My heart swelled with love for Demitri; for them all. As I kissed Ja' Monel, I guided him back towards the bed. I had already started to unbutton his shirt and was lightly caressing his bared chest. I had decided we would be fashionably late. One of my mates needed reassurance and that was more important to me than anything else.

A couple of hours later, we emerged from the bedroom. I wore my black jean skirt with the thigh high black leather boots. It was the best compromise I could come up with in satisfying them all. Although I had a sneaking suspicion that if they could just keep me in bed, naked, that would be perfect for them.

These last few weeks had me feeling so secure and happy, which had been a totally new experience for me. I didn't feel like I had to be on guard 24/7 anymore. I'd actually had a full week with no nightmares and slept through for a full ten hours with no interruptions in my sleep cycles. No insomnia. No jerking awake to pull myself out of a bad dream. No waking up with one hand on a blade that I always kept under my pillow. I had gotten into the habit of keeping weapons with me in bed from the time I was twelve and still did it to this day, but I wasn't waking up with my hand gripping the blades or guns anymore. I actually would wake up smiling now, which would probably freak out my kids if they knew, since they weren't used to that. I had prayed long and hard for years, for a home, a life where I could actually feel this safe and happy. My siblings had been noticing the changes in my attitude, as well. Often commenting on how much I was smiling now and that they were happy I was so at peace. Though, they had started to question my

58

leadership abilities more often, lately. Cassie wasn't the only one to have the "*talk*" with me. Gerard had a look of concern in his eyes more often when he spoke to me. Always asking if I was sure I could handle the tougher jobs now as well as I'd done before. That was very confusing to me, but I let it slide and assured him I had everything in hand quite nicely now.

I gently squeezed Demitri's hand, as we walked down the long hallway to start down the stairs together. I felt like my whole world was like some romantic song come true, with my men surrounding me with love. I moved down the stairs in matching step with Demitri and looked down to the foyer to see if Craven and Crimson were there, impatiently waiting for us. They were there all right, but the look on their faces was more than impatient; they looked strained with anger. My smile faded, as I saw who was standing with them.

My biological mother was there with her husband, wearing that look I knew so well. If I was still young and defenseless, I would be praying for a quick death or unconsciousness. Or both. I would be that scared. Now the fear came from me was the fear of not being able to hold my anger in check to make sure I didn't snap and kill her. Once, when I was a teenager and forced to live back at home with her at the age of fifteen because of a house arrest warrant, late one night I'd heard a voice whispering in my ear to get up and kill her. The night that happened, warrant or no warrant, I left the house and didn't see or call her for two years. Later, when I got older and heard of some teenager getting up at night and killing his whole family because he heard a voice tell him to do it, I had no doubt in my mind he was telling the absolute truth. I learned later, with my metaphysical training, where that voice came from and it wasn't from me. It was definitely an outside force. An evil one, at that. However, I never felt sorry for the teenagers who killed. They still had a choice. Anyone who actually acts because of that voice, have only themselves to blame for it. Blaming it on the voices is a cop-out. I had a choice that night and I chose to leave, instead. Again, saving her worthless and thankless life. From me, that time.

Pictures flashed in my mind of me at six years old, in my room and my mother bursting in and whipping me black and blue, screaming at me for being evil or a whore because my stepfather touched me. Calling me a demon child, because the knickknacks and cupboards would bang and rattle when my power would get away from my control. Images flashed and overlapped in my mind; the worst one was me begging for her not to leave for work, because I knew my stepfather would take me

59

to the basement to beat me. Or worse things would happen there. And still, she would go with this odd smile on her face.

The pain and the rage swirled inside me like an endless, black sea. I noticed I was shaking, squeezing Demitri's hand tightly with my own. If he had been human I would have crushed every bone in his hand. Thankfully, he was just like me. Vampire and Demi-God. I looked down, out of habit, just to verify I hadn't actually hurt him. I wasn't a child anymore and she hasn't had the balls to hit me again since I was twelve years old. She had slapped my face for just looking at her and I threw her up against the refrigerator and told her if she ever laid a hand on me again I would kick her ass. I snuck out my window that night and didn't come home for a year and that visit was a short one for other reasons. I looked at her again and glared. No, she couldn't hurt me anymore, but she had learned a new trick. Mental punishment and that was much harder to defend against then physical abuse. And a lot more damaging. She had made it her mission in life to make sure I was miserable. Any time before, if I was happy, she would have this sixth sense, it seemed like, and call or visit just to mess with my head. Once she saw that I was unhappy again, she would leave with her stern disappointed look on her face, but I could tell she was smiling inside.

I breathed in through my nose, out through my mouth and continued down the stairs. I could feel the worry and anxiety coming from my Kla' din mates. They knew I was very upset, but didn't understand where the feeling was coming from. I had never told them about my past. It just never came up. I had been too busy in spending time with them and my Earth-side mates; time with The Nightwolves, my kids and the Coven. My life was full to overflowing, but I was happy with it. I was content. For the first time in my life, I was happy.

And, Mommy Dearest came to town to rain on my parade. Go figure.

"Well mates, this should be interesting. I'll apologize beforehand, for anything my physical mother may say and please let me handle her," I asked my men, who had drawn closer to me, some caressing my back in comforting movements, others gently squeezing a shoulder or an arm. Whatever they could touch, because they knew I was close to letting loose my rage already and she hadn't even spoken yet.

I made sure she heard me, in the hopes she would contradict my words, by actually behaving herself; at least in front of them. It was already embarrassing to acknowledge we were even kin. Physically speaking, that is. Thank the Goddess, she wasn't my spiritual mother.

60

That would have really screwed with my head. My Spiritual Mother was also my Goddess and She had made it very clear She did actually care for my well-being. Thinking of the last time She had healed me when I was still fully human and had gotten badly hurt, made the rising tide of rage pull back into the space inside my soul where I had buried it. I grabbed onto those thoughts of my Spiritual Mother and cloaked myself mentally with them and moved down the stairs towards Mommy Dearest. She stood there looking like your typical successful business woman, though she looked about forty pounds heavier than me. We both shared many of the same facial features. Her hair had been dyed a nice auburn color to hide her gray, since she was over sixty years old now. Her blue eyes have never changed from that cold glare, as she looked at me.

A look of pure disgust shown from her eyes, as she witnessed my mates trying to physically comfort me. "Well, Catrina Lynn Garcia, I can see my suspicions of you living in sin were accurate. How dare you live like this, with your children under the same roof. What kind of mother are you?"

"Hello, Mommy Dearest and Robert. Nice of you to stop by." I completely ignored her vitriol, although my Kla' din mates had gasped at her rudeness and disrespect for me. My Earth-side mates were glaring right back at her, but so far, holding their tongues for my sake. "I'm afraid you came at a bad time, since we were just leaving." I had reached the bottom step and turned to my boys. "Why don't both of you go wait in the car. We will be leaving shortly." My mother's eyes grew wide with shock that I wasn't going to play her verbal game.

Her eyes started to narrow, then fill with fake concern. I knew it was fake, because I knew her. She wasn't getting the reaction she wanted so now she would play another card. Plus, she would want Robert to see her as the concerned mother, not the brow beating bitch she almost let out in front of him in all its splendor. I watched my boys scoot out the door and wished I could go with them just as quickly.

"Catrina, don't you see where this is going, honey?" her voice now gentled with care. "You are going to go to hell and you are dragging your boys down with you. When I go to heaven I want to see you there, honey. It breaks my heart knowing you won't be there in heaven with me."

I snorted, "We haven't been able to live in the same house since I was twelve. What makes you think heaven would be any better? Any heaven with you in it, would be hell for me, so if that's where you're going, then count me out. Between you and me though, we both know that isn't where you'll wind up." I almost smiled at the thought, but then remorse actually flooded into me. I wouldn't wish the lower astral planes on anyone, not even her. I felt like a chump.

"Catrina honey, you have to leave this house and move out, before it's too late. This is Satan's playground here, we both know that."

"Oh, look Demitri, instead of channeling Joan Crawford, she's now channeling Margret White," I said flippantly.

"Margret White?" he asked.

"Yeah, the mother of Carrie. Mrs. White." I saw that he understood the reference and he cracked a half grin in amusement. I turned back to my mother. "Have you been watching Carrie too often or reading Stephen King books again, Mommy Dearest?"

"Don't you get smart with me." She took a deep breath and reeled her anger back in. "My only concern is for you and my grandsons. You can't live here anymore with this trash. They'll only drag you and my grandsons to hell with them."

My anger slipped its leash. "Don't you dare call them trash. They have more honor, more decency then you'll ever have. They have more love and care for me then you ever did," I hissed at her.

"That's a lie, Catrina. I would die for you. I would lay down my life for you. That's why I am here now; to save your soul." She had just scored points with her husband, which was ultimately her goal. She was desperate to hold onto him, wrapping her life around his, since he was half her age. She would do anything, say anything, including selling me to him, if she could get away with it, if it kept him close to her. She had done it before with her ex-husbands. What she didn't understand was that she could do anything she wanted, so long as she left all her money to him when she died. He'd married her for her money, so he wouldn't have to work. He was a do-nothing, talentless, hypochondriac. He was my age, though, I looked a heck of a lot better than he did. And that was before The Triple Goddess turned me into a vampire. There was no way he would leave his meal ticket at this stage of his life. He wasn't even cute, with that scruff on his fat, round face and gut hanging over his very expensive designer jeans that I am sure my mother had bought him. Either she didn't understand the game Robert was playing, or she was just delighting in her new mental whip she'd found since she married him. How can anyone say she wasn't being the loving mother when all she wanted to do was to save my soul? Meanwhile, she would use this whip to try to make me feel like shit and hopefully pry me away from men who actually gave a damn about me. THAT, she couldn't handle. How dare anyone find me attractive and actually have a care for me. No, she wanted me to marry someone who would fool around on me and beat me. That would make her joyful. She'd loved my ex-husband and thought he'd walked on water. She got pissed when I left him and moved on, the first time he pulled his shit. A man only got one chance with me. The first time he hit me or fooled around, I was gone by dawn; and never went back for seconds, no matter what the prick promised. It was a habit that drove my mother nuts. I wouldn't stay around for more abuse from any of my exes, often kicking their asses, as I walked out of the door.

"This relationship you're in now is evil. The things you practice are evil. Satan wears many guises just to trick you. Anything to get your soul. You have to leave this place and these evil men; I mean it." She looked like she was about at the end of her rope. She knew she had no hold on me. Never had. Especially now, that I could so obviously afford anything I or my boys needed or wanted. No more would I have to call and beg for fifty bucks just to feed my kids and me for a week when things got bad. She thought her money would be a hold on me, but she was so wrong. Even without my mates, Craven was only two years away from turning eighteen. Once that happened, I would have had no problem telling her to take her money and stick it up her ass. For my kids, I would beg, if they needed something. But, for myself? Screw that, I can take care of myself and often did, before I had kids. Though, I knew she smiled her happy, quiet smile, imagining me struggling on the mean streets when I was on my own.

"Mom, if you make one more insult to my mates, I will show you just how strong my refrigerator is. Feel me?" I stepped closer to her, invading her personal space. "You are in their house and while you and this man you married to are here, you will have respect for them. If you can't recall your manners then there's the door and don't let it hit you in the ass on the way out."

"Respect for men who show you the way to hell? First, Dar ruined you and now these men are finishing the job..." I cut off her tirade.

"That's it.... Move.... Now... Out." I grabbed her arm and moved her towards the door, hissing in her ear on the way, "Dar didn't ruin me and you know it. You know I have been a witch all of my life. If you recall correctly, I tried showing you the witch's alphabet when I was fifteen. That was fifteen years before I met Dar. But no, you have a convenient way of remembering things the way you want." I opened the

63

door, pushing her outside and glared at Robert, silently telling him to follow her quickly, or else. "If neither one of you have nothing nice to say to me, my mates or my kids, then don't bother coming for anymore visits. I'll email you for Christmas this year." I slammed the door in their faces and turned to see my mates looking at me with pity. That pissed me off. I was embarrassed over the whole ordeal and that pissed me off. That she would dare visit me now, in Corpus Christi, when she had lived only ten hours away from me in Arizona for years and never bothered once to see me or her grandsons in all that time pissed me off. I picked up the table by the door (usually used for sitting down mail or purses) and threw it across the room. Out of the corner of my eye, I saw Demitri hold back Ja' Monel and Ja' Kelo from coming near me.

"Don't. The things can be replaced, we don't care. Let her blow this off in her own way."

"Isn't there anything we can do to calm her?" Ja' Kelo asked Demitri.

"No. Her anger has gone beyond reasoning. Just help us keep her from hurting anyone human. Otherwise, she can break every fucking thing in this house if it helps." Ja' Kelo nodded to Demitri and they fanned out to keep anyone living out of my range. We had household staff that might come to investigate the smashing sounds in the mansion.

I didn't care what they did, so long as they stayed out of my way. I grabbed an antique chair and threw it against the wall, breaking the mirror that was hanging on it. Glass shattered and sprinkled the floor in a silvery dust. I picked up the coat rack, shaking the jackets off of it and banged it against the door frame, turning the rack into kindling and putting dents into the wood work. I broke and threw things in a rage until I picked up a Japanese ceramic vase from the Sueki Period, roughly from the 7th century A.D. Demitri had gotten this the last time we were in Japan to celebrate our bondings. He had been teaching me antiques and the personal history behind each item he showed me. He loved sharing the history of an object with me and we could talk for hours about Egyptian and Japanese excavations. Archeology was a hobby of his; one I enjoyed learning with him.

I held it in my hand, looking at the colors of the vase and recalling the ancient history of it. Once broken, it could never be replaced. My power flared with a vision of a middle-aged man sitting in front of his hut with a small spinning wheel. He had a lump of clay that he was tenderly shaping, gently applying more force to make it more elongated. He looked much smaller then Japanese men looked in present-day Japan, but so much strength exuded from this small man. His muscles were

64

corded in his arms and parts of his chest that I could see in my vision. The forest setting around him seemed lush and a deeper green then what it was today. I didn't know if it was my imagination or an actual detail of the vision on the vegetation of his area. I knew the vision was a true one, but the details could easily be exaggerated in my mind.

He had a calm smile on his face; his thoughts happy as he spun his clay in his moistened hands. Hands that were rough and heavily callused from many long days in the field, then hours spent on his craft of making vases, pots, and bowls. At that exact moment, he had been thinking of his two sons and how happy he was his most recent addition to the family was female. His boys already strong and helping in the field, his new daughter would be a help to her mother when she was old enough. He could smell the meal his wife was preparing for the family and he knew his newborn daughter wouldn't be far from her sweet gentle mother. He had been worried over this last pregnancy and was happy she actually survived as many of his friends wives did not. Women dying in child birth were a common occurrence in his day and losing his loving wife would have been an ordeal he never wanted to fear again. He would be more careful now not to quicken her again, he was thinking. They had enough children and they were healthy. They would most likely survive to adulthood and that was good enough for him. He wanted to spend the rest of their time together and hopefully live long enough to see grandchildren. He considered himself a rich man in spirit, having such a solid family. His wife was ever a source of peace and contentment for him; his children respectful and hard working already for all their young age. He felt blessed and at peace with his world and those feelings flowed from his callused hands into the clay molding he was shaping, although he didn't consciously know he was doing it. I could feel this man from so long ago had such a bright, good soul. If I broke this vase, that link to that man and his life, his family, would be gone forever.

I took a deep shaky breath and slowly moved towards Demitri. I gently placed the vase in his hands. "Put this in a safe place. It deserves to be to be protected." I moved away from it, afraid my anger would shatter it even from a distance. The beautiful feelings that went into making that vase are probably what had made it last all this time. Those who had owned it before us, may not have had the power I did, but they most likely subconsciously picked up the peaceful, gentle feelings that were imbued into the vase from the time of its creation. It was likely what had drawn Demitri into buying it and bringing it home, though, he too, had the same abilities as I. He just controlled his powers much better than me.

I sat on the steps of the staircase and breathed in and out, trying to bury my anger again.

"Meshama?" Ja' Kelo moved slowly towards me, as I closed my eyes.

"Don't...not yet," Demitri warned him. He had seen me fly off the handle before. He knew I didn't have my control back in hand yet.

Ja' Monel looked to Demitri, "That was her physical mother?"

"Yeah, that's her mom here on Earth." His voice was sounding tired already. He always does when he is in a situation he can't do anything about it. He would love to tell my mom off. For years, he has been aching to call her to the carpet for the many things she had failed me on, but didn't, because I asked him not to. First off, she was my cross to bear. Secondly, for most of those years, he couldn't do anything, even if I had let him because we only had astral contact and not physical. The only way he could have done anything before would have been to use magick against her and that would have only added negative karma to his record. We were so careful not to do anything that would jeopardize our finding one another physically; we didn't dare do even a karma spell on her. No, what did I do instead for her? She'd asked me to get rid of a negative psychic vampire at work and I did. I did spells to make sure she kept her cushy job and found her a husband that would make her happy. And this is the thanks I get? No good deed goes unpunished, I supposed.

"Why does she treat her that way?" Ja' Kelo looked confused. In his world, a daughter was treasured and valued; kept from the smallest harm. Every single male in the family would gladly spill his blood in defense of a female child. Never would a Kla' din parent treat a female child this way.

"She hates Catrina," he simply stated. Shock grew on the faces of my Kla' din mates. They couldn't grasp the idea of a parent actually hating their child, male or female.

"Why? She has been blessed with an Ama child. Blessed with a female. How can she hate her own child?" Ja' Callum voice was rising with anger of his own. Anger I still felt beating though my veins.

"She doesn't understand that Catrina is the spiritual Daughter of The Triple Goddess and Her Consort. Even if she did, she would most likely put Catrina on a stake herself and burn her to death." Shocked gasps went through the room.

Finding my own voice, I said, "She had me to try to trap my physical father into marriage. Once that didn't work, I was nothing more than a burden to her. Something that dragged her down. She never really cared about me one way or another. She doesn't know how." They looked at me with pity showing clearly in their eyes and that made me angry all over again. "She, herself had been broken inside, long before I was born. We really can't blame her now, except, maybe she should have given me up for adoption when getting my father to the altar didn't work. That would have been the only other thing she could have done differently. But, I still think my life as a child would have been hell, in one form or another." I stood up and walked towards the door. "You can't have a strong sword without the fire to burn out the impurities," my tone of voice dripped with sarcasm. "We mustn't forget that."

Ja' Kelo pleaded, "Meshama, please tell me what to do and it will be done." He had dropped to one knee in front of me.

Ja' Monel followed suit. "Meshallima anyone, anything, I will kill for you and bring back its bleeding heart, if it would bring back your smile to us."

Demitri came up behind him and put his hand on Ja' Monel's shoulder. "Don't bother. Catrina cannot kill her physical mother, no matter the provocation. It would kill a part of her to do it or have it done. Damn it. I would have done it myself years ago if I thought it would make her world safer in the long run and fuck the negative comeback for it." He turned his eyes to me. "But sweetheart, don't let that bitch take away your happiness. Don't let her keep winning against you in your mind or your soul. You've been so happy lately. I have never felt such freedom in your spirit before and it would kill me if you lost it now." Tears were starting to make tracks down his cheeks and I pushed away from the stairs to go hold him.

I could hear his heart beating underneath my ear and I cuddled against him letting the rage pass away from me. "I won't. I'm sorry. I didn't mean to lose control so badly like this."

Demitri pulled back to look at me. "You have nothing to be sorry for. I wouldn't care of you brought the house down. Just don't let her bring you down, as well, is all I ask."

I reached up to wipe the tears from his face. "I won't. Not this time, ok?"

Demitri leaned down; his lips met mine, warm and gentle. I felt the others gather around us like a shield. They offered their strength, their protection and most of all, their love and there was no way I would let my mother destroy that.

Chapter Seven

Double attack

General Robertson snarled into the phone from his hotel in Corpus Christi. "I need more information than this. She isn't at the bar. She never is, no matter how many times I go in there. There was no one but military men. Where does she live? Where does she work? These are the things that will get her back into my hands. I'm running out of time."

"Sir, he is still cagy. I can't even put a watcher on him. He is so careful about going home, constantly scanning around him before he moves to another block. I can't even ask directly," his operative tried to inform the General. "The one time I did, he left immediately and didn't come over again for a week. I can't take a chance of him dumping me by pissing him off like that."

"Then, I say you aren't doing your job very well. Maybe I need to come and remind you of your own obligations?" The menace was thick in the air.

The General could hear the fear entering her voice. "No Sir, that won't be necessary. I will find something for you. I promise. Please, just give me another chance."

"It's been over a month. You have until tomorrow night. I'm on a deadline myself. So, get me something, anything and make it good." He hung up the phone, not wanting to hear any more excuses from his spy. He had until the next full moon or he would have to give Prince Barreiro free reign to find her himself and he would lose his prime bargaining chip for his own agenda. Although having his young niece in his control might make up for it.

General Robertson sat at the table in his room and closed his eyes. His attaché watched him warily, since he was still getting used to the General's moods. His previous attaché had had been one of the men killed in his home when the target had gotten away from his grasp. That little bitch was proving to be very troublesome.

He opened his eyes. "Major," he barked.

"Yes, Sir?"

"Give me that file on the Special Forces team again."

He was quickly handed the file that he'd gone over, it seemed like a million times, these past months, trying to find a weakness in getting what he wanted. Though true, what he wanted had changed from straight out killing the competition to trapping one of their most valuable tools again. And this time, keeping her until he had everything he wanted. He never did anything without making sure his plan was foolproof. Yet, the plan to kill both the Special Forces team and General Pierce in one straight shot had seemed perfect until they had surprised him. Now, he was forced to move carefully; much more carefully than before, since it seemed they had more tricks up their sleeves then he had previously known about. They had to have a full Coven, as well. It would be the only way General Pierce would have survived the attack he'd sent with his hell hounds. He knew for a fact, that Catrina was in Saudi Arabia at the time, so someone else had to have protected General Pierce from the assault here stateside. General Pierce himself was not a practitioner. He knew that from feeling his power levels when Robertson grasped his hand in greeting at the meeting in Pierce's office. Pierce was a mundane at best and not trained in the arts. Yet, his office was heavily shielded from any magickal attacks or spying. Pierce's military records show he came from White Head, Montana. An only child from a well-to-do sheep rancher, he'd joined the army at eighteen and had quickly risen in rank, fitting into the military life as one born to it. His grandfather was an army hero, also a General in his time, which had probably helped his career along so quickly. Pierce had never married nor had any illegitimate children, making the military his whole life; and Pierce served the military well-decorated with a silver star and three purple hearts before he was thirty. No connection with any covens and none of his family was even rumored to have been practitioners themselves. There was one curious blank spot in his military record which spanned over a year and a half of his life when General Pierce was still a Major.

Yet, there is no record of what he had been doing or where he was even stationed at; just a blank dot on his otherwise clean and spotless military record. None of Robertson's contacts could fill in this blank spot. That infuriated him.

He turned his attention to Captain O'Hara's records, showing him to be born in Tulsa, Oklahoma, the eldest son of six children. Joined the army to help out the family finances and still sent money home to his parents though the children had grown and moved from home themselves now. He'd wound up at the same base that General Pierce was overseeing, though not with as many stars on his shoulders and it seemed for some reason General Pierce had taken the then young O'Hara under his wing, guiding him to join Special Forces when he was an E-5. The most interesting thing was, O'Hara had the same blank spot at the same time as Pierce's. Again, Robertson had been denied access to finding out what these two had been up to within that time frame. He seriously doubted O'Hara had any power beyond that of a mundane. The other men of his unit were odd, though. Most Special Forces teams went with eight to nine men to each unit and O'Hara's had run with just himself and two others until Sergeant Logan, call sign Wizard, joined to become a permanent member nine months ago, serving as their Tech and Comm specialist.

Logan came from California as the son of a movie producer and a mother who was a washed up has-been of an actress that never made it really big. Highly unusual for a Special Forces team to run with so few men in a unit, but O'Hara had gotten away with it for a very long time. His reputation for getting the job done when he made Operational Commander and General Pierce's influence, had given O'Hara room to run his team as he saw fit.

Major Jonathon Harris, their demo and tactical specialist, had been on the team the longest of any of the men. His past was more colorful, with his father having died in prison doing time for assault and battery. His mother died two years later from liver failure due to being an alcoholic. The Major's sister died from a drug over dose a year after their mother passed away and Jonathon Harris, with a juvenile record still managed to get into the Navy and made it through to become a Navy Seal. His military record was dotted evenly with commendations and citations for misbehavior, until he was requested by O'Hara himself to join his Special Forces team. Apparently, on a mission in the UK, their teams had been unified for a particular mission and things went well enough that O'Hara wanted Harris on his team.

71

Clarissa Lee Moon

Sergeant Watson's, transportation and heavy weapons specialist, record showed no irregularity, until one bar fight that O'Hara had been in with Harris on leave that had gotten out of control. O'Hara tagged Watson for his team, pulling him from Watson's Ranger unit. According to the file, Watson was in a fight due to some young girl that was with another man who took exception to Watson trying to pick her up. The man had friends in the bar and when they joined the fight, O'Hara and Harris had pitched in to help Watson out. Pierce had gotten them all released from the stockade the next day. Born on a farm in Mesa, Texas, again, there is no indication that Watson or any of the other men could have had training in the arts, either from their parents or an organization within the military itself. The only time it seems that Pierce or O'Hara's Special Forces team had any connections to anything paranormal was during the attempted hi-jacking in New York a few months back, bringing Robertson back to the girl again. Yet, there has to be more than just this girl, her mates and her three children. Neither his spy or any connections or favors could get him any more information regarding General Pierce's activities and who else he might be involved with that could explain how easily and lightly the base had gotten off from the attack he'd planned against Pierce. Only one death was reported, and that meant Pierce had had a lot of help that day. The girl and two other unknowns were in Saudi Arabia that night, so there had to be more. Not knowing how many and what they were, meant he couldn't move against Pierce as quickly as he would have liked. Yes, he would have to tread very carefully this time, but Catrina would be in his grasp yet again one way or another. And then, he would use her to gain access to destroying anything she was connected to.

72

Chapter Eight

Initiative

Ever since he had walked through that door tonight, something had felt off. Crimson sat on the couch, waiting for her to make the tea she had promised, thinking of what could be wrong. She'd greeted him as she always had, but she seemed more distant tonight than ever before. Vanessa had been after him for some time about meeting his mother; maybe he ought to give some serious thought about it if he wanted to keep seeing her.

She came out of the kitchen carrying a tray with two steaming cups of tea and a honey jar. She set the tray on the table in front of him and silently served him. She didn't look up at him, nor did she smile as she usually did. This was starting to really concern Crimson.

"What's up, babe?" he asked her.

"Nothing. Here, drink your tea." She had poured a generous amount of honey in his but didn't add any to hers.

She sat down next to him as he drank his tea. It was sweeter than he usually liked it, but drank it to make her happy.

She rested her head on his arm and asked quietly, "Did you miss me?"

"Of course I did." He wrapped his arm around her and pulled her close.

She sighed, relaxing against his body. "Caro, this is hard for me and I don't want to anger you, but I need to know where I stand with you."

Crimson narrowed his eyes at her. "What do you mean, Vanessa?"

"Are you just playing with me or are we going to take this to the next level in our relationship?"

Crimson sighed heavily and rested his head against the sofa they were sitting on together. "I really don't need this right now, Vanessa."

She pulled away and looked at him, "I'm sorry, Caro, but I can't keep going on like this. I need to know."

"I just got back from a bad..." He stopped, before he could finish the sentence. This was NOT to be repeated anywhere outside of the family. He knew this, yet he'd almost spilled out how sore and tired he was from this mission. Nobody was supposed to know he had even been on a mission. He must be more tired than he'd thought.

"A bad what, Caro? You can tell me. I love you and want to be the one you can talk to. The one you can trust above all others. Please, let me in, my love." She started to move her hand up and down his chest in comfort. Unfortunately, she rubbed against a bad bruise and Crimson hissed in pain. He should have let his mother heal him before he slipped out the backdoor to The Nightwolves Lair but he had been in a hurry to get here to Vanessa so he could really relax. This was not what he had in mind.

"What's wrong, Caro? Let me see." She reached up to unbutton his shirt and he grabbed her hands, pulling them away from his body.

"Don't, Vanessa."

"Why?" She stood up, her face furious. "Something is wrong and you won't let me see to help."

"It's nothing. Just a bruise from getting hit with the pommel of a..." Damn it, what was wrong with him tonight? He shook his head to clear it.

"A pommel? Like from a sword? Have you been fighting, Caro?" Her voice had gone back to being sweet and seductive. A strong change from the strident tone she'd had but moments before. Crimson was feeling that something was really off, but he couldn't think of what it was exactly. His tongue felt thick, swollen and coated with cotton. This wasn't right. He looked around the room and saw things through a fuzzy blur. He shook his head again. He must be really fucking tired.

"Caro, tell me why you come to me with bruises and cuts sometimes? Where do you go? Is something or someone hurting you?" She knelt by his feet and slowly moved up his body.

"No, nothing. It's nothing."

"How about your mother, does she know? Where is she now?"

"Nightwolves Lair. She is trying to drink too much tonight." Why did he say that? Oh yeah, the bitch that was his Grandmother had come by tonight and upset mom. She really needed her ass kicked, he thought to himself.

"Really, Caro? Why don't we go there now and meet your mother? She would want to meet me by now, don't you think?"

Warning bells were now going off in his mind. "No. Not there, Vanessa. We can't. The rules. The Laws. Can't be broken."

"What, so I will never get to meet your mother? Have you been toying with me, then? Your personal booty call, when you feel the need? I am not a whore, Crimson," her tone had risen again, into that strident tone that was irritating him.

"I have to go now. I need to get home."

He moved her away from him and went to stand up and that's when the whole room slid off to the side and he swayed with dizziness.

"I think not this time, Crimson. This time, you will tell me everything I want to know. I'm tired of playing your whore. Tired of playing the slut for you."

"Not a slut. Not.."

A fist came out of nowhere and slammed into his head. He fell to the floor with the blackness threatening to edge out what was left of his vision.

He heard Vanessa walk over to her phone and opened up the cell to dial out. He groaned and tried to move off the floor, but he felt so heavy. So tired.

"General, she is at the Nightwolves Lair right now. No, he isn't fully cooperative yet, but he will be by the time I have him tied to a chair. Yes Sir. I will be." She clicked the phone shut. Why would she be calling General Pierce?

"Let's get going, Crimson dear. Time for you to learn some new things tonight," she chuckled, "Though, I don't think you'll find these lessons will be as pleasant as tutoring you in the fine art of love was." She walked over to grab him. "No, this I am afraid will be very, very painful and no love for it in the end."

She leaned down to his face and what he saw wasn't the same sweet face she usually wore for him. It was evil and gloating with a sick, deathly smile. "You might even find out how it feels to be shredded with the same whip my General used on your mother."

Everything clicked at once in his brain. He shot his fist up and into the side of her head and she fell back and away from him. He rolled up to stand, trying to keep his feet steady. He had to get to his mother. Had to warn her. He never wanted to see her beaten like that again.

Vanessa had jumped to her own feet and swung out with a kick to his stomach, but he pulled his body inward to absorb the blow like his mother taught him, so he wouldn't lose his breath. He could hear his mother's voice in his head, '*A fighter can't fight if he can't breathe. Roll with the punches and kicks; don't lose your breath, son.*'

Telepathy? No, just the training. Over and over again his mother trained him harder than the rest and now he knew why. For this, as he grabbed Vanessa's follow-up round house kick and pulled her backwards so she lost her balance.

'*A fighter must stay in control at all times. Nothing can impair your motions. Your fluidity. Emotions will defeat you in a fight. Stay focused. Stay calm.*'

OK mom, but what about drugs? What do you do when you're fucked up?

'*Control.*'

He took a deep breath and steadied himself through sheer will power. Control-I have to control this.

As Vanessa struggled to stand up he backhanded her, making her roll across the floor.

She reached the wall and grabbed something he couldn't see clearly. A wooden cane snapped against his jaw spinning him around. He went with the spin and nearly lost his balance when Vanessa grabbed him from behind. He reached over his shoulder and grabbed her shirt and threw her down in front him on the floor in front of the fireplace. She tried to stand up and he kicked hard enough to put her out.

"Stay down, bitch." He wiped the blood from his mouth and spat out what was in his mouth, lurching towards the doorway to make his escape, before Vanessa regained consciousness, but his steps felt so heavy.

As he opened the door, he heard scrambling sounds and Vanessa groaning behind him.

"Crimson," she growled. He turned around to defend himself again and got a face full of powder, as the bag she threw at him broke open upon impact.

"I curse you, Crimson. By the power of three, I curse you. The first animal you see, that is the animal you'll be ...unto the end of time.

Let the Dark Goddess hear me and grant my desire. I call upon The Goddess of Transition, The Goddess of Change to make this man,

Crimson, walk as the animal he should be, so shall it be." Her eyes were afire with her power as she threw the spell on him. He felt it settle around his aura and he immediately closed his eyes.

She laughed and said, "You'll never make it home now, Caro, without opening your eyes. Like the tom cat you acted like, I know you'll see an alley cat and be turned, forever, into a sweet, fluffy little kitty any dog can chew on." She was manic with her glee over his predicament. She knew this part of town was saturated with cats; either strays or home kept cats let out for the night. Being a small cat really didn't appeal to him, but neither did turning into any kind of animal. The curse she laid would keep him in that form and no other. How could he keep his place with the Nightwolves now? But worse, how could he warn his mother before General Robertson showed up at the club and took her?

He growled, "Don't come near me or I will kill you, you sick bitch." And he walked out the door and felt his way down the steps to the sidewalk in front of her house.

"Go home, Crimson and show your mother my power. Your mother won't be able to help you either, not with the ancientness of this curse laid upon you. Go home, boy and see the truth of my words." He could hear the sneer in her tone.

Getting his bearings, he moved towards what he thought would be the next street corner where he would turn left and head on through the middle of the town to the other side where he lived. He needed to get to a phone; something, anything, before General Robertson showed up and grabbed his mother.

Walking slowly, he could still hear everything around him. Thankfully, with the training his mother had given him, part of it was learning to fight blindfolded. So, walking down the street was hard and he tripped a lot, but he didn't fear going through town with closed eyes. If he could only get home, he knew someone would be able to help or at least keep him safe from seeing any animals since they didn't own any pets themselves. With them gone so often, mom didn't think it would be fair to have a pet and not to be there for them, so she nixed any ideas of a house pet. He was thankful for that now, even though at the time, he thought it was highly unfair and bitched about it often.

Behind him, however, he could hear a familiar footstep. He kept walking cautiously and measuring the footsteps behind him. He had always been careful going home; making sure he was never followed, either physically or psychically.

As he turned another corner, he still felt her behind him. Damn it, he can't let her follow him home. What would be the point of keeping his mother or the rest of the Nightwolves safe, if this bitch just followed him back to his home or heard the phone call, assuming he could find a phone booth? Wait, how could he be so stupid? He had his own cell phone to check in with the base when his pager went off and it should still be in his pocket. He felt inside and took out his cell, only to find it hadn't survived the kicks Vanessa had given him. It was useless in broken pieces. Frustrated, he threw it away from him and could swear he felt Vanessa smile behind him somewhere. She was being prudent staying far behind but he knew she was there. Most likely, she was waiting for him to screw up and see a cat or something and then grab him. His mother had always taught him that if someone had him or his brothers in their control, she would be screwed. Powerless. They, him and his brothers, were her only weakness, the only tool someone could use against her. He'd be damned if he put his mother in that situation. He had to think, but it was hard with this shit running through his system, making his brain work so slowly most of the time. He had to remain in control. Had to stay focused and think, damn it. Vanessa wasn't looking forward to another fight, which is why she was taking the easy way now. She was just waiting for the time the spell would work. He could use that. There was an alley coming up that had a huge trash bin he could hide behind and ambush her. Nausea roiled through his stomach, thinking of what he had to do after that. Fighting her was hard enough. He hated men who hit women, but his mother taught him that if a woman hits you first, she has declared herself a fighter and to treat her as such. The rule of no hitting women wasn't valid at that point. But, the thought of killing Vanessa made him sick. She was his first. He thought she loved him. How could he end her life after all the nights they have spent together making love? He could have killed her back at the house, but he just couldn't pull a blade on her. All he could think of was this was the woman who was his first lover...his first love.

He couldn't let her use him against his mother, though. He couldn't let her hurt his family or The Nightwolves, which was the same thing these days.

His face grew grim with determination as he found the corner by feel for the alleyway he wanted and took a chance to run to the trash bin that was always there, hoping he didn't trip on anything in the process. He reached out with his hand to feel for the steel bin. He found it and used the edges to find the farthest side and hid to wait for her to follow him into the alley.

He took a deep breath and steeled himself for the next act. He faked the sounds as best as he could.

"Meow. Meooroow."

Laughter rolled down the alley towards him.

"I knew you wouldn't make it, Caro. I do hope you're not a black cat. I like black cats." Giggling, she rushed towards the garbage bin and he struck out with his hand, feeling for her neck. She gasped in surprise, as he cut her throat with his blade.

He felt warm wetness stream down his hand through his fingers and knew he'd hit his mark.

He let her fall to the ground and leaned against the alley wall.

"Caro, how could you?" she gurgled and then he heard her last breath leave her body.

His head bowed back and he screamed with rage, howling into the night with pictures of her loving him racing through his mind. The tears wouldn't come. They couldn't. He did this to his lover. He was a monster. Why couldn't he think of anything else to do? Someway to subdue her?

Pain lashed and tore through him, making him heave with sickness.

'Crimson. What's wrong?' His mother's voice rang loudly through his head; louder and clearer then when he was remembering her instructions. He never liked using his powers and had refused to be trained but in the most basic forms of magick. The prescient dreams he'd had scared him so badly he never wanted more power, afraid it would make the visions worse, but he needed it now. "Mom. Get out of there. General Robertson is on the way. Meet me at home. Run. NOW, MOM."

'Are you ok? Do you need help?'

"No. I will be fine, just get out of there. Get out of there. Get out of there." He kept that phrase going, not knowing if it was because he wanted his mother out of his head so she wouldn't see what he had done or out of there so she would be safe from the General. He moved away from the wall and pulled the now dead body closer to it, tucking her behind the trash bin to give him time to think of how he was going to clean this up. He couldn't think straight now, though it wasn't as bad as it was before, but he was getting sleepier. Maybe, by the time he got home, he would be able to think of a way to get rid of the body the proper way for a black witch. He couldn't believe Vanessa was a black witch, and worse-working for the same S.O.B. that had tortured his mother. How could he have been so stupid? It had to have been a set-up from the beginning. She was always asking to meet his mother. That had likely been the goal to recapture her, and he'd almost led The Dark Coven, not only to his mother, but right to his whole family. The Black Coven wouldn't have stopped with just his mother this time. He stumbled down the alleyway, feeling sick and betrayed. How could someone sleep with a person and be so callus, so cruelly calculating? So cold as to have it mean nothing but their own personal, evil issues?

His hand fisted to his stomach as he almost blew up when he felt someone touch his shoulder. "Hey man, are you all right? Do you need help? Whoa, you're bleeding."

He didn't feel anything wrong with this person, although for all he knew, Vanessa could have had someone else on the sidelines to help her trap and curse him. He really needed a clear way home, though.

"I cut my hand trying to feel my way along. I lost my cane."

"Oh ok, I see now. I mean…err…"

Crimson gave a small grin. This guy was ok. If he played this right, he could get a ride and he needed one soon, because he was about to fall asleep on his feet.

"I can't see and I need to get home."

"Yeah, you do look hurt there. Are you sure you don't need me to call you some help, like the cops or an ambulance?"

"No, no please. I just need to get home. I'll be taken care of once I get there."

"Where do you live?"

"On Lighthouse Drive."

The guy whistled through his teeth. "Nice. So, off we go. My car is right over here."

Crimson again, grinned ruefully. He hated lying to this good Samaritan, but the faster he got home, the quicker he would find out if mom was all right. Then, she would fix whatever it was Vanessa had done. At least, he hoped she could. If she couldn't, then no one could. And going around with his eyes closed for the rest of his life didn't seem too realistic. Sooner or later, he would fuck up. With his luck, he would wind up turning into some canary or sparrow, or something. That would bite; or would that be pecked? He shuddered in his seat.

The good Samaritan led him up to his door and it took some doing to get him to leave him there. He didn't think it would be a good idea for this guy to be a witness to what he knew would be at the very least, an ass reaming in the extreme. Damn, his mother was going to kill him. He opened the door and his eyes, since he knew it was safe now. He saw Andre walking towards him with concern growing on his face, as he took in his appearance with blood all over his hands and shirt. He'd spent most of the ride convincing the good Samaritan that it looked worse than it was, and no, he hadn't been mugged or beaten up by street hoods. It had been an aggravating ride in many ways.

"Crimson, how bad are the wounds?" Andre's hands were already glowing with power, to help speed up the healing process. He was almost as bad as mom was in not letting him or his brothers suffer any wound for very long.

"Don't worry, most of this isn't mine. So, is mom safe… is she here?"

"Yes son, she is in the living room. She isn't happy," Andre warned him. He could imagine how pissed she was. Sneaking out without guards for one, and once she sees his condition, she'll fly off the handle for sure. He dreaded having to tell her about Vanessa, but they had to move fast to clean up the mess, before someone called the cops about a dead body in an alleyway.

Andre went to move his hand away from his stomach, thinking that's where the wound was, and he looked down to stop Andre and saw Andre's tattoo on his forearm. A tattoo of a black panther. Pain ripped through his entire being in one large, hot flash. It felt like heat-lightening was making its way through every cell of his body. Crimson screamed in pain and went to his knees, buckling under the strain, from the intense agony he was feeling.

He heard Andre yell, "CRIMSON. NO. Catrina, get in here now." But he was past the point of caring about anything now, except for wanting the pain to just stop and then, in a split second, everything went black.

Chapter Nine

Chasing Shadow

J was running towards the Foyer, when I heard my son screaming and Andre yelling. What I saw once I got there shocked me to a standstill. Andre was bending over this huge, black panther that was lying as still as death.

"What the fuck is that?"

"Your son, baby."

"You've got to be kidding me."

"I wish I were, but it really is Crimson."

"How…?"

Craven came bursting into the foyer next and stopped just as fast as I had, with most likely the same look of shock I had on my face.

"What's up, Mom? Andre?"

Andre stood up and turned to Craven. "Son, take a deep breath and remember what we have been training you to do with control."

"OK, I'm breathing, but where is Crimson? I heard him. I smell him, but I don't see him. Just a big, fucking cat on the floor. What's up with that?"

Andre pointed to the black panther lying in the middle of the floor. "That's Crimson."

Craven's mouth dropped open. "No way." He turned to look at me. "Mom?"

I walked over to where the panther was lying down and placed my hands on its body.

Breathing deeply, I let myself sink into its aura and saw what had happened, at least on a spiritual level. Animals have no soul; therefore they do not have many colored aura bands like a human will have. Most humans only have two aura band colors. Animals do, however, have a spirit, so they have one color to their aura. This panther had two aura bands, like Craven did, even in wolven form. That meant this creature had a soul and a spirit and therefore was human inside. This creature was not a pure animal. It had the two aura band colors that were Crimson's colors-being purple and green; but, surrounding the aura, was the most insidious black gunk I had ever seen. Worse than a possession or an astral parasitical entity. It flowed in and around the entire aura and even into the soul levels. This was not good. Craven's main two aura colors were purple and blue, but had a grayish, misty cast around his aura no matter what shape he wore. But, it was gray; there was no black. Having blackness to this degree, meant that this was a curse of the darkest form. I wouldn't be surprised to find out a person had been sacrificed in order to make this curse happen. A violent death had to serve a curse this black, this vicious.

I stood up and rubbed my hands off on my skirt. "It's Crimson, honey."

"No, Mom not...it can't be.." his voice grew rough and rumbled, letting us know he was about to lose control and shift.

"Not Crimson...noooo. It's my fault...mine.." which had turned into a howl of pure pain. We could hear how deeply Craven was feeling and he was losing his human shape, straight into the Dire Wolf form.

"Craven, calm down, calm down," both of us were cajoling him not to shift. Others who had made it to the front of the house were begging him to control his rage.

It was too late and nothing was going to stop him from shifting now.

"Craven, don't." It was too late. He stood there, towering above me, howling in rage. The sound reverberated throughout the house. I saw out of the corner of my eye, that a few siblings went to get the house staff out of the main house and into the smaller house out back, for the live-in staffers. I knew they would concoct some bullshit story to cover the 'weird' noises coming from the front of the house.

I stood in front of him, blocking his way to Crimson. Now that he had shifted, he was scenting the room and focused solely on the panther on the floor.

"Don't hurt him, Craven. That's your brother."

He moved a step closer to me, crowding me.

84

"Back off, Craven."

His lips pulled back in a snarl and moved closer, almost touching me now. I put a hand on his hairy chest and pushed him back.

"I said, back off-now."

'Won't hurt. Want to see. Smell.'

His telepathy had gotten better in this form, but his thought patterns went more animalistic. More in the now, with little ability to think beyond the moment. Wants. Fight. Food. These things were uppermost in the Dire Wolf or werewolf's mind. The ability to think logically or to reason any situation that didn't have hunting involved, went completely out the door.

The only thing that gave me alpha status with him, in either shape, was somewhere deep-down, he knew I was his mother and therefore someone to obey. Plus, the fact I had to bash his head into the concrete floor a few times when he'd shifted as a werewolf for the first time. I always kept the illusion going on that I was stronger than him. The truth was, in his Dire Wolf form, he could take me easily if he had a mind to. Nothing got in the way of a Dire Wolf in full rage.

"Ok, but take it easy and slow." I moved away and he crept forward and bent down to sniff the panther. His lips drew back again and he sneezed and coughed in wolf form.

Drawing back, he growled in my mind, *'Bad. Evil.'*

"What's around him is evil-not your brother. That's your brother in there."

'Hunt the one who did this. Smell blood scent of one who did this. Find. Kill.'

"No, Craven. Not yet. We have to wait for the hunt. We need more information before we hunt."

'Smell evil scent. Need nothing else.' He made to move through the door and I moved to stop him, as did Cassie. He seemed to hesitate with females more then he would a male, so my mates were letting us handle Craven's rage and kept silent, so as not to add to it.

"Craven, no hunting, yet. We will hunt, I promise you that; but not right now. Your brother needs us here to protect him. To heal him. He doesn't have time for us to hunt."

Cassie added her plea, "You want to hunt, right?"

'Yes.'

"Crimson needs to be there. He wants the hunt just as badly. So let us help your brother, so we can all hunt as a pack."

85

He moved back in compliance and settled near the wall, far enough away from his brother, but to where he could still see him. His wolf's head leaned back and he howled with pain, with his muzzle pointed up to the ceiling. The sound pierced through my ears that were already sensitive from being a vampire.

Cassie went to stand near Craven and slowly touched his clawed hand to offer comfort, unafraid of being hurt by him. I went to Crimson, to see about changing him back to his human form. Then, I too will be on the hunt for the one who did this and Goddess show them mercy, because I sure as shit wasn't going to.

Andre moved down next to me. "What do you think happened?"

"I don't know yet. This stuff is sticky. Like tar or sludge." I moved my hands up and down the cats' body, trying to find the root of the spell.

"I can't find a center for it. It's like it is everywhere, on all levels, at the same time. I have never seen anything so complex, besides the curse that had hit me way back when."

We looked at each other and Andre asked, "Do you think it is the same source as before?"

"No. This one is even more invasive and into the cellular level now. I can't find anything to grab onto and pull."

"Maybe, scooping it out?"

I shook my head. "No, we need to find the root. The source of the curse. Pulling it out in pieces won't work with this."

A knock sounded at the door.

"Fuck, I hope that isn't the cops."

Demitri went to answer the door and Andre and I tried to cover as much of the cats body as we could, to hide it from sight.

"Hey, what's up? Crimson make it home, yet?" Demitri opened the door wider to let Captain O'Hara and his team inside.

"Whoa." Sergeant Watson, otherwise known as Romeo, looked about the room. "So, what's with wild kingdom night?"

Craven snarled and inched towards him.

"Easy, Craven. He didn't mean anything by it." Captain O'Hara went to stand in front of Romeo, in case Craven went to take a swipe at him. "What happened, Cat?"

"We're trying to figure that out, Rock." I stood up and faced them. "What happened after we left?"

"Like you said, General Robertson came busting in...again. He checked every single persons ID there, then his cell phone went off. He took the call and went storming out of there, looking like he was going to explode." He shrugged, "So, we thought to check up on you here." He gave me a look that clearly said, 'your turn'.

"We came home, and fifteen minutes later, Crimson shows up at the door. Andre answered it." I turned to look at Andre for his side of things.

"He came in normal, but with his eyes closed, until he made it past the door frame. When I asked about the blood on his hands and the front of his shirt, he told me it wasn't his. I went to grab his hand to make sure he wasn't hiding a serious wound and that's when he started screaming and changed into that," pointing to the panther on the floor.

I grabbed his arm and took a close look at his tattoo. "Sure looks like your panther, babe."

He looked down then at the panther on the floor and swore. Rock, too, leaned in and took a close look.

"So, was he bitten?" Rock asked.

"No, he was cursed."

"Come again?"

"Cursed, hexed, bespelled. Take your pick."

"I thought, to turn into a Were, one had to be bitten or maybe even scratched badly enough?"

"Nope. There are many ways to become a Were. Though, being a Were is not so bad. Crimson's situation is worse."

"Why is that?"

"I'm willing to bet that he's been cursed into this form and won't change back."

Shocked gasps echoed around us.

"Why? Craven did, once he calmed down and got control."

"That's just it. Look at him. He is asleep. A shapeshifter of any flavor will revert to their normal, human shape when relaxed, by will or in sleep. He is asleep, but he hasn't shifted back, yet. Therefore, I am surmising he won't shift back at all. This is a pure black curse. Oxymoron as it sounds."

Romeo uttered the understatement of the year. "Shit."

"Yeah."

Andre came up behind me and hugged me close to him. "We'll find a way to help. I swear it."

"I know we will and the person who did this pays with interest. I won't settle for anything less."

The Rock cocked an eyebrow. "Do we know who did this?"

87

"I don't have a clue."

Craven growled and went to move towards the door again.

"No, Craven. Not yet. We aren't ready. We have no idea of what we will be walking into. We need to plan. Calm down," I urged him.

'Scent strong. Hunt. Kill.'

"He says he can follow the scent. That the blood on Crimson isn't his brother's, but someone evil and he wants to hunt it down and kill it."

"That sounds like a good idea, actually. There are enough of us here to start our own war on anyone if we wanted to. Why not let him track it down?" Romeo looked like he would enjoy a good smackdown right about now.

I snorted. "Oh yeah, great idea. Let's go for a walk through town with a Dire Wolf leading the way. No way would that cause a scene or expose us to the civilians in the area."

"She's right," Rock looked at me again, "but there has to be a way to trace it, isn't there?"

I thought about it and then an idea hit me. "Craven, can you shift into your wolven form?"

He swung his massive head at me and stared hard.

"Think of your wolven form. Picture it in your mind and shift to that form. That way, you can hunt, but not draw so much attention."

He snuffled though his nose and closed his solid blue eyes. In either form, he had no pupils to speak of; just a deep glowing blue eyes that shown with anger. It was eerily beautiful to see.

His breathing deepened and his body started to shake. He had never before attempted to shift into his other form. He'd switched from human to wolf or human to Dire Wolf, and vice versa. I didn't know if he could pull it off but if his desire was strong enough, I was hoping for a miracle.

"Cat, a werewolf would look as out of place as much as a Dire Wolf, don't you think?" Sergeant Logan aka Wizard looked confused.

"Actually, not really. I mean, sure a 250 lb wolf might be startling, but if we are walking beside it, like it's a normal everyday thing, people will most likely shrug it off as a really big wolf cross breed, like they have in Alaska. Just ask Gerard," I pointed to my youngest brother.

"She's right. They breed huge dogs for sled teams in the Alaskan Wilderness. If anyone asks, we can say he is an Alaskan Champion breed or some such nonsense. People have a strange way of taking the unusual and giving it plausible explanations."

I nodded my head in agreement. The last thing anyone would think, was that a real werewolf was being taken out for a walk by his owners.

We kept watch on Cravens progression. It looked like he might actually do it.

"Cassie, can you get some of our mates to move Crimson's panther form into the silver cage?"

Gerard stopped her. "Wait a moment." He bent down to touch Crimson's side and closed his eyes. I saw his breathing deepen, and after a bit, his eyes snapped open again. "Someone died for this curse." He turned to look at me. "I am sorry sister, but there won't be anything we can do, unless we find the person responsible for this and make them undo the spell. It is the only way."

I nodded at him, knowing he was right. He knew more about the dark arts then I did, but, I too, felt the death entangled into the spell. It still felt like my heart was breaking. If we couldn't find the black witch that did this, Crimson would never be human again.

Gerard stood up and nodded to Cassie.

As they moved Crimson down to the cell in the basement we'd had built for Cravens uncontrolled shifts, I looked over to Rock's Special Forces team.

"This isn't going to be a normal mission and if you want to stay out of this, we all understand, since this isn't a military problem."

He narrowed his eyes at me. "Crimson is one of ours. This is a military problem. Just tell us what to do."

"You understand that there could be some heavy, dark magick thrown at us. If you guys get caught in the middle of a Coven war, I can't guarantee that none of you will be hit like Crimson was, or worse."

His face hardened. "Crimson is one of ours, too. We'll go."

I loved that about this Special Force's team. Nothing would make them back down. I recalled the last time Rock had to ride one of my dragons. Well, maybe a dragon might stop them. Maybe.

I smiled to myself and turned to the rest of the group. Cassie and our mates had made it back up the stairs.

"I need three people to stay here and guard Crimson. When he wakes up, he will be pissed and hungry. There is Elk meat in the freezer the guys hunted a few months ago. Just defrost a bowl full of that and feed him as soon as he awakens. Who will stay to guard my son?"

Half raised their hands and I chose three at random. Two of Cassie's mates and one of Cendra's.

"Grant, I'll need you and Gerard with my group, we'll go on foot with Craven, as we hunt. I want my mates with me and Rocks' team. The rest, I'll need you to follow in the SUV's, with two of them empty, but for drivers, so we can all jump in one if needed."

Craven had finished shifting, but I could see in his bearing the toll that it had taken him to do it.

"Good job, Craven. Do you still have the scent?"

He snuffed at me. He was still huge in his were form, but looked more like an oversized, giant wolf with a beautiful coat of russet brown. Yet, those eyes of his would give him away, though it was a chance we had to take.

I grabbed a belt off the rack and slowly bent to put it loosely on him.

"Easy, Craven. This is only for show. If civilians see that we have a leash on you, they won't fear you so much and we can hunt." He shivered, but took it around his neck. Unfortunately, I had to add yet another belt, so there would be slack while he ran and not feel so trapped.

We walked out the front door and the rest of the team followed behind. Craven went to the edge of the property and even I caught a strong whiff of exhaust fumes.

"A car was here. Someone must have dropped him off."

"Will that stop you from tracing this back to the source?" Rock asked.

"This is different than when I was taken. A spell this dark, this extensive, lingers in the air. If they had even one window down, it will leave a trace in the air until sunrise."

"What happens at sunrise?" Wizard asked.

"When the sun shines, it will burn away the evil and the scent will be lost."

He looked at his watch. "We have three hours then, and some change."

Craven was pulling at the makeshift leash, anxious to start the hunt.

"Ok, let's go, but you guys are going to get winded. I don't think once Craven gets going that I'll be able to slow him down."

"Just go, we'll keep up," Rock stated firmly.

And they would, too.

I heard doors closing and engines starting to get ready to follow. "Craven, the hunt's afoot."

He gave a wolfy bark.

Andre looked at me oddly as we started to run.

I shrugged my shoulders. "I've always wanted to say that. This seemed like a good opportunity."

He started to laugh, as we ran down the street, going in an Easterly direction, to the other side of St. Padre Island.

As we neared St Padre Island highway, I grew uneasy, thinking if we had to go into Corpus Christi itself, where there were a lot more police cruisers, which could make our night extremely uncomfortable.

However, before the turn to go onto the highway, Craven turned again down a street filled with small shops on either side. We saw the flashing lights before we saw the actual alleyway that the police cruisers were blocking, not only with their cars but with police tape. We stopped, before we could be spotted, and I waved to the others behind us, catching Cassie's eye, who was driving the lead car.

Contacting her with telepathy, I said, 'Cassie, lead the cars to the back of this street and wait for us there. I don't want these cops to see a bunch of military SUV's going by a crime scene.'

'*I agree.*' And she made the turn and the rest of the vehicles followed her.

Rock's team was a bit winded, but they did keep up. I was proud of these men.

"Craven, is that where the scent leads?"

'Evil here. More evil here. Death, too. Prey dead. Hunt is done.'

"Wait a minute. Are you saying the one responsible for your brother's curse that's evil, is dead?"

'*Yes*'

Shit, this wasn't good. If the caster was dead, Crimson's chances in being turned back, just went down dramatically.

"But, there is now more evil?"

'*Yes. We hunt?*'

"No, I have a better idea." I was willing to grab at straws, now, "Grant you're a Corpus Christi Detective. Can you go over there and ask if you can lend a helping hand and find out what happened?"

"Sure, but you had better make yourself scarce."

"I agree. We will wait by the cars. Contact with telepathy when you find out what the hell is going on."

"Will do."

I moved the rest of the team to the backside of the street where the SUV's were waiting. We climbed in to sit and let the humans get a rest.

"You guys need to learn how to go to the well."

Rock cocked his brow at me.

"It's a place on the astral that you can send your spirit-self to and get a drink. It's how the 'Fountain of Youth' myth got started. You go there and drink, and physically you can re-energize."

"Does it keep you young?" Wizard asked hopefully.

"I don't know for sure, but I do know it does help replenish your energy levels and can also add to your power levels of magick. It would be hard for me to tell whether it would keep one young or not, since I was already born immortal."

"That's so not fair," Wizard complained.

I chuckled, "Who said life had to be fair?"

"Oh, don't throw that old saying at me."

Rock cut in, "Can you show us next time, where this place is? It would be helpful on missions to be able to keep going."

"Our next astral lesson, no problemo."

'Sister, a woman was killed here earlier tonight. Time of death was roughly 3 am. Her throat was slit. The most interesting part is, that General Robertson is here, and is trying to have the investigation moved under JAG jurisdiction. It appears the woman is also military and was stationed in Kansas. Quite the coincidence, don't you think?'

'Make sure they don't get that changed into a military jurisdiction. Call in every favor you can, to have Corpus Christi take this over, since ultimately Corpus Christi would investigate a murder here on the Island. The police station here on the island isn't equipped for anything this big.'

'Done.'

I told those who didn't have telepathy what Grant had found out and what was being done.

"Do you think Crimson killed her?" Rock asked quietly.

"He had blood on his hands and on his shirt. Yes, I think he did. The question is, why, and why didn't he cover this up before he came home? Why didn't he call for help? There isn't one person in this family who wouldn't have backed him up on this. It is obvious whoever this woman was, she was evil and cursed him. It had to be self defense. But, why didn't he call us?"

"He warned you the General was coming. He must have found out somehow that this woman and the General were connected. For whatever reason, he had to take her out. But you're right; this is sloppy for Crimson or…"

"What?"

"Maybe he didn't have time. Remember, he came home with his eyes closed. Maybe he didn't have time to tell us anything, before the curse hit him."

"But, he could have used telepathy," I argued.

"Baby, you know how he feels about magick. Killing a woman, even an evil one, might have rattled him too far for straight thinking. There could be a number of reasons why this went down the way it did."

"True, we will just have to wait to see how this plays out. Meanwhile, why don't we leave a car here for Grant and get Craven home before anyone sees him. It's been a miracle no one has spotted him, as it is."

Wizard snorted, "Most normal people are in bed."

I gave a half grin, "Well, I never claimed to be normal."

Wizard laughed, "No shit."

It wasn't until we got home, that I had noticed how quiet Craven had gotten. He padded into the house with his tail between his legs and curled up into a ball.

"Craven, what's wrong, boo?" I scooted down, so I could stroke his fur.

Everyone had gathered into the living room, taking seats where they could. My sister's mates were still downstairs, keeping a vigil of Crimson's progress.

Craven's wolf form started to shimmer and I knew he was shifting again.

When he completed his full shift, he was again human, with tears trailing down his face.

"I'm sorry, Mom. I am so sorry."

"What, honey? What are you sorry for?"

"That girl in the alley that's dead, is the same girl Crimson has been seeing on the sly. He made me promise not to tell, but he's been sneaking out to see her for weeks now." His shoulders were shaking with grief.

"You mean he was dating that bitch?"

He nodded, his head sobbing. "I didn't know she was evil, Mom. I know Crimson didn't either. Her scent, I recognized though, but polluted with evil tonight. She didn't smell bad before. I swear it or I would have warned Crimson, Mom. I would have."

"Shh, baby, I know you would have, but you know you were both to be guarded at all times. That asshole General has been looking for all of us. Now, I don't know how much he knows, if she was sent in as a spy. But, that explains the leak, Rock. That's where our leak was."

93

"I'm sorry, Mom. I didn't know."

I held him closer. "It's all right, boo. I'm not mad at you or your brother. We'll find out what happened. Ultimately, this is Crimson's bad, but you should have told me about the sneaking out."

"I know. I am sorry."

"No more secrets. Promise me."

"I promise."

"All right, then." I couldn't lose my temper now. Both of my boys were hurting and needed me to be strong for them. When this was over, I was going to kick some General's ass, though. He is so on my list.

Chapter Ten

Castling Queen Side

As we waited for news from Grant, Rock had called General Pierce to let him know what had happened and to see if General Pierce could circumvent JAG from taking over, or if JAG did wind up assigned to the case, if it could be our JAG division here that handled it and not a division controlled by General Robertson. Most of my siblings were sleeping upstairs in guest bedrooms, which we had for just such an occasion, but my mates and I were vampires, sleeping mostly in the day and rambling all night. My Kla' din mates had switched their sleeping habits to match mine, so we could spend more time together.

Had I been so wrapped up into my mates that I had been letting my parenting slip? How could I not have known that my son had been sneaking out? I should have had some sort of clue that Crimson was in a dangerous situation. What good was being a demi-Goddess, if I can't keep my sons safe? Though Crimson was nineteen now, since he and Craven just had their birthdays last month. Technically, he was an adult and quite capable of taking care of himself. I snorted.

Sure he can, that's why he's a panther now. I groaned inwardly. No, shit just happened. It could have happened to any one of us. The fact that Crimson was the one who'd gotten tagged by the Black Coven, was just chance. Well, not chance on the Black Covens part. They must have had this whole thing planned out. A general spell for locating a person who could help them find me. A bit of my blood and a crystal and it would lead them to anyone near me or even to me directly, if they had gotten really lucky.

Luckily, with my metaphysical shields in place 24/7, the likelihood of that happening is pretty small, but with Crimson shying away from anything dealing with magick unless he absolutely needed to, he wouldn't have a shield and it would leave him as the next easy target. Whamo, mission accomplished, contact made. Then, find his weakness and set up a scenario to play upon it. Yeah, they worked this one real well. She must have used his most vulnerable emotions and made herself seem like the only safe harbor in his life. Then, just sit back and milk him for information on the Nightwolves. I would bet she'd even had tried to get a meeting with me. Once physical contact had been established, she could have dropped a crystal or a stone near my home and things would have progressed from there. See who came who went and take down license numbers. Know your enemy. Learn their habits, and then hit them when the time is right.

I knew how these things worked from when I was being trained as an assassin many years ago. I could see their whole outline in my mind now and was pissed at myself for not seeing it sooner. I knew Crimson was up to something, but I let it go, trying to loosen the apron ties and let him be a man. You can only protect and mother your kids for so long, before you have to let them go and give them room to grow. To have a chance for experiences that will help them become self-sustaining grown adults. But, damn it, I should have been able to keep an eye from afar, couldn't I?

I had tried that with Craven and look what happened. Bitten by a werewolf. Some mother I was. My children were being hurt and their lives changed from what would have been a bright future, if not for me and what I was. There has to be a way to keep them safe from all of this. I couldn't walk away now that I was in so deep. But, maybe more guards, step up the protection-something has to be done.

"No, you couldn't, without making them feel crowded and resenting you for being overbearing." Demitri had walked into the library where I had been sitting, mulling things over, trying to get a handle on exactly what had happened.

"How?"

"You're thinking loudly. We all heard you, honey."

"Shit, I'm sorry. I didn't realize I was broadcasting out loud."

"It's all right. But, will you please quit beating yourself up, mentally? You're a wonderful mother. You have done a phenomenal job all on your own. My only wish, is that we could have been there for you sooner, to help you raise these great kids so we could have shared in the credit." He grinned wickedly at me. I could see he was trying to tease me out of my bad mood.

I slapped his shoulder. "See, trying to steal my thunder. Just like a man."

He settled down next to me on the couch and pulled me into his arms. My other mates slowly drifted into the library and set themselves on seats around us.

"I can't stand seeing my kids hurting, Demitri. This isn't the kind of life I had envisioned for them. They should be dating, going to college, meeting their one true love, getting married and having kids."

"Have their life all mapped out for them, do you?" Andre quipped.

"It's a life I never got a chance at. A nice, normal life. They deserve that much; for me to give them what I never had."

Antonio picked up my free hand and squeezed gently in comfort, "They can't be normal, baby. It's not in their blood, for one. And with the Prophecy coming into play, no one even mundane will have their nice, normal lives for very much longer. But, you did the right thing in training your boys to be strong by giving them the tools they will need when that time comes, to be able to survive what is going to happen. Maybe after all this is said and done, then they can have nice, normal lives like everyone else mundane. But, for now, it is really unrealistic, Catrina."

"Meshama, even in the Domija, accidents happen when we train our young. But, leaving them untrained, would be more hurtful to the child where they would be vulnerable to attacks."

"But your world is different from our world, Ja' Callum. Children here just go to school and come home to do chores and so on. They don't have a world filled with vampires attacking their home in the dead of night."

"Not yet, they don't, Meshama. And, what will happen now to those children who have been kept just so, when your portals open? They will be nothing but food with nothing to help them fight."

"You keep trying to give them the June Cleaver world honey, but the reality is, Leave it to Beaver is and always will be, a fantasy world. With, or without, vampires in it. People are not cookie cutter copies. If that were true, we would wind up with the Stefford wives world and I am sorry, but that doesn't appeal to me in the slightest."

"Nope, but it would appeal to the control freaks," I laughed.

"That's their fucking problem. But listen, honey, you have done well. And you have been letting them grow just as you should. Too much mother-henning now, would seriously add problems. You know this." Antonio patted my hand and stood up walking towards the liquor cabinet we had hidden in here. I was surprised that they hadn't had another hidden bedroom installed in here until I recalled Demitri's penchant for making love in libraries. He had this thing about being surrounded by books and laying me out on a reading couch.

"How about a margarita, love?"

I cocked my head at him, grinning mischievously. "Think 7 am is a little too early for drinking, baby?"

"Nah, it's happy hour somewhere in the world. Don't worry; I'll cut the alcohol level, so we can keep sharp through this ordeal. An almost virgin drink, for now."

"Cool. Almost a virgin, huh?"

Demitri started to growl and nuzzled into my neck, making me shiver from the sensation. The tingling he was making me feel was spreading up and down to my back. The sexual tension shot up in the whole room, with the rest of my mates looking on. That was another trigger for Demitri-being the exhibitionist he was, which only made him more aggressive with his tongue, licking along the side where my jugular was and lightly scraping his teeth against my skin.

Was the room getting hotter, as the sun rose higher?

I heard a throat clear at the door to the library "Umm hemm, Cat? You have a visitor that won't go away." Cassie's words were stressed and clipped, letting me know whoever it was had pissed her off. From behind Cassie, another form strode right into the room, like she owned the place and following her was her trusty lap dog.

Mommy Dearest.

Oh, joy. And just when my day had been getting somewhat brighter. Damn.

Demitri stopped what he had been doing but the growl in his throat had turned menacing. My Kla' din mates stood up, each reaching towards a weapon they had stashed on their bodies. Oh yeah, this was going to be fun. Not.

It struck me as odd though, that my Kla' din mates would actually draw a weapon on my mother. Interesting.

"So, Mommy Dearest, what brings you here on this bright and sunny day to darken my door?"

"Do you have to be so rude, Catrina Lynn Garcia?"

"I apologize. You're absolutely right. It has just been so long since you have come for a visit as you could have done in Arizona many a time, but chose not to, I have fallen out of practice with dealing with you. Always let you start the rudeness and then fight back. I quite forgot. My pardon. Now, here you are in Texas, hundreds of miles away from your home in Arizona, and I get two visits in quick succession. Fascinating really, and I should be honored. Would either of you care for a drink?" I looked at both of them archly. "Oh, that's right, neither of you drink. We were just about to have some margaritas, but I'm sure we have some juice in the bar or would you prefer coffee?"

"Really Catrina, drinking at 7 am? You just woke up. Have you picked up your bad habit again of waking up with a drink and going to bed with one?"

"I only did that when I had no choice but live with you under house arrest. It was the only way I could cope in your house, but if I recall right, you did your fair share of drinking or did you forget that, Mommy Dearest?" Her face was turning a nice shade of red. "Besides, I have yet to go to sleep, so actually, a Margarita is appropriate for me."

I stood up from the couch and walked over to the desk to put it between me and her. Not that I felt threatened by her. I was again only trying to protect her. With the desk between us, I wouldn't be tempted to hit her. If I hit her now with my strength, it would snap her neck if I forgot to pull the power back from it. My Kla' din mates had moved in behind me, as I sat down in the leather office chair at the desk. Antonio brought over my drink and I took a deep swallow and noticed this was fully loaded with alcohol. I glanced over at him with the question clear in my eyes.

'I figured you'd need it if you have to deal with that bitch.'

Ahhh yeah, he was right and I took another drink.

"Again, I ask, anything to drink Mother? Robert?"

"No, thank you," Robert said in a disapproving tone. Like I cared what the toad thought of me or my habits.

How could my 'bring love to my mother' spell go so wrong that it brought this slug into her life? True, he'd got her to stop drinking and smoking cigarettes. She'd had high blood pressure and with his regime of a healthy diet and mild exercise, he had gotten my mom into good shape with weight loss and a normal blood pressure. It was these things that had stayed my hand in either having him killed or doing it myself, when I found out just how badly he had twisted my mother's mind and made her into this fanatic I now had to deal with. Before, she had just been a bitch. Now, she was a fanatical bitch, which is worse.

I looked at my mother, as she just shook her head to my offer of juice. Maybe it is not all him. She is enjoying having a whip to hit me with, mentally speaking. She hasn't had this much control in making me feel like shit in such a long time. Maybe this is just what she wanted.

Since there were no chairs in front of the desk, my mother and Robert were forced to stand in front of me, looking like children being called to the carpet. I needed the power move and didn't request chairs be brought for them to sit on. Besides, if they were made uncomfortable enough, this would make this lovely visit shorter.

"What can I do for you, Mother? And please don't start with the whole 'I want to save your soul' shit. I am not in the mood for your pontificating."

"Catrina, why else would I be here? Why else would I expend the finances to come here and pay for a hotel suite, if not to try to help you?"

"Oh, I don't know. Maybe some normal Grandmother reasoning, like spending time with your grandsons, taking them to the zoo, or the movies, baking cookies. Oh wait, your grandsons are men now. You kind of missed your time with them and just think of the money you could have saved had you done that when you lived only ten short hours away from us in Arizona?"

Like she ever had to worry over money with her cushy job. A job I made even cushier for her when the company had moved to another state and instead of having her move with the corporation to keep her job, I did a spell that made them pay her to work from home. A nice 60,000 a year job where one fourth of her house expenses got reimbursed by the company and written as a tax write off, so she gets a nice tax return every year. Her monthly house payments were only $700 a month. A nice three bedroom house, with high vaulted ceilings and a bricked-in fenced yard. I paid $718 a month for my crappy 2 bedroom trailer on disability (from a terminal illness when I was purely human) and had to often go hungry, just to make the mortgage payments. That was the difference in having triple A credit and a good paying job and a person with bad credit on disability. Yeah right, she was hurting for money and needed to save every penny, my ass. Then again, I had no idea how much Robert cost in his upkeep. He didn't work; he just sat in the room in a corner watching my mother work all day on the computer and listened in on every conversation she had on the phone. I knew this, because when I would call, she always would put me on speaker phone so he would hear every word I said to her. It was why I'd switched to emailing her a few years ago though he most likely read those too, the creep. Demitri snorted and I snapped my head towards him.

'Sorry, but you're broadcasting again.'

Damn, the drink made me lose my shielding.

My mother had started in on her tirade and I didn't get the chance to reprimand my mate for the heck of it. Demitri gave a small chuckle.

"Catrina really, I had to work. And there was no room at your house to spend time with you or my grandsons."

"Yet, you could afford to go to Las Vegas once a month?"

"How did you... Never mind, we went there for Costco's shopping mart. It is the closet one to our hometown."

"Costco's? Really? Ok, how about the two week vacation trips every year, sometimes twice, if you could talk the company into it?"

"Catrina Lynn Garcia."

I cut her off, "You know, I really hate that last name, so don't bother using it. I will be changing it anyway, so you better get out of the habit."

"I would think your father would be hurt..."

"Hurt, really? He's dead, so why should he give a fuck? Besides, he wasn't my real father anyway, right? I have no blood right to the name, so get over it."

"Raymond is dead?"

"Yes mother, my stepfather died a few years ago, as did your past best friend, Katherine. You remember her?"

"You're lying. How would you know any of that?"

"You wouldn't believe me if I told you but, it's all a moot point now, isn't it? Katherine's dead. Raymond is dead and I am changing my name. End of subject." I sighed heavily, already tired not just from the sun rising which did affect us being vampires, though we didn't burn up in it. It just made us sleepy. But I was also already tired of dealing with this pod person, who claimed to be my mother.

"You have to leave this house and your...husbands, Catrina. This life will do you spiritual harm. Please, believe me."

"Mother, you don't know anything about it. You don't even know your own religion so please don't go preaching to me about it. It only makes you look stupid and you used to be such a smart woman."

"I won't have you talking to my wife like that," Robert was looking down his nose at me.

"Look dickless, you ain't got shit to say about it. Not here in my house."

My mother leaned over the desk in a pose that I think she thought would look intimidating. "Catrina, this isn't your house and don't you dare talk to him like that, or else."

That was Ja' Monel's last straw, apparently.

101

"You will step back away from our Meshallima, now, woman."

I could see by all of my mates' expressions, that the telepathy warnings were flying in between my Earth-side mates and my Kla' din mates, though they spoke on a private path, blocking me out of the conversations.

I stood up and placed myself between Ja' Monel and my mother. "Sweetheart, please let me deal with this."

"She shames you. She threatens you. This should not be allowed." His chin jutted out stubbornly at me.

"Demitri and his brothers do not get in the middle of things between my mother and me. I would appreciate it if you and your cousins did the same thing."

"They made that promise to you, Meshama. We have not. Nor we will allow anyone to threaten you."

"I thought all females were to be protected to pain of death?"

"Females, yes. But, in our world, if a female is caught breaking the law, it is her mate or her father who gets the punishment." He turned to give Robert a look that would have a normal thinking man start to run for his life, if he had half a brain. "It is he who would pay the price for your Mother's disrespect or threats."

Oh, shit. I turned to see how Robert and my mother were taking this new turn of events.

"Who are these men, Catrina, and what do they mean by 'in our world'?"

I was confused for a moment, then I realized something. "Oh, I am sorry; I forgot to introduce you to my other mates. Just in case you're not clear, these men too, are my husbands. All six are now mine by right."

Shock made her face turn white. "You flaming Jezebel. You whore."

I heard Ja' Monel growl behind me, "Woman, you dare insult our Meshallima so flagrantly?

"What did you do, Catrina, marry some flaming..." and before she could finish that sentence, I had jumped over the desk to land behind her and put my hand over her mouth.

I moved so fast she didn't even have time to breathe.

"Mother, if you utter one single insult out loud within my hearing about anyone in my family, I will personally beat your ass black and blue."

Robert made to move like he was going to try to remove me from my mother. "I wouldn't, slug. I will fucking nail you so hard in your nuts, they'll have to fucking remove them just to save your life."

At that moment, a loud roar echoed throughout the house, coming from the basement.

'*Crimson is awake and he is pissed,*' came the warning in my mind from one of my sister's mates.

'*He is feeling your anger. Control yourself, Catrina,*' Demitri cautioned.

I removed my hand from my mother and was about to tell her to leave when she started running her mouth, yet again. "What was that? It sounded like a lion. You don't have a zoo animal here do you, Catrina?" She was ignoring all my warning signs of just how pissed I was getting. The more I swore in a sentence, the higher my temper was getting and soon it would be to the point of no return, and I would kill someone. Another roar ripped through the air. I did as Demitri suggested and tried to reign in my rage.

"It's none of your business, Mother. Get out of my house; I have other fucking things to worry about now."

"You can't live like this. You can't bring your children into this house of inequity. This den of sin. And a large dangerous animal. You don't have the right."

"Mother, run, don't walk to the airport, get on the plane and get the fuck out of my state. Your vacation is over."

"No, this isn't over, Catrina." She turned to walk out of the house with her slug toy trailing behind her, trying to look hard with his pudgy face and scruffy beard.

Stupid, fucking woman, I thought to myself. I could hear her whisper hurriedly to Robert, as they went out the front door as yet another loud roar rent throughout the house. We went running down to the basement to see what was going on.

When I got to the basement, with my mates hot on my heels, I came to a halt to see Crimson pacing back and forth in his cell, growling heavily, then flinging himself against the bars, scratching at them with his massive claws. Howling in spitting rage, then he would resume pacing, his tail constantly flicking behind him from side to side.

"Did anyone defrost some meat?"

"Yeah, I'll get it."

Lee, Cassie's mate, left the room to return a few minutes later with a huge bowl piled high with red meat. I took it from him and moved slowly towards the cage to lift the trap door to slide the food inside.

"Think she'll go inside the cage?" Demitri asked the room at large.

"I'll spank her again, if she does," Antonio growled.

I shuddered in memory and turned to glare at Antonio. He was grinning the most wicked smile I had ever seen on him. I couldn't stay mad.

Chapter Eleven

Cover

rimson had curled up at the far end of the cage, glaring at me with his jaw half open, showing me an impressive set of sharp, long teeth. Getting into the cage with him now held no appeal to me and wouldn't do a damn bit of good. It wasn't like I could show him how to shift, since he couldn't pull it off anyway. Wrestling with him would be a futile exercise for both of us. I may put myself in danger often, but I never did it over stupid reasons. At least, that's how I felt about it. I pushed the bowl in and blood slopped over the edge of it, leaving a bloody trail on the floor.

His nose sniffed and he coughed with this slight hacking sound, then continued to lightly growl like a large cat warning off another predator. I dropped the trap screen and moved back, so he could come get the meat without feeling like he would have to fight for it. I had no idea how much of his human intelligence was working or if that part of him had gotten totally obliterated. My heart clenched at the thought, because if that were true, then getting him to at least be a part of the family in some form would be impossible and he would have the future of being a really big pet.

NO. I took a deep breath and sat back against the wall, making myself small for him. I would, by The Goddess, find a way to have my son back. Nothing was impossible. I just needed time to find something. With the black witch dead, I couldn't torture her into turning him back, but there still had to be another way.

I went still and breathed to calm my emotions and center myself. Crimson had edged towards the bowl in a zigzag pattern, low and close to the floor, getting ever closer to the bowl. Then, suddenly, he snapped out and grabbed a huge chunk of meat and dragged it back to the far side of the cage.

As he ate, I put a shield around my body and relaxed every muscle, one by one. Using astral projection after drinking alcohol was never a good idea even though it was only one drink, but when I was learning how to be an assassin one of the tricks of the trade that even the CIA used to train their field operatives was to quickly process drugs and alcohol out of their system and release it through the sweat glands in your body. It took months of practice, but by the time I was seventeen nothing could affect me for very long so long as I had conscious warning something was going into my system. It made taking pharmaceutical drugs and antibiotics a bitch because they would go through my body so fast, as to not help me when I actually did need a drug to work. I would build up a tolerance to high blood pressure medicine in a matter of weeks compared to other people. It made my doctor work double time in trying to find me something I wouldn't process so quickly, but we finally did find something that worked continuously; though I had to play with the dosage often, to keep my body off track so it wouldn't learn how to fight even that medication.

So, I sat there, pushing the alcohol out. Once I was clear of the drink, I let myself go out of my body and focused on the big cat. Before attempting to enter the body of the big cat, I made a strong white shield around my spirit self, to protect me from the curse.

He was tearing into the chunk of meat with a wary eye on the people outside of his cage. I made my astral self very small and slid into the cat, near its brain area. From here, I let my senses roam throughout his body, searching for the spark that was my son. I could hear the tearing of the meat; I could feel the muscles move as he ate, and I also got a glimpse of what the cat saw as he chewed. Every object was hyper sharpened and everything had lost its color. Just shades of gray, black and white. The cat's vision was amazing to see with my spirit self. Then, I felt a shudder run through the cat. Had my son been in control, I wouldn't have been able to enter into the big cat's body so easily. Not without permission from the owner of the body. But, Crimson had withdrawn himself consciously so far into its mind, that it seemed his human spirit had vacated the premises. Astrally sliding into a human's body that had a soul still inside was much harder to do in comparison, but the panther still felt me inside him and he didn't like it. I withdrew from using its vision and felt around for Crimson's soul self. I finally found him huddled in a dark corner of the panthers head.

"Crimson, honey."

"I didn't want to kill her. I didn't want to kill her." He kept repeating it over and over, as he sat there in that dark bubble with blood coating his hands and dripping down the front of his shirt. A steady drip was pooling around him and he didn't seem to consciously see it. He just kept staring at his hands. The blood was fresh and wet as if he had just killed her. He was mentally and emotionally stuck in that moment

"CRIMSON."

"Mom? He started to breathe heavily, "Run, Mom, run. He is coming. Get out of there. Get out, now." He closed his eyes and buried his face into his hands, smearing the blood. "Crimson, look at me. I am here with you now. See me." I kept my voice as even and calm as I could for him, but I had to get him to snap out of this nightmare he had put himself into.

I moved closer to his bubble. "Crimson, I am here with you."

He looked up again. "Mom? I didn't want to kill her."

"I know, sweetheart. You did what you had to do. I understand and I love you."

"I am sorry. I didn't want to."

"Let me in, Crimson. Let me help you."

"She's dead now, Mom. I loved her. I just didn't want to share our time with anyone else. I wanted something apart from the family and now she is dead."

"I know this and I understand. I am sorry you had to, but, I am ok now. We will help you. Just let me in."

"In? I don't...I want...I am sorry." He started groaning, as if he just couldn't let the tears go, but he wanted so badly to cry. He needed to cry; it would be a start for him to begin to heal from the experience. I had to get to him though this shield he had subconsciously built around himself, but I was afraid of taking something away that might be the only thing that made him feel safe inside. If I tore it down, he might lose his mind completely and there would be no reasoning with him then. He would be soul lost. I couldn't take that risk of breaking through to reach him.

I moved as close to his shield as I could and knelt down, so I could make eye contact with him. "Crimson, look at me."

"I didn't want.."

"Crimson, stop. Look at me now."

"I.."

107

"No, look at me. Forget everything else and just look at me. Come on, look at my eyes now." I started to put power, slow and warm into my voice, "Crimson, look at me."

Slowly, he raised his head and met my eyes.

"Good. Now see me, look at me. Who am I?"

"I didn't want.."

"No...who am I?"

He looked confused, then his eyes started to clear a bit, "Mom, you're my Mom."

"That's good. I am here. Focus on me. Control, Crimson. You need to regain control."

His eyes started to close again. "No, look at me now, Crimson and see me. Get control. You're stronger than this. See me."

His eyes snapped open and he strained to really see my face before him. I could tell he was struggling not to get trapped again into the hell he had created out of guilt.

"Mom, how? Where are we?"

"Never mind about that right now. Just keep your eyes on me. Don't break eye contact. I need you to break this shield, Crimson."

"Shield?"

"Yes, you built a shield around yourself. I need you to make it go away. Just think it to be gone. That's all you have to do."

"I don't do magick, Mom. It's a pain in the ass. I hate it."

"I know, honey, but I need this one thing from you right now. Make it go away."

"I'll try." He started to close his eyes again.

"No, Crimson, keep your eyes on me and just focus on what you want. You want the shield down. Make it happen with your mind, but don't take your eyes off of me."

If I lost eye contact, I would lose what small conscious bond I had gained with him. At least, his broken guilt record had stopped. That was progress. I needed him out of this shield before I could do anything else for him, but it had to be his decision to take the shield down; his power, not mine. Finally, I felt the pop of the shield disappearing from around the core of his soul and feelings came flooding out; anger, despair, guilt, grief and betrayal. An avalanche of emotions that almost overwhelmed me and would have, if I had not had to deal with very similar feelings from my own past. It still took everything I had not to break eye contact with him and not to let his feelings overcome my common sense. I couldn't be of any help to him if I broke down from feeling his internal pain.

"Good job, Crimson. Now, breathe. Breathe deep and easy and keep your eyes on mine." I edged slowly and cautiously towards him, so as not to startle him. Carefully, I took his hands in mine, though they were still covered in blood, which I knew was an illusion. His mind couldn't get over that moment of killing someone he cared about. The next step I had to do with him was to let go of that moment in time. From there, I wasn't sure how to proceed with helping him deal with what he had done. But, I figured we would just take this one step at a time.

"Crimson, I am not going anywhere. Mommy is here now and we will get through this together, I promise."

"I didn't want to kill her. I really didn't."

"I know that, but she gave you no choice. It wasn't your fault, Crimson."

"She is dead by my hand. How is that not my fault?" He raised his hands up to show me the blood.

I needed him off this track of thinking and now, or I could lose him again. I understood that he was actually reaching out to me for comfort, but we didn't have time for that. Our relationship had always been so distant and now, here he was coming to me for help and I couldn't be the comforting mother he needed. I had to be the trainer, the warrior. I couldn't be soft for him. There was no time for that.

"Right now, this blood, here in this place, is not real. Make it disappear. Let go of it, Crimson."

I was repeating his name every chance I got, so he wouldn't lose his identity along with everything else he had already lost.

"How?"

"Just make it go away. It's not there for real, it's an illusion. Crimson, you need to think rationally and not with your emotions."

I know I sounded cold and ruthless, but he had to get out of this darkness and in conscious control of the animal mind. If he didn't, and soon, the animal could quite possibly keep him locked in here and there would be no way for Crimson to get conscious control of the animal's body. He needed that much control or anything else I might be able to do, would be a moot point. The animals mind was strong as it was, being able to feel me and try to shake me out as he did, when I looked through its eyes. Crimson needed to establish a mental dominance, before the animal learned how to adapt and keep total control on a subconscious level. Animals may not be able to reason as humans do, but they are exceptional at adapting and overcoming for their survival. In the end, to an animal, that was the main and only thing they cared about their continued existence, by any means. Crimson needed to take control and hopefully learn to live in peace with this animal now that it was a part of him. It would make things easier for all of us, until I could find a way to reverse the curse. And I needed time. I had to get more ruthless, even though he was my own son. I could feel the animals mind expanding his mental dominance bit by bit, as we sat here inside its brain. Soon, the mind expansion would include even this dark corner of its brain and Crimson would be lost to us forever.

"Crimson, it is done. She is gone, so bury it. Bury it now and get control of this. Make the blood go away, it isn't real. None of this is real."

"She was my girl, Mom."

"I know, but this isn't the time, Crimson. You need to step up and get tougher. You need to be in total control, here and now, Crimson."

"Why? What's wrong?"

"Make the blood go away, first. Bury your grief. We will deal with it later. Just get mental control over this illusion now, Crimson."

I could feel the cat gaining ground and we were running out of time.

A look of pain crossed over his face, but the blood was slowly receding. Soon, the area was cleared of blood and his hands were clean. At least where we could see them, but I knew in his soul the blood would always be there. I would help him later with that, but first I had to get him to fight for dominance over the cat's body. This would be harder than when Craven had to gain control over his wolf. At least with Craven, his soul was installed throughout the body of the wolf. Not so with Crimson; and this would make things so much harder for him.

"Good. Now, feel this?" squeezing his hands hard.

"Yes."

"No, you don't. It's not real either." I tapped his chest. "This body isn't real." I brought his hand up to my face. "I am here in spirit only, so this isn't real. I need you to look around. Have you ever seen this place before, in the house or anywhere on Earth?"

He looked around and saw as I did, just darkness that seemed infinite; but even that was an illusion.

He looked confused. "Where are we?"

"We need to work fast, Crimson, so listen to me and believe me." I threw power into that command, because I just didn't have time to convince him of the reality of our position. With his soul exposed like it was, it made it unbelievably vulnerable to suggestions and he had no

110

tools to counter anything I did to him. He was lucky it was me in here with him and not an enemy. One's soul could be totally destroyed in this situation; or taken as a slave, even on a spiritual plane. He was as vulnerable as an infant and I felt some of that was my fault in not pushing him to learn the Arts more than I did. I couldn't let that get in the way now. What he needed was to learn quickly how to expand his soul throughout the cat's body and wrestle for control. I knew he had the ability. He had more untrained power than both of his brothers put together. I just never wanted to force him to learn, feeling he would come to me when he realized just how important it was to learn the Arts. Now that he finally recognizes the need for learning, I had to be relentless in getting him to use his power to win control.

"This is the spirit of the panther your body turned into. You need to let go of the illusion of a body in here and allow your spirit to flow throughout the body of the cat, Crimson."

"What panther?"

"You were cursed with a shapeshifting spell. You need to gain control now. If you let your power flow out, you'll see the spirit of the panther flowing throughout this body taking absolute control. You can NOT let that happen. If you want me to help you, you need to go now and gain control of this body."

"The tattoo. I saw a tattoo and then felt nothing but pain. I remember. Mom, help me. What do I do?"

Good, now he was thinking rationally again, though I knew that in burying all that emotion so quickly, there would be a price to pay for that later. I knew from experience.

"Let this body go and become spirit again and flow out all along this body and control it as you would your own body. It IS essentially your body, but the spirit of the cat is taking it over. You have got to stop it. I can't do it for you."

His face hardened and it actually made my heart twist in pain to see it.

"Let go. See yourself as energy and flow out and with WILL; take over, no matter what the cat does. No matter what it throws at you or how it hurts you; you must be the winner."

He closed his eyes and I allowed it, as his breathing deepened and his body became more transparent. In an instant, he was energy and flowed outward, meeting the spirit of the cat's head first.

The dark area I was in trembled and echoed with the sound of roaring. I almost lost my balance in there, until I had to remind myself that I, too, was nothing more than an illusion. I felt Crimson's spirit weaken and flinch from pain and I poured my power and energy out to him filling him with confidence and strength. The battle turned back to his favor, as the cats spirit fought and clawed for dominance to regain his lost territory. Crimson poured out and around with a heartlessness that scared me. He had never been so hard before. Now, he would never be soft again. I felt that in my soul and I wept for him.

Crimson's spirit had grown so much from anger and ruthlessness that it literally threw my spirit out of the dark place in the cat's brain and I was again in my own body.

My body felt like it had been shredded, but I ignored the pain as I crawled toward the cage and reached for my son. "Crimson?"

The cat yowled at me with defiance. "Show me. Show me you are in control, Crimson. Lift your paw to me." I reached my hand out toward him. The cat lifted his paw and briefly touched my hand with claws retracted.

I smiled in relief and went to rub his head. "Crimson, let me back in your mind so we can talk about what happened, now. I promise, we can work this out. Let me in."

He shook my hand off and lightly growled at me and stalked away. Once he reached the far side of the cage, he refused to even look at me.

"Please, Crimson. I am sorry I had to be so hard, but we have time now to talk. I am so sorry, babyboy. Please, let me in."

The growling grew louder and he flashed his teeth at me. It felt like my heart had split into pieces. He wouldn't let me in to help him and I couldn't blame him for being angry with me. Though, I had no choice in handling things the way I did, it was still my fault I couldn't help him with everything. That was a mom's job-to be there for anything, large or small. I had failed my son.

Pain welled up inside, and yet, I refused to cry. A hand gently gripped my arm, trying to pull me up into his arms. I found myself surrounded by Demitri's scent of patchouli and cedar.

"Come on, baby. He just got done fighting. He needs time to cool off. It'll be all right." But, I knew it wouldn't. I had lost my chance to heal Crimson's soul. I wasn't the comforting mother he'd needed me to be. I had to be hard to get him to fight for his cat's body. I knew Crimson would never let me in again. He had needed his mother for once and I gave him the warrior side of me. I couldn't blame him for hating me for that. I often hated my own mother for not being what I had needed her to be.

112

Unlike my own mother, however, I would regret this moment until the end of time.

As Demitri carried me away from the basement I prayed to the Goddess, that I would be given another chance to be the mother that Crimson had needed me to be.

Chapter Twelve

Blockade

O'Hara met us in the kitchen where Demitri had fed me blood from his neck and was now trying to get me to eat regular food to regain the calories I had lost. That was the main thing about having such strong psychic abilities when they were used, it burned calories four times as fast as a human working out for eight hours. We could literally burn out our powers if we didn't replenish what we'd spent. Even my siblings, who weren't vampires needed to feed often with red meat. It was part and parcel of being a heavy magick user.

"How is he?" O'Hara asked.

"He is consciously in control now, but I think whatever happened between him and that girl really fucked him up."

"Did you find out exactly what had happened?"

"Not much, except he had killed the girl in the alleyway. He was dating her apparently, and she turned on him. Obviously, she backed him into a corner where he didn't have much choice in killing her, but it is still tearing him up inside."

"Maybe Grant's cousin, Timothy, can have some counseling sessions with him or something?"

"Crimson doesn't let anybody close to him. Not even us and we are the closest people he has. I don't think Tim would have much luck, but we could give it a try in a day or two. First, I want to know everything there is to know about this bitch. I want her address, her relatives and their addresses. Everything. If we have to tear her house apart, piece by piece, we will. We need to find her spell book, all her tools, everything that could have cast this curse. If I can find the spell, I might be able to reverse the damn thing."

At that moment, O'Hara's cell phone rang.

Flipping it open, "Go," O'Hara said. "Right."

He turned and ran out of the room towards the bedrooms where the rest of his team was sleeping.

"Wizard, front and center now, with your computer."

One thing about Special Forces, it always seemed they were ready to go at a moment's notice and this time was no different. Before O'Hara could even make it to the steps, Wizard was at the top of the stairs making his way down. O'Hara stopped. "Where is your room for computer hook-ups?"

Antonio pointed to the room on the left side of the stairs, next to the library and O'Hara nodded for Wizard to precede him into the room.

"Grant is at the station. He says they got a print off a broken cell phone. Most likely Crimsons'. We need you to make Crimson disappear off of the grid in this state, STAT. They are running the prints now."

Without wasting time asking any other questions, Wizard opened up his laptop and pulled out a few cords to hook it up to the main computer in the house and got it booted up.

Unlike our computer system, it took no time getting online and his fingers were flying across the keyboard, erasing Crimson's Drivers license and photo from the states DMV's computer system. Highly illegal if we were caught, but that wasn't the worry. What was a main concern, was that even if we erased his tracks they would still have the copy of the print and might be able to trace it, sooner or later, using the high tech capabilities of the Pentagon. General Robertson wouldn't hesitate to call in favors from his buddies there. And the list of names that were tied to Robertson's was long.

I waved my fingers at O'Hara gesturing I wanted the phone. "Hey bro, how bad?"

"Bad, real bad. General Robertson got an injunction on searching the house, even though I managed to get myself appointed as lead detective and keep this a Corpus Christi police investigation; he still pulled some favors in getting things his way. He also has his own people guarding the house so we won't be able to search it on the sly, either." Damn this was real bad, and Grant wasn't done with the bad news either. "I couldn't make the phone disappear before they had lifted the prints off of it, but its gone now and General Robertson is foaming at the mouth over it."

"Good, so the phone is gone, but he has the print. Sooner or later, he will find an address to match that."

I heard him sigh over the phone. "Yeah, sorry sis. I tried to move fast, but this prick is hovering over every aspect and I can't get him kicked out of here because of the favors he pulled. Also, he has declared himself as being the closest relative, so I can't dispose of the body properly."

Shit, this was so not good.

"Just do what you can. Wizard is making things as hard as he can from this end. Thanks for the heads up."

"How is Crimson?"

"He's messed up in the head over the killing, but he has control over the panther's body now. Maybe Tim can help him?" I asked doubtfully.

"I'll call and fill him in later; right now I have to watch this prick."

Wizard nodded at me. "Ok bro, Wizard has cleaned house; see about getting the dill rod out of our territory."

"Will do."

I closed the phone and handed it back to O'Hara.

"What's the situation?" O'Hara asked, as he took his phone back.

"Robertson has an injunction on the house, so we can't search it. He also has the body, stating that he is her closest relative, so we can't remove the head."

"Is that really necessary?" Wizard looked a bit green.

"Yes, actually it is, for this level of magickal use. There is no end of things that could be done with her head still attached to her body. It all depends on how far General Robertson is willing to go."

"Are you saying she could be brought back?"

"In a manner of speaking, yes. And what will come back will be twice as hard to kill."

"Ok, that's not only sick, but it majorly sucks," Wizard said.

"Well, we can hope the General isn't willing to go that far. The price of bringing someone back is rather high and only the most desperate or the most foolish would try it. If he attempts it and fails, he could wind up losing his own soul and life. And believe me, there is a difference between the two."

"I hope he isn't strong enough to try raising her back from the dead, then. Sounds like it's nasty business," O'Hara stated.

"It's the blackest of magicks, and also one of the worst things a person can do. The number of Gods ones pisses off doing it and succeeding, is long. Salil being one of them and a God I wouldn't want to piss off."

"Salil?" Wizard queried.

117

"God of souls, basically. He gathers them for the Boatman. There are a few strong enough to resist dying when they should. He sends out one of his minions and they just need to touch you, kinda like a Grim Reaper, but these guys are physical humans. They search for those who refuse to die at their time, touch them and they die. That way, their soul goes to the afterlife for its cycling, judgment and then rebirth in some cases."

"So, Salil is a light-side God?"

"No, not really. He is a God that is neither light nor dark, but what he does is dark, for a good purpose."

Confused, they both looked at me.

"I know, but it's one of those weird things when something bad is actually a good thing in the long run."

They still looked confused. "Balance, everything is about balance. It creates an imbalance when a person fights their time of death. Some are strong enough to try to overstay their welcome and when they do, they can change things for the worse for others, because they aren't supposed to be here. And that's just one for instance."

O'Hara's face cleared in understanding, "So, by taking them out of the game they weren't supposed to be playing in, balance is restored, though killing them is technically a 'bad' thing."

"Right."

"There are human people who do this?" Wizard asked.

"Yes, they work for Salil, while they live. It's their only job."

"Sucky job."

"Not for them. They seem to be peaceful about the whole thing. It fulfills their destiny and they know they are part of keeping things in balance here on Earth. They do get slightly energized, once they've tapped a person for death. It's all symbiotic, actually."

"Ok, so why would Salil get pissed about her being raised?"

"Because her soul would be dragged back from her place in the underworld. That's circumventing the whole death, judgment and rebirth process. That tends to piss a lot of Gods and Goddesses off. Not just Salil. I just used that one as an example. He is just one of many who would be displeased and could wreck havoc on the magick user who does it. That's why it is rarely done but to play our part, we take the head so this is never even a consideration for the rest of the Dark Coven."

"Kinda like taking temptation off of the plate."

"Right. Again, balance is kept for all concerned."

"So, Robertson having the body with the head still attached-that is a real bad thing."

"Yes, if he is that stupid."

"Do you think he is?" Wizard asked.

"No," before they could relax though, I added, "but, he is desperate. Look how many times he has tried to raid the Lair looking for one of us. Most likely me, but he would make do with anyone of us, hoping to eventually get me I'll bet. The repetition of coming in and then setting this up to gain information from Crimson... yeah, I'd say he is definitely desperate enough."

O'Hara took a deep breath. "Well, let's hope his common sense outweighs his desperation."

"Here, here," Demitri added.

Chapter Thirteen

Counter Balance

The day passed in sleep for me needing to regenerate from having astralled into the panther's body. O'Hara and his team went back to the base to update General Pierce on our situation and keep a weather eye on the goings on of General Robertson via the computers there, which were more advanced then what we had at home.

When I rose for the night, I tried, again, to get Crimson to let me in and help him with his grief, but he wasn't having any of it. I knew he had conscious control, asking him to show me his paw again, which a wild panther would not do. I should have been relieved with at least that much, but the mother in me was desperate, not only for his forgiveness, but for him to open up and let me help. I didn't want him suffering as I had with guilt and grief marring his soul and his outlook on life. I never wanted to see any of my children carry such a tremendous weight in their minds or souls. I wanted things easier for them then it has been for me. And, with him going through these things, I felt I had let him down as a parent.

Demitri constantly repeated to me, that there was nothing else I could have done. I had a choice to make, and at the time, it was the right one. He needed his warrior mother, not the safe mother part of me, at that particular time. He told me, sooner or later, Crimson would realize this and open up to me someday; that I would just have to be patient.

He didn't know Crimson as I did. Often, throughout his life, he had retreated from forming any bonds with me or his brothers. I never clearly understood why. I did know that again the fault was mine, in that going to college while raising such young children, I might not have hugged him enough or paid much attention to him as a child as I should have. But he was always so quiet, even at a young age. Often ghosting around the house, it was hard to recall he was in the home and may have needed me to be the one to reach out and hug or give him kisses.

The other two boys often tugged my side asking for attention, which I would immediately give them, but not Crimson. Crimson always seemed alone, even in a house that I'd tried so hard to fill with love, no matter what was going on with my life. That is until I got hit with a terminal illness when I was still human in body, and Crimson was around nine. When I fell ill, I had retreated to my room, so I wouldn't burden my children with my physical pain or my mental depression. I felt kids weren't meant to deal with something as serious as that. But doing that nailed the coffin shut on Crimson's habit of being a part of the family but still apart in his own world. When I had finally started to make a comeback with my health, the damage had been done. Though, I still had tried to reach out to him often, making it a point to ask for a hug or kiss at least once a day, to try to get him to open up and connect with the family again. Some progress had been made, but now this happened and I didn't know if I ever would be able to regain the ground I had lost with him.

It was these thoughts plaguing me, which drove me to the base to work out my frustrations on the obstacle course. I had to slow down my pace to human slow so the other soldiers there that were also training wouldn't see anything out of the ordinary, but it still allowed me to blow off some steam, regardless. I just went through the obstacle course many times to get my relief.

My third time through, I was nearing the end of the course where one had to run as fast as you could to the goal line, but I slowed my pace so I wouldn't be a blur of movement and give myself away as something other than normal. Bad enough I was a female, who could beat the bases record if I chose too, but flaunting my vampire abilities would be beyond stupid. Though the daylight did naturally drag me down, so it wasn't such a chore to reduce my capabilities.

At the end of the course, watching me was Captain Holland. He led the 53rd Marine Recon force under General Pierce and he had hated me on sight. Whether it was because I was female or a mercenary, or both, I still haven't figured it out. I'd had to take him down in the ring once, hoping to at least gain his respect as a fighter regardless of being a female, but it seemed to only make him hate me more.

"You know, sell-sword, men who go through this course once are pretty well spent. Few could go through it a second time. Three times and someone around here is going to realize something is off, especially for a fucking female." His chin was set in the expected hard pose, as if he was gritting his teeth inside his mouth. A pug face with a bald head and gun-metal blue eyes made his visage look like your typical Marine career Captain with the bulldog mentality to go along with it. Not my favorite person to deal with, even on a good day and today was not a good day.

Under these particular circumstances, I could keep my cool and deal with it. We weren't in a hostile situation and he wasn't the real enemy.

If I were in a situation that demanded quick cooperation, I would nail his ego to the ground. A female can't deal with an emergency and a male's macho crap at the same time, but this wasn't an emergency and we weren't on a mission, so I let the insults slide. Besides, the man had a point.

I had on my green fatigues and a black t-shirt to blend in with the other soldiers around us. But, he was right that nothing could hide the fact I was female with my long hair braided down my back. The whole sell-sword comments, that really meant, "bitch for hire", I always ignored.

I learned early that words like those were just a way to elicit a prescribed response. If one didn't react to them, the one using the words would have one less tool to use against you. You would have the advantage in any fight if you kept your cool. Marine training was not so different than what I had had. Calling the men maggots or dog shit was pretty much standard training and it was for a very good reason. Military men were trained to be fighters, to be killers. Having men sensitive to someone calling them a bastard or worse, and not have control, could land the soldier in Leavenworth for the rest of his life. It wouldn't matter if the civilian had started it. The fact that the soldier had lost his cool and would proceed to beat the shit out of the dumb-ass would still pretty much ruin his life. So, Drill Sergeants would use such derogatory remarks in training to de-sensitize the men from name calling by others. If some asswipe came up to a soldier in a bar and called him a motherfucker, the soldier would remember being called worse in training and be able to not respond with a fist in the dumb-asses mouth more often than not, thus, saving his military career.

I had gotten good at ignoring being called names, but if someone was bad-mouthing someone I loved, then all bets were off. It was a major flaw in my own training.

"You're right; I should have remembered that fact." I had to give him his due.

123

He still hadn't moved away and his expression was still set in a hard cast, "Is there anything else you needed to remind me of, Captain?"

"Sergeant Satori is due to leave Pearson's team now that he has put in his twenty. As you know, he is their NBC when the mission calls for it."

NBC was short for Nuclear, Biological and Chemicals specialist. They were the best and the brightest and had nerves filled with ice water. They had to be, to deal with the very scary shit one found on a mission which had nuclear bombs or chemical gases.

All right, we were losing a team member that has served his twenty and has opted to retire with his benefits. I was still trying to figure out why he was telling me this without me having to drag the information out of him or getting it from O'Hara, who always was the one before, who'd kept me abreast of the stats of any member on his Special Forces Team and Recon's.

Maybe the old boy was softening up to me? Nahhh. But, I decided to play nice. "Ok thanks, for the update. When will his replacement be coming?"

"Sergeant Loman will be here at the end of the week. *Sergeant Alice Loman* is finishing up her evaluation requirements in the new procedures for the latest missiles disarmament. Since it looks like she will pass with flying colors, headquarters has given me the heads up early, to prepare the rest of my platoon to the fact a soldier who has to squat to fucking piss will be joining us. This PC fucking crap is really pissing me off." His tone of voice had gotten louder and rougher towards the end of his update. That let me know he was so not the happy camper.

"And you have no say in it?" I was surprised. I had thought the Captain of any given platoon would have the yay or nay-say on any soldier coming into his platoon.

"Apparently, not with the General trying to gain brownie points with the Joint Chief of Staff. The Brigadier General has a soft spot for females being allowed in any military branch and given a chance to prove themselves fit for war. I don't give a rat's ass if having females in the military are good for our image. My main concern is that of my men. I can't have them slowing down in the field to cover a female who can't keep up."

I noticed he had a file in his hand and assumed it was Sergeant Loman's military records. "But, she had to have passed the physical requirements, didn't she?" I was confused about his problem with the situation.

"Fucking barely." He shoved the file at me.

I opened it and scanned her details within the folder and saw his problem. 130 lbs wet, if that, at 5'6. Fighting skills barely acceptable for a fighting unit like Recon, which was still pretty impressive but with what we did, one needed to be top notch or there could be complications. Even if Recon did just usual missions, she might still be a liability in seriously tough situations. I was all for equal rights and opportunities being a woman myself, but when up against a fighter who weighed twice what you do AND was trained as hard as a Recon Marine, most females would be outclassed. It was just a fact of nature.

What made her exemplary, were her skills in disarming anything from a saran gas bomb to a nuclear warhead in record time. She was a freakin' genius at neutralizing chemical hazards and explosives. Her skills as a NBC were above and beyond what even the best Recon had right now in the Captain's Platoon. It was just that she was so damned small and light: in a physical fight or an out and out long run, she would become a problem and not an asset. Her marksmanship with a rifle and gun were fine. Could be better, but good enough for the platoon. Her weight and fighting skills though, were woefully below what we needed for this particular team and our peculiar missions.

So what, was the Captain using me as a whipping boy for his headache? "Her skills are excellent except for the physical part. On paper though, she passes, if by the skin of her teeth, but she passes." I let the sound of a question hang in the air.

"Your sister is smaller than her."

I nodded cautiously, "About ten pounds lighter and two inches shorter."

"I've seen her run. I've watched her fight with you and with the men. And, she is still basically human." It was both a statement and a question.

"Yes, she is still fundamentally human." I added an addendum, "Physically, that is."

He grunted, "And you, you could fight like she does before you became a ..." He still couldn't say the word 'vampire' without wanting to spit nails, "what you are?"

"Yes, I was just as lethal as either of my sisters." If not more so, they had always had a conscious. At one point in my life, I did not.

"Since I have no choice but to accept this female into my troop, can you two evaluate her to see if she can be brought up to snuff for this particular platoon? I don't have the patience or the knowledge of

125

knowing how to bring her up to speed." This was a huge concession from him. To admit he didn't have the skills necessary to make a female tough enough for his squad and still ask someone else for help made me respect him and feel like shit for thinking he was just here to yank my chain about the problem. This was not my day.

He also wasn't going to take the easy way out and let her fail on her own with no blame falling on him for her failures. He was actually doing everything he could to make sure she had every opportunity to make the grade here with us. I was astounded.

"So, basically you are asking my sister and I to check her out and see if we can work with her?"

His lips tightened, "Yes."

"I have no problem with that and neither will my sister. But, we would ask one simple thing from you as her Captain."

"And, what would that be?" he said through gritted teeth.

"Don't make remarks about fucking female this and that. We need to have her confidence up. It will make our job easier."

He was now spitting. "See, the fucking special considerations because of being a fucking female has already started."

"You misunderstand me. It is the ONLY thing we will ask. You may ride her just as hard as the other men in any other circumstance. It's the mental bashing we need to curb, until we can get her prepared for it. For the things we will need her to learn to compensate for her weight and stature, she needs no mental road blocks to overcome. In anything else, she will have to pull her weight, just like any of the others here. Fair?"

A low grunt and a slight nod of his head was the only assent I was going to get and I would take it and be happy.

'Danger...invasion...backup needed.' Then, silence rang in my head again.

My eyes went wide and I pushed the file back at Captain Holland. "I've got to go. My home has been infiltrated somehow. Crimson is in danger."

I took off for my car at a hard run which was at the other side of the bases compound. Surprisingly, I heard Caption Holland hot on my heels, keeping up with me. I didn't look back, however. I didn't really care why he was still hounding me. I needed to get to my son. I couldn't translocate with this many witnesses around me and would have to drive off the base and pull off the road and hope for no traffic, before doing my disappearing act.

We both whizzed by security and out to the parking lot to my car. Holland was breathing hard, but went to the side of the car as if expecting to ride along.

"What are you doing, Captain?"

"Going with you. You said your son is in danger and your house has been compromised. Let's go."

"I was planning on translocating once I was down the road a bit." I opened my trunk and started pulling out my gear, putting on my wrist sheaths and gun holsters and popping open my gun box to add that hardware to my holsters. Then, I slid on my leather jacket and moved for the car door.

"Translocating?"

"Yes, instantly going from one place to another. No, I can't take you… you're too heavy." I had seen the question in his eyes before he even voiced it.

"I'm still going with you. You have no idea how many you'll be facing and Crimson is a Nightwolf. I may not agree with having Mercs mixing with military operations, but I will not stand by and let one of ours be without backup."

That bulldog face was there and unmovable. I gave in and allowed him in the car. Once I hit the highway, I floored it and opened all four carburetors.

His eyes were slightly widened at the speed which my '69 Nova was making, but he didn't make a comment about my driving. Instead he said, "We may need more than just you and me."

"I agree. Call O'Hara, then my brother Grant and fill them in." I let him make the calls while I slid in between cars, hearing honking behind me as I passed others on the road. I ignored them and focused on making up for the time not being able to get there by translocation.

We were in my driveway in record time, as I slammed on my brakes seeing a trailer backed up to the door with a metal cage with half of it tarped over. I saw a group of people and my mother standing around, tying off the tarp from the front. They were working their way to the back of the cage with large straps being thrown over. Inside the cage was Crimson's still body. My heart was in my throat and I tore out of my car and pulled my weapons from the holsters. I snapped the safety off of both nine mils. and locked on the two people with rifles in their hands. Captain Holland had his own pistol out and aimed at yet another target with a rifle who was showing he was wearing a sidearm still in its holster at his side.

127

In a tone that would make any drill instructor proud, I snapped out, "Who the fuck are you?"

Rifles started to point our way. "If those rifles lower any further I can and will shoot to kill."

"You're not military, Catrina," My mother raised her voice over the shouts from the people gathered around the front of my house.

"This is Texas. You've trespassed on my property. That gives us the right to shoot and kill any trespassers."

"You're not going to shoot your own mother, Catrina."

Captain Holland didn't care who she was related too. "Drop your weapons now or we will open fire."

Behind us I could hear my brother's car coming into the driveway with his sirens blaring. O'Hara was coming up behind him and suddenly we had more guns in our favor pointed at the asswipes trying to take my son.

"There is a lot you don't know, Mommy Dearest, and there is more that you're not cleared for. What you need to realize is that you've put these people's lives in jeopardy and I will kill these fuckers if they don't drop their weapons now."

"They're Animal Rights Activists and they have the right to take an animal they deem in trouble. You have no right to have such a large animal in your home, Catrina, and we will take the panther with us. How could you be so irresponsible and selfish as to trap a panther and cage it in your basement? I am ashamed of you."

I knew how things looked, but she didn't understand what, exactly, was going on. Even if she did, she would still be having kittens, but with the witch burning scenario instead of this vigilante crap.

"Personally Mother, I really don't give a damn how you feel about me anymore. What you need to worry about is how you're going to get yourself and your slug out of jail, because you have violated so many laws, I can make sure the both of you do time until the day you both die. I am so fucking close in giving those orders as it is, so I suggest you shut your fucking mouth before I bitch slap you for being a fucking idiot."

The look on her face was priceless. Any other time, I would have basked in it just for the sheer perverted joy in getting some kind of payback on her finally, after all these years. But, my main concern was what they might have given Crimson and what kind of harm it would do to him. I have heard too many stories of Animals Rights Activists going in and taking a large animal, only to put it down later, because they had no place for the animal. No zoo, no wildlife sanctuary. So, they put the

128

animal down and have the gall to say it was for the animals own good. Never mind if the owner of the animal had everything in place for keeping such a large breed. No, their only concern was getting the animal out and calling themselves heroes for doing it. Then, to add insult to injury, some of these activists sell the body parts to black market curios and places in the East where they sell Lion hearts and powdered brains that are supposed to be some herbal miracle cure for some serious illnesses and they use the funds to further their agendas.

I didn't agree with people owning large beasts as pets, either. They were meant for the wild and I had always thought these people were idiots for buying such an animal for a pet. But, the Animal Rights Activists weren't any better, in their supposed attempts to right wrongs for the animals by putting them to sleep and selling the parts to fund their next righteous vigilante mission.

Good intentions paving the way to hell and I would be damned if they were going to do that to my son. I would kill every single fucking person here and that included my own mother. She had finally crossed a line with me. Never fuck with my kids. I didn't give a shit that she didn't know that it was Crimson in that cage; it was the fact she had him in a dangerous situation, all for her fucking pride and phony righteous indignation.

"I am a Detective for the Corpus Christi police department. Drop your weapons and turn to face the wall. You are all under arrest."

A weaseled face guy, who looked to be the leader of this vigilante group, puffed up his chest in self importance. "What are the charges?"

"Trespassing, breaking and entering, assault, assault on military personnel. That one could have gotten you all killed on sight and saved me paperwork. Those charges are just the beginning. You people have no clue whose house you have entered and the harm you have caused. But, I promise you, you will regret it before the day is out. Now drop those weapons before the military drops you permanently; we will not ask again."

Slowly, they started to drop their weapons. About damn time. Did these people have no sense of self preservation or were they that freakin' ignorant?

As the weapons were put down on the ground, Grant directed them to raise their hands and face the wall. Except my mother, she wouldn't do as instructed. "That's my daughter."

Grant snorted and pushed her shoulder. "I don't give a fuck who you're related too. You're under arrest and will be charged right along with these folks."

"Catrina, your own mother. How could you?"

"Very fucking easily right now. Now shut up and do as he says."

Shock again raced over her face, but she finally turned and raised her hands above her head.

Since Grant and the others had everything under control, I raced to the cage and opened the back door to crawl inside. I put my ear to his chest and felt the rapid beating of his heart and breathed a sigh of relief.

"He's alive," I shouted so all our people could hear. Hoorahs roused and Captain Holland had crawled inside with me, tracing his hand over the big cat's chest to feel the beat. "Is the tempo normal? It feels fast."

"I have no clue about big cats. Small cats, yes, it's normal. Their heart rates are faster than a human, but I don't know about big cats being the same way." I was going to have to wait until all the witnesses were gone before I could remove whatever it was they had pumped into his panther's body. His heart rate was steady though, and not dropping, so I knew we had time.

"Do you have a vet for this kind of thing?"

"Well Lee, one of Cassie's mates, is the closest thing we have to an expert on big animals. He used to work at a zoo as a keeper. He aided the vets there in handling the animals because they always calmed down around him. He picked up a ton of knowledge there, but was working his way through college for a degree in computer programming. That was years ago, before he met Cassie."

"Where is he now?"

My face went white. "He was supposed to be here, watching over Crimson while I was gone."

"Shit." Captain Holland echoed my thoughts, as we both slid out of the cage and raced into the house.

We reached the basement only to see Lee lying there with a dart sticking out of his side. I removed the tranq dart and put my hands on his chest to feel a heartbeat that was too slow and slowing down even more, as I counted beats.

"How is he?"

"Dying. Quiet, while I work." My hands glowed bright with power and I heard Captain Holland's sharp intake of breath but I ignored it and focused on Lee. With his consciousness blacked out because of the tranquilizers, it was easy for me to invade his body with my spirit. I found the tranquilizers throughout his entire bloodstream and gathered it with my power of WILL. With my mind, I dissolved it into nothingness.

After getting rid of the poison to his system which was especially dangerous to one of our kind, I poured energizing energy into him and started to back out as his spirit awoke. I didn't want him to find me inside and take it the wrong way. He could zap me with magick without realizing I was in there only to help him. I had no clue what his first instinct would be in this situation. Most practitioners though, were of the sort to fire first and ask questions later. Normally, it was the right response.

I slipped out of Lee and into my own body, just as Lee started to groan.

"He's coming around." Holland had his fingers on his pulse. More than likely he was feeling it become stronger and steadier, now that that crap was out of Lee's system.

"He'll be fine now but there are still more people in this house. Stay here with him while I go check."

He nodded and I went back upstairs looking for the staff that was usually in the house as well, doing their chores and getting meals ready for us when we came home. I found most of them in the kitchen and went to work. Behind me, I felt a storm of power coming within my range. My mates had arrived, as well as more of my siblings. Grant must have called everyone in for the emergency. I was glad, because some of these people were critical. The dose of the darts had to have been gauged for a large animal that could metabolize such a strong dose, but for a mere human, it could overdose them easily and cause death, if not attended to quickly. In Lee's case, it was even more dangerous, since our metabolisms often didn't deal well with any kind of sedative. (except for me and my three earth-side mates). Since becoming vampires, it didn't mess us up too badly anymore.

My mates poured into the room and I nodded to the sleeping people. "Tranquilizers, large animal dose." Then I went back to focusing on Marie our head housekeeper. A gentle lady I was fond of. She'd never hurt anyone and was kind to anyone she met. She would never think of fighting back or doing another person the slightest harm. She must have been so scared when they came in with rifles and pointed them at her.

I could hear Demitri snapping out orders for some to heal and others to search the rest of the house and grounds for more casualties.

As I finished with my healing, I looked at the rest of the room seeing everybody was taking care of the rest. I looked down into my hand and stared at the dart and stood up.

I stalked outside and saw that Grant had everyone on their knees and in handcuffs. I went to the weasel guy I had pegged for the leader of this sad excuse for human beings and grabbed him by his shirt, easily lifting him off the ground. I back handed him across his face with a loud slap and threw him back down where he landed on his side. Grant had grabbed me from behind. "Chill out, Catrina. We got them. Easy."

Shaking with anger, I spitted out, "I want them charged with attempted murder." I went to kick the punk and missed, because Grant had moved me bodily out of range of connecting. "I want every single one of these fuckers charged with attempted murder. They damn near killed Lee. They damn near killed everybody in there. I want their asses." My voice was shrieking. I was close to losing it and killing them myself. I didn't care what happened after I did it.

I felt O'Hara land on top of us, bringing me down to the ground. A dog pile of bodies landed on me in a mountain of flesh following him. I groaned under the weight and tried to move.

"Move off of her. I got this," I heard Demitri's command. Slowly, the weight lifted off me and I could breathe again.

"Are you sure?" Grant asked. "I've only seen her this pissed off once before and the fallout was nasty."

"I got it. She won't kill anyone today." All the weight lifted off me at once and Demitri reached down and grabbed me by my jacket, lifting me up against his body and immediately sinking his teeth into my neck in one smooth move.

It happened so quick, I was shocked into immobility for second. And that was all he needed, as I felt the sting of a needle slide into my flesh through my pants.

Looking down, I whispered, "Shit."

Just as before, it was too late to stop the tranq from sending me into blackness.

Chapter Fourteen

Blind Sided

Grant's shocked look was echoed through the group surrounding Catrina as she slept in Demitri arms. "What the fuck did you do?"

Demitri's voice was hollow, "Tranqed her. She'll sleep for a while now."

"She is going to fucking kill you when she wakes up."

Demitri sighed heavily, "Yeah, she is going to be pissed."

"No, she is going to fucking kill you," Grant was pissed and at Demitri.

"Grant, you didn't see her aura. She was going into a rage. She would have thrown you off and ripped the throats out of everyone here. Being pissed at me will seem like a cake walk in comparison to that. Or did you want her to kill?"

"We had her under control."

"You had shit. Once she got her leverage, she would have been out and killing."

Grant stopped his tirade long enough to try to understand what Demitri was saying. "Ok, maybe you're right, but man, you are in deep shit once she rouses. How the fuck are you going to deal with that mess?"

"Better that kind of mess then you having to order more body bags and Catrina being brought up on charges for murder."

"The law here would have covered it. We have clearance to shoot to kill in this kind of situation. It is a miracle no one here was shot." His face had the look of 'yet' on it. As if he was looking for any excuse to kill any one of them, handcuffed or not.

"The laws here, yes, we could have cleared her, but what about the Coven's Laws? No one at the time was under threat of body or spiritual harm. She would have had no defense in an astral court. Her Mother would have had no choice but to punish her...again... for acting without just cause or permission from on high. And that on high is her Mother Goddess. Your Mother. Or did you forget what happened last time?"

Grant looked at Demitri and remembered just how harshly Catrina was dealt with the last time she'd taken the law into her own hands. He looked sadly at his sister as she slept cradled closely to Demitri's body.

"You're gonna need knives. Lots and lots of knives."

"I'll deal with her when she awakens. Just get Crimson safely inside and tended to, and get this trash off my lawn." Catrina's mother glared at him, whether it was because of the way he had held Catrina as if she was a precious burden, or in response to what he'd said. He didn't really give a shit.

Demitri carried Catrina inside and up the stairs to gently lay her in his bed. On the way up, he had cautioned everyone to stay away from this side of the house until he and Catrina had dealt with their issues. Then, he calmly waited for her to wake, no matter how long it took. He didn't feel bad for what he'd done. No, not at all; but, he'd be damned if he would let her put herself in such a situation again. He'd sell his own soul first, before letting her suffer through another ordeal like that. Better her angry at him, then the shit she had already been through, he thought. It will be worth it.

Hours Later that same day

The sun had set and the house was quite. Too quiet. I could hear the familiar breathing of one of my mates in the room with me, but not much else stirred within my hearing.

I sat up and looked around, seeing Demitri sitting in the chair near the bed with a look of grim determination on his face.

I watched him wait for my reaction and I knew what he was expecting. I also knew he wouldn't do anything to hurt me, even to defend himself from any attack I might throw at him.

I moved to the edge of the bed and sat there, seeing that I was still dressed. I even had my jacket on with all of my weapons. Man, he must love me or he'd overlooked everything I was carrying on me. I was betting on the first part.

"Is Crimson all right?"

"Lee tended to him. He'll be fine."

"I am really pissed at you."

"I know that."

"That was underhanded."

"I won't apologize for it."

"I didn't think you would."

I stood up, feeling slightly dizzy still from the tranquilizer, but made myself move towards the door. Demitri moved quickly to block me.

"Where are you going?"

"Out."

"Please don't leave. I had no other choice."

I looked at him and saw his fear. He was afraid I would pack my things and walk right out the door. If he was anyone else, other than a mate, I would do exactly just that. However, I loved him. I loved him deeply and unconditionally. I also remembered the pain I had caused him before, when we were just starting out, just trying to get bonded so we could search for each other physically. Pain I swore I would never cause him again. I reached up and caressed his face. "I'll be back."

"Promise?"

"Absolutely," then I glared at him just a bit, "then we'll have that talk."

I felt him relax and he moved out of my way. Having me bitch him out was more preferable to him than me leaving. I inwardly laughed at the situation.

"Promise me, too, you won't do anything irrevocable?"

I stopped and turned to him. "I'll try." I wouldn't lie to him, but I couldn't absolutely promise him, and he knew this. He let me walk out with what he could get out of me.

I drove carefully to the police station, knowing my brother would still be neck deep in paperwork. Sure enough, he was at his desk with a pile of sheets on both sides of him and a smaller stack right in front that he was working his way through.

"Sorry about this." I waved at all the work in front of him, knowing he hadn't gotten shit for sleep for days now.

He looked up, shocked to see me there. "Not your fault. Demitri alive?"

I gave him an evil grin, "For now."

He shook his head and leaned back, "Unbelievable."

His face looked haggard from lack of sleep. I wondered when the last time was that he'd had a meal with his mates. One of them was due to give birth soon and if he hadn't been home to eat, he also hadn't been home to sex any of his mates, but especially Sheryl, who was carrying his baby. We needed sex often, not only for the energy, but if pregnant, the females needed it for the enzymes in a male's sperm that helps with dialation for giving birth. Without it, labor was long and hard. It also could get extremely dangerous for our kind. Humans, too, needed this enzyme for easier birthing, but our female bodies burned through them too fast or were incapable of creating the enzyme for ourselves, like me. The only other way for us to get that enzyme was through sex. He'd had to put his female's needs aside to deal with my bullshit and that just made me angrier with my physical mother.

"I need another favor, bro."

His expression turned cautious. "What kind of favor?"

"I need you to get me into the pen, so I can have a chat with Mommy Dearest."

"You're not going to do anything stupid, are you?"

"What do you think?" I gave him my best innocent look.

He snorted in disbelief. "Don't even try it. I know you better than that."

"Just get me in there."

"Fine, but cleaning up dead bodies in the pen is harder than you think. Please don't make more work for me," He pleaded.

"Trust me."

"Fuck." But he took me downstairs to where the prisoners were being held, until they were either moved to the main jail or they had a quick arraignment at the courthouse a block away.

My mother was there sitting on the edge of the small bed in her cell. I had never seen her in a cell before. This was a nice turn of events. Usually, it was her staring at me through the bars, telling me to get myself out, because she'd be damn if she'd bail me out. The first time, I was a mere thirteen years old and I had been framed for the crime. She didn't care. She never did.

"So, have you come to your senses and come to get your mother out of this cell, Catrina?"

Her tone of voice still hadn't changed. No remorse. No guilt. Just this judgmental 'I am holier than thou' sound rang through her mouth.

"What was it you said to me time and time again? You got yourself into this hole, you get yourself out? Yeah, that was it. I think you need to learn to practice what you preach."

She went to give me the up and down disapproval glare she had down pat, but stopped when she saw I was still wearing my guns in their holsters. My jacket was open and one could see the flashes of weapons hanging at my sides.

"Who or what are you, Catrina, that you can come into a police station wearing guns, can call in military people and have them back you up and have a large panther in your basement and no one fines you for it?"

"That is none of your business and you'll never know now. The main thing you do need to know is this, woman. If you do manage to worm your way out of these pretty damn serious charges, you are never to email me, call me, or even write me a letter. You are to never come near your grandsons again, in any form. If you come near any one of us, at any time, for any reason, large or small, I will pull in favors you wouldn't believe, have you up on charges as a potential terrorist, where they will lock you up and throw away the key. You won't get a lawyer, you won't get past go and you won't ever see the light of day again. Are we clear?"

"How could.."

"Shut up...ARE.WE.CLEAR?"

My eyes were burning a bright green with power now, I could tell, but I didn't care if she saw it or not, and didn't bother putting on my sunglasses. Power she hasn't seen me use since I was a child. I let her see that there was still something unusual about me. I let her see, and finally I saw the fear grow in her eyes.

She let out a breathless, "Yes."

I let her see and then I walked away from her. I was done trying to be her daughter. I was done trying to be anything to her. She was now on her own and I hoped her God helped her if she ever got into trouble, because I sure wouldn't... ever again.

I sat with my brother at his desk and helped him with his paperwork using a little misdirection spell, so no one would see me actually sitting there doing paperwork that should be for cops only. It was barely legal for me to cast the spell, but my brother needed to get home and be with his mates. Some serious family time with food, sleep and lovin' and in that order, I told him, as I helped him with his paper avalanche.

I drove back home to my own mate, who I knew would be waiting anxiously for me. I wanted to go to a home to people who loved me. To people who cared about my wellbeing, even before their own. I went home giving thanks to the Gods I had such love in my life, finally.

Right after I tortured my mate with a feather for a few hours. It was either that, or the couch; but he did deserve something for sticking that damn needle in my ass instead of his dick. True, fucking me on the front lawn might have been a little excessive, but damn it, being sneaky with the needle like that? Oh no, my sweetheart must pay. Yeah, hours of teasing ought to be just the thing to teach him better. I smiled an evil smile all the way home.

Chapter Fifteen

A Pincher

Thanks for saving Lee yesterday." Cassie was in her stance and throwing knives at the board with a steady thump, thunking it into the wood. The board was four feet wide and seven feet tall with a human target painted in the middle with small bulls-eyes targets where each major artery in the human body would be. Though, in real life your target is usually moving, it still helped to train for aiming for the arteries to bleed out your enemy faster in a fight.

We had been taking turns for the past hour practicing with knives, Shurikens and Cassie's favorites, Senbons. Small, two and a half inch long needles with feathers like a dart, to help in accuracy when throwing at an enemy. Hit an artery and they bleed a person out pretty quickly with its tiny barbed hooks. Most didn't see or know about the hooks and went to pull them out and wind up doing even more damage. Some didn't have hooks and were made for hitting the pressure points in a human body. If your throw was dead on you could paralyze a person or a body part on them and kill them with ease. I didn't like them as much as she did, because they could be thrown off the mark because the tips were so fine and wind up just pissing off your target, if they didn't hit their mark, they didn't do much harm. With a knife, even on a bad throw you had a better chance of doing some major damage.

"No problemo. That's what family is for, isn't it?"

She smiled, "Your mate is all right, now?"

"Which one?"

"Demitri."

I felt my cheeks turn a little red. "Yeah. He'll live."

She started chuckling. "I'll have to remember that one the next time one of my mates angers me."

I had gone home and stripped Demitri, handcuffing him to the bed. I used an aphrodisiac cream that tasted like honey and rubbed it all over his body. The cream heated up the skin, making it sensitive and tingling with need. For hours I teased him to a fever pitch then made him watch Ja' Monel, Ja' Callum and I have sex while I tasted him with my tongue. Never enough to satisfy, but mercilessly kept him hard and aching for me to finish him. He was begging profusely, before I showed any mercy and uncuffed him. After that he was like a hurricane in bed. He was everywhere and everywhere in a hurry. I still had tender spots when I walked too fast. So, I felt like he had gotten his revenge on my body. Though, the revenge he took on me was pretty enjoyable.

"You're thinking about it again."

"How the hell do you all know our entire sex life?"

She just shook her head and laughed.

"It's not fair. I don't know shit about what goes on with you and yours."

She said with a touch of rebuke in her tone, "You've been too busy to look around."

"Well gee, sis, let's see how many things I have to keep track of now."

She held up her hand. "Stop. I know how much you have to deal with and more mates on top of that, but I will be taking General Pierce's Brigadier General across the portal tomorrow and you haven't even asked what kind of plans I have in store for him."

I threw another knife into the board. "Why should I worry about that? You know what you're doing in that regard better than I do. I don't know shit about Brigadier Generals or what makes them tick. You'll have a better chance of feeling him out and knowing how to get him to do what we need. I'll just piss him off, if it were me talking to him."

She growled, "You aren't really here are you?"

"No, not really." I threw another knife.

She gave a small shriek. "That's what I have been trying to tell you. You haven't been *here* for a while now. We're happy you're happy, but you are losing your edge and you could not only get yourself killed, but us, too."

I put the rest of the knives down and turned to face her. "I have my astral 'I' in Trinidad right now taking care of my business that I should be doing. I have half my brain on General Robertson, who is having a meeting right now with Williams and I have been trying to hear the conversation since they are not under a shield," I paused. "Damn it.

They just went into the hotel room and he has that heavily shielded now." I continued my list, "I am running every shape shifting and dark spell I have ever read or heard about with another part of my brain to help my son and let's see. Oh yes, a little more responsibility in training a human female soldier to fight as near to our level as I can get her, who starts in two days. Is there anything else you'd like to add to my plate, because I'm sure I can find more room?' I added sarcastically.

She gazed down to the ground. "I'm sorry."

I started to walk away and she grabbed my arm. "I am sorry, Catrina. I didn't realize you had so many parts of you in so many different places, too. You know having your inner selves split apart like that is dangerous, if done for too long?" Her eyes were back on me with worry in them now.

"Do you realize I had over three hundred babies I needed to give names too? I had let my responsibilities slide for far too long on Trinidad, but she'll be done in another day or two, I'm hoping, then I'll be more whole inside again."

She gave a half grin. "This has got to be some kind of record to be split apart for so long and not lose your sanity or your soul part."

"It's probably what made me so slow in Kansas when I got caught."

Her grin left her face. "You need to be more careful, sister. We can't afford to lose you."

Wow, she cared. It still shocked me when one of them would say something concerning my wellbeing. Nobody had ever cared before, except my kids.

I gave her a hug, saying, "I'll be fine but we need to find out why Special Agent Williams is in Texas with General Robertson. That can't be good and I didn't hear anything worth noting."

She patted my hand. "I'll send Danny on it and see if we can't get close enough physically to pick up on something. He can't keep his secrets forever from us."

I could feel when she mentally contacted her other mate, Danny, to give him his detail. Her mates were quick to respond to anything needed so I knew the hotel would be covered in a matter of minutes. Danny was the closest one to the area out of all our mates. My Kla' din mates had returned to their world to oversee their holdings and would be back in two more days. My Earth-side mates had gone to the Corpus Christi downtown office. Another board meeting via telecom, another round of paperwork to be had by all, I supposed. Being heads of a huge corporation meant ten times the work of say a manager of a small business. It's no wonder heart attack statistics were up, since most CEO's and the like, worked an average of 120 hours a week. It was one of the points I had brought up to Demitri when he was still human and also had high blood pressure. What good was all that money, if one didn't take the time to actually enjoy it? His own physical father had died practically at his desk from a heart attack. I had started begging him to slow down and enjoy the fruits of his labor, damn it. These power movers worked even while playing golf. Many business deals were made on the golf course. A game that was supposed to be for fun and relaxation, has now turned into a place for even more work. At least Demitri had listened to me and was pulling back his work hours by delegating to others. Though we were immortal, now he and his brothers needed to spend time not only with me and work on building our relationship, but the mission The Nightwolves went on so frequently also demanded a lot of time. Great; so much for slowing down. We were still working, ughhh. Well, at least we had time for our sex life now. And that reminded me.

I snorted, "No shit, you guys know my sex life. Finding out what Robertson is up to should be a piece of cake." More work instead of sex- just freakin' fantastic, I snorted to myself.

A wicked look came across her face. "You're not exactly quiet, dear."

My mouth dropped open. "What?" And she ran for the house, escaping my question.

I took off after her. "Hey, get back here."

I shook my head as I chased her. Well, we were friends again and that made me happy. I would hate to lose the closeness I'd found with Cassie. Somehow Cendra, Gaston and I would have to find a better relationship too. A Coven was only as strong as its weakest link and we couldn't afford any weakness within our Coven. So one way or another, Cendra, Gaston and I would have to mend our fences. That should be interesting. If only it could be as easy as it was between Cassie and I.

142

Chapter Sixteen

Cheapo

Robertson sat at the table in the hotel with Williams and showed him everything he had gathered from the crime scene of the murder of his spy.

"This empty bag is coated with a powerful spell. What was the spell for?" Williams carefully handed back the shredded bag that Robertson had found by the front door of Vanessa's home.

"From the powder we found on the floor, it is called The Deatramvomacrum. An ancient, powerful, shapeshifting spell I helped her manifest. She was to use it as a last resort. A plan that obviously went wrong, since I don't have the animal in my hands," He growled.

"What animal?"

"If all else failed, she was to turn Catrina's son into an animal, like a cat or a dog. Something we could control easily and use to make Catrina come to us. There was no animal found in Vanessa's house or the alleyway," he grunted, "Well, we found a few alley cats, but there was nothing special about any of them, so we disposed of the bodies."

"Well, you have the print. It is a start in finding her house. You can go to D.C. and see what they can find there?"

"It may be the only choice I have left. Or I could turn the Vampire Prince lose and let him track her. He has tasted her blood."

"That is something, but then again, having those two meet up might not be a wise thing. What if they make a deal? Things could go badly, then."

"It is my last resort option. I will keep going until all else fails, before I open that can of worms."

"Prudent," Williams smiled.

"How goes things with placing more of our kind in office this coming election?" Robertson asked.

"Things are looking up. The people are in an uproar over the present administration. It will be easy getting enough of ours into office this term. By 2012, we should be able to take over any other branch we don't control at the end of this election. And your agenda? Any problems?"

"A few, but nothing I can't overcome before my deadline. It is harder to get the right kind of people placed into positions of power in the Pentagon with offices that are not elected, as yours are. Some of these people are career officers. Some of them refuse to leave their desks, until the day they die. For those, we make that day happen sooner, rather than later, but we can't do it too often or too close together. Thankfully, the first part of our plan went off without a hitch and we can move more freely now."

"Yes, making sure the AI computer at the Pentagon was disrupted during the 9-11 attack, was a stroke of genius. Now, they don't have the tools that would have warned them. It will be too late before they realize just how much we have taken over their seats of power."

Robertson grinned. "They still can't get that damned machine to work right or find the missing money we used up." Over a trillion dollars gone and will never be found now. He laughed, "It is amusing to watch them try though." His face grew serious. "Yes, that machine had to go. It was too damned accurate in predicting things happening before they happened, whether it was financial or a natural disaster. The AI computer was dangerous to us." He leaned back in his chair. "But, no more. They'll never get it to work the way it did. They never knew exactly how they'd gotten it to work the way it did in the first place. The damned thing was an accident from its conception."

Williams laughed, "Much like the making of Champagne eh?"

Robertson grinned. "Yes. You and I will be opening a bottle for ourselves very soon."

Williams grew serious again. "As soon as you get this Catrina out of our business. We must do something about her and soon, or all could be lost for the both of us."

Robertson was about to comment when they both felt the same bone chilling air fill the room. A few seconds later, there was an authoritive knock on the door to Robertson's room.

Robertson opened the door, feeling dread pulse through his body and soul. Two tall, gray cloaked figures were standing there. Without a word, they moved silently into the room, not waiting for Robertson to invite them in.

Williams stood up quickly and dropped to his knees with his head bowed, before the terrifying duo.

Robertson quickly followed suit, after he had closed the door.

"My Lords," both of them echoed in greeting.

Robertson and Williams may have been High Dark Priests of their respective Covens, but these two represented two of the Seven Lords of The Grand Coven. They were the true beings of power that all Dark Covens the world over followed…and feared. From Robertson's position, he could see the upside down gold filigree Catholic Cross hanging from a belt tied around the gray cloak. The Seven Lords wore these crosses in this fashion, not because they were Satanists, but in honor of Grand Master Jacques De Mollay, who had cursed both King Phillip of France and Pope Clement who had turned on the Templar's in 1307. A curse that came to fruition within the year had commanded the deaths of them both. After being betrayed by The Church, The Templars had left Europe with eighteen Galleys loaded with gold. Ships filled with a treasure to outdo any treasure in history that was never seen again. Not only were those ships filled with gold and jewels, but with thousands of years of Occult knowledge. Papyri scrolls from the Alexandrian Library and many others like it that were not turned over to the Church. The Church had demanded all such esoteric knowledge and objects of worship be taken to the Vatican and put into its' vaults, never to be seen again by the heathens they'd conquered. Objects of power the Church used themselves, from time to time. When conquering a heathen nation, they would make it look like they were burning such pagan items in the name of God, but secretly hiding them away. Some of it went to the Church, but some the Templars kept from them, not trusting the Church wholly in not using the more dangerous objects of power. Yes, more than gold went into those ships that night and General Robertson knew his history well.

The Templars then formed The Grand Coven and renounced the church and civilization, swearing someday they would take over the world and rule. Seven Lords who could trace their bloodlines to the surviving Templars that fled Europe that night hundreds of years ago. Each generation swearing Allegiance to the Grand Coven and slowly, insidiously taking over world financial trades and businesses of power using magick, assassins, or stealth. Some called them Freemasons, some called them Bilderbergs and some say Illuminati, but the true name was known only to gray cloaked Lords.

145

To the other smaller Dark Covens worldwide, some hiding in plain sight as Freemasons, they were known to them as The Grand Coven and all did as the Seven Lords bid. Their power was absolute and ruthless; and they were here in Robertson's room. May the Dark God help him.

One of the gray cloaked figures spoke. "Why hasn't the woman been captured, yet?"

"My Lord, please we..." Williams started.

"Silence. We do not want excuses," commanded the first gray cloaked Lord.

The second one hissed, "You both are failing us. Failing The Grand Coven after we gave you the ancient spell for transformation."

The spell Robertson had begged for from the Gray Lords so he could use it to control Catrina. He'd had to tell them about her and her abilities to gain their interests and aid in capturing her again. Robertson's plan had been to grab Catrina, using her to get The Prince to turn him, and then he would turn Catrina over to the Gray Lords for more knowledge in the Ancient Arts. But, the plan had failed and now Vanessa was dead. Another thing Catrina has to pay for. Vanessa was a favorite of his and quite powerful in her own right.

Robertson's forehead was beading with sweat. "I have tried several times to reacquire her. She is always slipping away. I have gone to the club many times to try to catch her. She always eludes me."

The first gray Lord barked, "Then, fool, make her come to you."

"How? She knows the base in Kansas is filled with men loyal to us."

"IDIOT. Must we do everything? Create a situation she will have to investigate. Chose a place far from either her base of power or yours and grab her there."

The second cloaked figure spoke menacingly, "Lure her away from her base of operations and into territory she is not familiar with. We have been shown children are her weakness. That should put the odds in your favor and you had better not fail us again."

"Yes, My Lord. It shall be as you say." His mind was already spinning with plans.

"We have allowed you two to combine your covens, since America's Pentagon and Congress are so tightly bound together. No others have had your advantage and still, you fail us."

"Others, My Lord?" Robertson dared to ask.

"Yes, there are others. It takes more than one area of power to take over a nation. Financial, Medicine, Agriculture and Education must be controlled, as well. Military, Congress, Senate are critical to our plan.

There are seven areas that must be in our hands for us to rule this nation. If we can control The EU, America and the U.N., we can bring the whole world to its knees, finally. The New World Order shall be ushered in."

"Our Grand Ancestors will rest in peace. The first two stages of our plan have gone off without a hitch. There will be no other time more advantageous, as the Prophecy grows nigh. With the Magickal Races coming back, we can utilize their powers and strength and rule till the end of time."

"You will help us to bring America in line with the others, and this woman and her Coven will bleed for us," The second cloaked figure gloated.

The first gray Lord stepped closer to Robertson. "She and her Coven must be brought in chains. If we control her, we can control her Coven, and also her Goddess."

"But, a Goddess, My Lord?" Robertson was shocked; no one could control a God or Goddess. It was impossible.

"Not impossible, you fool." Robertson was surprised the gray one had read his mind so easily. "She is favored by The Triple Goddess. We have seen this in the Mirror. If we capture her, we can use her to make The Triple Goddess our very own slave."

"A vampire favored by a Goddess? Why is she so privileged?" Robertson was now shaking with fear. To take on a Goddess was suicide. Others have been cursed until the end of time with horrendous outcomes. Yet, The Lords knew of things he didn't. Knowledge of the Arts he would kill for. His determination grew, despite his fear. Determination and greed.

"That hasn't been shown to us...yet. You will find out for us when you have her in your possession. Is that clear?"

"Yes, My Lord." Any other answer would be impossible and Robertson knew if he succeeded at this task he would be able to ask for more training. Training other High Priests didn't have and never would. He could be almost Godlike with the knowledge of the Arts the Lords knew. Any risk was worth gaining that knowledge. And Catrina was now his key to it. The Prince would be his key to immortality. He would be invincible. He quickly shut these thoughts out of his head, before it was picked up by either of the gray cloaked Lords.

There was still that pack of dogs in Louisiana that could either be brought to heel or used to entice Catrina out the safe nest she has built here. Yes, those dogs that had turned him down before, still had their uses. It will be a pleasure to yank on their chain yet again.

Chapter Seventeen

Queen's Pawn

assie had taken off with Brigadier General Halbert Bruhest and his men, along with her mates, except for Lee, who had stayed behind to help me with Crimson. A Recon team went with them just in case, but I seriously doubted anything untoward would happen to any of them. Trinidad was peaceful and Kla' din only had the Draugralls to worry about, who weren't due for another attack for three weeks. They had missed the last cycle, which was both good and bad. Good, because no one was attacked during the last conjunction of the three moons phase; but bad, because it probably meant they were up to something unusual. With the schedule the Kla' dins had, the Draugralls were at least pretty much predictable and could be dealt with. Now, however, they have recently changed their habits and that left us worrying about what new tricks they could be cooking up and what it might mean for Kla' din and its people who were already beleaguered under the systematic attacks.

Danny had reported back to us of seeing something highly unusual going into, then out of, the hotel room of General Robertson. He would have missed it, if he had not been looking out of his third eye at the time, trying to find a weakness in Robertson's shield. He told us of two dark beings walking in and staying for over a half hour in the room. Then, they had left the room the same way. The thing that was incredible Danny said, was no one else could see them. When he used his normal vision, there was nothing but a cold feeling in the immediate area, but when he used his second sight, he could see the two beings walking down to the parking lot when they opened up an astral doorway between two cars and disappeared. What freaked him out was that these beings seemed human, but with very large auras, meaning they held a lot of power. There was no third band of color in their auras, so they

149

weren't demi-Gods like we were, but with the amount of power they held, they were damn close he said.

The fact that they had enough power and knowledge to even open up an astral doorway without being near a node of power was impressive and worrisome. In Ancient times, the only ones we were aware of that could transport from one place to another using astral doorways were The Druids, who were mostly massacred by St. Patrick, and Egyptian Mages of old. What was also in the old texts belonging to our Coven was the fact that they used power nodes and ley-lines for the energy boost. Yet, these two people or beings didn't, and that was very odd.

Today was my meeting with Sergeant Alice Loman. O'Hara and General Pierce had already filled her in about the Mercenary part of Special Forces and The Marine Recon 53rd fighting force and our special 'abilities'. O'Hara had told me she took it rather well on the surface, but to watch her while training to see if she had dissimulated during the debriefing. I hoped for her sake she hadn't, or she could find herself serving the rest of her career in some arctic outpost where a few have already been sent; or worse, sent off to Leavenworth.

Both Captain Holland and Sergeant Loman were waiting for me as I reached the obstacle course on the base. I took my position to the right of Captain Holland and faced Loman as a superior officer would.

Captain Holland barked at her, "This is Commander Catrina Garcia. She will be overseeing your adjustment here with this platoon. You are to follow her orders to the letter, as you would a superior officer. Is that clear?"

"Yes, Sir," came the sharp response.

"She's all yours. Keep me updated." Without a backward glance, he stormed off the obstacle course and left me to it. Well, he did keep his word about not making any nasty female comments. It was a start.

She stood there, not quite looking at me, but still at attention. She had dark brown hair and hazel blue eyes. She was pretty without being too pretty for a soldier. She'd clean up nice though, if she had a mind to. She didn't look soft, but not as defined in muscle tone as I would have liked. A few months with the weight bench will change that, though.

I asked in a conversational tone to throw her off guard and watched for her reaction, "Sergeant Loman, how are you enjoying your move here to the base?"

"Sir... Ma'am?" looking slightly confused, but not afraid or put off. That was good.

"Call me Cat. Are you warmed up?"

"Yes Sir...Ma'am."

I sighed. This was going to be a long day, I could tell. "Good," I pulled my stop watch out of my pockets. "Hit that course now and move your ass."

She took off like a shot and was running to hit the first line. I watched her run, climb, swing, and jump over the various equipment placed around the course and saw her run out of steam halfway through it. Her speed slowed down even more once she hit the barbed wire, where a soldier had to get on his or her belly and scramble underneath the lines of wire without getting caught up. She was panting as she made it through and was hitting the home stretch in a flat out run to the end of the line.

I clicked the watch, as she crossed and she slowed down, out of breath and turned to look at me.

I pressed my lips together. "Not good enough, Sergeant." I showed her the time.

"But, that's 33 seconds faster than the bare minimum."

"Not good enough," I growled.

Her eyes widened and her back stiffened. "I'd like to know what is good enough, Sir."

Good, this kitten had claws.

I handed her the watch, "How about I show you what is good enough?"

Never ask of someone else what you wouldn't do yourself, came the old instruction in my mind. Though my old teacher was a first class sociopath and an assassin, but he was good at what he did.

Once she clicked the timer, I took off and ran the course with only half my abilities opened up. If I had a mind to, I could be a blur for about five miles, before I used up my energy and would still be faster than a normal human. I wasn't even breathing hard when she clicked it, to see the time I had made. Her mouth dropped open.

"That's impossible."

I snorted, "Obviously not."

"I won't be able to do that. I'm not like you."

I gave her a hard stare. "Nothing is impossible and yes, you can do this."

"I don't see how."

"Either you learn how to do this or you will be bounced out and transferred elsewhere. Is that what you want?"

"No Sir," snapping to attention again.

"Cat," I corrected her. "Nothing is impossible. Let me here you say it."

"Nothing is impossible."

I repeated loudly, "I can't hear you."

She said it louder, "Nothing is impossible!"

I put my arm around her and guided her to the workout room. "Good, now come with me, grasshopper. You have much to learn."

Chapter Eighteen

Central Pawn

Apparently, the Brigadier General still wanted to meet with me, regardless of having seen Kla' din and Trinidad. So, I scheduled a meeting with him before another training session with Loman. This way, I had an 'out' of a potentially difficult meeting. I really hated smoozing. I was really bad at it.

"It's nice to meet you Catrina Garcia. You've become something of a legend, I hear."

His greeting was warm and he motioned me to the seat before General Pierce's desk. General Pierce was not included in this meeting and that made me nervous.

Taking the offered seat, I replied, "I doubt that. I haven't been associated with the military for very long."

"Ahh yes, but it's what you've accomplished already, that has made you a legend. That nuclear missile in Pakistan, for instance."

"Sergeant Miller's NBC took care of that. I was already unconscious by then. Don't see how that could have made me into a legend?"

"True, but you got them in there. You also disrupted things enough for them to do their jobs and without losing men doing it. That's something of a miracle. No matter how well laid a mission is there is usually loss. You've cut down those statistics drastically. That's legendary."

I didn't comment, not knowing what to say about that. If he wanted to think legendary, let him, so long as he helped us keep doing what we were doing. I didn't give a shit.

He looked at me with a sideways glance. "So, what do you think of our current administration?"

Well that was a question out of left field. "I hate politics. Not my problem."

"So, you don't vote?"

"Oh, I vote. I vote religiously now, ever since 'he who must not be named' got put into office illegally."

"Excuse me?"

I smiled at him. "You don't watch movies, do you?"

"No, I'm afraid not. Would mind clarifying that for me?"

I sighed inwardly. No wonder those in Congress were so out of touch with the people.

"The last President got appointed by the Supreme Court, violating our Constitutional voting election. That pissed me off. Now I vote."

He nodded. "And this President?"

"He who has no balls."

His eyes widened, as if looking for that definition, as well, "He lets people, other leaders, bad mouth America. He doesn't back up his own policies with any conviction. He has no balls."

"So, you voted Republican?"

"No, mostly Green, actually."

He gave me a quizzical look, pointing to my file. "But, it says here, you are a registered Republican."

"Being a registered Republican allows me three things as a citizen and a single mother."

His gaze looked at me expectantly.

"One, when I was in college, I was allotted more grant money then if I had been Democrat or not affiliated with politics. Two, it allows me to slap the Republican Party in the face every time I vote for the other guy, despite being registered in their party. Three, it amuses my twisted sense of justice."

He shook his head. "You are a rebel to the core aren't you?"

I shrugged.

"But, throwing your vote to a small third party won't do much in the grand scheme of things."

"I know people say that it is wasting my vote, but if more people threw to a third party, then it wouldn't be a two party system anymore and both Dems and Reps could be brought into line."

"That may be wishful thinking."

I shrugged, "It's my vote."

"True. What kind of politician do you vote for, then?"

"One that keeps the laws off my body as a woman, who keeps their damned laws off my guns and leaves my house the hell alone and respects the Constitution without using it for toilet paper."

He pursed his lips for a moment. "So, you're for neither main party, but you vote. That's amazing, really. What do you consider yourself?"

"A Constitutionalist with Green party leanings."

He was silent for a minute. "A Mercenary who is a Constitutionalist with Green party leanings." Then he started to laugh in this deep belly laugh.

I smiled at him until he finally stopped.

"Why all the questions about my political habits?"

"I'm just trying to find where you fit into all of this. How the things you do may affect America as a whole, culturally, politically and socially."

"I'm just here to stop the bad things from taking over. That's it; that's all. I don't have anything to do with 'changing' anything for America, except when I vote and my one vote is one in millions of other voices. Not exactly world shaping, now is it?"

"It will be, when some of the things General Pierce has told me about, come through those portals. America will be changed forever by that, no matter what party is in political control."

I couldn't disagree with him completely, but it wasn't all doom and gloom, either. "Some of those creatures and beings are peaceful and just want to be left alone. It's the ones who want to dominate that I plan on stopping. So, how does that affect America as a whole?"

"Sooner or later, the public is going to know about the other races and when that happens, things could get ugly. People will most likely run scared; politics could change on a dime. People voting in laws out of fear. Martial law might be evoked. The face of America will change and I need to know if you are going to be the best bet for keeping America as whole as possible through those ramifications or are you the kind who will make things worse."

"Ahh, I see. A person is smart, but people are dumb panicky animals." I quoted MIB. Fear is a great whip and used often by the wrong hands, like Robertson and his ilk. 'He who must not be named' used it on a daily basis during his two terms and it worked extremely well for him, too.

He nodded, agreeing with me, but probably not understanding the reference. However, Kla' din and Trinidad were filled with the unusual, and for the most part, they were peaceful beings, again an MIB-type situation in a way, which I proceeded to point out to him. "You've seen Kla' din and Trinidad. I don't see what the problem is."

155

"Your sister, Ms. Wong, showed me those worlds, true. But, I can't pretend I understand everything about those worlds and the people, or beings if you will, who live on them. Nor do I understand how you and your brethren could be demi-Gods and Goddesses and yet be American, too." He took another breath. "Before I back this, I need to know how much of an American you are, as opposed to someone who is used to ruling, using your powers to do it." He stood up and started to pace the room. "You have a tremendous advantage over the normal human. You have a whole Coven that can combine these powers. What chance would we have, if you and yours were the type to conquer and control?"

That is exactly why I didn't remind General Pierce or O'Hara of the fact that we weren't the only ones on this planet. I had accidentally spit it out during the first mission on Kla' din, but I had laid a lot of mental bombs on O'Hara and the team that night. It's quite easy to forget one mention, since they had so much to freak on as it was.

There were at least nine other Covens worldwide, that I knew of, filled with demi-God children, like my siblings and I. If they were still having kittens over my siblings and me, I sure as hell wasn't going to remind them again. Either General Pierce thought those other Covens were filled with just strong magick users or had forgotten there were many other pantheons that had done the same thing as ours did. I decided to keep that particular information Coven business only, as well as other facts, just in case. So, I played it out with the Brigadier General. "Ok, I see your point, but also remember this." I looked him square in the eye. "We're the only game in town." This wasn't a lie. In this town, we were the only ones. Truth can come in many forms. "Without us, as you said, you have no hope. Missiles don't work on some of these creatures, your guns would be useless, and they don't give a shit about anyone's civil rights."

He looked pissed for a minute, then his face cleared and he moved back to the desk to sit down heavily in the chair. "So, it will be about a leap of faith. At least, you and yours vote, so that shows you do care about the system that is in place. You may not agree with all of the policies, but you're willing to work within the system to make changes and that's good."

"You really care about that? About the system, I mean. The system is corrupt and kind of on the broken side right now."

He threw it back at me. "But, you still vote, don't you."

"Yes, because there are a few white knights in office. People who went into politics to make positive changes in the system and get things

156

back into proper working order. They're fighting an uphill battle but they are in there fighting. So as long as they are there, I will vote to keep them there and help all I can."

He smiled and nodded, as if he'd finally heard something he was waiting for. "You care about the system. For all your 'rebel without a cause attitude', you still care." He took a deep breath. "That is why I and my people will help you and yours."

I grinned ruefully at his ploy. "That would be nice."

Oh, this guy was sneaky. I was going to have to watch this one closely. He motioned me out the door, knowing I had another training session scheduled with Sergeant Loman and seemed to want to walk with me to the training grounds.

"Well, now that that's out of the way, how's the Sergeant's training going?"

"She is coming along nicely, actually." Almost as fast as O'Hara had when I'd first took him on training him. Though his aura being larger than a normal mundane human when he first started still baffled me, his power levels have grown tremendously since. As a result, his aura was even bigger and much denser with power today. Almost seventy-nine percent of Recon and all the Special Forces under O'Hara have grown and learned under the Covens tutelage. Those that were left, were nulls, and would never be able to work magick. It just wasn't in their genetic code. For them, we provided talismans and power stones for their protection against negative magick. It was better than nothing, for the time being.

The Brigadier General went on, knocking me out of my musings, "That's good to hear. You know, I have a granddaughter in the military."

"I didn't know that."

"She and I have always been close. A regular tomboy, when she was little. When she turned eighteen, she wanted to follow in her Granddaddy's steps. It upset her mother, of course, but she allowed it, so long as I promised the very best training for her."

And I bet he watched out for her too, but nothing wrong with that. I did the same thing for my boys.

"No boys in the family to take over?" I asked curiously.

"No, afraid not. But, even if there were, I'm not like some who are against having women in the military." He gave me a gimlet stare.

I got it. He wasn't opposed to what I did either as a female.

"Women are strong. Giving birth is hard, painful work. Keeping a family together takes diplomacy, patience, and budgeting. Society doesn't give enough credit for the strength and perseverance of the woman's role at home, in business, or the military."

"Not that I am disagreeing with you, but that seems like a very wide, open-minded view point for a career military man."

"You didn't know my mother or my wife," he chuckled, then quieted for a second. "God rest their souls," he said, with a sad sigh.

"So, they're not amongst the living, then?"

"No, no, but I still remember everything they both taught me." He gave me a slightly reckless smile. "Never underestimate a woman."

"They sound like they were both good women."

"I was lucky. Luckier than most, I suppose. My granddaughter too, you can't underestimate her. Problem is, she doesn't have the genius smarts like your Sergeant Loman." I looked at him and his look turned more serious. "Don't get me wrong; she is smart as a whip, but the level of an NBC is not her forte."

"What is her forte?"

"Marksmen, sniper, anything with guns. She is also quite the fighter for all her small stature; she is quick and fast." He sounded very proud of his young granddaughter. I also saw where this conversation was now going.

"And her goals?" I asked.

"Special Forces."

Stunned, I stopped walking. There were no women allowed in Special Forces, The Rangers, even Navy Seals had the rule of no women...period. Though, the Navy Seals had a small point that if the woman was in her menstrual cycle, she could attract sharks. This was true, but then my remark would have been to take her out of rotation until she isn't bleeding anymore. Problem solved.

America though, was still in the dark ages when it came to women's rights, for all its vaunted democracy. Shit, even Austria allowed their women to have the vote twenty years before America conceded. For some reason, women had to fight tooth and nail for every inch of equal rights in any area of life in America. Now, here was a female wanting to join Special Forces with a Brigadier General for a Grandfather who loved her. This should be interesting.

I laughed out loud.

"You don't think she could do it?" His voice was getting a tad gruff.

"Oh, I don't think that at all. But, she has one hell of a battle in front of her-the military having its status quo and all."

"Not with you training her." His grin was back. "Well, it could ease the road before her."

I knew it, I just fucking knew it. I sighed deeply. One hand washes the other; this was politics and life in general, actually.

"Listen, I can take a look at her and see if she can pull the training off, but I can't guarantee being able to turn her into a special killing machine. Some people have no gift for it at all, as well you know, if you have studied Recons averages. Over twenty percent will never be able to master the kind of training we go through."

"Why is that? Some are pretty impressive and a few haven't made any progress at all."

"And they never will; it's not in their blood. They are nulls."

He looked to me for clarification again. "People who, no matter what, will never be able to do magick. It's not in their genes, spiritually or physically. Men have a higher average of this then the women, though."

He looked surprised. "I find that interesting. Why is that?"

"A male can be a fine fighter, the best. They have strength and the muscle mass to pull it off. That's just nature, but women have their own strength and that is their intuition; their strength of WILL that most men can't compete with. It's what makes us the yang to the ying, but most don't realize this fact. I was hoping to actually get more females into Recon to pair them up with those who were nulls, so they would have a magickal fighting edge, regardless of their own blood heritage in the field. Men have strength, women have intuition-put those two together and you have a very strong fighting team. It's what the Celts did back in the day and it is also what made them so fearsome in battle."

"Our society doesn't see intuition as a fighting strength, however."

"I know this, but with what is coming, we'll need this edge in the field sooner or later. It's why I have been working so hard with Loman, so Captain Holland will see the benefits and not be so hardheaded when I request more females in the unit when the time comes."

He looked pleased. "Oh, so you do have more plans then I see?"

Yeah, me and Machiavelli; always have plans under your plans and then another layer to those plans. I never did anything without having a few other things in the fire at the same time. However, I wasn't going to give this particular man anymore insights to my thinking patterns.

"It just makes sense to have every tool we will need when the time comes. Most of Recon has gotten used to working with women after going on so many missions with my sisters, my female in-laws, as well as me. Only a few hard-heads are left to enlighten."

He chuckled. "I'll send over her files and get her over here for evaluation by you. We'll see what we can pull off later."

I realized right then, I wasn't the only Machiavellian in the hallway.

Chapter Nineteen

Dark Squares

eneral Pierce was happy with me now, that his chum was on board. We could breathe easier at the base knowing our activities would be covered up from the eagle eyes of The White House. General Brigadier's granddaughter, Lieutenant Bruhest, would be joining us attached to General Pierce's staff on paper. In reality, she would be trained as hard as she could take, before trying out for the pipeline. A Special Forces training program that was brutal and unforgiving of any mistakes, large or small. If she made it through that, her request was to try out for O'Hara's team. Wizard was quite taken with that idea as he watched her push herself through the obstacle course time and again, until she dropped. I admired her determination and guts. Her training in the esoteric Arts was well in hand, since she was definitely not a null. She was picking up the tricks of the trade even faster than Loman, who I could tell was slightly jealous of this fact. To stem any animosity, which isn't a good prodding tool in the Arts, I instead encouraged them to work together as a team. It worked for the 707th White Tigers, a Special Forces Elite unit in the South Korean Army; all of them female and lethal. Later, in their training, I would pair them up with a null in Recon and get them used to working together, but for now, they needed to learn together and grow more confident both in mind and spirit. They will achieve this faster if kept separate from the males, for the time being.

I knew statically, it would be easier just to remove the nulls and replace them with men who could learn the Arts. It would be what some pencil pushers would do, not thinking about morale of the unit as a whole. These men, nulls or not, have become family to us and still had immense value as fighters...and as friends. I would keep things as they were and just do what we could magickally to keep these men safe in the field if…no when… the shit hit the fan. They've showed their loyalty to us; now we would return that favor.

General Pierce called a meeting of The Nightwolves three days later with a report of incidences of a civilian going into an emergency room with large claws marks on the face a few weeks ago in Louisiana. The emergency room attendant and police had put it down to an attack by someone on meth and that the patient was traumatized from the incident; that he only imagined the guy who had attacked him had claws growing out of his hands, since he came back negative from a drug test, but over the limit for alcohol in his bloodstream. The police had an ABP out for the attacker with a warning of being a meth user and considered dangerous.

This one attack would have gone unnoticed by General Pierce if it wasn't for the body of a young woman showing up yesterday that looked like she had been ravaged by a wild animal. A large wild animal. Pieces were missing from the body in a most gruesome way that it had made the Picayune News in New Orleans. The fact that Hurricane Katrina had hit New Orleans in '04 and yet no portal was registering on our PETS, we made it a priority mission, hoping to find one of General Robertson's hidden portals and gain control of it. The mission was to be twofold, in finding out what attacked the man and killed the woman and also see if I could make contact with the Vaudoun underground and see about getting them to lay off the weather curses against America. Two birds, one stone; I liked it.

I took Craven with me since it was a stateside mission and some sort of animal was involved. Most likely a large breed of werewolf with the information we were able to glean from the police report. They had found paw prints in the mud near the body of the victim, but the size didn't match with any known breeds in North America. They were just too large and the depth of the paw print suggested the animal weighed over two hundred and fifty pounds. No North American wolf breed ever got that large. But, werewolves did and Craven could be very useful if that was what we were facing in New Orleans-if he could control his Dire Wolf form.

New Orleans in October was mild, but still heavy with humidity. Wearing a leather jacket in this type of weather was uncomfortable, but necessary to hide all the weapons I was carrying. None of us was very comfortable and were headed to the crime scene as fast as we could, after dropping off our travel gear at the hotel. Many of the businesses were open and the smells of New Orleans cooking wafted on the breeze, making me desire the food far more than blood. That didn't happen very often for me, since I had been changed. Even before the change, food was just something to fill the stomach for fuel. Very rarely did I crave food for its own sake, unless it was Sushi.

New Orleans was vastly different from Japan with the weather, shop stores and food. Not only was the air heavier here, but the stores themselves were a mix of vibrant colors; each adding their own uniqueness, with window decorations to tempt the tourist to visiting inside. Japan was more demure with reds and greens being the main colors of their stores and homes. New Orleans blasted with many different colors, smells of seafood grilling and the spice of gumbo while the air echoed with sounds of jazz blowing festively all around us. We were nowhere close to the time of Mardi Gras, but New Orleans didn't care; it was still a party town; at least on the surface. Streets behind the main causeways still showed signs of destruction. Though, some were cleared of the debris, the damage was still devastating. Large spaces of now empty lots that once probably held homes and side stores before Katrina flooded through their neighborhoods and wiped it all away. It was in one of these areas that the crime scene was still taped off with police tape which we ignored. We saw the spot almost immediately of where the body had lain, with large spots of dried blood marring the ground around it. Now that it was a rust-colored brown after drying out, it almost matched the dirt and mud around it, but Craven and I could still smell the scent of blood and feel the trauma of death. That meant the murder happened right here. We looked around, but there were no other homes close enough for any hope of a witness to at least to hear the sounds of screaming. Near the murder sight, we could see where the police had taken a mold casting of the paw print. With the chemicals and clay used to make the mold, any scent of the actual predator would not be lingering, so I scented around the area instead and just picked up the scent of humans and negative energy. Nothing that smelled of a possible werewolf or even a large animal. I looked at Andre and Craven and they, too, shook their heads. Just small alley cat smells and rodents, but nothing large enough to have done the damage we could tell happened from the blood patterns splayed around the death sight. A lot of humans had tracked through here, so if any of them were the killer, there was no hope of picking it up. All the clues we needed to track the killer with, had been obliterated by modern technology and police forensics.

"What now?" O'Hara asked me. I turned to Andre to see if he had picked up anything that I may have missed. He shook his head silently.

He knew enough about forensics to know that the blood splatter that was left showed the woman had died horribly and brutally. From the autopsy report, there had been teeth marks on the bones and some of those bones had been crushed into powder, proving that whatever it was that ate parts of her, had huge, powerful teeth and really strong jaws. Normal wolves wouldn't be able to completely crush bones into powder within the arms or legs as it showed in the x-rays taken of the female victim. It had the local police baffled.

The crime scene bothered me as much as it did anyone here, but the best thing to do was to track this creature and put it down. Permanently. Then, find its' portal and close it. This tribe of werewolves were obviously too blood-thirsty for any sort of treaty, the same as the ones in Saudi Arabia had been.

"Let's head over to the first victims house and have a talk with him."

O'Hara nodded and we loaded up into the cars to drive over into what used to be, and still is, called the Ninth Ward District. An area for people who lived with little or no steady income. Wizard was able to get the specifics of the hospital report pretty easily. The guy, who had been drunk at the time of the attack, lived in that neighborhood, which was also where the attack itself happened. So, if the two cases were related, this werewolf had a large expanded hunting ground. The two attacks were far apart and vastly different, but the level of increasing violence wasn't unusual for a werewolf who had gotten the taste of blood and liked it.

For a civilian investigation, General Pierce had provided us with fake Federal Marshall's badges and phony files had been placed in the mainframe, in case some local cop somewhere got a wild hair up his ass and ran our names and badge numbers through to verify our bullshit story. On the surface, it would hold up, but any serious digging and we might have a problem. Also, even Federal Marshals usually ran alone or at the most, in two man teams. With one whole squad, plus Special Forces and my three man team, it was a bit much to swallow that Feds would need this many men for just an investigation. Which is why only O'Hara and I were going into the house with our phony badges and the rest of the team would be in their SUV's down the street. O'Hara was dressed for the occasion, with his suit and tie looking every inch the cop. With his crew cut and military stance, he would pass just from sight alone. I, on the other hand, would have a hard time with my leather and blue jeans, but we could always say I was dressed for any undercover work that might be needed on the fly. That was the story we were going to stick to anyway.

I could tell Craven didn't like waiting behind with the others, but he was holding to his promise of following orders to the letter. Bringing Craven along was helping him get some space from the problem of his brother being a panther permanently and I knew the guilt weighed heavily on him. No matter how many times I told him it wasn't his fault, he still felt he could have done something to stop it. All of us felt that way and all of us felt useless being unable to do anything to help Crimson come back to us in human form. We had tried every magickal spell we knew. We tried a full Coven ritual, and still, nothing happened to bring Crimson back to being whole. I even called my Mother Goddess, and as usual, I got nothing but silence. That usually meant the problem was fully in my hands and up to me to solve it. Just like my previous curse had been back before I'd had found my mates. Again, the same situation of nobody being able to do a damn thing, despite the wealth of spells and counter-curses we knew. Despite the vast amount of power we could bring to the table when we combined our forces. The Goddess Herself silent, patiently waiting for me to break myself out of it. It was just as aggravating now, as it was then, and I was losing my patience on this matter. It was one thing for me to be held up by a curse, but quite another, when it was my own son who was suffering; and suffering alone in silence, stubbornly refusing to let me or our family counselor in, to help him deal with it emotionally. If it hadn't been for the diligent work my mates had done with me in releasing most of the rage and becoming less volatile I would have blown up days ago. As it was, my anger was slowly seeping back the longer I had to see my own son in a cage; not himself, not only in body, but in mind and soul, as well.

I quickly buried these thoughts, as we pulled up in front of a one bedroom house in bad repair that belonged to the live male attack victim. We both got out of the car and walked up to the door that had a screen door with a rusty broken screen mesh hanging from the sides. By the looks of this house, even before hurricane Katrina, the owner hadn't put much work into repairs or up-keep on the home. Though, with finances being what they were, food had to come first with most folks in this neighborhood. There wouldn't be enough left over for repainting the house annually, as well as the smaller repairs needed. I carefully knocked on the door, afraid the screen would fall off and waited for someone to answer. I could hear a slow shuffle staggering to the door as it cracked open for the owner to see who was standing on his porch.

O'Hara flashed his badge, as did I, but I let him take the lead. "Mr. Howard Frankton?" The man nodded his head suspiciously to O'Hara. "I am Federal Marshall Hamstein and this is my partner, Wilks. We've come to ask you some questions about what happened to your face." Through the dim lighting shining from behind him we could see angry, healing, pink-ragged lines slashing down the left side of this guys face. That meant the attacker was right handed, if he had been standing in front of him, as the claw marks suggested he had.

"I already told the police everything. They didn't believe me." The guy was only about two inches taller than I was and had an old t-shirt and ragged jeans on, and was already slurring his speech, though it was only ten in the morning. This guy had a drinking problem or the attack messed his head up pretty good.

O'Hara just looked at him. "We're not interested in the police report. We want to know what you have to say about it."

The guy opened the door wider. "Well, it's about time. There's something weird about that whole damn family and that includes that stuck-up sister."

He motioned for us to come in. We walked into the living room and he moved stuff off of his tattered old couch and invited is to sit down with a motion of his hand. The place had a smell of mildew and mold, from the flooding, I assumed. Very few homes made it through Katrina in the Ninth Ward. Most of them were made unlivable for their previous owners. This guy was extremely lucky in having a semi-habitable home left.

O'Hara kept the lead with the questions while I surreptitiously looked around. "What family and what sister are you talking about, exactly?"

"The Norwell's over on Tenth Street. A month ago I was there visiting with a friend who lives down the block. I don't go over to his house anymore, though," he said gruffly.

"Why is that?"

"Because of that weirdo family. If her brother can make claws come out of his hands, I don't want to mess with any of the other family members. They're freaks, all of them."

Mr. Frankton sat down on his seat across from us, picking up his beer from the table that he'd had been drinking until we interrupted him.

I leaned forward. "Why don't you start from the beginning and give us the whole rundown."

He gave me an odd look but did as I asked. "I went over for my friend's birthday party. After the party, I walked home and I saw Amanda sitting on her steps. I thought she might want some company and went to make conversation with her. Her brother came out and started some shit. I yelled back and then he went all spooky-like and slashed at my face with his hands, except they weren't hands anymore. He had claws; big, hairy, paw-like claws. The cops at the hospital didn't believe me and said I was drunk." He shook his head, "I wasn't though, I only had a few beers at my friend's party."

That was a lie. The toxicology report from the hospital showed his alcohol level way above the legal limit. Luckily, he hadn't been driving, or he would have been charged, but since he had 'just been walking home', they had let it slide, was my guess. The New Orleans Police Department had to deal with drunken disorderlies all the time; it wasn't anything new to them. They only came down hard if you had been driving while under the influence. Otherwise, so long as there isn't any damage, they don't sweat it much in this town. I knew this from when I had come through this town several times, back in my more illegal days, before I was a mother. Partying was a way of life here-or it used to be.

"What's her brother's first name?" O'Hara asked him.

"Ashton, Ashton Norwell."

"And he lives at the house?"

"Yeah, but the cops went there twice and he ain't showed back up yet. Might have taken off for another state or something 'cause they didn't find him." He leaned forward. "But, if you asked me, I think he is still in that neighborhood and his relatives are just hiding him."

"At the house? But, I thought you said the cops checked there."

"No, in the neighborhood. His whole damn family took over the neighborhood after Katrina hit and washed everyone out. They showed up not too long afterwards and started buying up the property there, no matter what kind of condition it was in. Folks was glad to sell to them and make money, so they could move elsewhere and not have to worry about repairs."

"So, the entire neighborhood is Norwells?" I asked.

He nodded his head. "Yeah, most of them, so he could be in one of those houses within six blocks. Lots of them freaks there now and it seems they get more all the time. Like it's some kind of fucking permanent family reunion."

"We'll do the best we can to track him down," O'Hara told him.

He reached up to gently touch the wounds that were scarring. "You do that, boyo, but you should get that whole damn family, too. I know they're just like him."

Once O'Hara and I had gotten outside, we looked at each other. "Sounds interesting, doesn't it?" He said.

"Oh yeah. Wonder if we brought enough guns?"

He grin grew cocky at the edges. "Let's go find out."

Chapter Twenty

Pawn makes Knight

We caught up with the rest of the team and let them know what we suspected. Everyone started to strap up for a possible dust-up.

Craven was grinning from ear to ear in excitement. I shook my head at him. Kids, they always think the fighting is fun. That is, until they learn their first painful lesson that either makes or breaks them. Fighting can cost you more than you're willing to lose and once it's done; there is no taking it back. No deposit, no return. You can't ever go back and change what happened and that reality, unfortunately, never hits them until something really bad goes down. Craven had gotten a taste of it in Saudi, Crimson had just fully learned that lesson himself, and I still didn't know if it had broken him or not.

I, as a mother, wished Craven would have never had to learn such a painful lesson. I, as a leader of a family of Mercs, knew he would and it was a lesson he needed to learn, no matter how painful the transition may be. I just hope it didn't break his spirit in the process. His inner spirit was so much gentler inside than Crimson's was. Either that, or Crimson just hid his better. Craven wore his heart on his sleeve and having to watch the Mercenary life take that from him, made me want to hit something. Really hard.

O'Hara looked at me. "Hey, you ok?"

"Just fucking perfect." I snapped on the straps for my inner blades and Shurikens before putting my leather back on.

That was O'Hara being the Rock for the team. The steady one for everyone and making sure no one was about to go bug fucking postal on anything or anyone. He knew, whatever the problem was, I had it under control. If I didn't, I wouldn't say anything. My silence was his clue that I

169

was about to go off in a real bad way. Since I'd answered him, he let it slide.

Andre moved closer to me, but kept his distance; letting me know with his body language, he was right there if I needed him. It took some of the bite out of my anger at the situation and let me focus back on the original problem.

We drove toward the neighborhood where the house of the 'alleged' attacker lived. As we got closer, I felt we had crossed a metaphysical shield that was strong enough to make me take notice of it. "STOP. NOW."

"What the hell is that?" Rock asked, as he slammed his brakes and came to an abrupt stop. He was getting really good with his metaphysical training-even he had picked up the psychic backlash. The SUV's behind us stopped as fast as we did; several of them skidding to avoid hitting the one in front.

"That is a real big psychic shield, Rock."

"Ok, that means we're on the right track then, I would assume."

"Yeah, it also means we have a very big, fucking problem," I retorted.

"Explain." Rock never minced words on a mission, especially when the danger of a mission has racketed up a few notches in the dangerous category, as this one just had.

"It means these fucking wolves have magick. Now you take into consideration how many of them we might be facing in a gun fight living within a six block radius. I was thinking of several hours of fighting, but eventually, with the team we have with us, we could take them. Add magick into that mix with these many fucking wolves and only two highly trained magick users and the rest of you still playing catch up, means we got a very big problem."

Andre was looking all around. "She's right."

"So, we pull back and re-evaluate this situation then, and come at it with a different plan."

I was about to agree with Rock and signal for everyone to get back in their SUV's and turn around, when Craven growled out, "Too late, we've been spotted."

Five men were walking right down the middle of the street towards us in a vee formation with a blond-haired leader in the front.

Rock signaled the men to maneuver the SUV's as a barricade across the whole street and take cover behind them, as the four of us remained right where we were. I amped up the shields around myself and Rock, knowing Andre would do the same for himself and Craven. We drew weapons, but kept the barrels either pointing up or down, since the group coming at us didn't have a single weapon in their hands.

I heard the SUV's move, then the men getting ready behind the steel barrier they had created, and getting their rifles pointed and ready to fire on our signal.

"What do you think?" Rock asked me.

"Stay steady. They don't have weapons and I am not feeling any power surges, as if they were gathering energy for a magickal duel, so maybe they want a pow wow?"

"That would be nice," he said through gritted teeth, since he could see other faces peeking around corners and through the windows of houses all up and down the street. I had already counted over twenty-six potential hostiles and if I knew anything of how these types of situations went down, no one would be calling the police. Not in this neighborhood. If they were all werewolves, they wouldn't want the attention of the local police. This could work for us and against us, if it came to a fire fight with guns and claws.

We didn't want the attention either, but we weren't in a good position if they had magick, as well as claws, to throw at us.

"Then again, cops got better things to do than die," I muttered to myself ruefully.

Andre gave me a weird look. "Big Trouble in Little China," and then focused back on the oncoming gang.

I laughed. He got it. It's why I loved him so much. He got me, when others would look at me sideways in confusion.

The leader of the gang got within five feet and stopped. He didn't look happy, but I could tell he was definitely a werewolf. His aura showed the expanded aura colors of a shapeshifter and his face showed the predatory angles, not only in the clean lines of his face, but in the blueness of his eyes that held the hint of a hunter in his gaze. Although he looked only around twenty-four or so, he held himself like a leader. Strong and sure of himself in his place with his pack and his world. And this neighborhood was his world now.

"You've come into our territory," he stated simply

"We're tracking a killer," I said, with a matching even tone in my voice. His eyes widened that it was me, a female, that had started the pow wow and not one of the males, as he had assumed. Good. Keep him off balance and we might live through the day.

He looked at me more directly than he had before. "We've no killers here."

"Someone clawed up Mr. Howard Frankton's face, and the man responsible lives in this neighborhood."

"I didn't kill him."

Ah, the elusive Ashton Norwell himself. This was good.

"True, but a female victim on Trade Avenue wasn't as lucky. Someone got hungry with the meat."

"None of mine did it."

"Did you?"

"No."

"Then, we still have a problem. We have one man with wounds on his face and a dead woman whose attacker needs to be put down."

"I didn't attack or kill the female. I never left the neighborhood."

The thing was, I believed him. He admitted quickly enough to the man, but he wouldn't budge with the statement about the woman. And why would he leave his territory in the first place? Wolves were very territorial in the wild and werewolves tended to be the same way. If he hunted, it would be within an area he could control and this neighborhood was it, as far as I knew.

"You hunt?"

"Yes, we hunt."

"Do you hunt humans?"

"Not unless they start the hunt," came the warning, laced through his words. Craven was answering with his own low growl at the perceived threat to his mother, no matter how slight that threat that was being delivered.

To distract them both I asked, "Where are your hunting grounds?"

"Far from here, from any city." He wasn't going to tell me exactly where, I could tell, but I didn't need to know the specifics. Only the fact that his hunting grounds for this pack was not in the city. There would be no reason for him to have killed that woman, unless it was personal.

"Do you know a Brenda Shelby?" I noticed the men he had came with, were slowly spreading out and sniffing the air, as if they wanted to smell inside the SUVs themselves.

"No, I don't." Ashton had noticed me noticing his men and they all stopped- still again, in sync, without a word or gesture from him. Wonderful; it most likely meant they had some sort of telepathy or something between them. This just kept getting better and better.

"If I showed you a picture would you look at it?" going for the extra cautious approach with this situation.

"Yes." Damn, he was more monosyllabic than Rock was on a mission.

"Wizard, I need that picture of the woman." I didn't want Ashton to know we had telepathy among most of our people now. An ace in the hole, if we needed it.

"Coming to point," Wizard warned us, so his approach would not trigger the melee. He moved up slowly and handed the picture to me, which I in turn showed to Ashton.

"No. Never saw her."

"How about your people?"

"None."

"Can you really guarantee not one of your people stepped out of the territory for a midnight snack?"

His gaze had turned hard with rising anger, "Yes, I can verify no one of my family left this neighborhood at any time," his voice turning more deeper and edging with a growl. He also had taken another step towards me and I held my ground, letting my own hardness fill my own eyes, showing him I wouldn't back down and wasn't intimidated. "Someone killed the woman. Someone not completely human. You're the only game we know of in this town that fits the profile for something like that."

"Game? We are NOT prey." He took another step towards me and Craven didn't like it.

Craven's chin was tucking under and his own suppressed growls were coming out louder and louder.

Ashton glanced over to Craven and his eyes widened. "You bring another wolf here? This is Cadian territory. This is challenge!"

"Stop. He won't attack unless we're attacked first," I tried to shout over the howls that had erupted all around us. Craven lost it and let out his own challenging howl to the sky. Andre's shield shattered from Craven's psychic outcry. A shield meant to keep magick out, not to hold magick in, which is why it shattered, and that was when they could all smell that he was wolven.

"Cat?" Rock was asking in that one word, 'do we shoot or what'?

I yelled out, "What does 'challenge' mean here?"

A female came forward from the crowd that had quickly gathered. An alpha, judging by the way she held herself, with just as much fearlessness as Ashton did.

173

"It means the intruder will fight Ashton."

"Why? Craven didn't start anything."

"He walked into our territory. That is challenge. His temerity for walking into the middle of our pack is how potential outside alphas fight for rank. He growled at Ashton. The outsider chose his opponent. Challenge has been issued and answered. Ashton must fight."

"Craven is only here because of us. He didn't come here to challenge anyone."

"Too late." She nodded over to where Ashton had been standing, but he was now on four feet, instead of two.

Craven had held his human form by sheer will. I could tell he was fighting his wolven instincts with every fiber of his being.

"Mom?" came the question, laced with anger just barely contained.

"Cat," I corrected him, seeing Ashton was not waiting and this could place Craven in a weaker position. "Go kick ass."

Craven's face lit up and with a wild yelp for joy, he let loose with his Were form and met Ashton wolf to wolf.

They collided together with teeth bared, jaws snapping, and claws trying to rip into the other. Ashton was gorgeous as a wolf though, I had to admit. With a pale, honey coat that looked soft and silky, it was oddly set off by the huge white teeth he used to try to bite into Craven's russet coat at his shoulder.

'*Cat*'? came from the others of our team, who had mastered telepathy, and Andre too, was asking what we should do.

'*Kill Ashton if he goes for Craven's neck.*'

I heard several of our men move into a better position to cover Craven if it looked like Ashton was going to rip out his throat. There was no way I was going to let anyone kill my son. I didn't care that Craven was essentially a werewolf and no longer under the influence of human urges, but more animalistic ones. He was still my son and I would kill every single wolf here to protect him.

From the beginning of the battle, however, it looked like Craven was holding his own pretty well. Several times, he had almost gotten a hook into Ashton's neck with his teeth, but at the last second, Ashton would swerve and dance out of the way. Then he would whip around testing Craven's skills in fighting in Were form.

Damn, I could see it now. Ashton was just playing him. Luring Craven into a false sense of security, before he would strike for his kill shot for real. Ashton must have dueled a lot if he knew how to fight like this. Craven has had no other werewolf to practice his fighting skills with in that form. He knew how to fight as a human only. This battle here, he was fighting on pure instinct alone. That would not win this duel in the long run, with an accomplished fighter, such as Ashton appeared to be.

My heart was in my throat when I saw the plan unfold. If I warned Craven using telepathy, I could do either of two things or possibly both- distract him while he was fighting and he would then be exposed and/or make him lose his confidence as he fought.

Right now, all he had was adrenalin and instincts to help him through this. Taking his confidence away or distracting him with a warning, could spell his doom. I looked around the group, seeing a mix of our people and theirs and mine were shouting words of encouragement, not seeing the danger Craven was in.

On the surface, it did look as if Craven was gaining on Ashton and wearing him down, but it was Ashton who was gauging my son's abilities and tiring him out, waiting for the right time.

That time came a minute and a half later, when Craven had misjudged a lunge to Ashton's neck and lost his footing on his back hind legs. Ashton whipped around, and with his teeth, tore a long strip of flesh from Cravens left hind quarter. Blood gushed down from the wound, staining the blacked pavement. Shocked silence took over the ring of spectators, seeing that first blood had been drawn. Ashton was doing his laughing in werewolf form, circling around Craven, confident now that he had my son right where he wanted him. Hurt and off balance.

I could feel Craven's pain echo through me and I almost went into the ring to rip out Ashton's throat myself, when I felt Craven's psychic heat rise along with the pain.

Craven turned to face Ashton, snarling, his eyes glowing blue with pain-filled hate. Craven breathed in twice and shuddered all along his werewolf's body, which seemed to be growing larger.

His werewolf muzzle that had been long, was shortening and drawing inwards, while the rest of his body seemed to bulk out and grow in length and height. Within seconds, he was on his hind quarters, in his Dire wolf form and he was pissed.

Everyone in the ring backed up and gasps went throughout the mob seeing this seven foot tall Dire Wolf. Craven didn't wait, as he closed in on Ashton with three long strides, grabbing him up by his throat, and slamming him back down into the ground.

Several times, Craven picked him up, only to slam Ashton back down, growling and snarling his anger at the werewolf who dared hurt him.

The Dire Wolf finally saw he had taken the fight right out of Ashton and with a final slam, he covered Ashton's body with his own, grabbing him by his throat with his large, gleaming teeth and bit in, drawing blood.

I heard a cry of alarm from the woman who had approached me at the beginning of the fight. Tears were streaming down her face. She shifted into werewolf form and I drew my gun and aimed it at her, slowly squeezing the trigger, until I saw her get into crawling position and inching her way forward on her belly, whining and whimpering. I held off from shooting, until I was sure she wasn't going to try to take Craven with her teeth, in defense of Ashton.

When she was close enough to where Ashton laid, defeated and bleeding, she flipped over, baring her belly to Craven. Whining at him and giving licks at Craven's claws hooked into Ashton's back.

That was when I noticed how excited Craven had gotten. And how, exactly, he was covering Ashton. Almost as if he was going to dominate him sexually, as some wolves do, even in the wild. The alpha male will mount a beta male or a young untested alpha to keep him in line. The female baring her stomach to Craven must be Ashton's mate and is offering herself up so he wouldn't rip out Ashton's throat after mounting him. That was something the more aggressive werewolves did in some tribes. It kept the threat of any upcoming alphas from trying to issue any further challenges. Craven was now being ruled by his wolven instincts fully and I didn't know if he had enough human in him at the moment to stop what he was doing, but I sure as shit didn't want to witness it.

Craven's clawed hand reached over and lightly caressed the female's belly. I still didn't know if he had fucking on his mind or killing, because he could so easily rip into her tender stomach now. Dire Wolves were notorious for being more homicidal on the drop of a dime, for no apparent reason. I held my breath, not knowing which way I wanted to see how this ended. The mother in me was in direct conflict with my leadership as a Merc.

One simple way to solve this would be to kill both female and male werewolf myself, before I saw anything at all. But that would be for my own benefit and not Craven's. This was his win, not mine. And Dire Wolves and werewolves sometimes were very sexual in taking their winnings and making a point of dominance. In our world, this would be normal, but I was raised human and I'd raised Craven that way as well. It was only our instincts that would take over in a fight, which made us realize how much we weren't human underneath our civilized veneer.

I breathed a sigh of relief, as he moved off the male and crouched between both female and male. He put his clawed hands on their throats and bellowed a roar in triumph. I quickly looked away from the scene before seeing more than I wanted to, and scanned the crowd instead, to gauge how they were taking this.

"Ok, that's weird. I've got to admit," Rock said.

"That's because you're human, through and through." I grinned at him, and then went back to the crowd, who looked as defeated as their leader was.

"I keep forgetting you're not purely human."

"You know, that could be taken as a compliment or an insult. Depending on one's point of view."

He laughed at me shaking his head. "Fuck you."

I shook my head. "Not my type." I wrinkled my nose at him, "too human." Then, I laughed at him. No way was I going to let him know I had that ick factor going on, as well.

We were joking around now, because we knew the danger was over. Or at least the danger to my son was, as we went back to scanning through the crowd around us, who now had the potential of turning on us in retribution if they had the mind to.

Chapter Twenty-One

Queen Covers Knight

Craven slowly stood up to his full seven feet and let out one last long howl, as if asking, "Anyone else'? He snarled and glared at everyone in the ring, waiting for an answering challenge. No one dared. One by one, then groups at a time, dropped their eyes to the ground and sank to one knee in front of him. The only ones left standing was our team and they were looking around at the crowd in confusion. As I took in the scene, I started to get a bad feeling about this.

Ashton was still dazed and his mate was furiously licking his muzzle, as if trying to revive him. I finally took my aim off her, since it didn't look like she was going to be doing anything sneaky against my son. She was just worried over Ashton. This pack, if nothing else, had some honor. They didn't attack en mass, before or during, the challenge. That spoke well for this particular tribe of werewolves. The killing of the woman by any one of these wolves was not adding up in my mind anymore. Howard Frankton's attack made sense if he was making passes at a mate or relative. They wouldn't want a mere human to mix with one of their own. Though, clawing his face wouldn't help them keep a low profile. A simple punch to the face would have made one's point just as effectively. So, the swiping seemed extreme to me and that kind of behavior would lead to an escalating level of violence, especially for a werewolf. Ashton firmly denied having anything to do with the female victim, but he admitted to the swiping without a qualm and no remorse for it either. This case was getting confusing. Maybe they had a rogue werewolf. It's happened before, with other tribes, according to the legends we had.

Rock interrupted my thinking, "Ah Cat, what's up with this?"

179

This being the fact the Ashton and his mate had reverted to human form. She was now helping him to his feet and both were buck-assed naked in the middle of the street.

"Werewolf politics." And this wasn't good. Craven was only seventeen. Much too young for being what I thought this pack would make him, now that he has defeated Ashton in a fair battle.

I thought it was odd they didn't have the magickal ability to transpose their clothes, as Craven did, if they were magick users themselves. Whatever Craven was wearing went into the mists until he shifted back into human form. Everything, but swords or rifles. Jewelry, knives and hand guns had no problem shifting through the mist.

The mists is a transcendental dimension where part of a shifters physical being and soul went when they shifted on the physical plane. When they were in human form, it was their shifter selves who waited in the mist. That's why they were so animalistic when they shifted into their animal form on the physical plane; too much of their human-selves went into the mist in place of their shifter animal spirit. I then noticed the piles of ripped clothes on the ground from Ashton's shift. The female had just thrown her clothes off and shifted. Neither bothered with getting dressed; instead, gazing at Craven's Dire Wolf form with a look akin to worship.

Oh, this wasn't good at all. They both staggered to stand in front of Craven. Craven pulled back his lips with a warning growl. Ashton answered by baring his throat to Craven, as did Ashton's mate. Craven bent down to take what was offered from Ashton. The shift had healed the wound from Craven's bite while Ashton was in Were form, but there were streaks of blood marring the flesh on one side. I held my breath, as Craven licked at the blood and bit into the neck offered to him. I was hoping the blood smell wouldn't trigger Craven's blood lust, but he did well in putting just enough pressure into Ashton's neck to draw a bit of blood in this form. Not enough to do any real damage. Ashton shuddered from the biting and leaned in towards Craven. My ick factor was rising, as I saw Ashton was also excited over this ritual. Craven then turned to Ashton's mate, who had also been waiting patiently with her throat bared, and Craven had repeated the movements with her. She, however, reached out and stroked his muscular arm, feeling the fur and the corded muscles. Craven gave a warning growl and she pulled back quickly, with her eyes going down to the ground in immediate submission and obedience.

Ashton dropped to one knee. "My Lord, the pack is yours. I respectively beg of you that you do no harm to the men who have served me. They have no interest in challenge and want to live in peace, free to raise their young without worry of them being killed at birth. It is their only desire. I offer my life for theirs, if you demand it." His mate gasped at this, but did not stop him from the offer.

"Shit," Rock said, closing his eyes. I silently agreed with him. However, Andre had an odd look of admiration for Craven, as if a proud daddy seeing his son gain another title, earned through teeth and blood. I rolled my eyes at him, which he couldn't see through my sunglasses, but he could feel through our bond. He grinned at me. Damn males.

I knew this was going to be bad. Craven was now leader of the pack. Most alphas of werewolf tribes will kill the previous serving guard of the defeated leader. This was done to assure that the lower ranked alphas wouldn't plot an overthrow and reinstate their previous leader. It was a political move that conquering nations had done in our own history. Some countries still did that to this day; attack a country, kill the leader, serving guard and any person who could give hope to the people for rallying under the previous national flag. They install their own people in the offices of power and reign as they see fit, with very little resistance to the changes to the country that had been defeated.

The Werewolf packs of many tribes that were written about in our books of legends had operated in the same manner. Ashton was also afraid that this is how Craven would operate.

I went to stand next to Craven. '*Craven, how much of you is here?*'
'*Want.*'
'*Want what, exactly?*'
'*Want male, female, pack. Mine.*'

And he had earned it. I couldn't deny him that, but I had raised him human all of his life. He wasn't ready for this emotionally or mentality. Once he regained his human form, he might be overloaded with too much otherworldliness and it could do a lot of damage to his human psyche. If he had been raised with a pack, then I would step aside and let things go, but Craven had no clue of the entire ramifications of taking on such a huge responsibility, let alone the fact of making relationship decisions in Were form. And that gave me an idea of how to handle this situation as his commander and not his mother. I also wouldn't be breaking any promises I've made to him.

'Craven, the job isn't done yet. You promised to follow my orders when on a mission. We are STILL on that mission. You will have to put this off until your duty to The Nightwolves is over.'

This would buy me time to get him back in human form and thinking as a human and not an animal. It was the best I could do. But Craven, The Dire Wolf, didn't like it and growled at me, 'Mine. Want mates. Finish mating now.'

I spoke aloud, "Don't you growl at me."

Ashton and his mate growled at me in turn, stepping up to support their new leader, who had turned on them and snarled heavily.

Ashton's face was shocked, "Dam?" He looked at me from head to toe. "She's your Dam? She isn't Were."

I think Craven had told Ashton and his mate not to growl at me because I was his mother. I could be wrong though, I didn't speak Were and the growls all sounded the same to me.

Ashton moved cautiously towards me and sniffed. "She isn't human, either." His mate drifted over and sniffed me herself and then cocked her head as a dog would, as if they were trying to figure out a strange, new scent or a puzzle.

"What are you?" Ashton asked.

"What I am, doesn't matter. What I am to my son at this very moment is his Superior Officer," I ground out, as I turned back to the reluctant Dire Wolf. "You swore allegiance to The Nightwolves. To me! And, by the Goddess, you will obey!" I hated to come down on him so hard and in front of his newly acquired pack, but they needed to know who was really in charge at this very moment. I also needed time to get Craven thinking as a human, which meant I needed him to shift into human form as soon as possible.

The ripple effect went through the entire pack as they digested that piece of information. Craven may be leader, but if I understood Werewolf politics, if a leader owed obedience to an outside source, that source had to be obeyed as if they were leader, as well. I didn't want to usurp Craven's position, but I needed the pack to back off until Craven could make decisions with a clear head and not his wolven instincts.

I could see Rock's face shine with admiration at my move. His eyebrow rose high and incredulous that I could think of this so quickly and manage to regain control of the situation. Craven's head had lost some of its height, hanging a bit from my rebuke. He knew, even as a Dire Wolf, a sworn word was absolute and could not be forsworn. Not without some serious retribution. He backed away from the two previous alphas and coughed out another low growl that sounded like some kind of order. The two of them backed off and eyes went to the ground.

"May I ask a question, my Lady?" the female alpha asked quietly.

"Yes."

"Is that why you and yours have taken some of our young wolves and a cub? To replenish your pack?"

"What the in the hells are you talking about?"

Craven's head went back up and the growling was back. Exasperated, I looked for Andre's position. "Andre, take him over to the trucks and get him to change. Craven, I will deal with this for now. Go change, so we can all sit and talk together."

He reluctantly went off with Andre and I turned my attention back to Ashton and his mate.

"Explain, now." Oh look, I was getting as monosyllabic as Rock was, but my patience was coming to the end of my endurance.

Ashton nodded towards the Black SUV's. "Trucks like yours come into our neighborhood from time to time. When that happens, we are always missing members of our pack, usually younger ones who have barely gained their adulthood. But, a few days ago we came to be missing a very young cub; a male, and his Dam is distraught over the loss. We thought you were coming in to take another one of our cubs or maybe returning him? But, we don't smell his scent on the trucks or you."

"You're missing werewolves?"

"Yes."

"How many?"

"You should know."

I shook my head at him. "I swear, by whatever Gods and my own Goddess, none of us have anything to do with your missing wolven of any age."

A strangled cry came from the mouth of a young female in the crowd and she had collapsed to the ground on her knees sobbing, as if her heart was breaking. A male leaned down to her bring her into his arms, shushing her and petting her back to comfort her.

Andre warned me on our private telepathic path, *'Get her calmed down. Craven is only in his werewolf form, now but he is getting agitated over the female's pain.'*

I gasped out loud and used my third eye to scan the area and saw something that almost broke my own heart. Bonds had been formed from Craven to every member of this pack. There would be no way now that my son could ever return control to Ashton, as I had hoped. He was bonded to his pack now on a psychic level, and that could not be so easily transferred or revoked. Craven, at seventeen, was now responsible for the well being of this pack and by extension, so was I.

Shit.

I went to the female and offered my own comfort.

"Listen, I need Craven in human form. You need to try real hard for me to control your grief and I promise I will do everything in my power to help get your cub back. I swear this." I would have offered anyway, being a mother. I could imagine the pain she felt losing someone so precious, but now it was my son's duty and mine to do this for her.

She sobbed, lurching into my arms. "Thank you, thank you, please. He is so sweet, please. Bring my baby back to me."

"Shush, I have sworn I would do everything I can, but let me get all the information of what the hells is going on and I still have my own hunt to finish here."

Wizard was standing nearby, watching everything.

'Wizard don't react, but I need you to look up any military planes coming in or going out or any other means of military personnel for the last three weeks.'

He nodded carefully at me, *'Done.'*

Ashton spoke up, swinging my attention back to him. "I swear none of us killed that woman. There was no reason to hunt her. She wasn't in our territory. None of us know her and she posed no threat to me or mine."

I believed him. Because of those strong psychic bonds, a leader would know every mood of his pack. A killing bloodlust would echo through him and he would have been warned one of his members was losing control. His own aura wasn't spiking red, which would happen when someone was lying. So, some other wolf or animal had to have killed that young woman on Trade Street.

"But, Howard Frankton is your responsibility."

"He offered insult to my sister. She is only fifteen years old by your calendar counting, two years away from her first heat by our reckoning of age, among our kind. She is still a child in our eyes and was doing nothing but stargazing. That scum came up to her and tried to put his paws on my baby sister, when she had told him repeatedly to leave her alone. I felt her panic and went outside to see what was wrong with her.

I saw him groping my sister and swiped him. It was my right and my duty."

My anger flared up in response, but not at Ashton. If Howard Frankton had been here, I would have bitch-slapped him myself.

Ok yeah, the scum bag had deserved it. Doubt the creep actually learned a lesson, though. Well, maybe he did. He had learned to stay out of this neighborhood. I'd call that a win.

Fuck him, let him live with the scars, then. Earlier, I had a mind to go back and remove them through healing, but not now. Let him look at his face every day and be reminded not to touch a female, a young female at that, that didn't want to be touched. Served the fucker right. Case closed. And I could do that, because I wasn't a cop.

Ah, it was good to be a Merc.

I met Ashton's hard gaze with one of my own. "Justice has been served, then. Karma's a bitch."

His hard gaze turned to one of relief and like-minded agreement on what we considered proper justice.

But, we still had a problem. Several actually, as I saw Craven trying to control himself and revert to human form. Going from Dire Wolf to Werewolf, then to human, was the only way and took much more time to shift back for him. So, I started the information gathering, hoping I could uphold my sworn word and justify it to General Pierce somehow.

"Why don't you two get some clothes on and let's get out of the middle of the street. This may be your neighborhood, but sooner or later, somebody is going to come down that road."

As they complied, I asked Rock to get the cars pulled out of the road and parked along the street, as normal looking as possible, for having four identical black SUV's in a group. They may seem a bit out of the ordinary going down the road together, but they sure came in handy when one needed to carry a bunch of artillery, med kits and Black OPs bags for each member; plus have room for any hostiles or dead bodies to dispose of properly. Gas guzzling fuckers, but they sure did the job.

Clarissa Lee Moon

Chapter Twenty-Two

j' adoube

J walked over to the house they had chosen to congregate at which still had its old style wraparound porch and Victorian architecture. I loved old houses like this. In their presence alone, one could feel the history in the style of the house. They don't make houses like this anymore.

Most homes now had a cookie cutter look for the Smiths and Jones' of the world. All alike, and most even had the same paint on them. I would go out of my mind living in such a neighborhood with the weekend husbands mowing their lawns all together, soccer moms driving their kids to their various sports, dance recitals and play dates. What happened to the good old days of the kids just going outside and playing together on their own? Now, some parents think they have to schedule every second of their lives, driving not only their kids into needing Prozac, but driving themselves into the ground, as well.

This neighborhood had more of that old time relaxation of weekend barbecues, kids playing together because they want to and moms talking about their husbands on the porch as they drank their iced teas and lemonades. I loved that New Orleans held on to the old and accepted with grace the new and unconventional. What a wonderful blend of cultures they had managed with aplomb, I thought to myself.

And these werewolves; I shook my head inwardly. Talk about new and unconventional, yet old at the same time. They blended in perfectly with this city. Ironic that it was a city many books had based paranormal myths and legends into their writing with imagination and old style charm, and yet here in this city there really were werewolves living amongst the humans and no one really paid much attention to it. Like it was normal for this city to have such occupants. I had to laugh out loud at the absurdity. Ashton looked at me with that confused look which almost made me want to scratch his head playfully.

I refrained, though it was hard, and just sat down next to the female alpha, who had a pitcher of iced tea waiting for me. She had put back on her sundress and sandals, but her demeanor was subdued.

"What's your name?" I asked her gently.

"Domica, My Lady."

Oh, here we go again with the titles. Well, it still beat Meshallima Ama Ja' Catrina all to hell. So, I didn't bitch about it.

"Thank you, for the tea. It's good."

She gave me a shy smile for that and sat down next to me at the small table they had on the porch with some seats set all around haphazardly, more for the comfort of having many guests, than to look good.

Rock, taking my cue at the ease I had set, also allowed his men to look relaxed as well. Though, I knew these guys could snap into action within a heartbeat if the situation demanded it.

"So, I think I would like Ashton to tell me everything, from the beginning to save me time. I want to know when you came here. When you saw the black trucks like ours and when each missing wolven happened and what was going on at the time and who put the shield up around the neighborhood. In that order, leave nothing out. I'll let him talk and ask my questions afterwards. Is that agreeable?"

"Of course, My Lady."

I ground my teeth and set myself up for Ashton's report.

He set down his glass and looked at me. "Several years ago, a doorway opened up from our world to this one. What we saw on this side looked like the place had been ravaged by something powerful. I didn't know about it yet. It was one of our lower-ranked alphas who discovered the doorway to a world not ours."

I almost broke my own guidelines in wanting to know about his world, but caught myself in time and let Ashton continue.

"He wandered around here, seeing people and broken buildings, but no shifters. Just these humans and signs of severe flooding. As time passed, the flooding went down and he ventured out further to gather more information about this place. A group of humans jumped him. We didn't know why at the time, but we surmised later it was for food or money. Many were starving and desperate here, but he beat them off easily. Very easily," he stressed. "He then knew we would have no competition or worry for the safety of the pack, as we did have at home. That's when he came to tell me everything he had found out."

I couldn't hold back my question. "Why would you be worried about the safety of your own pack on your own world?"

"Cadia is ruled by the five Royal packs. My father is the leader for one of the Royal packs. All of the rulers there are brutal and some are absolutely ruthless, killing young male cubs of alpha males who have mated when there are enough alphas in the ranks. They fear that if there were too many alphas, there might be more challenges to their seat of power. My own father had started to kill the young cubs when our lower echelon of alphas had filled to overflowing. I didn't agree with the decision and I wouldn't help with 'The Gleaning'. He had me banned to my apartments in the main citadel and I couldn't warn the lower alphas when he was coming to 'Glean'. It was also how I found out he had been spiking my food with a drug that sterilizes a male, so I couldn't breed with my mate, Domica. He would have used this on all the males if it wasn't so expensive to get, so only the upper echelon alphas and his own son were treated with the drug but it was still better then when the 'Gleaning' time came for the lower echelon wolven."

Man, that sucked and I felt for him and his wolves. His father is as much a bastard as my own is.

"I still have another three years before I can hope the drug has run its course and I can breed with my own mate and give her the cub she has wanted for so long. The drug lasts for seven years and costs a fortune to be made." He reached over to hold his mates hand. "That was when Lecaino came and told me of this place here and a plan began to form in my mind. I arranged for my mate and I and those of the upper echelons that wanted to come with me to run to this world. We took everything we could that might be used for trade to buy what we would need to live on this side of the doorway. We found gold and gems worked the best for transactions here into the local currency and with that, we bought these home and repaired those that were damaged in the storm. We found out that's what had caused all the damage here to begin with. Slowly, we would get the lower echelons here and give them a home, working our way outward in the neighborhood. After the first six months here, is when we saw the black trucks coming into the neighborhood, as if they were looking for something or someone. I was afraid we had let down our guard and someone had accidentally let a human know about the pack, but nobody came forward with such a mistake. The bonds between me and those who left my father's rule had transferred to me strong enough by then, so I could tell none were lying. I was of his bloodline, so the transfer was easy. We just needed distance from my father and being on another world did the trick rather well." He grinned ruefully at me.

Well, now that made sense as to why they would prefer Earth, as opposed to their home world. Werewolf refugees. This just kept getting better and better. General Pierce was going to just love this one. Not.

But, I couldn't make this pack go back to their world. They had broken no human laws until Howard Frankton, and the asswipe deserved it. According to the New Orleans Police reports, this is the first unusual happenstance. Other than the dead girl, who I was convinced wasn't this pack's kill. There could be another pack from another world that didn't have this packs wisdom in keeping a low profile, or something more insidious was going on. I was betting the latter. Two werewolf packs from two different worlds winding up here in New Orleans would be too much of a coincidence and there hasn't been another category five hurricane for another portal to form from. This had to be something else then.

Ashton continued. "Once we have another home ready for living in, one of my pack volunteers to go back and try to rescue more of our people and bring them here. We then set up and get to know the local language, habits and find jobs. The hardest part is the schooling. Some of our cubs are just too aggressive to hold themselves in control at school, without an alpha to keep them in line."

I interrupted again. "Home school. It's what we do. We have the same problem."

"Is that legal here?"

"I am sure it is, though each state has its own requirements for home schooling. There is always a way around it to get the set up you want for your cubs."

He looked relieved. "I have been racking my brain on how to fix this one. We have been hiding our kids in the houses during the day until school is out, then allowing them out in the neighborhood to play. I know it's illegal, but we couldn't do anything else that wouldn't eventually expose what we are."

"Didn't you ask questions to people around here or at the school?"

"No, we were afraid it would draw attention to the fact that we wanted some of our young at home. We don't talk to anyone here unless it is absolutely necessary. The realtor lady doesn't care if we seem odd, so long as we have enough money for the houses around here. I could tell we could walk down the road naked and she wouldn't bat an eyelash at it, but that's because we have made her very, very rich in buying up homes here from people and filling them with our own pack."

I believed him. Money can make even the most insane people just seem like harmless eccentrics to others here. Money lets one do a lot of things most can't even fathom getting away with.

"All right. You used the portal; that's what we call it here, portals, and you made a home for yourself. Then, the trucks came. Tell me about that."

"We had been here for about six months and the pack at that time was much smaller. Only about twenty-five or so. The black trucks came in, cruising at all hours of the night and day. Sometimes, two or three men would jump out of the trucks and walk through the neighborhood, sometimes with their hands out like this." He showed me his palms facing up with his fingers spread about half an inch apart. Then he mimicked their movements.

"Shit, they were casting for a psychic feel, searching for the portal."

General Robertson and his men, I'd bet. I would bet a lot of money on this one. Now, we may have something to justify helping the wolves out with their missing wolven to General Pierce.

"That's what we thought, but they didn't find it. Later though, we were missing Germund and then two days later, Sumini. We couldn't find them anywhere and I couldn't even track them through the bonding cord. It was like they were just simply gone. We even searched for them on the other side of the doorway, thinking my father had found out about our secret and had dragged them back, but they weren't there, either. I couldn't feel them there or on this world."

He wouldn't be able to either; not if General Robertson used the Moiré Mesh. It blocked out any psychic energy or magick use, either in or out. Bonding cords were useless for tracking in that instance, as we'd learned the hard way ourselves. My heart went out to them.

"Then, this human in a uniform came three months later, asking for a meeting with the leader of the clan. We knew he knew something but at the time, we didn't know how much, so I went to meet with him. If I hadn't taken so many with me that night, I am not sure I would have made it back from that meeting."

Now, that had to be a hard thing for a werewolf leader to admit to. Werewolves were not easy to take and they sure didn't like admitting any weakness. It made for more challenges later by the young and upcoming alphas.

"He said he was a leader of a military branch here in the USA. He wanted an allegiance with my clan for anything that he and his troops might need. He said he would help keep our secret if we aligned ourselves with him and his agenda, no matter what it was. He said he could also provide humans if we had a need for them for anything we wanted to do for hunting, mating, and for killing. That was when I told him no, not under any circumstances. He smelled bad to me. I know the scent of a ruthless leader. My father is one but he smelled purely evil. I bluffed our way out, by saying we could go right back home that second and he wouldn't have anything to tell anyone else about. No proof. So he had no hold on us. It was a nerve racking time after that, always being on the lookout for some military vehicles to pull in. We had escape routes set up and someone was always on guard, so we could move everybody out if we needed to. I knew we could handle a group of humans, but we've watched TV here and know there are many thousands in the military. Too many for us to hold our own against, even if it meant going back to Cadia. That's when one of my people met a powerful Vaudoun Priestess."

My ears perked up over this, as this was the second thing I had to do on my list- make contact with a true voodoo practitioner and get the word out to stop the curses being thrown at our people here with weather magick. What was really interesting to me, was the fact General Robertson did not have this portal under his control, but a Voodoo Priestess did.

I frowned inwardly. Ok, that may be even worse news, actually.

"I went to meet her and told her of our problem here and she said she could protect our neighborhood, but I had to allow a bonding cord between her and me, since I was tied to all of my wolves."

I knew it; this was not good. I leaned back into my chair and used my second sigh to gaze at his solar-plex chakra. I saw his tie to his mate but the ties to his wolves had transferred to Craven. There was still one blackish cord going from him to somewhere outside this group and if I had to guess I could follow this all the way to voodoo priestess herself.

She won't be a happy camper, when she finds out about Craven taking over and I'd be damned if I would allow her a bond to my son. NO fucking way. Pieces of the puzzle were coming together in my head with General Robertson and this Voodoo Priestess at two centers. I could see a real bad scenario unfolding for these people, hitting them from both sides. Goddess help them.

192

"She said she would protect our neighborhood from any malicious magicks and also cloak the doorway from the military. It was the only other option we had at the time or face having to go home and back to my father's rule and his gleanings. I know he would take me back, as I am his only Heir, but the others will suffer more from returning. So, I took what she offered. It's been quiet since until three days ago when Takani there," Ashton pointed to the female who lost her young son, "took little Nicus to the park to play. She said she had only taken her eyes off him for a minute and when she turned back around, he was gone. There was no scent trial. Nothing she or any of our best hunters could track with."

He sighed and picked his drink back up. "Then, you came and we thought you were here to either bring the cub back or grab another. Well, we didn't know exactly what the plan was and now your son is our leader."

He hung his head. "I have failed my people here, if you've come to take us or kill us. None here want challenge. We just want a safe home. That's all."

Craven had shifted back to human form and joined the group sitting at my other side. He gave me an odd look. *'Why is he so sad?'* he asked on our private path.

'He thinks you will take out his serving guard and place your own in their place.'

'Oh, classic takeover tactics!' He knew his war history better than most adults did and knew too, the strategies that went along with a hostile takeover. *'No. I'll just give back control to his wolves. I don't want this. Too much shit, already. I feel everyone's pain, worry, fear, anxiety. It is too much for me, Mom. He is much more qualified for running his wolves. I don't know any of these people.'*

'Cat. And, it's too late for that.'

'Why?' he asked suspiciously.

'Look with your third eye and see the psychic bonds that tie you to these people.'

He did as I asked and then jumped up to his feet, growling and cussing. Ashton and his people looked at him, with alarm in their faces. Takani was whimpering in fear, huddled next to her mate.

'Craven, control yourself.'

'I can't do this. I don't want this,'

'You have to; these people need your help.'

193

'*What do you mean?*' His anger deflated and he took deep breaths to calm down. I didn't do anything to calm the wolven. A little bit of fear was good and Craven needed all the tools of leadership, Machiavellian or not, to keep things as stable as possible, both for his own safety and that of this new pack of his.

With the clues I have been putting together in my head, things didn't look good for any of us right now. I needed time to come up with a solution for everyone. For the time being, having Craven as the leader of this pack served my own purposes very well in making things easier for me to plan around. I told him everything Ashton had related to me so far.

I added my own order as I finished. 'You need to follow my lead and make sure they do as I say but the orders have to come from you, not me, or it will weaken your position in the pack. None here may want challenge, but their base instincts may drive them to challenge you if they sense any weakness. Do you understand? I can't fight three fronts; it's insane enough to take on two fronts in a battle. I need you to back me up all the way. Later we will see what we can do about this pack leader thing, but for the time being, just deal with it.'

'*But, the voices in my head, their feelings; it's making it hard for me to think.*'

'*Put all that in a tiny bubble and place it in the back of your head. If something comes through that bubble, it means one of them is in serious trouble. Then, you open the bubble, but until then, it should quiet the voices and dampen down the emotions.*'

'*Is that what you do with your bonds?*'

'*Yes.*'

He shut his eyes and started his breathing exercises, creating the images I had given him in his mind and shut the pack out. Once he was done, his face had cleared up a bit and he didn't look like he was going to bolt anymore. Having a lot of voices and emotions in one's head can drive a person insane if they don't learn how to shield from it. Now, he knew what I had to go through every day with our family and the Coven.

Craven looked around and saw the fear in their faces. "No one dies. So, don't worry about that."

Ashton came up and dropped to his knees in front of him, placing his arms around him, "Thank you, My Lord."

Craven pasted a smile on his face and gently moved him off. I knew why. It wasn't because Ashton was male, but blocking out other people was much harder, bubble or no bubble, when there was skin to skin contact. Werewolves would even be harder than a human to block, because of their psychic strength.

I gained Ashton's attention again to help out Craven. "Ashton, so what you were telling me about the Voodoo Priestess being the one who cloaked the portal and putting up the shield around your neighborhood, says to me none of you have any magick beyond the telepathy and empathy through the bonds?"

Again, Ashton gave me that odd look. "No. None of us can wield magick; we're wolves. Werewolves can't do magick."

'Quiet, Craven. It's another tool in your arsenal if you ever need it.'

He nodded his head to me slightly, letting me know he caught on and agreed to play along. We didn't know everything about these people or if what was going on in their world was a fact. Yes, I believed them, but I didn't have hard, concrete proof of anything. Until then, it was best to keep a close eye and play this with caution.

"I'll need the name of this Voodoo Priestess and where she can be found."

Rock was looking at ease again, seeing I was still taking care of business, even though we now had personal shit going on with these people. Andre was sitting across from me, thinking his own thoughts. If I knew my mate, he would have seen the clues, as well and was as disturbed by them as I was. And I was about to make things worse for these wolves.

"Why?"

"I'll need to go and have a talk with her about a lot of other things that are on my to-do list here in Louisiana."

"So, your territory isn't this state?"

"No, Texas, actually."

Ashton's worried look was back. "What are we to do then, if our leader leaves this state?"

Craven took a deep breath. "I think it would be best for now that you run this pack as my second in command. Your people know you best and they are already used to you commanding. I need to finish out this mission and then we will see what needs doing."

Ashton relaxed a bit. "But the others through the doorway? Our plans to bring more across? What do you want done?"

Craven looked to me and I spoke in his stead. "Actually, I need to see this portal."

Ashton was looking leery again, but stood up to show me the way.

195

I was amazed that between two sheds was the portal. with a black, psychic smoky curtain covering it. Damn strong sheds to have withstood the hurricane winds that ripped through this neighborhood. But, there it was.

Andre walked up to it and psychically felt for the energy signature.

"We can rip through this easily, Cat and close it."

Ashton gasped, looking to Craven. "But, My Lord, you said,"

Craven glanced at me again and I shook my head at him, answering his silent question. Out loud, to ease everyone, I countered Andre's assessment, "Andre, we can't close it right this second, but we can take her cloak down and add one of our own, until we get the Bokaris stones in place."

My cloaking would hold for a while, but once I ripped through this black shield, she would know another major magick user was in the neighborhood. Ashton apparently had the same thoughts as I did,

"She won't be pleased."

"She is forsworn. It's now our responsibility to take care of this and we will, but I can't let another magick user have control of this portal."

"How is she forsworn?" The angry glare was back in his eyes.

"She didn't protect this neighborhood from ALL malicious magicks or Nicus wouldn't be missing. Those were Dark Adepts that rolled through here taking your people. They are obviously stronger in some magicks than the Voodoo Priestess is, or she underestimated them; either way, Nicus is missing, so she cannot have control of this or you anymore. That also means, I have to cut that black bond off of you."

He backed up, until Craven growled at him.

"I am sorry, but that black cord is connected to you and will eventually hook into Craven. This is not allowed by our contract with him. That cord will place him in danger, and by extension our Coven."

He thought about what I had said and then nodded his head silently.

I walked up in front of him and gathered my power, making an astral white sword. You couldn't see it with physical eyes unless I used a lot of power, but that wasn't needed. I only needed to cut the cord spiritually, not physically. I reached for the cord and grabbed it. I took the astral sword and swung down on it. It snapped with a hiss of sulfuric odor filling the air.

Oh, this was so not good. She had been siphoning off psychic energy from the pack all this time. Like a psychic vampire. Rock looked at me with questions in his eyes but I shook my head, letting him know this was not the time.

"Andre." He nodded, knowing I wanted extra shielding put up around us until I was done. I made my hand glow pure white and cleansed the astral wound I had made in Ashton's solar-plex chakra area. I then turned to the portal and slashed at the shield, bursting it. There was a small backlash of power, but our shields deflected it.

I then quickly put up our own cloaking on it, adding a few surprises for any magick user crossing this area until I could get the Bokaris Stones to close the portal. No practitioner would know how to deal with an otherworldly device such as a Bokaris stone. I wouldn't breathe easily about this until we got those stones here or we shut the portal all together, but that would be a last resort right now.

I looked at Andre. "Oh yeah, she is going to be pissed. What a way to start negotiations for stopping those curses, eh?"

Andre shook his head at me, laughing and Rock just gave me the eyebrow. The rest of the team? I looked over my shoulder and sure as shit, they were taking bets. "Twenty, in my favor," I shouted to them.

Clarissa Lee Moon

Chapter Twenty Three

Adjournment

J left several of the men behind to patrol the neighborhood, along with Ashton's wolven guard, to keep watch for any more military vehicles coming in and to prevent any more kidnappings. There was no way we could now leave this pack unprotected. With General Robertson in the picture, it wasn't hard to figure out he had something to do with that woman getting killed. I was also willing to bet he had taken the cub and I had a sneaking suspicion of why and what for. Wizard was still gathering the Intel I needed, so hopefully by the time we got back, he would have a report for us and I can asses just how bad this was going to get. I had a lot to process and not very much time to get everything in line.

Rock still had a hard look on his face over something, but I ignored it for now. I focused on trying to balance my son's position in the pack and still get what I needed done, with as little time wasted. In most kidnapping cases, you had eighteen to twenty four hours to find the victim, if you wanted any hope of getting them back unscathed. The more time that went beyond the time limit, the chances of getting them back unharmed, went down drastically. Typically, in cases such as this, with a three day late start, the chances would be slim to none in finding the kid even alive in any kind of shape. This, however, wasn't your usual kidnapping. The cub was taken as bait. This was both good and bad. Good, because the likelihood they were doing anything bad to the cub was slim; bad, because it placed me and anybody going after the cub in a weaker position. They'll know we are coming, for one thing, and more to the point, ready for us.

Then, we had the Voodoo Priestess, who was going to be very upset that I cut off her power supply. I will also have to deal with her very quickly, before she can find another power source that could match

199

Clarissa Lee Moon

mine. The fact that I needed her to not only pass along a message to every major practitioner from here to Haiti but also to leave the pack alone, has already put me in a bad position in negotiations with her. Her price for both things could be high. She sure wouldn't do it out of the kindness of her heart. Most Vaudouns don't. You always have to give something, in order to get something, when dealing with this particular pantheon.

I got a picture of the cub in human form and the address to the Priestess' home. I was pretty sure she knew we would be coming. I was going to leave Craven with the pack, until I saw the moon eyes Ashton and his mate were giving my son. Sure, most seventeen year olds were hyper aware of any sexual attention, but Craven was still dealing with the fact of being a pack leader and having to focus on keeping his shielding in place with the new bonds that had formed. His mind was on anything but sex now...and I wanted to keep it that way for as long as possible. I may be just his Commander in the field but I was still his mother. I made a promise and I would keep it, in treating him like any other soldier in the field. I wouldn't worry for Romeo's sex life for instance, but for all of Craven's training he was not only my son, but still just a kid in some aspects. I wanted to try to keep him as innocent as I could, for as long as I could and I would use my rank as his commanding officer to do it, if I had to. So, the decision to take him along into a potentially magickal blow-out with a Voodoo Priestess versus leaving him behind safe from the magick (but not safe from the interests of the alphas) sucked. It was a hell of a choice to make as a mother and as a commanding officer.

We drove from Ashton's neighborhood to the address he had given us for the Mambo's home, taking Craven with us. I figured Andre and I had a better chance of keeping Craven safe from the voodoo priestess than leaving him back there with no one to guide him through the choppy waters of relationships before he was ready for it. Werewolves were a horny lot.

Voodoo people, on the other hand, were very volatile and yet we walked right through her shield and up to her door, without an invitation or a gift.

It was rude, it was ballsy and would either let her know we considered ourselves tough enough not to be fucked with or just piss her off more. It was a tossup. We had four men down the street just on the other side of where her shield began. I took the strongest military magick user with me as a show of force and the only other one who was up to

200

snuff was O'Hara. Andre and Craven would show the family level power along with me. Hopefully, that would be enough to give her pause.

The door opened before we had the chance to knock and a young man was standing there looking at all of us very slowly and carefully.

He was a slender young man in his early twenties and smelled of a practitioner, though a young one. I couldn't tell if he was a light or dark practitioner due to all the protective gris-gris and charms hanging everywhere. Some had been made with the death of a creature, which made my gag reflexes kick in. I hated being surrounded by death, like trophy rooms and such. The echoes of the animals' death still rung through my soul and it has always made me ill.

Using the deaths of animals in a voodoo ritual, didn't necessarily make them black practitioners. It was a way of life for them to use animal sacrifice, a way to gain enough energy to make their magick go. My method of magick was different, with very few rituals calling for a sacrifice, though they were in our BOS's, too. They were just used as a last resort with our family. Still, with all of these protection charms and whatnots being made with death energy, it made me slightly queasy.

"The Mambo said to ask you, do you come with war or talk, in your intentions?" He spoke with an interesting mix of French Creole and Jamaican accents, but still clear enough for me to understand the question.

"Talk, only."

"Your word?" I knew he was asking me for an oath from one magick user to another. He was most likely her protector and related by blood. Depending on the Priestess's age, I would be better able to guess if he was a son or nephew, or if she were young enough, a brother. Though, I was leaning more toward having to deal with a much older practitioner. The level of power that went into making the bond, cloak for the portal and the shield, spoke of someone with a lot of wisdom that came only with age.

"My word we will only talk, unless I or anyone with me is attacked first... on any level for this day."

I added that last part, because it would have created a loop hole for her to attack with magick and still not be held responsible for it.

"Who is calling upon the Mambo?"

"High Priestess for The Nightwolves Coven."

I had already warned O'Hara not to give any names because they could be used against a person in sending curses out. So, I didn't give her

201

my name or the true name of the Coven but calling ourselves The Nightwolves Coven was close enough not to be a lie to others. We of Fae blood, were good at not telling the truth without actually lying. We were Nightwolves and the whole Coven was a part of it, so it really wasn't a fabrication.

The young man took my word and let us in the door. He led us to what seemed to be the main living room of a pretty good sized house. If she made her living by selling voodoo spells and charms, she was making a very good living from it. There were soft brocaded red couches and a glass coffee table with gilded gold around the edges. Hand stitched tapestries graced the walls, depicting various mythical scenes. Some had verves interlaced around the edges and these gave off an ebbing of power. The creatures shown in these pictures might even be in the mists in spirit and these tapestries were her physical representation of her familiars that was much like my own astral familiars. They were probably there for protection and cloaking for her home.

"Have a seat. I will return with the Mambo."

None of us sat down. I wanted easy access to my guns or my magicks if things were going to get nasty. I was sure the others felt the same way.

A woman walked in wearing a red caftan and a turban styled head-wear. She looked every inch the Voodoo Mambo, with dark coffee-colored skin that was still smooth and free of any wrinkles. She had dark, almond-shaped eyes with high cheek bones, giving her an Egyptian cast. Her full lips colored with red lipstick, emphasizing their fullness perfectly. She was a very beautiful woman and a very pissed off one, as well.

Her dark eyes glinted with anger, as she looked at each of us in turn, then came to face me.

"You are tha one who took my wolves from me." Her statement was heavily laced with a Jamaican accent with very little of the French Creole undertone that her son had. I knew he was her son now, from the way he placed himself with her. Her husband stood on her right-hand side and you could see the family resemblance in the males, except for the eyes; he had his mother's eyes.

"You were forsworn. We took control and have given our oath to protect them from now on." I wanted her to know there was no way she was getting those wolves back into her control to siphon from. A Lao needed energy to work; the more energy the stronger the Lao. But, taking energy from living beings, as she had been doing, is more of the left-hand path, then that of the sweet Lao. If she was a Bokor, we could be in a world of shit.

"I an I', am not forsworn. I an I' have protected t'em."

"A cub was taken three days ago by Dark Adepts. That is not protecting them."

"No dark magicks can get t'rough I an I's protection," she scoffed.

Her aura had seemed to grow, slightly testing against mine. Power was sparking between her and me, though no one in the room could see this unless they were using their second sight abilities. She was testing my shielding and my magicks to see just how strong I was. It was both rude and underhanded at the same time. It also did not bode well as her being a Priestess of the sweet Lao.

"They have magicks that can cancel anyone's magicks."

"If t'at is true, w'at make you t'ink you can protect t'em now?"

Again, her power flashed out towards my shield and I sent it back at her.

I looked at her with a glint of anger in my own eyes. "We've kicked their asses once, and we can do it again."

"Why t'en, have you brought your talk here to me?"

She had not given up on testing the waters. She had sent a small tendril towards O'Hara now, which I blocked. I didn't want her to try testing him when he didn't know how to fight back yet, metaphysically speaking.

"I need to get a message out to all those who practice voodoo from here to Haiti."

"W'at is tha message?" She had snaked one towards Andre and I let it go , knowing Andre can easily block it and slap her with it, if he had a mind too.

"If anyone is throwing weather curses, to please stop. There are already enough natural disasters hitting everywhere. We don't need anymore and innocent people are being hurt."

She sneered, "Innocent...no one is innocent." Her voice then turned into a purr, "If I an I' send t'is message to my people, you must do something for me."

"What might that be?"

"A skull t'at belongs to my family is in Texas. T'ey call him Max. I an I' want it brought to me."

Andre and I went deathly still, knowing what it was she was really asking for. Rock must have picked up our vibes, because his eyebrow was rising in his, 'what the fuck is going on' classic move.

The skull she wanted, she cannot have. It would give her access to untold power, if she knew enough to unlock the secrets.

"You owe for the life of the cub. The skull is with its keeper, where it should be. I know Max's history."

"Tha cub is not dead." She dropped the bullshit story of the skull once belonging to her family. I knew for a fact, the skull used to belong to a Tibetan Healer who had given it to its new keeper before his death.

I had been watching her husband from the corner of my eye, inching slowly towards Craven. He seemed to be sniffing the air around him.

"No, but he is missing."

She seemed to have finally figured out we weren't easy meat and was behaving, metaphysically speaking, for now.

"You will get him back or be forsworn. T'en t'ey be mine again. Or you get I an I's skull, to replace w'at you took."

"The skull is not mine to give, but we need the message sent out."

"Why should we stop w'at t'ey have brought down on t'eir own heads? Even Legba's spirits are angry over preacher mans words of hate. He dances on tha graves of our people here in tha city. He and others like him dance over the graves of our people in Haiti. T'ey try to take our children, our future, as t'ey did when t'ey owned our ancestors. Why should we show t'em mercy, when t'ey dance their joy for their God and we die?" Her voice was rising in anger and I couldn't really blame her. If it had been me and my people, we would have sent out a psychic backlash ourselves. But, we would have been specific in our targets.

However, I couldn't fault her for the hate. I, too, had learned to hate a people when I saw others dancing in the street when 9-11 happened. Innocent people killed and others danced. I had not hated them before, but I hated them now. Before, I had been sad for them and would wish peace for all involved, but no longer. My heart just isn't that big, to wish for good on someone, when they danced for death.

But, there were other truths, too, "The power would be better spent in helping your people, don't you think?"

This is something I could say I practiced what I preached. Instead of bringing more grief to them, I took my power and used it to aid others here in the States where it could be helpful instead of spiteful. Defense is one thing, an eye for an eye another, but actively using power to harm in revenge so generally is wrong.

"I an I' help my peoples. I an I' protect my peoples. But, I an I' will not help you. Not even tha Sentinels will help your peoples."

"The Sentinels?"

"Keepers of tha Black Gate; or don't you know of t'em?" She started laughing low, "T'ey try to hold tha gate closed by blowing tha sweet in tha crack at tha Dark Shadows, but soon tha gate will open and tha Shadow Lords will come and no one will be dancing in tha streets anymore. Much blood will spill, much eating of tha souls for tha hungry Shadow Lords, and I an I' will show t'em where to eat first." She started ambling slowly towards Craven. "I an I' smell something animal, something powerful. I an I' will send your message if you give me t'is one."

I stepped in front of her, blocking her path, "No deal."

"T'en no message."

Power flared up between us again and this time I let go with what constituted a light metaphysical slap. She narrowed her eyes at me.

"Fine, we'll leave in peace for today." I had her pegged now. She was definitely a Bokor. There would be no talking with her, no reasoning.

"For tha day," she agreed. "But, when tha night comes, so do tha shadows. T'ey may be small now, but t'ey can still do much and t'ey grow."

I motioned for the guys to proceed me out the door. "Even the darkest night has to flee, when the light comes."

"T'ere are places so heavy with darkness, tha light cannot escape," she countered.

"There are places so bright with light, the darkness cannot live at all," I made it sound like a promise.

Her lips tightened with anger. "We shall see."

Clarrissa Lee Moon

Chapter Twenty-Four

Advanced Pawn

Rock ground out as soon as we were in the truck and driving down the street going back towards Ashton's neighborhood, "All right, what the fuck was that all about?"

"That was making a nice, new enemy really pissed off at me and throwing down the gauntlet at it."

"What's the Black Gate?"

I threw a question back at him instead. "What do you know about the Bermuda Triangle?"

"No. Fuck no. I really don't want to hear this right now."

I shrugged, "You asked."

Andre piped in, being a smart ass, "You did ask her."

Craven was sitting back, laughing at us all.

"Why is it with you folks everything has to be the fucking twilight zone?"

"Hey, we didn't put this shit there."

"No, you didn't. Ok, so what's the Black Gate got to do with The Bermuda Triangle?"

I saw a young black teenager walk out into the street. "First, you better stop the car."

"You're right." Rock spotted him, too. The kid just stood there, as we stopped.

"Well, let's go see what the problem is."

We all got out and moved slowly towards the kid.

"Are you all right?" I asked.

"My Houngan said to stop the black truck coming down this road at this time."

"Your Houngan?"

"Yes, he said to give the woman who stepped out this."

207

This was a white piece of paper that was folded and had a wax seal on it.

'*Babe,*' I could hear the warning in Andre's mind-voice.

I ran my free hand over the folder paper, but felt nothing malignant. I smelled it and the scent of frankincense wafted off the paper. That was a good sign, since the scent is used for pleasing the Gods and Goddesses in our pantheon. I assumed most other pantheons used the scent for very much the same thing.

"My Houngan's Lao is sweet," the youth said, with a knowing look in his eyes.

I opened the paper, breaking the wax seal on it and read it.

What I read made me smile, "Tell your Houngan that our Coven sends our thanks and may blessings shine down on him and his Lao."

He smiled back at me. "My Houngan added one more message for you. He said, 'Someday soon, you will have to do what you fear the most- not once, not twice, but three times more. He said the power of his Lao will be there for your draw when you need it." He reached into his pocket and drew out a golden necklace and handed it to me. I took it and felt the power throb through the medallion. On one side, was the symbol for closed doorway; the other, held a symbol for open doorway.

"Keep the closed side outwards, until you need his Lao, then flip the medallion."

"Again, my thanks to him and his house." I put the chain on my neck with the sigil for closed showing and tucked it into my shirt next to my skin. It resonated with my power, until a harmony was settled between the two powers, then it went quiet against my skin.

The young man took off, having done his errand and Rock had his eyebrow trick working overtime.

"Wait until we get back to the wolven's 'hood. I don't want to explain things twice." Things were speeding up and we were running out of time for many things, but the one I worried about the most was the cub.

Wizard was waiting for us with a few sheets of paper ready for us to look over. He must have found a printer around here.

We all looked over this new information and all of the pieces fell into place for me. I was going to have so much fun tearing Plum Island apart. But first, I had deal with this shit here.

Rock got a hard look on his face. "This is what we have been waiting for."

"What?" I asked him, as I was envisioning beating the shit out of some scientists.

"Not right now. First, we need to call General Pierce." He snapped around to Wizard, "Forward the Intel and a report of everything that has happened with the investigation."

Ah, I am not the only one who has put the pieces all together or was there something more going on then I knew about?

Right then, a sharp pain bent me over and made me gasp for breath. That was a warning signal that my shields had been infiltrated by another practitioner had come into the area not cleared for entry.

"Shit. Breach," I yelled. I turned to look towards the park and went into a full-out run. Andre and Craven were hot on my heels and Rock was pounding right along with them. He had learned how to take his energy and turn it into inhuman speed for short durations. Ashton and his main guard kept up with us easily. We got to the park in mere seconds and we all saw the voodoo priestess bending down sniffing the ground. She saw us coming and stood up, sneering at us. With her left hand, she threw something on the ground and turned sideways and went through an astral doorway and was gone, closing the door behind her.

"Damn it." That slippery bitch.

"What was she doing here, Cat?" Rock asked.

"Getting a scent for the ones who'd made it through her shields. If we're lucky, she'll go after them first, for breaking her protection, aiding in her loss of the wolven." I approached the area carefully, trying to find what I had missed earlier and what she'd obviously caught, or she wouldn't have left so easily.

I bent down to the exact spot where she had stood and sniffed at the grass. I could smell her and the herbs she had used for a summoning of an astral doorway. I snorted; amateur. I didn't need no stinkin' herbs to call a doorway, but I did need an exact direction to go- some sort of line or tie to the place or person I wanted to find or get to. I didn't know her or her haunts, so trying to track her through a doorway would be suicidal. I could wind up in an infinite number of planes of existence and an equal amount of different levels of those planes. Then I smelled it; the scent she had found. She would be looking for the power signature, but I knew that scent. The personal scent of General Robertson and the muscles in my back started to jump and twist in remembrance of my time with him.

I stood up, breathing in and out slowly. Andre's eyes widened and he came over to hold me, offering his emotional support. I could deal with this. I know I could. This was nothing more than bad memory and I was used to that. Feeling Andre hold me tight made me remember just how bad things had gotten for me and physical pain was nothing in comparison to that time without my mates. No, I could deal with this. The General had no hold on me. I smiled at Andre, letting him know I had it under control now and he stepped away.

'*I love you,*' I said to him on our private path.

'*I love you more.*'

Sexual heat started to rise up between us; but this, unfortunately, wasn't the time or place.

Instead, I turned to Rock. "General Robertson personally took this cub. It's his scent on the ground, though faint." I loved being a vampire sometimes.

He took out his phone and hit speed dial for General Pierce.

He filled him in on the bare essentials and then listened for a minute. "Acknowledged."

"Cat, we have to return to the base for debriefing."

Ashton's worried look came back to his face. They all looked worried. "I can't leave them unprotected, Rock. I gave my word."

Obviously, General Pierce heard me, because Rock handed me the phone, "Cat, we need you here for debriefing. The situation has changed."

"I understand that, Sir, but can't we leave the squad here and my men and let me call in one more?"

"Who?"

"Gerard. I know he's there at the base waiting for us." We always have at least one person on the base when any one of us is out in the field. This way, we can get things done quickly if the situation called for it like it did now.

"Fine. You and O'Hara's team come in and I'll have another squad waiting for you, but we can't wait for the time it would take for Gerard to get there, even if I sent him out right now."

"Sure, you can just tell Gerard I said code Dark one on one."

"Code Dark one on one?" General Pierce asked, confused. "Hey, he's leaving. Where is he going?"

"Not to worry, he'll have one of my other siblings show up there in about 15 minutes. He'll be here with me in about 2 minutes."

"Catrina, you have left something out again, haven't you?" Oh boy, he used my full name again. That usually meant he wasn't amused.

"I'll fill you in at the debriefing, but look at it this way. I just saved you time and money."

I heard him sigh heavily, "Fine, just get back here, STAT."

"Yes, Sir," I snapped out and gave the phone back to Rock.

Rock said, 'Yes Sir' one more time, then shut the phone with that look back in his eyes.

Rock looked at me, "You really like pushing people's buttons, don't you?"

"My psychological evaluation said I have problems with authority figures."

"That wasn't in the FBI file."

"No, it wasn't."

"Why wasn't it in the files, Cat?"

"I paid a lot of money to a very talented person to take some of the worst things out of all of my records."

"So, you're telling me, there is more about you that we don't know?"

"Yup. Seems like I got my monies worth, huh?"

"Shit." Rock closed his eyes

"You have been pushing everybody's buttons today, Cat. What's up?" Wizard asked.

"I haven't been laid in a few days," I snapped.

Wizard turned red from my frank answer and a few of the guys in the squad started laughing. I heard a few 'well, that explains a lot comments', too. Damn males.

'I can fix that,' Andre was smiling.

'How? I have to leave as soon as I get Gerard here.'

'Damn.'

'Yeah, see what I mean? I am getting cranky, damn it. All these fucking interruptions and shit are cutting into my time with all of you lately.'

'I'll make it up to you later.'

'Promise?'

He got a lecherous grin on his face, *'Oh yeah.'*

Heat ran through my body again, but since I couldn't do anything about it, it was making me even crankier.

I whirled around to face the crowd. "Ok folks, give me some room and move it now. You're about to see something most folks never get to see in their lifetime." I put my best circus entertainer voice into the order.

They backed off and I made a circle in the ground, blessing the area with white light.

I then focused on my inner power and also tapped into my mates powers. Then, I focused on my altar at home and the node of power I had built up there and tapped into it, as well. It may sound like I was tapping into a lot of power and I was. Bringing a whole person to you, took a lot of power. I wouldn't even need half of this power if I was just going myself from here to there on this plane. Closing down portals was a lot like that. It took an F-5 hurricane or tornado or a 6.5 earthquake to get enough energy to make a portal but it took very little to shut them down. At least for me. A typical magick user would need this amount of energy and then some, to close one himself. Being the daughter of a Goddess had some benefits.

I turned my attention to the bond I had with my brother, Gerard, and found him in my mind's eye, standing and waiting patiently for me in a field outside of the buildings at Truax Field base. I made a doorway from the circle to him and like bending time and space for one single minute, folding the distance with WILL, making the two places meet for the time he needed. He then was able to step through the door and out the other side, appearing in the circle in front of me. I closed the doorway immediately, since it took a lot of power to hold it open. It also took a very strong mind to hold the focus that precisely. One single mistake, for even a split instance and he could be trapped betwixt and between forever, with very little hope of ever being found.

"Greetings, Sister."

"Greetings, Brother." And he hugged me.

"So, fill me in. What's the emergency?" he asked.

I told him everything that had happened. Since I knew his knowledge in voodoo and how to protect against it was as deep as, or deeper, than mine, I felt the wolves here would be well protected until I got back. But, I thought I had better prepare them for the bad news now, before I left. I needed everything in place if I felt the shit was going to hit the fan, for them to be able to move fast, if it did.

"Ashton." He looked at me, finally taking his eyes off my son's bod long enough. Wolves were a horny lot, but I was not calling the kettle black. Nope, not me. "Craven and I have talked about the possibility of the Voodoo Priestess making life very hard for you here and now we also have a very bad General taking your people when he feels like it. We can't be here 24/7. We have other things we need to do a lot of the time. For now though, we are leaving these men here to watch over the area. They'll fight, if needs be, but I have to ask you, how tied to this place here," pointing to the surrounding area, "are you and your people?"

"We can't go back home." His expression had turned bleak.

"I didn't say that. I asked how tied to this particular place are you?"

His face cleared a bit. "Oh, well, we have seen other places through the TV and magazines we buy. As long as there are hunting grounds nearby- deer, elk and such, we would be happy, but..." his voice trailed off.

"But, what?"

"There are more that want to come here, too. They don't want to be there anymore and we have been bringing them over, bit by bit, as we rebuild here."

"How many are here now?"

"One hundred and thirty two."

"Including children?"

"Yes."

Not bad. I knew of several places I could put them that we could guard better and easier.

"How many more want to cross over?"

"Another two hundred give or take a few." I looked at him. "Some get scared at the last minute and decide to stay. They don't want to leave so many friends behind."

Another two hundred plus or minus. Shit, that overtaxed my own and my Earth-side mate's personal resources. We owned a lot of land all over the world, but nothing big enough for so many people and with cubs. Children? What world would love to see more children playing in the streets again?

"How well do any of your people fight?"

"About fifty here now are strong fighters, alphas all."

"How many are waiting on the other side wanting to defect?"

"Over a hundred, all with cubs marked for gleaning. We're trying to build as fast as we can, before the Solstice in our world. That's when my father has started Gleaning. Every Solstice now."

Those people would not turn at the last second. With children, you would face hell rather than see them killed. But, hell wasn't what I had in mind for them, though it could get hot for a bit there.

"What do you know about fighting vampires?"

"What is a vampire?"

213

CLARISSA LEE MOON

Shit. I took a deep breath and let my fangs slide out and hissed lightly at him. He didn't back up, but I saw his nostrils flare in agitation. This was a good sign.

"I have a place, maybe, if I can get permission where there will be no gleaning, no military threats and where people will appreciate the fact that you are wolven and would welcome you with open arms. There is, however, one small catch."

His eyes took on a predatory look. "What's the catch?"

"There are bad vampires called the Draugralls that have been hunting these people for food and women. You would be asked to defend the people against these vampires."

"You are Draugrall?"

"No, I am a different tribe of vampire." I kept it simple for him because we didn't have much time and I still had much to do. "There are many tribes of vampires some good, some bad, some so-so. Do you understand?" I went into my drill instructor mode, as I did when training my children.

"Yes."

"These kind though, are very evil and very fast. Their fangs are longer than mine." I started circling around him. He crunched lower in his stance, keeping me in front of him. This was really good.

"They have claw-like hands with razor sharp nails they use like knives." I pulled my knives out of my wrists sheaths. "Now, I don't have claws like those guys, but I do have blades. Silver-made blades that will burn you, just as the poison that is in the tips of their nails will burn you, if you get slashed. Do you understand?"

His chin tucked in and watched me closely, as I twirled my blades in front of him. "Yes."

"You can't let them bite you. I have no idea what a vampire bite will do to a wolven, but I do know what it does to others and it can enslave the victim if it's not cleaned out fast enough or if the vampire who bit the person isn't killed. Do you understand?"

I could hear the men behind me and Andre making bets and joking around. Ashton's pack though, watched every move and soaked up everything I was telling them, as well as Ashton and this boded very nicely for what I had in mind. Kla' din could gain that badly needed ground force. These guys had kept up just fine, on Rock's heels, when we made for the park during the intrusion.

"Yes." And this came out in a low growl.

"There is a lot of advantage in fighting in human form, if you have swords and blades made of silver. Have you or your alphas ever trained with such, as a fighting technique?"

His grin grew sharp and evil looking. "Yes. Many of the Alphas are proficient sword-wielders."

"That's very good. Then, that leaves shifting for quick recuperation if you get wounded. Guard yourself, wolf." And that was the only warning I gave him, as I headed in for an attack, slashing my blades going for his chest. That damn wolf went right over me in a front flip and landed behind me. I turned to guard myself from this new direction. "Hey, why didn't you do that when you fought my son?"

"As you said, there is an advantage in fighting as a human, but a challenge fight has to be in wolven form, when one is making a bid for a higher position."

I laughed out loud and swung my left leg out to swipe him off his feet. He countered by jumping in the air and swinging out with his leg, clocking me across the face.

I spun around from the blow and my men were silent for once. I actually got hit and they couldn't believe it.

I swiped at my lower lip, coming away with a bit of blood. I narrowed my eyes at him. "Oh, that's gonna cost ya."

"Honey?" Andre sounded a tad worried.

"Got it, babe." I went up in a defensive crouch and waited for him to move. He came at me with a whirl of blows and punches aimed at the upper half of my body. I countered and got a few fast kicks into his lower rib cage. Every time he pulled the acrobatics, I pulled back and guarded the flank he was trying to expose. Then, by making him come after me, which was proving to be his downfall, I back stepped and slashed out across his wrist. The second his eyes went down to look at the cut, I went in for his neck, lightly nipping it, then jumping back out of the way as he tried to punch me.

"Never let them get to your neck. Their bites are contaminated."

I whirled in behind him and jumped in for a draw across his neck again with my blade. I pulled back at the last second, so I wouldn't make the cut for real.

"Never let them get behind you. They'll rip your throat out and gorge on the blood."

I tapped into the power of my brother and mate.

Gerard was in my head, '*Cheater*,' he tsked at me.

'*Not if you win. You win- you live- Not cheating.*'

215

I took the power, and faster then he could track me, I lightly cut him several more times on the arms, chest and once on his leg.

The pain of the burn from silver made him take pause, which had to be corrected.

"No matter how many times they slash you with their claws, don't stop to look. Don't let the pain be felt; keep fighting, so you can live."

I put on a burst of speed again, moving around him and taking him down. "Once your enemy is dead," I put the blade to his throat, "then you can see to your wounds. But, in battle, there are no wounds, no looking to see how bad it is. It isn't bad, if you ain't dead. So don't stop fighting until your enemy is on the ground not breathing, before you do anything else."

I let him up after he saw he had lost the fight. "A vampire isn't safely dead until you have taken its head off completely from the body. When the battle is over, burn all the parts of the vampire each and every time. Do you understand?"

For Ashton, getting his ass kicked twice in the same day, wasn't good for morale for him or his wolves, which he reminded me when he said, "If they move like you, how can we beat them?"

"We," pointing to my family and back to myself, "are different, even from the norm for supernatural creatures such as you, such as the Draugralls. The Draugrall, you can easily take, if you are properly prepared for them. Plus, you'll have a back up of dragons and Sorcerers making victory easy enough with team work. That's why we are here and not there. What's coming here will really be bad, so we have to stay here until the battle is over."

"We've seen nothing but mostly mere humans. They don't seem very dangerous."

"But yet, you are missing people and a Dark Adept came in here after a Voodoo Priestess threw her magicks around and took a cub? Ashton, that is only the beginning. I swear, I am not lying, when I say things here are going to get worse. And because of that, we can't be here in this state all the time. There is more, but Craven and Andre will fill you in on the Prophecy and what it means to this world here."

He could tell I meant a lot more and turned his focus back onto what mattered to him personally, his people, "What are the chances of getting them and the cub back?"

"I'll be honest with you. The first two, slim to none." I had a feeling they were the ones General Robertson had experimented on. I doubted there was anything left, but I would look. "The cub, I have higher hopes for, since he is being used as bait." Or, I swore to myself, I will take it out of Robertson's hide myself-piece by piece.

He sighed heavily. "If relocating again will keep my wolven safer, then so be it. But I want the right to bring everybody across now who want to come. It would be wrong to leave them behind."

Admirable; I was liking this wolf more and more. "Done deal, if I can get my other mates to agree. It is, after all their world I am offering for home-steading. Give me a minute." He looked around to see if another was coming, confused at what I was about to do.

I just closed my eyes and put out my sweetest vibe in the call. Hey, it couldn't hurt.

I reached out to my Kla' din mate, Ja' Callum. *'Oh sweetheart, light of my life, sweet release to my soul, gentle ruler of my heart.'*

'Meshama,' he groaned, *'please tell me you haven't done something extremely bad again?'*

Oh, how well he knew me, but for once it really wasn't a bad thing I'd done. Not really. *'I need some help for some people and you and your cousins are the only ones I can turn to on this one.'*

'What people?'

'Three hundred strong of wolven that could make a very nice ground force that we've been looking for, to defend Kla' din. But, they need homes; they are refugees in a way.' I explained fast what had transpired. Information going mind to mind was faster than a computer. Pure information downloads that a highly trained Adept of the Arts can rapidly assimilate and use. You just have to be careful when you take information or give information in such a manner. The first time we did this, I had blocked out much of my brain from him, so he wouldn't be able to hurt or put something in my mind I didn't want. At the time, I didn't know him very well, but since then, there isn't anything I wouldn't trust him with, including my own soul.

'Oh Meshama, our son is too young for such a heavy burden.' Inside, I melted with love for this man who knew me so well already; of the pain I had buried, filled with concern for my young son. That he shared that same feeling and saw Craven as his son in spirit, showed me just how blessed I really was. Reluctantly, I had to push all personal feelings aside and look at this situation as objectively as I could. And use the incident as best I could.

'There is nothing that we can do about it right now. Maybe not ever, but be there for him when he needs help. These wolven now belong to him and by extension, to us. We have disrupted their plans here and they are also in danger,

not only from General Robertson, but from the Bokor. We can't stay here to protect them, so the next best thing would be to move them where they will have safety from these people and be useful to us at the same time. I see it as a win-win situation right now. If you and your cousins agree.'

'Have Andre make a tunnel for us, I'll bring them and meet with these wolven of our son.'

'Thanks. You guys deal with this while the team and I go to debrief. Bring Bokaris Stones for the portal. My love to you.'

'My soul to yours, Meshama.'

I turned back to the group. "All right, here's what's needed. Andre, Ja' Callum needs a door to get here. He is bringing stones. With the portal cloaked by something so alien, General Robertson and the Priestess will just assume the portal has been shut down, as we did with some of the others. Ashton, get as many of your folks here, if Ja' Callum agrees to the deal. Fill them to the rafters of your homes until we can get a plane here to transport everybody in one shot to the portal of Kla' din. Gerard, take care of protection against voodoo on these people. She has had direct spiritual contact with them for quite some time. Especially Ashton here. Major Pearson, patrol the neighborhood and kill anyone looking like they want a piece of the wolven." He nodded to me and went to deploy the men. Andre waited for me to move, so he could start the tunnel and I blew him an astral kiss goodbye.

"Craven, these are your people now, too; stay and help them get ready for transport. Make some plans for consideration and we'll hash them out later."

On our private path I added, 'I am sorry so much now rests on you, but I have faith you can step up and do well. If you need help or advice, you know the family is always here for you. I love you, son.'

'Love you, mom. Hurry back, please.' He sounded so lost right then, I wanted to give him a hug, but had to refrain since we were on assignment as Mercs and not home as family. I settled for giving him a smile and moved off to get with the team and head back to the base while everybody here got things in order.

I thought I had done a good job holding my own personal feelings in, when I really needed to hit something, anything. One son on a quest that could turn into the nightmare I'd had to endure, another son cursed into the shape of a panther and now my youngest, loaded down with a responsibility a grown adult would have had a hard time with, being unprepared for it. I held my silence and did the job I had sworn to do.

Everyone had been quiet for the car ride to the airport, until Rock asked me, "Think he'll be all right?"

"He'll have to be."

Chapter Twenty-Five

Active

Cassie and Demitri were waiting for us to arrive in the war room back at the base in Corpus Christi, Texas. General Pierce was not a happy camper and asked for O'Hara and me to step into his office before the debriefing.

"Andre called me not five minutes ago asking for another plane for transport. I thought there was only supposed to be three hundred werewolves moving through?"

"That was the estimate I had gotten right before I left. We didn't know their solstice would scare so many into taking their families into an unknown world in order to keep the babies alive." Though, as a mother, there wasn't anything I wouldn't face if it saved my child.

Andre had called after Ashton's spy had gotten back from Cadia, with the news that even more were prepared to flee than even Ashton had guessed at. It put a snag in our refugee movement. The rulers of Kla' din, though, were ecstatic at the thought of having so many ground force fighters added to their world that could keep pace in a fight with a vampyre. They had a huge male population, but only a small percentage could wield magick on any level. Those who could, were elevated to the status of a Je' and taught how to flex the power of their world into inhuman speed. Then, they were taught how to wield blades and fight hand to hand.

Their female population was only fifteen percent of the world's population, though a higher percentage of those could wield power. However, the females were kept out of any form of danger, because they were what little future the Kla' dins had in repopulating their world. The females were taught how to bury their powers, so they wouldn't be so easily located by the Draugralls and taken by force. It was truly hellish for a female with very strong gifts, to constantly have to keep them

221

buried down within herself. Young female children, with any power were never left alone, until they could withhold their gifts without having to think about it. Until that day, she was in the constant care of an adult who could dampen her powers, until she learned how to suppress them on her own. I could empathize for those young girls. I had to bury mine, so my mother wouldn't have me exorcized. Still, it's a hell having to hide abilities all the time, no matter what the reason was. Until we could find a way to keep the Draugralls out of Kla' din, it was the only way to keep the girls safe.

"I sent two more planes, just in case. But, do you have any idea how hard it is going to be for me to not only get those people, those werewolves, through airport security, not only in Louisiana, but through Okinawa? And how hard it's going to be to get them through the towns to where the portal is? The logistics is just begging for an incident, and what we're doing here could come to the attention that we can't shut up." Oh, he was not happy.

O'Hara stepped in, trying to calm the waters. "My friend in Okinawa could help with transporting them to the portal under the radar, if I can call him, Sir?"

General Pierce rounded on him. "And won't he be asking questions of dropping off all those people and they disappear, not to be seen again?" He then turned his suppressed wrath back at me. "Because of the spell weaving your Kla' din husbands sends, it's been hard enough keeping up with the women who show up in Japan. And, those women are never seen again after their passports and visas run out. The Japanese Consulate is asking why we haven't lodged any complaints over the number of missing women having disappeared into Japan recently. That has been hell sidestepping why we aren't concerned. And now, we aren't the only country missing women on supposed Japan vacations. And their governments are lodging complaints. It makes us look bad when we don't do the same thing."

"Having a bad day, General?" I asked, flippantly.

O'Hara rolled his eyes.

Before the General could take me to task for it, I said, "Listen, the Shaballum's mating season is almost over. The callings will go down drastically, since only the strongest Je's will be able to send a spell out through the portal after that time. It's why the Ja's have allowed so many of the weakest Sorcerers there to call first, rather than the strongest. It was also the only way not to have Sorcerers traipsing all over our world searching for their mates. Even low leveled Sorcerers could cause a lot of havoc here. This, in the long run, will save you many headaches. After the heat is over for the mares, the strongest Je's will call and the toll of missing women will go down."

"That will still add up at the end of the quarter and how to we explain our lack of concern?"

"I have an idea, but it is a tad illegal?"

"Anything, please."

"Some of our people are very good with computers; I can send a family to Japan and set them up to take note of the women being drawn to the portal. Once we have their names, we can clean out their existence here, but we'll have to hack into other countries computers, as well. It has risks, but smaller in comparison to the missing women toll going on now, I would assume."

He looked at me, incredulous. "You call that a tad illegal?"

"Well, yes; we aren't killing anyone." I was confused.

His smile started small, and then the laughing started. "Cat, there are some days that I just don't know what to do with you."

"A raise would be nice."

That only made him laugh harder. O'Hara soon joined in. I don't know what their problem was; I was being serious. Replacing leather jackets and boots as well, as the silver blades I would lose on missions, was expensive.

"No raise?"

He just shook his head at me. Oh well, I tried.

"Fine, but if I save the world, I want a nice bonus."

"Cat, please. Seriously now, get those people over there after they talk to Wizard. He'll have codes we aren't supposed to have that will keep the risk down to a minimum."

I was being serious.

His own expression turned taciturn again. "Now do you mind filling me in on how you got your brother there so quickly"

"I bent time and space for a minute."

O'Hara interjected, "But, I thought you couldn't do anything larger than fifty pounds."

"For one, Translocating and opening an astral doorway are two different things. Translocating is instantaneous. You have to have been at the place before and your aim better be dead on, balls accurate." I have been wanting to use the term for a while now and smiled. "Opening astral doorways is another way of getting others from one place to another if they have never been there before. However, opening a doorway and holding it takes a lot of energy. Also, there are other downsides to an astral doorway. If I bring people to me or send them through the door, I wouldn't be able to follow safely."

"Why couldn't you follow after everyone has passed through?" General Pierce asked next.

"Because, the power needed to hold it open would drain me too badly for me to also safely cross. I would barely have enough left to safely and properly close the doorway again."

General Pierce sat back into his chair. "What happens if it's not closed right?"

"A rip in space and time can happen, causing a rift. That would be bad."

O'Hara looked at the General, who nodded his head at him. "When we were at the Priestess' house, there was talk of a Black Gate and the Bermuda Triangle?"

The General's eyes widened, but he waited for me to reply. "There are twelve natural dimensional gates on Earth. The Bermuda Triangle is just the most active and famous one you would recognize, right off the bat." There were thirteen actually, but the thirteenth gate wasn't a problem and something they didn't need to know about. "The Black Gate is more commonly known as the Mediterranean Triangle covering both land and sea of the top part of Africa and the Aegean Sea. The Sententials are strong voodoo practitioners who pass on the knowledge of this gate to each successive generation. Their mandate, which they've kept for millennia, is to keep that gate closed by building positive energy and sending it into the small cracks of the Black Gate keeping The Shadow Lords at bay. It's called, 'Blowing the sweet through the crack'. Whenever you hear a voodoo practitioner speak that sentence, they are talking about the Black Gate."

"So, what was she talking about when she said, 'soon the Gate will be open and the shadows come'?" O'Hara asked.

"Bokors like her are waiting for the shift to open that gate and let the Shadow Lords out to rule once more."

"Cat," the General interrupted, "What's a Bokor?"

"A Bokor, is a voodoo practitioner that worships the left-hand path; General Robertson's equivalent."

"Wonderful, so now we have another host of people and a gate to worry about?"

"Yes and no. That's the Sententials job, not ours, but we must back them up, if they call. The Shadow Lords aren't really the warm and fuzzy type. It would be a real good idea to lend a hand if the Sententials ever call for it."

"And the skull called Max she wanted you to steal for her?"

Damn, O'Hara would have to remember that part.

I sighed, "The Skulls are part of the prophecy. There are thirteen ancient crystal skulls, the most famous and also the biggest, weighing eighteen pounds, is called Max and he is right here in Texas."

The General reached for his notebook and was taking notes. "You talk like it's alive."

"It and the others are alive, in a way."

O'Hara continued to dig for more information, "So what do they have to do with the prophecy?"

"The thirteen crystal skulls will come together to aid the Ancient Gods and Goddesses back into our world. So the legends go."

"Why isn't Max with you then? Who is this person who has him?"

"The Skulls aren't our mandate and Max, as the others, are with their proper keepers, except one."

The General rubbed his eyes. "I know I am going to regret this, but where is the one who isn't with its proper keeper as you say?"

"In a government installation locked away in a steel box and put with a great many things the government has neither knowledge nor any right to have. They are messing with fire and it will burn their asses some day." And that day was coming sooner than they realized.

"Why did they lock it away?"

"It wouldn't stop moving."

"Excuse me?" the General asked.

"It was in a museum, but it didn't like it there. It wanted to be with its proper keeper, so it kept moving. It freaked the curator so much, he called in the specialist and they were freaked and locked it away. What they still fail to understand to this day is that when the time comes it will move where it ultimately needs to be, locked steel box or not. They ALL will move when the time comes. It just wants to be elsewhere at the present time, is its problem."

Stupid mundane mortals thinking they could play God or control something made by the Gods, I snorted to myself.

"So, it moves-by itself?" O'Hara wanted this completely clarified.

"Frequently; it's not happy."

"Where does it want to be, then?"

"I have no clue. I am not a keeper."

"Is this a problem for us?" The General was probably afraid I'd ask to break into a federal building to steal it.

I smiled at him. "I haven't been told it's my problem; so no, I would say not."

He blew a sigh of relief. "Good, but these werewolves are a problem."

"Not really. They'll be on Kla' din when if I think it's best to move them out of harm's way. They'll be Kla' dins problem or an asset actually, since they will be much safer fighting vampyres and won't have to worry about voodoo priestesses, lab experiments or dark adepts. Compared to all that, vampyres will be a cake walk."

They both just looked at me for a long moment.

O'Hara shook his head at me. "There is something so wrong in what you just said, but I haven't figured out exactly *what* it is, yet."

"What? Vampyres are an outside threat, right?"

"Right."

"Werewolves always need something to fight, it's in their blood. Ashton can say until he is blue in the face, that all they want is peace, and that may be true, but sooner or later, some of those alphas instincts are going to kick in and it won't be peaceful. Being in Kla' din, they'll have an outside source to fight that will keep the pack cohesive until it's been solidified. Trust me, Ashton may be a good leader, but on some things, he is still wet behind the ears. His alphas would have challenged him sooner or later and then he would have had major guilt in taking out one or two of his men to make his point."

O'Hara's face cleared. "Ah, I see-dominance games. I keep forgetting they're not just people."

I answered both of O'Hara's points. "Not games really, just instinct until enough blood has been spilled. And it's easy to forget they're not humans, when you don't see them on four legs all the time."

"And now your seventeen year old son is the pack leader," the General reminded me.

"I know. Why do you think I am happy to give the Cadians an outside force to fight and bleed over until the pack becomes banded in spirit and blood?" I knew what I was doing when I suggested Kla' din. It filled so many needs, but mostly it kept my son from having to spill the blood of his own pack. That would have ripped him apart. Ashton would survive and eventually be all right about it, since he had grown up with dominance battles all of his life. But Craven hasn't, and it would have permanently damaged something inside of him, making him vulnerable and eventually some alpha would go in for the kill. It was the best thing I could think of to keep something like that from happening to him. He already had enough on him that could break him so easily, with his big heart.

"Well, the werewolves are going to be dealt with, the Black Gate is not a Nightwolves problem, and the skulls are not a problem; but this is, Catrina. This concerns us very much." General Pierce slid over a news article dated two days ago.

The caption read, "23 young women kidnapped from two Churches, Parents and Church officials are frantic."

I snorted, "I know why the Church is frantic. They're afraid of getting busted. Again."

"Is this that Maggie problem we talked about?" O'Hara took the article to read it.

"Catrina, this is nothing to make light of," Pierce rebuked me.

"I don't see why not."

"Why didn't you inform me of this mission?"

"It was a civilian problem, not a military one."

He looked upset again. "What isn't in that article, O'Hara, is one of the priest's was castrated. What's amazing is the wound looked weeks old, but the priest swore he had just woken up with his genitals removed, Catrina. Would you mind explaining this?"

"He must have been caught doing something very bad."

"This borders on vigilantism, and you know it."

"I don't know anything. If you recall, I have been here the whole time. None of your people were involved, so it shouldn't be a problem." I had been voted out of going, since no one in the Coven trusted me to keep my cool and not kill anyone on our way out. The whole mission was done with our second string family defenders. They needed the experience anyway in doing civilian OPs before taking on a military one. Personally, I thought they had done a bang up job. Gerard was quite happy, too.

"Where are the girls now?"

"Safe, until we know that the girls won't be turned right back over to the church. If so, I am sure they'll have other options available to them. The ones whose parents can be trusted to keep their daughter safe from the church will have a happy reunion."

Our family counselor was working overtime helping each girl deal with the aftermath. Hells, we needed more help for the psychological aid these girls needed. Everything else, we had covered.

"Some of those girls are pregnant, Catrina." Again the General used my whole name. He must be pissed as hell.

"And they'll also be taken care of. All has been taken care of. We could use one or two more shrinks though, if you have them?" I asked hopefully.

"You can't mutilate people like this and not expect some kind of blow back, Catrina."

Then, O'Hara dropped his bomb. "This is why I think she ought to be taken out of rotation for this next mission, Sir."

"What?" I was now the one getting pissed.

"You're a liability for this mission. It's obvious from the Intel that this is a ploy to get their hands on you again. Plus, we are going into a government installation, where it is alleged that they are doing illegal scientific metaphysical experimentation. You're unstable in your emotions when dealing with anything to do with children or science on metaphysical beings. Your judgment becomes impaired. Finally, it is inadvisable to walk into a trap that is so obviously meant for you. We can't take the chance of placing you in extreme danger and giving them what they want. So, I recommend you sit on the bench for this round."

"Catrina?"

Oh joy, the General was going to let us two leaders hash it out.

I took a picture out my pocket and showed it to O'Hara. "Look at him."

He did, but his resolute face didn't change.

"That's an innocent, three year old little boy. Yeah, he may turn furry every now and again, but he is still just a child, a baby."

"But, he's not yours."

"No, he's not. He is an innocent who needs help, and the faster we get out there, the better his chances will be."

"They know you're coming. They want you to come. It would be stupid to give them what they want."

"Yeah, they know I am coming. I know that they know I am coming, but they're idiots if they think I am coming in the front door. That's your job." I smiled evilly at him.

"I can't trust you not to kill anyone once you get there. This isn't Pakistan, Brazil or even Saudi. This is an American OP on American soil. It has to be a clean snatch and grab; I can't trust you to do that."

O'Hara had never tried to stop me before. He never got in my way with a situation that was clearly more of a paranormal situation than a military one. He was out to cockblock me on this mission and he was pissing me off.

"If you can promise me I can bring every single paranormal out of there and send them home. We get their files and burn their computers; then I can promise not to kill any humans unless my life, or an innocent's life is in imminent danger and I have no other choice."

With what I will be walking into, I was guaranteed death and mayhem which was why I could promise this so easily. The General and his men would give me every opportunity to have my revenge.

"No killing? No mutilating?"

Why was I getting the blame for somebody else's work?

"Unless absolutely necessary."

"All right. How to you plan on getting past the General's men, so they can't grab you?"

"I'll think of something," I said, smiling up at him.

"That's what I'm afraid of." O'Hara gritted out.

"Enough, you two. I won't authorize you on this mission, Cat, unless you can show me how you going to keep your exposure down to an acceptable level."

"Fine, let's head off to the war room then and I'll see what we've got to work with."

Neither looked happy, but they agreed reluctantly and we set off to meet up with the rest of the teams going in.

Wizard had gotten the blueprints of the plant and some history of how and why it was built. I scanned the information letting ideas come and go in and out of my brain. It had always been weird how my brain worked the way it did. I just let it go, doing what it did best while Wizard filled us in on his report. "Plum Island was built back in World War II and is still headed by a German Scientist that worked under one of the most evil Nazi Death Camps that used Jewish prisoners to experiment on, then kill them when they were done with their bodies, providing they lived through the experimentation. Our people got a hold of this particular German scientist, because of his knowledge of viruses and biological warfare. His genetics knowledge held him in good stead in splicing together cells our own scientist hadn't even conceived of. So, our government made him a deal; work for us or die. He's been there ever since leading the labs in making viruses and genetic splicing of cells for various mutations."

I interjected, "It's been rumored Plum Island is responsible for allowing the West Nile virus out along with Lyme disease."

"Lyme disease is definitely at their doorstep. The department investigating the West Nile virus; still hasn't gotten concrete proof yet." Wizard affirmed.

I snorted, most likely because they'd gotten pressure put on them from someone higher up in the food chain. Or paid off really well, to slow the investigation.

General Pierce added his report. "There have been two bodies of unknown origins wash up on the East Coast, not far from Plum Island."

He showed me pictures taken of these grotesquely malformed bodies, which looked like a cross between something vaguely human and many parts of an animal. What kind of animal, was anyone's guess, but the end result was really awful.

"How did they wind up on shore?"

Wizard was answering that one, "We don't know exactly, but since this place was built so long ago, security and safety measures are sadly and dangerously behind the times for the kind of experiments they are working on."

Which explained how two dangerous viruses, never known to man before, are now loose on our planet. Good job, dumb asses, I thought to myself.

"But, these creatures are extremely larger than a virus. How could they have gotten loose?"

The General said quietly, "Autopsies show they may have had extra abilities that nothing on Earth has."

Meaning that these creatures had been spliced from supernatural beings with possible abilities of shapeshifting, blending or even cloaking. Son of a bitches must pay. But I held the anger off of my face and just took the information as outwardly calm as I could.

O'Hara looked at me with a hard gaze in his eyes, "So, how do you suppose to get on this island surrounded by water?"

"Recon and half the Special Forces can come in from each side. It should pull all of those men out to the outside to defend, right?"

"Yeah."

"At night, they should have no more than twenty people on the island during a normal situation, but since General Robertson will be there, we should count on another forty to fifty highly trained soldiers."

"Right."

"Since we are doing a snatch and grab, with as low of a body count as possible, we'll need tranqs dosed for normal human body weight and rifles for them."

230

"So far, so good. But, the exposure to you, personally, will be too high if you come in on any of the sections."

"Not if I come in by air."

O'Hara blinked, "What?"

My assassin teacher would be killing people right now; he once knocked me upside the head to get the point across. I didn't wake up for over an hour. Then he said to me, 'No one ever looks up. That's how you die, stupid.'

"If they're scattered outside in every direction, I drop in the middle, right on the roof. From there, I can enter either through one of these doors or preferably, through this completely antiquated ventilation system. Shit, look at this, a six year old could get through this," as I pointed out several easy entrances in from vents.

Captain Holland snorted, trying to hold his laughter in. He thought I'd just made a rookie move.

"Those vents can hold any number of viruses and disease which aren't probably guarded on the island to begin with. You want to die?"

I smiled, "I am a vampire, sucker. No stinkin' virus is going to harm me."

Captain Holland lost his smirk.

"Ok, but you can still carry contaminates from the island on your extraction."

"Not with magick to 'clear the air'. We can easily remove anything off of us before going outside of the building, even cells as small as a virus. Anything not normal to us, we'll fry with magick."

O'Hara was gritting his teeth. I couldn't understand why he didn't want me on this mission.

"You'll have to show me how before we go," was all he said. I knew I had won.

"Umm, Cat?" Wizard got my attention

"Yes."

"How do you plan on getting onto the roof?"

"From a plane or a helicopter."

O'Hara's eyebrow went up. "Do you understand the winds in that area?"

"Yes, I understand that on a choppy night it, can be damned dangerous."

He nodded. "Wind currents being erratic to begin with and manning a drop on such a small area would be a tad suicidal."

"Not with the right pilot."

He shook his head, "We don't have anyone among us that skilled."

"I know of someone."

The General was looking rather peaked again. These two really didn't want me going. My feelings were starting to be hurt over their lack of confidence in me.

O'Hara gritted out, "Who would be skilled enough... no let me rephrase that... who would be crazy enough and good enough, to make that drop?"

"Lieutenant Juan Rico."

O'Hara stared laughing. "The pilot that crashed and was in a coma? That one?"

I nodded, "The pilot who saved everyone else on that ride, landing a malfunctioned piece of shit helicopter. The pilot who has flown eleven missions, dropping off or picking up Special Forces teams just like yours, under heavy gunfire and brought you out. The pilot who has more flight time in combat than anyone else on this base. Yeah, that one."

If that wasn't crazy enough or skilled enough, I'd become a nun.

We went through the rest of the to-do list, while we were there. Mark 5 SOC boats that had minimal radar signatures made them damn hard to pick up if they were scanning, and with the outdated equipment they had on that island, I was secure with the Mark 5's. We also requisitioned several Zodiacs, small inflatable rubber rafts, which had a small engine that can get us back out to sea, to the Mark 5's waiting for extraction. And one Stealth Black Hawk helicopter.

"Sure you trust him to get you up there in one piece?" O'Hara asked me.

"Absolutely."

"Fine. Get him here and prepared for this," General Pierce ordered.

Oh, he was not the happy camper at all.

Chapter Twenty-Six

Alekhine's gun

Lieutenant Juan Rico and his co-pilot were waiting for us on deck. O'Hara had stopped to talk with the General before catching up to us on the tarmac.

"Ready to save the world, one mission at a time?" I asked him.

"Ready to roll." He was smiling; almost gleeful. Yeah, he was one of the crazy ones, all right. You had two kinds of pilots; those who were just flat out insane or ones who went by the book. I personally liked the crazy ones. They're willing to go that extra mile when you needed them to. Tonight's mission needed one of those.

The winds were pushing and shoving from different directions once we hit the coast. The shore line of the coast and the shore line of the island were making the winds wild and because of a storm that was still five hours away, it was making things extremely hazardous in the air. As heavy as the copter was, we were still being bounced around pretty good. Jumping from fifty feet in the air was going to take...well...crazy people like us. I took Cassie and Antonio with me, along with Gerard, one of his wives, Lucy, and Grant. I was surprised my baby brother brought along his wife, but he said he wanted all his wives to get the experience of fighting lethally and using their magicks. Unusual for an Italian man and his wife having such a young baby at home, but it was his decision and I personally agreed with it. The more she knew, the more effective she would be in protecting those babies at home with her sister-wives. O'Hara and Romeo made up the eight who would be dropping onto the roof. We'd use black ropes to do it, but that didn't make it any safer with the heavy gusts of winds that kept changing directions on us every few seconds.

Rico did his job and sounded off the signal for dropping. We threw our lines out and slid down the ropes, using power to keep them steady,

233

despite the hectic winds. I could see the ground teams moving stealthily from the shore into position, to start the fireworks as a distraction, so we could slip inside.

Once we were in place and the 'copter was out of sight, O'Hara gave the signal telepathically, so no radio signals would be used, giving us away. Right on time, and in perfect sync, all four sides started laying down smoke grenades and poppers. Poppers were used just to get attention but not really do any damage; they sounded big, but that's about all they did. We each slid into our chosen air ducts and went on in. Oh, I loved being a Merc. I was smiling underneath my cowl as I glided through the vents to reach my target of the computer room where Antonio was supposed to meet me with O'Hara. To get to the computer room, we had to pop out of the vents inside one of the lab rooms. I came out of my vent to a very surprised old man in a lab coat, with a tray in his hands of various vials and containers.

I recognized his face in a photo that Wizard had of the infamous Dr. Zimler. This man- this monster- was responsible for thousands, perhaps hundreds of thousands of lives, and yet, I bet he felt absolutely no remorse for a single one of them.

"Put the tray down."

"Vat....?"

"Shut up. Put the tray down now or I'll kill you."

He put the tray down and I walked up to him, putting my hand on his face, almost gently. I gazed into his eyes and looked for a soul and saw nothing but huge black holes. His decisions to hurt, to maim, even to kill with no remorse- no conscious- had torn pieces from his own soul, leaving behind a shredded black husk. He may have been human in form and in blood, but his inner self was that of a soulless monster.

I feed power through my hand with a spell, then took a Senbon out of a small case with my other hand and stuck him with it. He hit the floor and I didn't bother trying to ease his landing. The chemical on the small dart would knock him out, doing him no harm, just as I promised O'Hara and the General. The power I sent into his brain, however- well, if the good doctor ever performed another experiment that will hurt someone, or a supernatural, the magickal suggestion I had laid in his brain will automatically kill him, looking like a stroke. My promise kept, my hands will be clean. He'll be the one to bring his own doom upon him. Fitting, I thought.

Antonio had stepped in and looked at the body, and then walked right past it, going into the computer room as he took out his gadgets for hacking. We both had put on extra speed to get here first, so O'Hara wouldn't know we were searching for other facilities for supernatural creatures. Antonio worked fast, making copies for our own Coven and then stopped. "Cat, look."

I narrowed my eyes as I scanned the information, as it flowed across the screen.

"Copy everything and hide ours, then wipe the whole system clean."

He nodded and went back to work, knowing we'd only have another two minutes at the most to get the job done. I went back out to the lab room to buy Antonio some more time. Sure enough, Rock was getting good, making better time than I had thought, as he cruised in. He stopped, when he saw the body of the old man on the floor.

"Is that who I think it is?" he asked me.

I slowly looked down, and then back up. "Yup."

"You promised you weren't going to kill."

"I know I did."

"He looks dead."

I blinked, "Does he?"

He bent down to check for a pulse. "You knocked him out."

"I did, and gently, too."

He gave an exasperated sigh, "You could have just told me that."

"It was more fun watching you get mad."

"We don't have time for fun." He moved on past the sleeping doctor, as Antonio was coming out of the door, handing over a disk to Rock, "Here's the copy you and the General wanted. The computers have been wiped, too. Shall we?"

"That was fast."

"We aim to please."

Antonio went off to his next mark, which was the security system, so he could make it easy for Rock and I to get to the prisoners cell block. I was hoping Nicus would be held in one of them, since that was supposed to be the most heavily secured section of the whole compound on the island. Our other team members had their own blocks to check and free those within.

Antonio whispered in my head as each section was disabled, so we could just fly from one area to another until we made to the prisoners cell block. Rock and I would knock out the security guards stationed here and there, before they could get on their mics hanging on their shoulders. Rock used his tranq gun and I used my Senbons.

235

With two more guards down at the prisoner's station, our area was secured. I took a look at the control panel and saw a system very much like the one that had had Demitri trapped so many years ago. My blood started to boil seeing this contraption being used on these metaphysical beings. You wouldn't think how dangerous a magnet with the right polarity and sound waves hitting it could do to a supernatural, but they were excellent in stopping any metaphysical being or supernatural from using their powers.

Men in the clean white lab coats and their PH.D diplomas, thinking they had the right to keep a being in such damaging cages. Not caring what lives they were ruining, whose hearts they were breaking, or even what destinies they were changing; just as long as they got their quantifiable, empirical data with their cold, calculating, detached attitudes. They were delving into areas that were none of their business, and that they had no right to and someday I seriously hope The Gods would give me leave to hunt these fuckers down and kill them; slowly, painfully and with the same cold detachment they had probably shown their subjects. They were no better than those Nazi motherfuckers who used the Jewish people as lab rats.

"Cat, are you all right?"

My hands on the consul had heated up and were burning the table top. I quickly moved my hands away and got control of my anger. No amount of therapy or loving from my mates would ever wash this particular rage from me. But right now, a three year little boy needed me to keep my cool. So, I calmed down and quit burning things, gathering my thoughts together.

I looked for the switch that would open the door to the hall that led to all the cells. I flicked it open and went to look at how many cells there were.

The hallway was long and cold looking, with its blueish-gray walls. Every four feet there were steel doors with small windows with metal coverings you can slide back to peer into each cell. The floor was pale concrete, with large drain holes about five feet apart on the floor. Each drain pipe was covered with steel metal and what looked suspiciously like the Moiré mesh coating the surface. I counted at least forty steeled doors. Too many, so I looked around for a clipboard that would tell who or what was in each cell and found nothing. Fuck it, I needed to get everybody that I could trust out of there and there was only one way to do that.

"See this switch, Rock?"

"Yeah."

"Flip this up when I open my hand; down when I close it, ok?"

"Got it."

He manned the switch that would take the magnets offline while I stood in the main doorway and signaled for him to turn it off.

'Listen, we don't have much time. If you want your freedom you have to swear to me on your souls and your Gods that you will behave and harm no one in any way, large or small, until we get you to your homes. Swear now or stay here. Your choice.'

'Who are you?'

'No time, we have to go now. Swear or stay. Choose.'

Several 'swears' came to me, but what they didn't know was that I was watching on the astral plane for any red flares and saw three. I made note of their location.

'There are children here. I need you all to swear not to harm the children at all. Swear now or stay.'

They swore again, but two more red flares added to the three who'd lied the first time. These creatures might find children too tasty to avoid their instincts on not harming one. I couldn't take them with us. I couldn't leave them here alive to suffer and continue being lab rats, either.

I made a hard decision, with Nicus' face in my mind. He may not be my flesh and blood, but he was just a little boy. I could kill for him, to keep him safe.

I signaled Rock to close the switch again, turning it back on before the supernatural's knew about it.

I walked back to the panel and touched the button that corresponded to the prisoner's cells that had flared red on me.

"What are those?" Rock asked me.

"Kill switches. I remember these. They had them on a panel at the lab for each of the cells when we broke out Demitri and other supernatural's at the University when we lived in Arizona."

"And you're going to hit those buttons?"

"For those five I felt evil from, yes. We can't trust them." I reached up to the button for cell 10, pushing it. "And we can't leave them here for more experiments." I rapidly pushed each cell number where I had felt the lies, felt the hunger, felt nothing but evil and I ruthlessly killed them all. Maybe I was no better than the Nazis myself.

Inside each cell, gas was being sprayed to make them slow and confused, then jets of flame to burn every square inch of the cell. Without any protection or magicks, they were fried alive, screaming in their cells. I heard the screams, I heard them beg and the only thing I could feel was guilt in not taking them out with the blade, in honor. I still would have killed them but killing like this just seemed so cowardly. But, we didn't have the time for me to challenge each one, fight them and kill like a warrior of the astral realms should.

"You're killing in cold blood and your life or an innocent isn't in imminent danger."

I looked at him. "They weren't human."

He shook his head, "You'd think I would have learned better by now, with you and your wording."

"Clock's ticking." I ran back into the hall and signaled Rock to hit the switch again. 'Those who were killed were pure evil and weren't going to keep their word. I will not leave anyone here for them to experiment on anymore, but it's your choice whether you walk out or go out in a body bag. Now, for the rest of you, again, your word no harm to anyone and you follow my orders or those of my Coven, to the letter, until we get you to where you belong.'

Several 'my words' came quickly that time and I could feel they meant it. Nothing like a little fire to get their attention. I switched my power focus to their cell locks, which were on the side of each door. They were electronic mechanisms where you had to slide a card through them. I smiled. Anything electric was so easy to manipulate using astral energy. Then I frowned. Unless you had that damn magnetic plating turned on under a magick user. These scientists may be idiots for messing with things that was really none of their business, but they were sure getting diabolical in trapping our kind.

I switched the connection within the mechanisms and all the doors opened simultaneously. Slowly, they walked out, not trusting that they wouldn't be harmed or killed.

Some looked like they had been there a long time and had been badly abused. The children were even more cautious and I waved then to me. "Come here, little ones." I didn't see Nicus in the group of children, some ranged anywhere from what looked like six to young teenagers. I removed the lower part of my cowl, so they could see my face and smiled gently at them. Pointing to the eldest looking one of the group who was a young male. I said, "You, I need to gather up all the younger ones and get them in a line holding hands. My nice friend, Rock, will lead you out to boats so we can get you off this island and back home."

"My parents were killed, Miss. I have no home any longer." The young teenager answered.

"We'll figure something out. Just do as I say for now, so we can get you all to safety first. We'll find something, I promise." I turned to the adult paranormals. "Follow behind them; seven to a raft, with three of my people in the raft with you. They'll get you to a larger boat, so we can get away from here. Now, I need you all to move out."

Cassie came up behind me. "Where is Nicus?" Her question let me know they hadn't found him in any of the other cell blocks.

"I don't know. Get them out and I'll look around."

I went to the cell doors, looking into each, while Rock and Cassie led the now freed prisoners out to the boats. I saw a couple of blackened corpses in a few of the cells I had hit the buttons on. I then saw little Nicus, huddled on the bed, with his thumb in mouth, sucking it with his eyes tightly shut. As if, by keeping his eyes shut, nothing would harm him. I walked into the cell, calling softly to him. "Nicus, baby. My name is Cat. Your mommy, your Dam, sent me to take you home."

The sucking on his thumb slowed down, but he didn't open his eyes. "Sweety, I am going to pick you up. Your Dam is worried for you, so we need to go home right now." I gently reached down to pick him up, moving pure calming, blue energy through my hands to keep him calm, as I eased him into my arms.

"Shh, it's ok, I've got you. I promise, I am taking you home."

His eyes opened and he looked up at me, then he settled into my arms, tucking his head into my neck. I kept rubbing his back and crooning to him and started to move down the hall, when I heard another small whimper coming from further back, deeper into the cell blocks. I listened hard, as I moved further into the prison ward and I saw a cell that had a small crib inside of it. I moved in and looked into the crib, seeing a tiny female baby who couldn't have been more than three months old. Carefully, I reached out to touch the baby and her head moved towards me with her pale lavender eyes wide open. I gasped and moved her black hair from her ears. Seeing the tips of them, I knew exactly what she was and swore viciously to myself. They dared to take one of my Mother's people. I had to breathe deeply to keep my anger contained, so the little ones wouldn't be frightened and picked her up with my other arm, tucking her close to my body.

"Seel'la bethra, Mia'bitta calla, Seel'la." (Good girl, baby. My Little Lady, Good girl.) She may be only three months old, but she would be comforted by hearing her native tongue calming her, assuming I had the right dialect.

It's a good thing they didn't know what she meant to my Coven, to our people. How in the seven hells had they nabbed her, and when? It had to have been recently. General Robertson wouldn't have known an Elven child would actually be related to us, however small, and under my Mothers rule. She is the Queen of all Elves, Fae, Seeli or otherwise. All came under Her rule. She conceived their races many millennia ago and therefore they are most precious to our people. The Fae and all of Mother's races had retreated, for the most part, to other dimensions until the return of all the Gods and Goddesses, including Her. She would not be a native of Earth. That meant somehow these assholes had found a way to one of the Elven worlds and snatched this child from there and brought her here.

I walked out of the cell and moved towards the door leading out when I heard footsteps pounding down into this section. I had both hands now filled with children and couldn't get to my weapons. I also couldn't throw any magick around. I hurried out the door and cloaked us, which is a hell of a drain on my magick. The Generals men poured into the room and I held still, invisible to them, but I wouldn't last for long. I prayed the babies would be quiet, as I moved cautiously around the men and out the door they'd just come from

"She has to be here, then. She would come down here to get to the boy. Search the whole ward."

I watched one of the men peek down the prisoner's hall with his taser drawn.

Tasers would disrupt most paranormals abilities to use magicks but I was different in that it actually amped me up. Andre and I were the only two in the Coven that could use electricity in most cases. Tasers were one of them. But, I still didn't want to take a hit with babies in my arms. I had no idea how it would affect them.

"Sir, the cell doors are open."

"Check each cell and make sure she isn't hiding down there, damn it." General Robertson ordered.

Oh, I'd gotten him mad. I smiled. It was so tempting to put down the children in a safe enough corner, sneak up behind him and snap his neck. I could kill every one of them, but if a stray bullet or a stray bit of magick hit one of these babies—no, I couldn't chance it.

Someday though, he and I would have our time together and next time he would be the one screaming for me.

"Nothing and no one in the cells, except for a few corpses. She must have killed a few of the creatures, Sir."

He sounded confused as to why I would do that.

"Damn that bitch. Find her now."

I kept moving towards the door and down the second hallway that would get me to the East side of the facility.

Their voices faded away, as I hurried down the hall towards one of the outer doors. Now that the General's men were back inside the faculty, our time was up.

I could hear his men running behind me, searching each office as they went, and they were making good time in catching up to me. I couldn't move as fast, having to hold the cloaking and run with two children in my arms. If I used power to pour on the speed, I wouldn't have enough left for the cloak. I had already burned up my power stores and was now using what I had inside in reserve, so it was one or the other but not both, which made me human slow in running.

I reached for Cassie with telepathy. *'Coming out hot with two babies, cloaked. Need back up now. East door.'*

'Which door?'

'Southeast.'

'Copy.'

I felt power coming to me through the bonds from sources I hadn't dared tap into before, not knowing how well off they were in giving me their own energy. They might have been in trouble themselves, so I didn't draw from them, but once they knew I was in trouble, they gave me what they had. I took it and poured on the speed, turning down another hallway and seeing at the end of it, two figures standing there waiting for me, with guns pointing down the hallways. I uncloaked so they could see it was me and to not shoot. Babyface ordered, "Cat, drop now."

I went to the floor on my knees and curled my body over the babies as Babyface and Romeo fired at my pursuers.

Then, he yelled, "Go. Go. Go."

I got up and ran the rest of the distance, as they held the door open for me.

We spilled into the night, running hard for the shore, where a raft would be waiting for us. The Elven baby whimpered weakly, at being jostled so much and from the cold night air hitting her face. I got into the raft and the men climbed in after me. Babyface took control of the craft and revved up the small engine, taking us out to sea where a larger craft waited for us.

"Is the baby all right?" Romeo asked. I put her in my lap and waved my hand over her, using power to check her. She was so weak from hunger. Those bastards didn't have a magickal being who could feed this baby. Human milk or formula wouldn't do any good for an Elven babe. The milk had to be natural and from someone with power. Elven babes needed not only the nutrition but magickal energy, too. Another few days and this babe would have died from starvation. I gathered her back against my body, as Romeo put a blanket around us.

"She's cold and hungry, but otherwise all right. We need to feed her as soon as possible."

"What is she?"

"Very precious, so let's hurry."

Chapter Twenty-Seven

Indian Bishop

Once we were on board the plane, I told everyone on our private path what kind of baby I had in my hands. No one let their expressions change on their faces, but one by one, they grouped around us, as if making a protective circle around the babe from anyone else on the plane. It was instinctual for every one of us to do everything we can to protect this infant babe. Nicus, feeling even safer now, looked up at me. Seeing his beautiful, soft brown eyes, clear and bright and knowing he had such a winsome smile when he was happy that showed in the picture his Dam had taken, made me realize he was just as precious and deserving of our protection as the Elven babe was. I hugged him close to me, smelling his hair, so I would know his scent anywhere and never forget him. Holding these two sweet babies made me yearn badly for the promised dream I had of having twins. One boy and one girl.

I must have leaked out my needing, because I felt a hand start to rub my arm in comfort. Looking up, I saw Antonio too, was watching me hold these babies and I knew he wanted to see our own children in my arms, just as much as I did.

O'Hara looked at us oddly when we reached the ground at the airport in Louisiana to take Nicus to his Dam and then to move everybody out to Kla' din. My people had put me in the center of a circle made of their own bodies and wouldn't let anyone approach me or the babies.

We drove to the Norwells neighborhood where they were waiting for us at Ashton's house. Ashton came out to the porch with Nicus's Dam, who came running and my people let her through, so she could grab her baby from me.

She kept crying and kissing his face, then would snuffle his hair deeply all over. Then, she would hold him tightly and the snuffling would start all over again. I guess that was how a werewolf mother made sure her child was hers or something. I smiled, happy to see I was able to keep my word to the mother, and Ashton came as close as he could, "Thank you, for bringing him home alive. We are in your debt."

"Do you have a lactating Dam here, anywhere? This babe needs nourishment quickly."

His eyes widened and he coughed out a call. A small woman came forward from the crowd and timidly walked up to our group.

"That's Nissua. She just birthed two months ago."

"Nissua, would you mind feeding this babe? I can't take her to her parents through a doorway like this. She isn't strong enough to withstand the transfer right now."

She shyly nodded her head and we made room for her to sit and feed the babe. I was reluctant to let her go, but I knew she needed to be fed to gain enough strength to go through an astral doorway from a Nexus. I hated going through doorways physically, because it left me vulnerable. Also the last time we went through an astral doorway to an astral plane, it was there that my mates and I had died. Usually, when you die on an astral plane in physical human form you stay dead, body and soul. It was extremely dangerous to take your body though an astral doorway, especially when the end destination was not on this world or another world aligned on a physical plane. Any other existence and you take the chance of being killed, both in spirit and in body. So, now I had a deep phobia about it and once this child was fed, I would have to make that trip with her to get her to her home. Her home was not on this world and her world would most likely not be on any physical plane of existence, but on an astral one. And now my own personal energy levels were drained from this mission, in having to cloak three bodies for so long a period of time.

The Houngan had said I would have to do the thing I hated the most and he also said I would have to do it three times. Well, at least this trip would be to a world where it should be somewhat safe enough for us there. Especially, since we were bringing back their baby.

Andre called out on our path, *'Need help now.'*

I turned to Cassie and the others. "Don't let that baby out of your sight." I took off running towards the edge of the wolven neighborhood.

I could hear Craven howling with rage, as I drew near the area where they were. The scene before me almost made me gag and I saw

Craven tearing into the throat of a dark figure lying on the ground. There was blood everywhere and Craven was ravaging the body in sheer anger.

I yelled, "Craven, stop!"

He wasn't listening and just kept tearing at the body. I turned to Andre, asking, "What the hells happened?"

"That man there," pointing to the body on the ground, "came to the edge of the shield, as Craven and I were patrolling. He threw a spell at Craven which made him paralyzed. Then, he started to draw Cravens spirit out of his body and I threw a fire ball at him. When he blocked it, the spell on Craven became undone and Craven shifted into a Dire Wolf and tore into him. I couldn't stop him."

"Shit. Ok, I got this." I walked closer to Craven, who was gorging on the blood. "Craven, stop now." I put power and compulsion into the command on every level, which made him pause. "Craven, look at me. It's Mommy." His head reared up with blood dripping from his muzzle and teeth.

"The enemy is defeated. He can't hurt you anymore."

'Bad. Evil.'

"I know, but now he's dead. Come away from the body."

'My kill.'

"I know, it's all yours, but come away, now."

'Mine.'

"All yours." I wasn't going to disagree with him, though the blood did smell very good to me. I was so low on energy; I needed blood so badly that even this gruesome scene could seem somewhat tasty. I shook my head and almost gagged again. That helped me push down the need and I focused getting my son away from the body and changing. It took some time, but once he was in human form again and realized consciously what he had done, he broke down, sobbing in my arms. He was horrified at the scene and couldn't calm down.

"I got you, sweetie. It's all right, Mommy's here. You couldn't help it. It was his bad for trying to steal your spirit, honey."

But, he was irreconcilable and kept crying. He couldn't even construct any recognizable words, except I could catch the no, no, no's. Anything else out of him was incoherent.

A black shadow grew from a lighter shadow near where we were. I pulled Craven away from me and pushed him towards Andre. "Get him out of here now, and protect our son. I've got this."

"You sure?" He sounded doubtful.

"Yes, please. Craven can't take anymore right now."

"I'll send someone for back up." I nodded and he dragged Craven away from the danger that felt malicious and worst of all, vengeful. I reached down to the body and smeared some of the blood on my hands and around my mouth.

The Mambo had formed completely from the shadows and stepped towards the body.

"You killed my mate." She hissed, "I can't even raise him back from tha mess you have made of him."

Excellent, she bought it and I sure wasn't going to tell her I wasn't the one who did this. I wanted her to think I personally killed the creep who tried to steal my son's powers.

"You will pay for t'is." She reached out with her hands quicker than I could block and it felt like metaphysical dark hands were gripping my heart and my mind, paralyzing me from doing anything, even from drawing power from my Coven. I had already been so weak from the mission; I had nothing left over to fight back with.

"T'ree times you will see tha black; black of tha sea, black of tha night and black of tha snake will bring you tha black of your sight. T'ree times cursed, three times dead. Your worst time in life will be in your head.

Until tha end of time, you will live tha undead; breathing, but not living, heart beating, but no loving. Nothing in, on or of t'is Earth will break t'is in my stead." She then threw a bag full of powder in it, grabbed the body of her mate and they both disappeared into the shadows. I snapped out of the trance she had me in and fell to my knees, gagging on the metaphysical black air, like poisonous smoke, which had filled my lungs.

Gerard and Antonio came running up and picked me up off the ground.

"Oh, shit." Antonio could smell the power of the spell.

"Sweet Goddess, Cat, you've got to fight this." Gerard was holding me up, looking into my eyes.

"No energy. Hungry."

"Feed her," Gerard commanded of my mate.

Antonio grabbed me and spun me around, baring his throat. I took what he offered and drank deeply. Power not only rushed into me from him, but my other mates, too. He must have sent out an SOS to them, letting them know I was in trouble. I took the energy and searched inside my spirit, looking for the root of the spell, but every time I grabbed on to a dark tendril, it would only shift to a new location. I couldn't pull it out, not even with this much magick. I needed something else to draw out the spell then, if I could exercise it, and we were running out of time now.

"Thank you, for the blood, but we have to go now."

Gerard grabbed my hand. "It didn't work?"

"No, but we can't stop now. If she finds out Craven is the one who killed him, she'll be back. The General could now be on his way with more men. More magicians than we can deal with and keep everyone safe. Let's get home to our base where we'll be stronger and get these people off to safety. It will be one less thing we'll have to defend against."

They knew it was the best course of action. There was only so much we could do here and many more resources at our home base, so they agreed and we ran back towards Ashton's house.

The Elven babe had been fed and felt much stronger to me. "This child needs to be taken home now. Ashton, your people need to be moved, as well as the other paranormals. Gather everyone and whatever transportation you have and get them to the planes now."

He didn't argue and moved towards the group of wolven that was much larger now then it had been two days ago. Many were carrying young children in their arms and had cloth sacks hanging on their backs. I bet this was everything they now had left, after fleeing their home world before the next Solstice. Our Winter Solstice was still a few months away. I wondered briefly if their Solstice time was the same as ours here on Earth?

I moved over to where Craven was still huddled and shaken. His face was pure white from shock. "Craven, sweetie, I have to take this baby back home, but I will meet you at the base. Please, listen to Andre while I am gone and I will be there to talk with you then if you need me, ok?"

"Smell bad, Mom."

"I know, but it will all work out. I'll fix it later. Are you all right?"

He shook his head but replied, "I'll help Andre get the wolven to the new home. Just hurry back, ok?" His eyes looked at me pleadingly. I have never seen such pain in them before. I hated having to leave him right when he needed me the most, but this babe had to go back before the Mambo realized she was here or the General came with his men to take me and her back.

"You've had to go through a lot in a short space of time, but I am proud of you for being strong enough to carry the load."

"Proud I killed a man and then ripped into him like an animal?"

"That's part of being a Dire Wolf and not your fault. I still love you no matter what you do, as a Dire Wolf or as a man. You're my son."

He stared at me, then the baby made a noise. He switched his attention to the child. "You'd better go, Mom. She probably wants her own mother. She has been through a bad time."

I kissed his cheek and went over to my mates. "I'll be at the base when I'm done. Meanwhile, get these people moved and we'll figure out what to do about the other paranormals and those children."

"Are you going to be all right? Maybe you should take backup."

"O'Hara and the squad will need every single magick users they can get out of us just in case even one of these paranormals goes back on their word and get out of hand. There are too many children with this group to take any chances."

"It's a world that your Mother is Goddess on so you should be safe enough. Go, but don't take too long. The sooner we can remove this curse, the better," Antonio reminded me.

"I know. The longer it stays, the harder it will be to remove, but we really need to get these people out of here."

Gerard asked, "Do you know where the nearest Nexus is?"

"Yeah, I saw one about a mile towards the West end. I'll use that one."

I waved to them and wished them a safe trip and started walking to the nearest Nexus I'd seen earlier.

A Nexus was where power pooled from an intersecting crossing of a ley-line. Where two lines crossed in the center, a flame of power was built, looking much like a tall, white candle flame, but it didn't burn you. Well, unless you used it wrong. I couldn't just make an astral doorway like I'd done for Andre, because her home was mostly likely on another plane of existence. A straight astral doorway needed to end up in a place that was in line with Earth. If the place you wanted to go was on a different level, then you needed a Nexus to get there. It was a favorite way for Druids to travel from Earth to another dimension or one area to another, back in the days when Druids were revered in Ireland. That is until St Patrick drove the snakes from Ireland. And, I really hated St Patrick's Day.

St. Patrick was the son of a druid family, until he was captured by Christians and made a slave. Over the years, he had converted to

Christianity and was released. Helsinki syndrome must have kicked in hard, because he took his new religion and went back to Ireland on a Holy Crusade to either convert the Druids or kill them all. Those that didn't have enough power or knowledge to flee using the ley-lines were slaughtered by the hundreds. Only a few hundred had enough power to escape to other dimensions. The Church tells a different story; that Patrick did many wonderful acts of God and the Druids threw down their pagan religion and converted. That's why they have St. Patrick's Day now-to celebrate the "driving of the snakes from Ireland." Snake-looking tattoos were done on Druids who mastered a particular level of magick. The stories passed down by my people through each successive generation told another story of forced conversion or death. Luckily, those that had used the Nexus, took with them the knowledge for future generations to relearn and to hopefully someday, repopulate pagan families with Druids again.

First Columbus day; a man who committed genocide on millions of peaceful Arawak Indians, and then St Patrick's day- a man who slaughtered the Druids who couldn't run. Both holidays were instigated by the Church. Next thing they'll want is Hitler day; he'll have good company with the first two monsters of history.

Thinking of the church always pissed me off, so I turned to look at the baby. She smiled at me and cooed. I couldn't help but coo back at her. When I had reached the Nexus, I cautioned her though she was a babe, "Ok sweetie, this may sting a bit, but I'll try to make it quick."

Going through an astral doorway made from the center of a Nexus stung a magick users aura. Imagine walking through a wall made of electricity and that's what it felt like. It took a Master of the Arts to hold the focus while your body and soul were being stung with power. One little slip and magick users could be lost betwixt and between forever, so your focus had to be absolute.

I walked into the center and opened the Nexus' power, searching for a matching energy signal from the baby, using the baby as a focus to a particular doorway. Finding it, I shoved us towards the right door and stepped through, holding my breath.

Stepping into her world, I saw the scenery change to a bright day which hurt my eyes, but I still loved the breathtaking beauty I saw around me. Trees so large around they must have been thirty feet in diameter and swirled upwards into a maze of greenery and twisting thick branches large enough to walk on. They were even bigger than the Sequoias back in California and a lighter shading of brown with wide green leaves. The grass was thick, lush and soft under my feet. The wildlife around me was humming and squawking with happy abandon; some moving so fast you couldn't see if they were birds or just big bugs. I hated bugs. The thought of big bugs really icked me out, so I thought it would be best to hurry to her home. I gazed around until I saw in the far distance a tall building with a flag on top of a tower. It was a direction and even if that wasn't her particular city, it would be a place to start in finding out where a couple was missing a baby.

News like that would travel fast in an Elven world, where babies were just as rare as on Kla' din. The Elven were long-lived folk, so their breeding cycles were further spaced apart. Rumors had made it to Trinidad that the pregnancy rate had dropped even further than was normal for Elven, but no one knew why. So, therefore, this babe would be extra rare and easy to trace to her grieving parents.

I broke into a gentle run, so the babe wouldn't be jostled harshly and made good time to the front gate leading to an Elven city. The large beige wall surrounded the whole city and must have taken years to build. It was still in good repair but that didn't surprise me. Elven were a picky lot and very clean. They wouldn't let anything of theirs get into disrepair or look poorly.

They also didn't like strangers holding an Elven babe that obviously didn't belong to said person, as several arrows were notched and swords were drawn.

"Keoyaa Le dosen?"

'Who are you stranger' was shouted at me from an Elven, who stood slightly apart from his troops. I could tell he was a leader; whether a commander or just a troop trainer, I had no clue.

I sent the message out telepathically to all on a broadband, because I didn't want to chance saying something wrong if I didn't speak their particular dialect the right way. I could accidentally declare a war that way. Telepathic communication between supernatural's automatically put it into a universal language that was easily understood.

'First Born Daughter of The Triple Goddess and Her Consort in physical form, coming to bring an Elven babe back to her rightful parents.'

I had already taken off my cowl, but my hair was still braided down my back. I removed the block to my Godhead powers and let my inner spirit shine for them.

A gasp went through the crowd. Then, one by one, they dropped to their knees, sheathing their weapons.

The black curse was trying to seep into that part of me and I quickly blocked my Goddess powers again. That would be a very bad thing, if this curse meshed with my Goddess powers. It would be extremely hard to get rid of it then. Safer to draw it out first, if I can, than to try using my Goddess powers to vanquish it and fail. I didn't want to take that risk again, either. It was how the first curse stayed with me for so many years.

'Forgive us, for drawing weapons, but we have been in a state of high alert since the Dukes Daughter had been taken.'

A Duke? Whoa, what was General Robertson thinking? Pissing off the Elven was never a good idea, but a high born daughter was priceless. I bet that was why there were so many warriors around us. They had been preparing to come track her down and kill anything between this babe and them. A Duke's daughter was the lifeblood of an Elven tribe. Without her, there would have been no hope for a future for these people as a whole. A High born daughter was the symbol of their future, their very existence. She represented everything then to these people.

'She has been brought back. If you would take me to her parents, I will gladly hand over the infant in peace.'

'Right this way, Your Highness.'

A path instantly cleared for us and we walked through the town with people coming to see the impromptu parade we'd inadvertently caused. Whether it was to see me or the babe I didn't know. Maybe both.

One handed, I pulled my hair out, so they could see the length. It was another symbol of power here to these people. I took the band off and with just a twinge of power, I unfurled my hair and made it smooth. I didn't want to be shown to the Duke and his Lady looking so rough.

A bit of magick cleaned me of blood and my clothes were neat looking again. A trick Ja' Callum had taught me. The babe just cooed happily in my arms, obviously knowing she was home again.

Her tiny little hand waving merrily, trying to catch a strand of my hair. She had been fed, cleaned and now she was home, getting closer to her parents. It was all she wanted and I smiled at her happiness. We walked up the palace steps and there was no waiting to be announced. We were ushered right into the throne room where her father was pacing back and forth looking very worried. The Mother was sitting on her throne, the babe was a spitting image of her mother, with raven black hair and pale, lavender eyes. The look on her face made me wince and hurry forward with the child to wipe that look of pain off of it. She had been heartbroken. She didn't wait and stood up running to take her child

251

from my arms, ignoring decorum. Her husband was right behind her touching the infant gently, making sure she was real.

'Allegora, my daughter. The Goddess has answered our prayers.'

He spoke both verbally and telepathically, but I just focused on the telepathy.

Her mother was weeping over the return of her babe and kissed her gently all over her little face.

She reached out her hand to mine. *'Bless you, Princess, for returning my baby. We thought she was lost to us when we couldn't feel her life-force any longer.'* She quickly drew back her hand in horror.

'You've been cursed with a spell most foul.'

Her body instinctively turned the babe away from me, but I let it go, knowing it was an unconscious act. The babes safety must come before all else. I understood this as a High Priestess and as a mother myself. Her husband moved in between us and glazed his hand over my aura, feeling for the dark energy.

'How could this happen to a Daughter of The Goddess?'

'By not moving fast enough apparently,' I said, ruefully.

He nodded, as if it had made sense to him. *'You have returned our child for which we bless you and your Mother. Allow me to return the gift with a gift of my own. I can give you one great magickal gift as a reward for returning Allegora to us unharmed.'*

'What kind of magickal gift?' I asked.

'One that will be strong enough to remove that curse from you.'

Thinking of someone else who could benefit from this boon more than I, who meant the world to me, I said, *'I saved your child help me save mine, instead. Can you make something that can remove a curse that has shape-shifted one of my sons into the body of a panther permanently by calling upon the Goddess of Transformation and a live sacrifice?'*

'Show me your son and the events that happened,' he requested.

I opened my mind enough to the memory of Crimson and his transformation and the bits I had been able to extract, before he had gotten home that night and shifted.

'An Elden curse, Princess. How did your enemies know of such a curse? They haven't been used for thousands of years. The Eldens are older than even our race.'

'They have knowledge of spells that even my own Coven doesn't have.'

'I can't undo that completely. It outstrips even my own gifts, but I can twist the curse.'

'Anything for Crimson.'

He nodded, knowing my son meant the world to me, as his daughter did to him and removed a ring from his hand. With power, he made a diamond-looking stone come out of the setting and placed it in his hand. Everyone gave him room, as he started to glow, imbuing the stone with his power. He handed it to me when he was done.

'*Place this on his forehead and use the incantation. You'll have to hold him tightly so he doesn't move until the spell is done, but afterwards he should be able to shift back into a human while he is conscious.*' He told me the incantation to twist this cruse and I committed it to memory.

'*Blessings to your house.*'

One did not thank another in the Celtic Pantheon. It was considered an insult. I thanked my Goddess Mother often, just to yank Her chain, but I was the only one who could get away with it.

'*Be warned, My Lady, he will revert to the body of the cat when he sleeps, but he will have control over the change, so long as he is awake.*'

'*It will be more than he had. Blessings from my family to yours.*'

'*We have not walked on Earth in a very long time. Why are things so violent there now that they would take a babe from our world?*'

'*The Great Shift is coming, so if you could keep your warriors here and not bent on revenge, that would be greatly appreciated. Know the ones who did this, have paid dearly for it already and I will go back and finish the job.*'

He held still for a long moment, thinking it over. The need for revenge would be burning in his blood, but he would also need to put the welfare of his world and his people in the balance.

'*Fine, if you are going back to take care of the rest. I will trust you to see our Honor has been upheld.*'

He smiled at me. '*Never did I think I would see the living embodiment of our Goddess' Daughter in my Demesnes. If her Children are on Earth fighting the darkness, let me pledge my own forces, if you ever have a need of them.*'

Thinking of the things that could happen right before the night of the Great Shift, I replied, '*I just may take you up on that offer.*'

Smiling again, he pledged, '*Then here- use this ring when you have need of my men to fight. Just whisper my name upon the stone.*'

I took the ring and tucked it into my pocket, again with a blessing.

'*I and my dear wife will also pledge not to picnic in our forests anymore without a guard with us at all times.*'

'*Is that how they snatched her?*'

'*Yes, we were out playing in the forests.*' His face took on a slight shade of red. '*We were involved while Allegora was sleeping peacefully under the shade of a tree nearby.*'

Ahh, I knew things could happen when one was "involved". I wouldn't have thought twice about mating with one of my husbands on Trinidad if my child was sleeping somewhere close by to hear if they woke up. Times have changed it seemed, for peaceful worlds. I made a mental note to myself to be vigilant, even on Trinidad from now on.

'We never had any trouble for so long we let down our guard.' His expression hardened. *'I will not let that happen again.'*

I knew he wouldn't, either. We said our goodbyes and his Lady looked at me with pity in her eyes. She knew I had made the decision to help my son, rather than do something to save my own life. I also knew she would have done the same exact thing. It was how the all the Fae were when it came to our offspring. Nothing else mattered but their wellbeing.

Chapter Twenty-Eight

Bullet Chess

Jraced back to the Nexus and brought out the Medallion the Houngan had given me. I was out of energy and would need his Lao to get back home. This was not my world and unless I made a bond here I would not be able to tap into its powers unless I found a node and I didn't want to waste time doing it with my hurry to get back to Crimson and hopefully see my son in human form again.

I turned it, to open the Lao's power, and drew it to me, making the connection and visualized the bases grassy area at Truax Fields. Though they didn't have much grass. Stepping through the doorway, I hurried to the building where they had room for all of the paranormals while we processed them. As I had expected, my Coven had been busy at work getting the more reasonable paranormals home with Bokaris Stones for their portals, taking the control away from General Robertson and making treaties with each world. For the more aggressive ones, General Pierce was having kittens trying to find planes and time for a squad to go with each one, plus three Coven magick users to keep things civil. If a treaty couldn't be reached with their home world quickly, the portal would be closed from our side. The children we were saving for last. Not because we wanted to use them as a bargaining chip with their home worlds, but it was much harder to get the correct information where a particular child belonged to, especially the younger they were. The elder ones were more quickly ascertained, but with two of them, there were problems. The eldest boy I had put in charge of the children back at Plum Island had no living parents. They were killed by the General's men. Apparently, this would put him in a very bad position back on his home world, making him what he called a 'scavvii'. A youngling with no protector, which on their world would make him basically a slave. I couldn't, in good conscious, make him go back so we gave him the

255

option of being adopted into one of my families members home, or adopted into a family unit on Kla' din. He wanted to see the world before he made his final decision which I thought was wise of him. The other one was more confusing in a way until I looked into her eyes. I saw that same look in my own eyes as a teenager. She wasn't ready to talk yet, but I could guess what her problem was and gave her the same choice. She opted for Kla' din right away, stating she was too afraid to be here on this planet after what had happened to her at Plum Island. I couldn't blame her. I was itching to get back home, but had to fill out the paperwork on all these beings, what they were, where they came from and their personal brief history here. I wanted all this knowledge to go into our Covens BOS and, of course, General Pierce wanted a copy for his records. Being a Merc didn't mean there was no paperwork and it was also done in triplicate, just like the military. Oh, joy. O'Hara would get a copy, as well.

When I first arrived, I had asked for Craven, to deal with any trauma he might still be feeling, only to find out he had stepped up and was escorting his pack to Kla' din to help them in their transplanting. It was a bittersweet moment for me, which almost had me breaking down into a wet blob of tears. That same feeling a mother gets when her child leaves for school for the first time and you have to let him go and trust him with strange people. The same feeling you get when he takes his first camping trip and you can't go with him to oversee his every need. A letting go, a rite of passage every mother feels when their child steps away one more step towards independence and eventually adulthood, that you know there is no coming back from. And this was my baby's last step. Just a few hours ago, I held in my arms a tiny, precious bundle, remembering how Craven felt when he was that small. I realized how empty my arms felt to me now. The ache cut clear to my soul.

So much was changing and so fast, I felt like the world was spinning at a speed I couldn't keep up with. I did the only thing I could do. I poured myself into the work to hurry it along, so I could at least help one of my sons get back to some kind of normalcy.

The odd vampire I had noticed back on Plum Island stepped in my way, as I was making for the door, knowing the others had a handle on the rest of the work here.

"A moment, My Lady."

I stopped and looked at him. "Yes?"

"You are not of The Prince's Bloodline, I know that now, but my Prince would still like to meet with you."

"Where's your portal?"

"The territory you call Kansas."

My blood chilled in my veins. "General Robertson took you from a portal in Kansas?"

"Yes, though I didn't know it at the time, but I have since learned of it as the General gloated during my tortures."

"He tortured you?"

He nodded to me, I quipped, "I spent some fun time with him, too. Amusing isn't he?"

He looked at me quizzically, I sighed, "I'm sorry, but it's been a long twenty-seven hours. I still have to get home to my son and try to solve another problem."

"You have a child?"

"Well, not exactly," hating him in that moment for reminding me. "They are all grown adults, now."

His eyes went wide. "I will wait, then. My Prince will most definitely want to meet you."

"Why, you are not exactly a creature of the light?"

"Neither are my people truly of the dark. My word on that."

I nodded to him. "Fine. Let me go home and care for my son. I will return to see what we can do with your Prince."

"I will anxiously await your return."

I snorted and kept moving, letting people know where I was going and calling Andre to my side.

"I'll need help with Crimson, hon. I have something that may help him."

"Really? That is outstanding, babe. What is it?"

As we drove home, I told him of my entire trip, instead of the very short glossed-over report I had given when I had walked in the door a few hours ago. Everybody had been so busy, they didn't take note of just how short the report was.

"Why didn't you tell the General this?"

"Antonio hasn't filled you in, yet?"

"No. We have been busting our asses getting the more light-sided paranormals home using doorways and processing the rest the longer way."

"Ahh, well, Antonio found something very interesting in the computer program at Plum Island, as well as some files. Apparently, our good General and O'Hara were a part of a research group the CIA and the military had going on called Program Mind Spring. It's why O'Hara's aura is bigger than a normal mundane should be. I knew there was something about it, but I didn't feel the need to dig into it."

"Mind Spring?"

"Oh yeah, 'remote viewing' ring any bells for ya?" I sneered over the militaries wording for astral projection.

"Oh, shit."

"My sentiments, exactly. O'Hara has progressed faster than the rest and has an amazing capacity for storing energy. For someone who is supposed to be mundane, that is."

"Not so mundane, huh?"

"Nope. Not anymore."

Andre was getting as pissed as I was over the incident. "Why didn't they tell us?"

"I don't know, but I don't like it. It's why I had made sure one of our people was with each and every paranormal tonight, making sure they weren't shipped off to another installation. But, there is more."

Andre groaned, "What?"

"Remember when that plane I was on, going to New York was hi-jacked?"

"Yeah, I remember," he growled. He was still pissed about that one.

"Well, there seems to be a reason General Pierce and O'Hara's team just happened to be in the area at the time. Plum Island officials knew they were dealing outside their programs laws with illegal experiments. The General and O'Hara's team were to find out exactly what, and I think to shut them down, though that part isn't clear to me yet. I haven't read the whole file, but Plum Island had plans of taking them all out, until we botched their scheme in setting O'Hara's team up."

"So, that hi-jacking was a way to get O'Hara's team out in the open, then they were going to be whacked?"

I nodded my head. "Yes, and it was going to be blamed on the terrorist instead. Nicely wrapped, with a big ole bow on it and with the added touch of making the current politician look bad, so Williams could slide one of their darksiders into office, instead. A nice chess play all in one shot, but we fucked it up."

"No, you fucked it up," he smiled. "Good job."

"Smart ass."

"So, with General Pierce moving all of us and his men to Corpus Christi, it took them inadvertently out of the line of fire."

I added my own thought, "Now, I can guess where O'Hara and his team disappear to from time to time. He tells me it's for extra training for

Special Forces, but he could be making side trips out to N.Y., scoping on Plum Island."

Andre agreed, "And checking up on Williams."

"Yes, Williams' strong hold seems to be parts of New York and Washington D.C.; General Robertson has a foothold in Kansas and The Pentagon. If you wanted to take over an entire country, what would you do? Where would you set up your men?"

Andre thought and then said, "Shit."

"Yeah, it's what I would do, too."

"So, what's General Pierce's ultimate agenda?"

"I don't know, but think about this, babe. He has gotten his men trained further than they ever could in their program, 'Mind Spring', with us training them. Their program shut down publicly because of their low results. They didn't know by going after it with a scientific bent, instead of a spiritual one, they would run up against a brick wall, but they have since removed said brick wall with us, don't you think?"

"I'm so not liking this."

"I'm not either, but I still don't feel an evil intent. It's why I didn't go ballistic when we got back from the raid."

"You've been controlling your anger very well, baby. I'm proud of you." He looked over at me gave me a quick wink and took my hand into his, as he turned his attention back to the road. Of course, I had to get all gushy inside, because he said something nice about me. I still wasn't used to having somebody say nice things to me and it would throw me off balance, from time to time; but I was definitely liking it.

We got to the mansion and went into the basement where Crimson still stayed. He wasn't happy about it, but understood enough that letting him roam around the house would have the house staff in a tizzy. Lee was there as usual. I swear we saw more of Lee then his wife did lately, but that couldn't be helped, as there were so many doing duty on the base right now. Hopefully, this would work though and he could go home.

"Crimson, come here and look." I pulled out the stone to show him what I had. He ambled over in his slow catlike way and sniffed at my hand.

"It's a spell stone that can change you back if you let me try it."

He opened his maw and coughed at me. I understood a bit of what he was asking. "I'll need to put this to your head and it may hurt. Andre will have to hold you down and you have to try hard not to move, all right?"

He growled lightly, but not in menace and I opened the cage door and slid slowly inside.

Lee asked, "Will that change him back?"

"I think so. We'll find out shortly."

Andre came in and motioned for Crimson to come near him. "Lie down son, so I can get a better grip on you."

He went to the ground and Andre got into position and nodded at me to proceed. I curled my legs around Crimson's body and got his head into position with one arm and got the stone right above his head. I positioned the stone right between is eyes in the center of his head where his brow chakra would be if he were in human form. I spoke the incantation and breathed power into the stone, activating it and then let it touch Crimsons furry head. At first, not much happened, but the stone grew brighter by the minute. Then a slow sizzling was heard, as it burned the cat's fur underneath it. Crimson flinched but held back until the thing had gotten so hot it was even burning my fingers. He couldn't help bucking under our holds, trying to shake his head to get it off. "Stay still, Crimson. I know it hurts. Breathe with the pain."

The stone had literally melted into his forehead now and I could let go of the stone since it was now glued there and I used both hands to keep his head still. It was tearing me up to see him go through so much pain, but I was hoping the end result would be worth it. Crimson let out a roar, as the stone sunk deeper into his head and I knew the thing had attached somehow to his skull. I could smell burnt flesh and cat hair and the combination was not pleasant. There was a loud popping sound, then I felt skin under my hands, not fur, and I looked down to see my son was in human form.

"That fucking hurt, Mom," he croaked out.

"I know, baby. I am so sorry. But, look you're human again."

There was no sign of the stone in his head until I switched to my third eye vision and saw it gleaming there in the center of his forehead. It looked kinda cool, actually.

We helped him up and Lee brought in a robe for him. His clothes had ripped when he had shifted as the curse had taken over. He was shaky on his legs but he waved us off from trying to help him. He had always been so damned independent. I couldn't think where he got it from.

"I got one mean headache."

Andre moved near him. "Let me take it."

Andre was really talented at taking headaches away. Crimson was feeling better in mere minutes.

"Thanks. How did you do it, Mom? Reversing the curse, I mean."

I looked down at the ground. "I really didn't do anything and it's not really actually, technically reversed, son."

"Come again?"

"Well, you'll have control over whether you want to shift or not and when... until you go to bed. When you sleep, you'll revert back into panther form."

He hung his head and was so silent for so long. "Honey, I am sorry. It's the best I can do for right now."

He started to shake his head. "No, it's ok. It's better than before."

"Do you need to talk?"

"No, I just want to go to my room for awhile. I need a bath and some time alone."

I started to say something, then thought better of it. "All right. I'm here if you need me."

He gave me a half grin. "I know that."

He shuffled off to his room, getting used to using two legs all over again.

"I think we deserve a nice glass of wine before I go back to the base. And you, Lee, should go see your wife. I am sure she misses you."

His face lit up. "Yeah, there are a few equipment closets we haven't tried out yet."

I started laughing. "I don't want to know."

We went upstairs then and went into the family room as Ja' Kelo came walking in. He went straight to me, giving me a tight hug. "I have missed you, Meshama."

"When did you get back from Kla' din?"

"Just now." He went to kiss my neck and his hands roamed down to my buttocks, squeezing them. He pulled me tighter against his body and I could feel how hard he was. "Ja' Kelo, now is not the time. I still have to go back to the base." If he got going, he wouldn't stop all night long. He was like the damned energizer bunny. He and Antonio had stamina to burn.

"But, I have missed you." he pouted.

"I've missed you too, but I just got done twisting a curse on Crimson and I promised another vampire I would talk to him and this Prince of his, which by the way guys, says his portal is out in Kansas."

"No way," Andre said.

261

"Our son is human again? Wonderful, Meshama."

Lee almost choked on his wine. "That's too weird. We've been looking for that damned portal for a long time now."

"Yes, so we need to grab some Bokaris stones and head over there, talk to this prince guy, make a treaty and stick another one to General Robertson's ass." Later, I'd explain to Crimson's current condition to Ja' Kelo. I still had so much on my plate.

"Then, can I give you a good greeting?" Ja' Kelo asked, hopefully.

"Yes, then you can give me a most wonderful greeting. I'll need it." My Kla' din mates were more patient about getting their loving than my Earth-side mates were. They were more willing to wait, which I would wonder about from time to time, but since knew I had their hearts; I didn't let it worry me unnecessarily.

He moved away from me to do his second favorite thing when visiting Earth. Watch TV. I was beginning to think TV was an invention made by darksiders.

"Look Meshama, isn't that sea the one here where we live or part of it?"

I went to see what he was talking about and saw a newscast reporting on an oil spill in the Gulf.

"Yes, Ja' Kelo that is part of our sea here in the gulf."

'T'ree times you will see tha black', a dark voice whispered in my ear, *'Black of tha sea.'*

The scene panned to show huge, black oil slicks spreading out to where you couldn't see the ocean's true color anymore and the room went dark on me. I couldn't breathe, I couldn't move and that feeling of a hand on my heart and head was back and this time squeezing so hard I couldn't even think.

"Catrina, baby? Oh shit."

"What's wrong with her eyes?" Ja' Kelo sounded alarmed.

"They're black. Catrina, fight it, baby. I can't lose you. Fight it."

Their voices were getting fainter and fainter until the spell passed and sound came rushing back into my ears.

I started to take deep breaths again. "I'm ok. I'm ok."

"What the hells just happened?" Lee demanded to know.

Andre filled him in, while Ja' Kelo held me tight, listening to Andre's story.

"Why aren't we working on a counter curse?" Lee asked.

"Because, since it happened, I haven't had five minutes to even think about it."

"Now would be a good time to start then, don't you think?"

I started to agree with him, when I heard a calling ring through my head.

Christoph's voice was yelling, 'Mother, Ware dan..,' then silence. I stood up and opened every channel I had to Christoph, calling for him, but got nothing but silence. I couldn't even feel him through our mother/son bond.

"Christoph's in trouble. We have to go now."

Lee spluttered, "But the curse on you?"

"Will have to wait. Lee, tell the rest of them at the base, but I have to go now."

"Not without us," Andre stated firmly.

"Fine, let's go."

We ran outside to the backyard and I went to our circle there. I felt outwardly again, hunting for a signal, anything that was connected to Christoph and got nothing but a faint echo of my blade I'd given him. There were three of us, so we combined our power while I focused on the blade. Once the doorway was formed, we walked through it.

As we came out the other side, I saw my silver blade lying on the ground without the sheath. That meant, most likely, the sterling silver sheath was still in Christoph's possession. However, I couldn't feel it or Christoph anywhere.

"Where are we?" Ja' Kelo was searching around for any clues as to our location. An old stray newspaper fluttered and he ran to pick up the wrinkled page.

Looking at it, it said Portland Herald, Portland, Connecticut. I didn't know Connecticut had a city called Portland, too.

"Well, he is not here now, just my blade. What the fuck is going on?"

"I don't know, but let's look around," Andre suggested.

We started searching the grounds and the picnic table for any clues. Christoph was walking through a park in the dead of night for a reason, but what? He was supposed to be on a quest. Was this part of it, I wondered?

I finally gave up looking for physical clues and went to the ground where the blade had been laying and sniffed around.

"Son of a bitch!" I shouted.

"What?" Andre hurried over.

Pointing to the ground, I said, "Smell that. You too, Ja' Kelo."

Ja' Kelo looked stunned, "Draugralls? But, what are they doing here?"

263

Andre was shaking his head. "More importantly, how did they know to come here?"

"I don't give a shit. Those fuckers have my son now. If they lay a fang on him, I swear I will lay waste to their whole fucking planet."

"Babe, calm down. We'll get him back. I promise."

Right then my cell phone started to ring; looking at the number it was General Pierce, "Yes," I answered shortly. I wasn't too pleased with him either, at the moment.

"Cat, we need you here. Did you hear about the oil rig breaking in the gulf?"

"Yes, but that's not a magickal situation. The best we can do is have one of our people hold back the oil from spreading down near us and try to keep it in place as much as possible."

"Why can't you fix the leak?"

"It's a man-made problem; we can't interfere. They broke it, they have to fix it or reap the consequences from it. Karma can be a bitch and I'll make sure it hits them in the face." I was getting more pissed by the minute. I cared about the ocean a lot, but my concern had to be for Christoph, first and foremost at this time.

"But the ecological impact will be tremendous."

I was getting an idea of why the Gods had pulled back from man. Fix this. Fix that. Instead of taking responsibility for their own actions and fixing their own damned problems. There are days I really hated this world. This was one of them.

I barked at him, "My son has been taken by Draugralls. I am sorry, but someone else is going to have to have to hold the oil back. I am going to Kla' din now."

"Draugralls? Which son?" I could hear the concern rising in his voice. It made me feel better about him.

"Christoph. He sent an SOS and now he has disappeared from the face of the Earth. Literally. He isn't here, but the scent of Draugrall is still strong, so I am going hunting before they can harm him. I hope."

I swear I would kill them all if he was harmed. I wasn't about to lose another person I cared about. Why didn't I see the danger to my own flesh and blood? I saw J.R.'s death coming months before it hit, and did everything I could to stop it from happening, but it wasn't enough. I lost J.R. in spite of using every power at my disposable. He was a son of my heart, if not of my body. He had grown up with Christoph, mobbing around the 'hood, since young teenagers together, and they had been inseparable up until the day of his death. I lost Dar, the best friend and teacher I had ever had. She took the place of my mother when mine had left me hanging out to dry with a terminal illness eating away at me. I was not about to lose my eldest son. No matter who ordered me differently. I didn't care of the fate of the world was held in the balance.

"Fine, go after him. We'll send a team to the portal. I am sorry, Cat." I almost felt bad for yelling at him but held it back. He still hadn't told me the truth of his involvement in other areas. Him or O'Hara, and I was pissed about that.

"Thank you. I'll let you know where we stand on the hunt."

I hung up.

Looking up at the sky, I heard that damned dark voice in my head again, 'Black of tha skies.'

I couldn't see any stars. No opening of an astral door. No lights anywhere shining down. Not even the moon.

"Shit, her eyes are black again." Andre yelled at me, but his voice was further away now Ja' Kelo sounded frantic with worry but I couldn't hear what he was saying. The time spanned longer this time and I thought I was dying there for a second, when the air rushed back into my lungs.

"Sweetheart, please," Andre was pleading.

"I got it. I'm all right," I assured him.

"Baby, we have to do something about this curse right now."

"We can't. You know the Draugralls. If they feed from him and lose control, they'll kill him. No bringing him back, no return. I can't chance that."

"You're no good to him dead, either."

I replied, "If he dies what then? Besides remember what Ashton said?"

He looked confused, shaking his head

"About the bonds transferring to him with the pack once they were on this side of the portal?"

"Oh yeah, distance made it easier for the transference." Then the light came on. "Ok. Good idea. It's worth a shot."

Ja' Kelo asked, "What I am missing?"

Andre turned to him while I made the door to the portal in Kla' Din.

"If she can get into Kla' din fast enough, it might stop the curse completely, until we can figure out a way to get it out of her."

I certainly liked the idea. Get my son and stop the curse from going any further, buying us time to deal with it. Two birds , one stone again. Sounded good to me.

Ja' Kelo was all for it and Andre got Demitri and Antonio updated with what was going on and what the plan was on their telepathic bond. They agreed, as well, and were on their way to Kla' din to help with the hunt for both my son and a way to get rid of the curse on me.

I had the doorway made and we stepped through. This sure was easier than going through the regular channels at the base in Okinawa. I misjudged the distance a bit, but still, we could easily walk the distance. I saw Demitri and Antonio waiting for us.

They hadn't misjudged the distance. I was a bit envious about being outdone...again. But, they were here to help me save my son; always there for me when I needed them. It was a far cry from when I was alone all those years without them in my life. Back then, there was no one I could turn to until I'd met my best friend and mentor. Then she was killed and I was alone again. The loneliness had really started for me then and almost drove me insane.

That's when I heard the hissing and saw on the ground a big, black snake. It reared up and a voice, louder this time, hummed in my ear, 'Black of tha snake'.

The snake had a ball of cloth in its mouth, which it spit at me. It broke open and again my face and lungs were filled with powder. Choking and coughing, my lungs and soul filled with a black cloud. I couldn't breathe at all. I couldn't hear my mates yelling. I reached for Demitri and the world went black and I saw no more.

Chapter Twenty-Nine

Stalemate

emitri put out an immediate SOS to the whole Coven. One by one, Catrina's sisters and brothers showed up, using astral doorways to get there as fast as they could.

"Gerard, can you do anything?" Andre asked.

"I read through all my books on voodoo. The last line in the curse says 'nothing in, on or of this world will break this curse'. This is one of those rare, old curses. I honestly don't think there is anything we can do here for her."

Demitri eyes shut as if in pain, looking up at Cassie who also was well transversed on old curses.

Cassie was not herself though. She kept shaking her head, as if discounting all the counter curses she had learned from their books and other sources. In frustration that scared Demitri because he had never seen her lose it, "I told you something like this would happen if you didn't get your edge back." She shouted uselessly to Catrina. Spinning back on Demitri, she said, "Look at her. She's not even alive. Her soul is gone."

Demitri and her mates switched to their third eye and saw as Cassie did. There was no aura. No color, just a dead empty space of air around a husk of a body. Demitri put his ear to her chest. The heart beat so slowly, it was barely there; the blood pulsing through her veins seemed to slow for a living person, even if that person was a vampire. He pulled back to gaze into her eyes to see if he could find some trace of animation. Nothing looked back, but dead, unseeing eyes. Their color had turned a dull black, so oddly disturbing from the vibrant blue they normally were. Or even the green they turned to when she was using her powers. But, this? This dull, black showed no living soul was residing inside her body.

267

"No, Catrina. Please come back to me, baby," Demitri pleaded, tears starting to roll down his face, as his pulled Cat closer to him.

"Please, come back. I can't lose you. We can't lose you." He pressed his forehead to hers and sent power from his heart and mind to her. "Please, come back, baby. Come home to me."

The words echoed and bounced off of the impenetrable black shield around Catrina's mind; and for a moment, for a brief second, something flashed inside the bubble.

"Come home to me."

Black clouds swirled around me. "All I wanted was a home."

But, no one heard me and I was lost in the blackness surrounding me that seem to go on forever.

Bibliography

(These include the books O'Hara was directed to read to get him and his team properly started in their training in the arts.)

Scott Cunningham, "Earth Power"
Scott Cunningham, "Encyclopedia of Magical Herbs"
Scott Cunningham, "Living Wicca"
Denning and Phillips, "The Practical Guide to Astral Projection."
David Krieg, "Modern Magick"
Ted Andrews, "How to See the Aura"
Ted Andrews, "How to Heal with Color"
Ted Andrews, "How to Speak with Animals"
Silver RavenWolf, "To Stir a Magick Cauldron"
Silver RavenWolf, "To Ride a Silver Broomstick"
Gaston and Yvette Frost, "Astral Travel"
Raven Grimassi, "Ways of The Strega"
Raven Grimassi, "Wicca Magick"
D.J. Conway, "Celtic Magic"
D.J. Conway, "Astral Love"
Charles Fielding, "The Practical Qabalah"
Sayed Idries Shah, "Oriental Magic"
Dael Walker, "The Crystal Healing Book"
Phyllis Krystal, "Cutting"
Lynn Pickett, "Mary Magdalene"

Chess definitions used in the Chapter Title of this part of The Nightwolves Story of Nightwolves Siren's Song

Chapter One
White moves First

The **first-move advantage in chess** is the inherent advantage of the player (called White) who makes the first move in chess. Chess players and theorists generally agree that White begins the game with some advantage.statistics compiled since 1851 support this view, showing that White consistently wins slightly more often than Black, usually scoring between 52 and 56 percent. White's winning percentage is about the same for tournament games between humans and games between computers. However, White's advantage is less significant in rapid games and in games between weaker players.

Chapter Two
Double Space Pawn

These doubled and isolated pawns are just waiting to be picked off by your opponent. You opponent may elect though to simply ignore them since they are of very little threat unless they reach the back rank and get promoted to queens. This is easily avoided by blocking their path with a pawn of your own. The other disadvantage of having doubled your pawns in the game of chess is that you have also opened a file that your opponent can use to mount an attack onto your back row

Chapter Three
En passant

("in the act of passing"; derived from French) The rule that allows a pawn that has just advanced two squares to be captured by a pawn on the same rank and adjacent file. The pawn is therefore taken as if it had only moved one space. It is only possible to take en passant on the next move.

Chapter Four
Domination

A situation whereby capture of a piece is unavoidable despite it having wide freedom of movement. Usually occurs in chess problems.

Chapter Five
Fianchetto

Refers to a bishop developed to the second square and the longest diagonal on the file of the adjacent knight (that is, b2 or g2 for white, b7 or g7 for black), or the process of developing a bishop to such a square. It usually occurs after moving the pawn on that file ahead one square (or

271

perhaps two). The Italian word is actually a noun ("in fianchetto") and not a verb.

Chapter Six
Indian Defense

(1) A move or plan which tries to meet the opponent's attack; (2) an opening played by Black, for example the Scandinavian Defense, King's Indian Defense, English Defense, etc.

Chapter Seven
Double Attack

Two attacks made with one move: these attacks may be made by the same piece (in which case it is a fork); or by different pieces (a situation which may arise via a discovered attack in which the moved piece also makes a threat). The attacks may directly threaten opposing pieces, or may be threats of another kind: for instance, to capture the queen and deliver checkmate.

Chapter Eight
Initiative

The advantage that a player who is making threats has over the player who must respond to them. The attacking player is said to "have the initiative". s/he can often turn the play as s/he wills. The initiative often results from an advantage in time and/or space. The notion of the initiative was used by Steinitz (e.g. *The Sixth American Chess Congress*) and by Capablanca in his *Chess Fundamentals* (Chapter 4).

Chapter Nine
Chasing Shadows

A move where ones opponent will make false leads for the other to fall for while the real moves to victory are being made in another area. Causing your opponent to chase false trails.

Chapter Ten
Castling Queen's Side

A special move involving both the king and one rook. Its purpose is generally to protect the king and develop the rook. Castling on the kingside is sometimes called castling short and castling on the queenside is called castling long; the difference is based on whether the rook moves a short distance (two squares) or a long distance (three squares).

Chapter Eleven
Cover

To protect a piece or control a square. For example, to checkmate a king on the side of the board, the five squares adjacent to the king must all be covered.

Chapter Twelve
Blockade
A strategic placement of a minor piece directly in front of an enemy pawn, where it restrains the pawn's advance and gains shelter from attack. Blockading pieces are often overprotected.

Chapter Thirteen
Counter Balance
Practice of chess game indicates that controls chess opening is not easy. Elementary contradiction from all openings ranges from effort of White to have the advantage through exploiting of initiative in respect to White's first move right and Black's resistance in attempt to reach counter balance or creates a complication situation wherein both side has the same attack opportunity.

Chapter Fourteen
Blind Sided
"To move along the line of natural expectation consolidates the opponent's balance and thus increases his resisting power . . . In most campaigns the dislocation of the enemy's psychological and physical balance has been the vital prelude to a successful attempt at his overthrow."

Chapter Fifteen
A Pincher
Where two pawns are used to capture a piece in a pincher move.

Chapter Sixteen
Cheapo
Slang for a primitive trap, often set in the hope of swindling a win or a draw from a lost position.

Chapter Seventeen
Queen's Pawn
A pawn on the queen's file, i.e. the d-file. Sometimes abbreviated **QP**. Also **Queen Rook Pawn** (QRP), **Queen Knight Pawn** (QNP), and **Queen Bishop Pawn** (QBP) for pawns on the a, b, and c-files respectively.

Chapter Eighteen
Central Pawn
A pawn that is on the King file or the Queens file, i.e. on the d-file or the e-file.

Chapter Nineteen
Dark Squares
The 32 dark-coloured squares on the chessboard, such as a1 and h8. A dark square is always located at a player's left hand corner.

Chapter Twenty
Pawn Makes Knight

A pawn that advances all the way to the opposite side of the board (the opposing player's first rank) is promoted to another piece of that player's choice of a queen, rook, bishop, or knight of the same color. The pawn is immediately (before the opposing player's next move) replaced by the new piece.

Chapter Twenty-One
Queen covers Knight

Where the Queen is used to protect the Knight as it is moved across the board.

Chapter Twenty-Two
j' adoube

(from French) "I adjust". A player says "J'adoube" as the international signal that he intends to adjust the position of a piece on the board without being subject to the touched piece rule..

Chapter Twenty-Three
Adjournment

Suspension of a chess game with the intention to continue it later.

Chapter Twenty- Four
Advanced Pawn

A pawn that is on the opponent's side of the board (the fifth rank or higher). An advanced pawn may be weak if it is overextended, lacking support and difficult to defend, or strong if it cramps the enemy by limiting mobility. An advanced passed pawn that threatens to promote can be especially strong.

Chapter Twenty-Five
Active

Describes a piece that is able to move or control many squares.

Chapter Twenty-Six
Alekine's gun

A formation in which a queen backs up two rooks in the same file.

Chapter Twenty-Seven
Indian Bishop

A fianchettoed bishop, characteristic of the Indian Defenses, the King's Indian and the Queen's Indian.

Chapter Twenty-Eight
Bullet Chess

A form in Chess where the players have one minute to make all their moves.

Chapter Twenty-Nine

Stalemate

A position in which the player whose turn it is to move has no legal move and his king is not in check. A stalemate results in an immediate draw.

Memoirs of the Nightwolves Series:

Nightwolves Coalition 2nd Edition
Nightwolves on the Prowl 2nd Edition
Nightwolves Siren's Song (Dec. 2010/Jan. 2011)
Nightwolves Dawn to Dusk (TBA)
Nightwolves Battle for Kla' din (TBA)
Nightwolves Union on Trinidad (TBA)
Nightwolves Twilight - The Last Battle (TBA)
Nightwolves Companion (What was Real,
Mundane and/or Magick) (TBA)

Paranormal Erotica by Clarrissa Lee Moon
Celeste's Nites First Trilogy (short stories-Claiming Celeste, Hunting Celeste and Sharing Celeste)
Celeste's Nites Second Trilogy (short stories-Protecting Celeste, Contemplating Celeste and Loving Celeste) TBA

Author Bio

Clarrissa Moon would like to live like a tumbleweed, going from different states often, but her home base is in Tucson, Arizona. She's an avid reader and owner of more books and DVD's then any used book shop; she also enjoys Martial arts, swimming and raising pure bred Japanese Chins. She has written as a journalist for two E-magazines. She is also, the author of 'Celeste's Nites' Novelettes. She considers herself unique, unusual and unconquerable.

Celtic Circle + Pyramid 830
Connect with me at the Nightwolves Lair Blog -
http://clarrissamoon.blogspot.com/
http://clarrissaleemoonauthor.webs.com/

In Honor of our Planet's wild animals:
Please help these Organizations that save our Endangered Species, such as the Wolves and Silverback gorillas.
http://www.defenders.org/
http://www.bigoakwolfsanctuary.org/
http://gorillafund.org/

Clarissa Lee Moon